Temptation Rag

ELIZABETH HUTCHISON BERNARD

Temptation Rag

A NOVEL

BELLE
EPOQUE
PUBLISHING

F
ber

Published by Belle Epoque Publishing
PO Box 5554, Carefree, Arizona 85377
BelleEpoquePublishing@gmail.com

Author website: www.EHBernard.com

Cover design: Ghislain Viau
Interior design: Paul Barrett
Cover image: Dolly Zuckerman (aka Dolly Bernard), ca. 1924
Photo of Paul Laurence Dunbar by Kell / Courtesy of Library of Congress
Author photo: Tina Celle

Library of Congress Control Number: 2018907520
ISBN (paperback): 978-0-9984406-4-4
ISBN (ebook): 978-0-9984406-5-1

First edition

For my mother, Helen J. Hutchison,
who gave me the precious gift of song.

ACT I
1895–1896

Oh, de white ban' play hits music, an' hit's mighty good
*   to hyeah,*
An' it sometimes leaves a ticklin' in yo' feet;
But de hea't goes into bus'ness fu' to he'p erlong de eah,
W'en de colo'ed ban' goes marchin' down de street.

—From "The Colored Band," Paul Laurence Dunbar

Paul Laurence Dunbar, 1872–1906

Threads

SEDALIA, MISSOURI
NOVEMBER 1895

When the train pulled into Sedalia, it was evening. Late November was a quiet time of year. The traveling minstrel shows that made stops all through the summer were long gone. They wouldn't be back until spring. That was fine by Strap Hill. He wasn't looking for work. Not with a booking just a few weeks off in the biggest, richest city in the world—or so he'd been told, because he had yet to see New York City for himself. Lately, though, he didn't mind telling anybody who'd listen how New York was the answer to a poor man's prayer. With a good ring shout and a little bit of luck, no telling how far you might go. As for him, he was plenty happy to ride on the coattails of Mr. Ben Harney, the young Kentuckian fast making a name for himself as the originator of ragtime.

Standing on the platform, Strap took a minute to admire the view, the last rays of sun spreading a golden glow over the rolling hills of central Missouri. Looked to him like fine farmland. A man could probably make a half-decent living around here if he was of a mind to get his hands dirty. But that wasn't the life for him. No sir! His sights were set on making it big. Money was the answer to everything, and he was about to grab onto a whole bunch of it, just as fast as he could.

He buttoned up his brand-new wool frock coat and pushed his bowler down tight on his head so the wind couldn't take it. Carrying his old leather suitcase, he hurried down the steps and turned south.

The railroad meant there were jobs to be had, and the frontier town had grown to a population of about fifteen thousand. A wooden sidewalk ran the length of Main Street, the buildings mostly one- and two-story brick, some with corrugated-iron awnings. Strap passed by a row of storefronts—general store, barber shop, feed store, hardware store. They were already closed for the night, the shopkeepers at home with their families or maybe enjoying a little libation at one of the taverns down the street. Exactly where Strap was headed now.

"Hey, stranger, lookin' for a little fun?"

He eyed the half-open door but kept walking, chuckling to himself. He had no illusions about being a ladies' man. He could imagine how they might write him up for some "Wanted" poster back in Memphis: *Be on the lookout for Strap Hill, short and wiry, black as pitch, nose wide and flat as a pancake, a big gap between his two front teeth.* Not the prettiest picture, but still he figured he'd have plenty of opportunities with the ladies once he got to New York, after he made a name for himself as Ben Harney's sideman.

By the time Strap hit the center of town, it was like a whole different place. The doors to the pool halls and honky-tonks were thrown wide open, lights glowing and sounds of piano music filtering onto the street. Without too much trouble, he found the Maple Leaf Club and went inside. The place was packed, the smoke thick as fog. The crowd was mostly Negroes and a few whites, mingling together as if there were nothing strange about it. He headed across the room, past the pool and gaming tables, on his way to the bar stretched along the back wall. The colored bartender was sloshing a wet rag across the counter. He looked up and, seeing Strap, tossed it aside.

"What'll you have?"

"Whiskey." Strap settled onto a high stool, unbuttoned his coat, and shoved his suitcase under his boots. "Who's playing tonight?"

"Whoever show up, I reckon."

"You know Otis Saunders?"

"Otis? Sure, he's a regular." The bartender yelled, "Anybody see Otis?"

"Seen him playing pool little while back," somebody called out. "There he is, coming this way!"

Strap swung around on the stool and watched as Otis Saunders strutted toward the bar. His friend was just like Strap remembered him, with the sure step and easy smile of somebody who knows what he's all about. He couldn't help being just a little bit jealous the way all the ladies turned to ogle as Otis sailed by.

"Somebody asking for me?"

Strap jumped up and stuck out his hand. "Good to see you, Otis."

Otis's eyes lit up. "Why, if it ain't Strap Hill! I'll be dogged! What you doing in Sedalia, man?" he said, landing a hearty slap on Strap's back.

"Way you and Joplin was talking about this place, knew someday I have to see it for myself."

Strap had met Saunders and Scott Joplin during the world's fair, the Columbian Exposition in Chicago, in the summer of '93. He and Otis ended up in a scrape with a couple of cops on Colored American Day, when twenty-five hundred people gathered in Festival Hall for a celebration of Negro cultural achievement and the powerful statesman Frederick Douglass seized the occasion to make a fiery speech about how bad things were for his people—no jobs, no respect, no payback for all they had contributed to the country. Afterward, when everybody was streaming out of the big hall, it seemed like the cops were just looking to nab a colored man, with or without reason. Strap and Otis were the unlucky ones.

Strap noticed how Otis was eyeing him up and down, probably wondering what he'd been up to that he could afford fancy threads like he had on. But it turned out Otis already knew.

"Heard you're singing with Ben Harney."

"That's right."

Otis rubbed his chin. "He fessed up yet to where he learned how to rag, or still claiming to invent it all by himself?"

Otis's question put Strap on the defensive. "Don't matter to me if he invented ragging or not. Long as folks like it."

"Don't get me wrong, Strap." Otis rested his hand on Strap's shoulder. "I don't have nothing against Harney. I hear he's a good man, almost like one of us. Fact is, don't know any other white man touring with a colored band. Unless maybe it's that he's got some black in him after all. There's rumors about that, you know. What do *you* say? You seen him up close."

"He look plenty white to me. And the way he talk about his family, seem they's all big shots. Says his grandpa's in the government, a state senator or something. Somebody else a professor at the university, wrote a book about numbers. For Kentucky, the Harneys is kind of like blue bloods, I guess."

"Sure like to know where Ben Harney learned to rag," Otis said, shaking his head.

"What difference it make?"

Otis gave him a look, like he ought to know better. "Just ain't right, Strap. Ragging is *our* invention. That rhythm come straight from Africa, you know as well as me. Straight from the black man's soul. Ain't right for Harney to claim it's all his idea."

4

Strap didn't say anything. When it came to fancy talking, he figured he was no match for Otis. Besides, maybe his friend was right. But that wasn't going to stop him from playing Tony Pastor's vaudeville theater with Ben Harney billed as the bona-fide originator of ragtime. Why, he'd have to be a fool to pass up a chance like that.

Otis glanced over his shoulder. "Sorry, buddy, but I got to go. The folks are getting restless. I'm on tonight." He gave his fingers a good stretch, then rubbed his palms together fast and hard, like he was trying to start a fire. "How long you going to be in Sedalia?"

"Got to head out to New York pretty soon."

"You'll room with me while you're here. Long as you like."

"You sure I won't be putting you out?"

"Listen, Strap." Otis leaned in close. "I'm going to introduce you to my sister, Bess. She's a real looker and sweet as a tub o' honey."

"That sound mighty good."

"You're going to love it here. Fact is, I could see you getting real comfortable in Sedalia. Settling down with a nice girl? Doing a little singing and shouting on the side?"

Strap couldn't help laughing. No way he was staying in Sedalia! Not with what he had ahead of him in New York City.

Fame, fortune, and everything he thought went with it.

A Secret Life

May opened the top drawer of her French serpentine commode, inhaling the scent of lavender as she slipped her hand beneath a pile of silk camisoles and wrapped her fingers around the soft tooled-leather cover of her journal. Quickly, because she hadn't much time, she extracted the book and went to the fireplace. Leaning in to catch the light from the crackling blaze, she began to flip through the pages, unable to resist stopping here and there to read a few of her favorite lines. It was funny about her writing. Sometimes it came to her so fast and effortlessly it was almost like magic. At other times, it reminded her of making Christmas taffy, endlessly folding and twisting and pulling at the words until finally they assumed the desired consistency and shape. Her latest poem was like that. She'd still not finished it.

Her journal was one of a number of books she kept hidden in places where her parents would be unlikely to stumble upon them. She was sure neither of them would have any tolerance, let alone appreciation, for the verses she composed. Or, for that matter, the poets and writers she admired—most of them French and famously debauched. But wasn't it those writers who had taught her most of what she knew about life? Real life, not the kind lived within the sheltered confines of the Converys' Manhattan mansion or their sprawling country estate in neighboring Connecticut.

A few minutes earlier, she had quietly exited the lively party going on downstairs in the ballroom, feeling a sudden spark of inspiration. It would be wonderful if she could complete the poem she'd been composing for her piano teacher, Mr. Bernard, and read it to him before his performance tonight. She knew it might shock him that she would lay bare her feelings so shamelessly. But maybe that was the only way she would know for certain whether he felt the same.

There had been subtle signs that he might. A few times during lessons when by accident their hands touched and she had felt that fluttery sensation in her stomach, he'd quickly moved his hand away as if he, too, sensed the danger. And he often seemed reluctant to look at her directly, a trait she found both annoying and endearing. He appeared to be shy. That could only mean he cared what she thought of him, perhaps as much as she cared what he thought about her.

She recalled again the afternoon, just over a month ago, when she had dared to tell him of her aspirations to become a poet, afraid he might react the same way Teddy had. She'd mentioned her writing to Teddy only once. Casually, as if it didn't matter all that much, as if it wasn't the entire reason she lived and breathed. He'd not even been curious enough to read a single one of her poems so he could judge for himself whether or not her writing had merit. But then, why would she expect anything else? Teddy Livingstone was far more concerned about the next polo match with his buddies at the club than he was about her poetry.

But Mike Bernard . . .

She thought she would never tire of watching him at the piano, his fingers caressing the keys, a look of such tenderness on his face as if he would gladly die for each and every note. At those times, it was like she was peering through a tiny window into the most hidden parts of him. And yet everything else remained dark and mysterious. He'd been her piano teacher for nearly three months now, and still she knew so little about him, not nearly as much as he knew about her. Her poetry had given him exclusive access to her secret life, a glimpse into her private thoughts, her deepest longings. By now, he must know how trapped she felt by society's silly conventions, by her parents' expectation that she would settle for the same empty existence she saw other so-called privileged women endure day after day. How desperately she wanted to be free—like *he* was free! To live the life of an artist.

To fall in love.

Lately she had begun to imagine them together in all sorts of places, most of which she'd never been herself. Paris was her favorite—strolling down the rue des Martyrs where she'd read that the poet Baudelaire used to roam. She could picture them peeking in the windows of interesting little shops, listening to the distant bells of Notre-Dame-de-Lorette church, sipping coffee at a quaint café as the conversation turned to music and poetry. After a blissful day of sightseeing, the moon a silvery ghost in the darkening sky, they'd slip back to their little hotel on the Left Bank and sit on the scrolled-iron balcony drinking champagne until dawn, when they'd finally fall into bed amid giddy laughter and kisses and heartfelt promises of forever.

"May, what are you doing?"

May's younger sister, Emily, stood just inside the bedroom door, dressed in pink chiffon, her hair swept up in a style May argued was too mature for a fifteen-year-old. But Mother, as usual, had ignored her.

"I just came up to refresh my perfume, that's all," May replied, hiding the journal behind the billowy skirt of her silk gown.

"Mother has decided the concert should begin at midnight. She asked me to tell Mr. Bernard, but I can't find him—and it's already eleven thirty. Have you seen him anywhere?"

May knew exactly where he was. After their last lesson, she had made a point of suggesting that he wait in the gentlemen's dressing room until just before his performance. "That way, you can make a dramatic entrance," she'd advised, hoping to sound as if she knew all about such things.

"I'll find him, Emily. Don't worry. You go back down to the ballroom."

"Don't tell"—Emily giggled, covering her mouth with her hand—"but I've already had two whole glasses of champagne!"

May smiled. It amazed her sometimes to think only two years separated them. Emily was such a child. "Just make sure you don't get the hiccups, or certainly they'll figure out what you've been up to."

Emily nodded. Still tittering with guilty delight, she turned and disappeared. Reluctantly, May tucked her journal back in its hiding place, her thoughts again on Mike Bernard. He said the dates of his upcoming concert tour were yet to be announced, but it couldn't be too much longer before he'd leave, maybe never to return. The thought of it worried her. There might be little time left.

Little time to convince him of what she already knew—that they were meant to be together.

The Kiss

———

M ike scrutinized his image in the tall mirror of the gentlemen's dressing room. He was decked out for the evening in a glossy black tailcoat and formal trousers. His waistcoat was cut low, amply displaying the finely pleated shirtfront decorated with tiny gold studs. A white bow tie, kid gloves, and patent leather boots completed the ensemble, which had taken a sizable chunk out of what he'd earned in his nearly three months of employment with the Converys. But, by now, he was resigned to the fact that investment in one's appearance is a necessary part of climbing the ladder of success. And there was no doubt that tonight was to be a significant step up. Maybe the opportunity of a lifetime.

At that very moment, some of the most important people in New York were downstairs in the ballroom of the Converys' palatial Manhattan residence on Fifth Avenue. They were people with money and the inclination to spend it on worthy causes, such as patronage of extraordinary musical talent. Soon they would be listening to him perform Beethoven,

Chopin, and Franz Liszt's Hungarian Rhapsody No. 2, a technically difficult selection sure to impress even the least sensitive of listeners.

It was the possibility of a night like tonight that had been uppermost in his mind when he auditioned for a position as piano teacher to the Converys' two daughters, May and Emily. Desperate to make an impression, he'd presented himself as a budding young pianist in the process of preparing for an East Coast concert tour. In truth, though he had auditioned for a number of promoters, everyone told him the same story. He had no name, they said, no following. On top of that, they insisted, Americans believe serious music belongs to the Europeans. Despite his conservatory training, there was no way around the fact that he lacked the Continental mystique.

He came closer to the mirror and studied his face. It was thin but no longer had that underfed look. He recognized its flaws—the jaw was narrow, the nose a little too large, eyes deep set. But when you considered it all together, without separating the parts, maybe it wasn't so bad.

There was a light knock from the hallway. Mike quickly stepped away from the mirror, striking a pose by a small Louis XIV table on which he rested his hand with an air of nonchalance.

"Yes?"

The door swung open.

"Good evening, Mr. Bernard!"

May Convery was stunning in a sky-blue gown with enormous puffed sleeves and a trumpet-bell-shaped skirt, her slender neck adorned with a choker of sparkling diamonds and sapphires. The moody depths of her hazel eyes, her heart-shaped face, and her full lips with their high-arched Cupid's bow might easily make a fellow forget she was only seventeen. Mike recalled how painfully intimidated he used to feel around her, despite that she was a full two years his junior. But since that morning, a month or so ago, when she first read him her poetry, he'd begun to see her differently. Not as the spoiled daughter of a wealthy financier but as a lonely young woman. Accomplished, defiant, yet also fragile and insecure.

Maybe more like himself than he would have imagined.

"Where's the attendant?" May asked, glancing around the room.

"He was called out momentarily—an urgent problem in the hat room, they said."

"Good." She stepped inside, closing and bolting the door behind her. "I was hoping for a moment alone with you. Are you all right? You're not nervous?"

"Nervous? No, not really." He was, of course, extremely jittery. But admitting it would only have the effect of making him more so.

"I've been busy tonight telling everyone about my fabulous piano teacher and your upcoming concert tour. If I had a hundred tickets, I could have sold them all by now."

Though she obviously intended to put him at ease, her words only served to remind him how much of an imposter he was. Not only had he lied about a pending concert tour, he had claimed an entire life history that bore little resemblance to his own. Mike Bernard was not his name. His family went by Brown, a name derived from Braun, the change having been made on their arrival at Ellis Island. And the story of how he'd been raised by a wealthy uncle in Chicago, owner of a successful music publishing house? Another lie. But how could he possibly have admitted to Mrs. Convery that he grew up in the tenements of New York City's Lower East Side? That his father was a wallpaper hanger and his mother took in piecework.

That he was a Jew.

May glided to the full-length mirror, turning to admire her dress from several angles, though Mike noticed her eyes kept wandering to his face. "They showed this gown in Paris, at one of the fashion parades just last fall. Mother thought it would suit me well." She paused. "What do *you* think?"

There was no question she looked more beautiful than he'd ever seen her. The fitted bodice of her dress left little doubt as to the perfection of what lay beneath, making it difficult to focus his attention elsewhere. But he was determined not to give her the slightest reason to doubt the purity of his thoughts.

"Mrs. Convery is a woman of impeccable taste."

May swung around, appearing piqued. "I didn't realize you were such an admirer of my mother!"

"I only meant—"

"Men always think Mother is quite something," she continued, with an attitude that was surprisingly pugnacious. "Who knows, maybe they've never met a real Southern belle before."

"But I—"

"However much you may admire my mother now, I could tell you plenty of things that would no doubt change your opinion of her, and not for the better. Like the way she—" May halted, a blush spreading across her cheeks. "I'm sorry, I suppose I shouldn't be speaking so carelessly. Really, you must forgive me. It's just that I had hoped—well, I guess I'm disappointed. You see, I wanted to give you something tonight. Something very special. Personal. But, unfortunately, I couldn't get it ready in time."

Mike couldn't help but be annoyed. Right now, he had more important matters on his mind than childish intrigues. His performance in front of a hundred of New York's elite was in less than an hour. "There's no need for you to apologize—or to give me anything."

"It was just a little gift to wish you luck with your performance."

"That's very kind of you but not at all necessary."

"Obviously a gift is never *necessary*. It's something one *wants* to do." She hesitated. "I might as well tell you, it was a poem. One that I hoped would express—well, how I've come to *feel* about you." She looked at him intently, fingering the jeweled choker at her throat. "But maybe you're right. Maybe it's *not* necessary. There might be a better way."

She came at him in a rush of rustling silk, enveloping him in a cloud of rose-petal perfume. Before he could realize her intention, she had already kissed him full on the lips. Quickly, she stepped back, regarding him with what could only be feigned innocence. She had ambushed him! "What's the matter? You don't like kissing?"

"I-I-I—" He hated how he was stammering like an idiot. But this was *May Convery*, the daughter of one of the richest men in Manhattan! And what was *he*? A lowly piano teacher, only a notch or two up from a servant—and a fraud to boot. He must put a stop to this, and right away!

"Your behavior, Miss Convery, is—"

"*Your* behavior, Mr. Bernard," she interrupted, "is entirely unacceptable. When a young lady offers a kiss, it's a gentleman's duty to respond with a certain enthusiasm."

Again she flung herself at him, this time throwing her arms around his neck, firmly pressing her mouth against his, her bosom so tight to his chest it was as if they were joined. He wanted to push her away. He knew he must. But it was only a matter of seconds until his will collapsed. He was too intoxicated by her smell, her taste, the feverish warmth of her body to offer even a semblance of resistance. All he could think was, astonishing as it seemed, May Convery *wanted* him.

Or the person she believed him to be.

His hand found the curve of her hip, then the small of her back, the silk of her gown smooth as ivory beneath his fingertips. His eyes were closed, but the blood pounding in his ears made it seem as if everything around him was spinning. He never heard the urgent jiggling of the door handle, not even the sharp knock that followed.

"Hello? Open up in there!"

May wrenched herself away from him. "Oh, no! It's Teddy."

"Teddy?"

"We must act as if I only came to inform you of the change in schedule."

"Change?" he echoed, not comprehending anything.

Hurriedly, she wiped her mouth with the heel of her gloved palm and went to the door. Mike somehow managed to slink to the window. Parting the velvet drapes, he tried to appear as if he were watching for someone's arrival. Yet he remained in a state of confusion, not sure whether to be elated or horrified by what had just happened.

"May! What are *you* doing here?"

Out of the corner of his eye, Mike appraised the intruder, a tall, athletic-looking young man, handsome in that well-bred way he had often envied—wavy blond hair, straight nose, square jaw.

"I was just informing my piano teacher about the schedule for his performance," May replied breathlessly. "Mother changed her mind and wants him on stage at twelve sharp. By the way, I don't suppose you've met Mr. Bernard?"

The young gentleman approached Mike, rolling back his lips in a mechanical smile. "Teddy Livingstone." His handshake was pointedly indifferent.

"My father and Mr. Livingstone's are business partners. Our families have known each other just about forever, or certainly as long as I can remember—which is quite some time," May babbled, noticeably shaken.

Teddy's eyes had not left Mike's face. "Mike Bernard, the illustrious piano teacher. I've heard all about you. Seems Miss Convery imagines you're some sort of genius—or something."

"She's far too generous in her praise."

"You're right. She does tend to exaggerate. But then, that's part of her charm."

"Perhaps so," May chimed in anxiously, "but I'm afraid my charm won't count for much if I don't get downstairs to our guests. Mother will be wondering where I am. And it's nearly twelve." She cast a glance at Mike that seemed full of foreboding, as if she were warning him of something more urgent than only the time—and then she turned and hurried out the door.

Upstaged

———

Teddy Livingstone pulled off his white gloves and tossed them on the same Louis XIV table that Mike had earlier employed as a prop. "I'm curious, how did you manage it?"

"I'm sorry?"

"How did you persuade the Converys? They're not in the habit of inviting just *anybody* to entertain at their parties."

Mike threw back his shoulders, uncomfortably dwarfed by Teddy's superior stature. "It wasn't necessary to *persuade* anyone. I was honored to be invited by Mrs. Convery to help celebrate the holidays."

"I thought you'd say that, even though we both know it wasn't really Mrs. Convery who invited you."

Teddy sauntered over to the mirror, regarding his image with an attitude of smug satisfaction. "No need to take offense. I understand ambition. I don't have a problem with it." His eyes shifted to Mike, a few feet behind him. "What I *do* have a problem with is you and Miss Convery."

Guiltily, Mike flashed back to the heated kiss that had overwhelmed his better judgment. "I have no idea what you're talking about."

"I think you do. May is a very sweet girl. Not the kind who should be taken advantage of."

"I assure you, I've done no such thing."

Teddy stepped away from the mirror, standing directly in front of Mike, arms folded across his chest.

"I gather she didn't tell you about us. You see, it's always been more or less understood that she and I—let's just say our families decided long ago that we would make a good pair. In case you don't understand how these things work, empires aren't built by accident. That's why I hope I'm wrong about you."

"I'm Miss Convery's piano teacher, nothing more," Mike replied, trying to keep his voice steady. "And I resent your insinuations to the contrary."

"Is that so?" Teddy cocked his head. "Well, I've been away for a while, but from now on I plan to be spending a lot of time with May. Come to think of it, aren't you supposed to be leaving soon anyway? Or did your big concert tour, the one you've bragged to the Converys about, suddenly go up in smoke?"

Mike heard a clock chime from the hallway. With a start, he realized it was already midnight. He'd been provided scant enough notice of the change in schedule, but especially after everything that had just happened, he felt wholly unprepared to make his entrance downstairs. Yet he must, and without delay, or he would be late. He took a step toward the door.

Teddy blocked his path. "We're not finished."

"I'm expected downstairs."

"That can wait. I don't want any mistake about what I'm saying to you. I'm sure the Converys will understand that you simply don't have time to continue with their daughters' piano lessons."

"If you'll excuse me—"

"Let me put it another way, then." Teddy continued to stand in his way. "May's father wouldn't be pleased at the

20

notion of you taking liberties with his daughter. People who cross George Convery tend to regret it sooner or later." Teddy's smile was slow and deliberate. "I don't suppose it would be so easy to play the piano with broken fingers."

The clock chimed its final stroke.

"I have to get downstairs."

Mike again ventured a route past Teddy and, this time encountering no resistance, hastily exited the gentlemen's lounge. The moment he was out of Teddy's sight, he bolted across the hall and down the curved marble staircase. At the bottom, standing alone in the foyer, he stopped to catch his breath and wipe the nervous sweat from his forehead.

His hand trembled as he pulled out his pocket watch.

Two minutes past twelve.

Mike crossed the foyer. As he walked briskly through the candlelit reception hall with its floor-to-ceiling murals depicting tales from Greek mythology, his eye was momentarily drawn to the painted image of Icarus falling from the sky, his wax wings melted by the sun. Why had he let that fellow Livingstone unnerve him so? Broken fingers! It was an absurd threat. George Convery was a businessman, not a gangster. Wasn't he?

Arriving at the ballroom, he paused in the doorway while he struggled to regain his equilibrium. An army of liveried footmen hustled among the hundred or more guests, balancing silver trays with champagne flutes filled to the brim. Mustachioed men suited in black and white, clever power brokers and those lucky enough to be living off the cleverness of generations past, animated their conversations with the nodding of heads and polite laughter. Their wives, resplendent in silks, satins, and lace, fluttered their painted fans nearly as fast as their tongues. Off to one side, the younger women without escorts huddled together anxiously while the young men by whom they hoped to be approached, for a dance or possibly more, gave final consideration to the most advantageous pairing.

He finally spotted Isabelle Convery at the far edge of the crowd, gaily holding court with several distinguished-looking gentlemen. Even in his agitated state of mind, he couldn't help the fleeting thought that Mrs. Convery was, indeed, very attractive. Her beauty had a harder edge than her daughter's—high cheekbones, a slightly Romanesque nose, raven hair. Bedecked in an elaborate gown of apricot-colored silk brocade, satin, and chiffon, with a puffy train that spread out in back like the plumage of some rare species of bird, she would have been the center of attention even at an event that was not her own.

Brushing aside a footman who rushed over with a look of eager servitude, he took off across the floor. As he approached Mrs. Convery, she turned away from her companions, obviously with no intention of introducing him.

"Mr. Bernard," she said imperiously.

He leaned close, speaking in a confidential whisper, his heart galloping in his chest. "Good evening, Mrs. Convery. I'm terribly sorry to be late. I hope I haven't kept you and your guests waiting too long. But if you're ready for me, I can—"

"You'll never guess who's here," she interrupted, gazing toward the north end of the ballroom, where a forty-piece orchestra was assembled, silently standing by. A grand piano, bathed in the warm glow of a dozen footlights, filled a small stage just to the right.

"Pardon?"

She turned back with a triumphant smile. "Edward MacDowell! And he's agreed to play for us. Can you imagine?"

Mike's stomach plunged, along with his hope. Edward MacDowell! Everyone knew that the American pianist and composer was currently the toast of New York after having been favorably compared to Brahms by Henry Krehbiel, the city's most influential music critic.

Mrs. Convery's eyes swept over him. She took a step back. "Why, you're sweaty as a field hand. Go upstairs to the gentlemen's lounge and clean yourself up. I'll send someone for you later—*if* we need you."

She turned away and, assuming a beatific smile, began her promenade toward the new guest of honor. Mike was barely able to keep himself in check so desperately did he want to grab her, shake her until she admitted that it was all a terrible mistake. Of course she needed him—he would play for them now, this very minute. Edward MacDowell could wait.

But all he could do was watch as MacDowell, an intense-looking man with a thick black mustache, waxed and twirled at the ends, waited next to the piano, beaming with confidence. A few seconds later, Isabelle Convery joined him. They embraced to enthusiastic applause.

Mike felt as if he were standing alone on the bow of a sinking ship. The ballroom was a sickening blur of blinding lights, scraping voices, gaping mouths. A hostile territory into which he had mistakenly wandered and from which now he must escape or die.

Keeping his head down, he navigated to one of the open doorways and slipped out, passing through the candlelit reception hall and into the vaulted foyer. He thought of his silk top hat and his expensive new cloak hanging in the gentlemen's lounge upstairs. He wasn't about to go after them now, not with the chance of running into Teddy Livingstone.

On the verge of tears, he hurried toward the door. One of the attendants opened it for him with a smile.

"Have a wonderful evening, sir."

Conservatory Boy

It was past one a.m. when Mike arrived at the Eloise Hotel on Sixth Avenue in Greenwich Village. Nobody seemed to notice him enter the saloon, though in his black formal wear he hardly blended in. The bar was packed mostly with Irish and Italians, working-class men in canvas coats and rugged boots, but also a few suited clerks and skirted shopgirls. Bartenders in long, white aprons bustled about, refilling shots and steins and preparing endless plates of crackers, cheese, sausage, hard-boiled eggs, and pickles.

He'd been here once before, having nothing better to do than while away the evening over a beer. It was just another dive, nothing special except for the elegant craftsmanship of its massive mahogany bar ornamented with a finely sculpted relief of grapevines and romping cherubs. He recalled the piano player spinning out tunes in the back room, not one of the better ones he'd heard around town.

But then, maybe he'd come here tonight precisely for that reason.

His head down, he crossed the saloon and slipped through the half-open door. Once inside, he shadowed the wall, cloaking himself in the dense smoke, aware of a nagging ache in the pit of his stomach.

This room was smaller than the main saloon, the clientele also a notch below—raucous sailors and cutthroat gamblers attended by provocatively dressed hookers and rent boys, their faces rouged and powdered to perfection. In the far corner, a sinewy colored man with salt-and-pepper hair banged away at an old upright. He was dressed to the nines in a blue pinstripe suit, a bright-red handkerchief decorating his front pocket.

"Smokey, knock it off! You're giving me a damn headache," somebody yelled.

Smokey stopped playing and cupped his long fingers over his eyes, scanning the crowd. "I got just the thing for you, Mr. Jerome. This one would put a baby to sleep." He started up again. The sentimental tune was one that everybody seemed to know. Right away, an off-key chorus of assorted drunks joined in.

Just a little band
From my dear old mother's hand,
Far dearer to me now
Than wealth untold.
Though it's hardly worth a shilling,
Still to die I would be willing
Ere I part
With mother's little hoop of gold.

Mike was listening to every note Smokey played, judging him mercilessly. Still, it wasn't enough to distract him from the revolving scenarios playing over and over in his mind. If only he hadn't allowed that arrogant bastard to intimidate him! He should have called Teddy Livingstone's bluff, shrugged off his insults and his threats, stood up for himself like anyone with the least bit of gumption would have done. And Isabelle Convery!

Why didn't he compliment her on her gown, on the decorations, the success of the evening—*anything*? And why couldn't he muster enough confidence to follow Edward MacDowell's performance with a brilliant one of his own?

If he had done all that, instead of acting like some bedeviled miscreant fleeing the scene of a crime, then he might at that very moment be enjoying a glass of iced champagne with George Cornelius Convery, discussing the details of his debut concert tour, which Convery would readily agree to finance in its entirety. That he was huddled against the wall in the bleak back room of the Eloise saloon was damning evidence of the complete and utter disaster he had made of his golden opportunity.

And to think he had dreamed tonight would be the beginning of a new life.

A chain-smoker at a table of gray-faced card sharks flipped a penny in the direction of the piano player. "Here you go, boy. Take a break." The coin landed under the bench. Smokey quickly brought the number he was playing to a close. He retrieved the penny and a few more coins that had been tossed on the floor, after which he departed for the bar.

For Mike, it was the perfect opening. But should he take it? An argument raged in his head. He had spent nearly his last dime on the fancy getup for the Converys' ball. His rent at the Bowery flophouse he currently called home was due in a few days, and he had barely enough to cover it. But playing for pennies in a place like this? No matter how bad things were, he had never stooped so low.

A disjointed memory flitted through his mind. An image of the *shtiebel* in his old neighborhood—nothing more than a shabby storefront converted to a makeshift synagogue. A place where, long ago, he would sneak inside to play the piano he'd discovered there, hidden in a dark corner, dusty and out of tune. He had started by picking out simple melodies that he'd heard, at first only with his right hand, then eventually adding the left. Remarkably soon, his fingers became strong and sure, and the songs he played filled the *shtiebel* to its rafters.

He thought back to when the rabbi discovered what he'd been up to—that he'd been breaking in through a small, unlatched window in the back to practice when no one was around. That very evening, the old man had a private talk with Mike's mother. He could still picture them, their heads bent together over the Torah desk, speaking in hushed tones, mostly in Yiddish. Every now and then, they would glance his way, as if considering which among the dire punishments at their disposal might best suit his crime. He thought he was in for it, that his mother must be furious. Instead, the rabbi called him over, patted his head, and praised God. Eva Brown's eyes filled with tears, and she talked about miracles as if she were a Catholic.

"Someday you'll be famous," she said as they hurried past the huge oak beer barrels stacked in front of the neighborhood saloon. "Someday you'll make your mother proud."

How proud would she be to see him now, at this very moment, here in the back room of the Eloise among drunks, thugs, slatterns, and worse? If only he might suddenly awake to find that his performance at Isabelle Convery's ball had made him New York's newest musical sensation, and this place was nothing more than the scene of a grotesquely comical dream.

But that was not going to happen. Maybe this was where he belonged after all.

With no one paying the slightest attention, Mike strolled over to the piano and sat down. He rubbed his hands together, drew a deep breath. He'd never done anything like this before, which was the only thing that might make it even slightly forgivable. It was just an experiment.

Giving himself no further opportunity for remorse, he forced his fingers to the keys and broke into the hit song "After the Ball," easily navigating the simple melody, augmenting it with rich chords and lush arpeggios. Following several rounds of verse and chorus, he seamlessly transitioned to a second popular tune, calling upon every musical device of the masters to transform the rather pedestrian refrain into something closer to grand opera. Out of the corner of his eye, he watched for a reaction from the crowd. A few of the patrons had noticed something was different and turned to watch, but most were too busy drinking, laughing, and groping under skirts.

He picked up the pace. The music became a locomotive barreling down a straight track, the left hand pounding a steady bass, the right weaving intricate variations on a theme. In a moment of daring, he lifted his backside off the bench, half standing as his fingers scurried up and down the keys, faster than rats in a dark alley. He heard a cry of delight from someone in the crowd, and his excitement spiked. On and on he went, switching songs like he was switching hats, for each one inventing a new sound effect, a new gimmick. While he might dress up a melody any way he wanted, in the end it had to sound familiar enough to touch that special place in the listener's heart where music works its most powerful magic. And that was precisely what he set about doing. He captured his audience like he was reeling in a giant fish. Slowly, painfully, with every ounce of strength he had. Afraid to stop. Afraid to let go of this brash new persona that it seemed must have always been lurking beneath the surface, beneath the façade of everything he thought he was or wanted to be.

After ten minutes, his linen shirt soaked through with sweat, he rolled down the keyboard one last time and struck the final chord. Those who were not already on their feet leaped out of their chairs whistling, stomping, calling out to him. "Bravo! Bravo! Bravo!"

Smokey stood in the doorway, hands on his hips, brows drawn together in a scowl. A heavyset man with a stogie wedged between his teeth handed him a nickel. "Here you go, boy. Give this to the new piano player," he said, belly-laughing as he walked away.

Smokey strode over to Mike and slapped the coin down on the piano bench. "You just about finished?" he snarled.

"Nope. Sorry, old man." Mike wasn't interested in negotiating. He turned back to the keyboard and started in again, leaving Smokey to shuffle angrily off to the bar, muttering curses under his breath.

He never imagined it would be so easy to keep the crowd begging for more, so impossible to refuse each and every request, half of them for songs he barely knew but managed to fake convincingly enough. He ended up playing until nearly four in the morning. Not until the last cadre of inebriated sailors had stumbled out the door did he finally lower the lid over the keys, sitting perfectly still for a minute or two, his body drained of energy.

The floor was littered with pennies, nickels, and dimes. With a sigh, he got down on his hands and knees and began to gather them up. He'd done well for himself. Yet even as he stuffed coins into his pockets, he grappled with mixed emotions about the night's success. On the one hand, he was as ashamed of being here as when he first walked through the door. He had debased his talent. If any of his old professors could see him now, no doubt they would disavow any knowledge of him whatsoever.

On the other hand, he was aware of having experienced a peculiar sense of elation. There was a certain challenge in turning the mundane tunes of the day into something larger than life. Granted, it was nothing like the joy of rendering a difficult Chopin etude with flawless execution, knowing that the educated ear of every rapt listener was attuned to the same perfect wavelength. But these folks tonight—unsophisticated, even depraved, as they were—they had recognized his talent.

They had shouted and cheered. Proclaimed him fantastic, incredible.

Mike stood up. Wiping dirty hands on his fancy black trousers, he exited to the main saloon, planning to slip out through the front as anonymously as he had slipped in.

"When you coming back, kid? Tomorrow night?" called out one of the bartenders.

"Can't say for sure," Mike answered, opening the outer door to a cold blast of winter air. He raised his collar in the back, knowing it would do little good. He thought again of his fine new cloak and hat, forever to remain unclaimed in the gentlemen's dressing room of the Converys' mansion. Suddenly remembering his fancy white gloves, he retrieved them from his pants pockets. Gratefully, he pulled them on.

"Hey, what's your name, anyway?"

Mike hesitated, debating whether he might as well go back to being Michael Brown. He supposed it made no difference.

"Mike Bernard," he tossed back.

He stepped outside. Smokey was leaning against a light post, puffing on a cigar stub. He wore a thin, shabby overcoat, the sleeves too long, no hat or gloves. Mike felt a sudden stab of conscience.

"Hey, thanks for letting me play tonight." He reached into his pocket and pulled out a few coins—enough to constitute a peace offering.

But Smokey ignored his outstretched hand. Blowing a cloud of smoke in Mike's direction, he flipped the butt onto the snowy sidewalk. Mike withdrew his hand, dropping the coins back into his pocket.

"Where'd you learn all that fancy playing, anyway?" Smokey said, giving him the evil eye.

"Berlin. Studied at the conservatory there," Mike added, his conceit getting the better of him.

"Ohhh—you's a conservatory boy." Smokey broke into a malicious grin. "Where you playing next week, Carnegie Hall?" He spit on the ground before pointing a long finger at Mike. "Listen, I got a pretty good thing going here. Don't need you coming around to mess it up."

Mike bristled. He was done letting people insult him, push him around. "Seems like the folks tonight had a different opinion."

"I seen your kind before. Got the hot stuff now, but I put five dollar on your quarter you gonna burn all your bridges behind you. That's what they always do. Thinks they's too good for anything 'cept the big time. But they never gets there. Never do."

"Well then, guess I'll see you back here tomorrow night." Mike turned to go.

"I was you, I wouldn't do that. I got friends, and they don't like nobody cutting into my territory."

Forcing a laugh just loud enough for Smokey to hear, Mike set off down the deserted street, his shiny boots making scrunching noises on the covering of packed snow. He had already rounded the first corner, was just recalling again that kiss from May Convery, when he felt a hand on his shoulder from behind.

"Hey, wait a minute." The man's voice was deep and slightly hoarse.

Mike swung around, wishing he hadn't been quite so cavalier. He fully expected to see Smokey with one of his cronies, come to rough him up. Instead, he found himself face to face with an innocuous-looking white man, heavyset, with unkempt gray hair and a cockeyed smile.

"Heard you playing tonight at the Eloise," said the stranger. "How long you been around town?"

"Not long." Mike was still wary. Could be some kind of trick. Maybe this fellow was out to rob him. Inside his pocket, Mike curled his hand into a fist.

"You're way too good for that joint, you know."

"I know."

The stranger reached inside his baggy overcoat. Mike braced himself.

"Here." The man pulled out what looked to be a business card and handed it to Mike. "Be at this address tomorrow morning, eleven o'clock. I'll tell 'em you're coming. When you get there, just say Jimmy sent you." He peered through the dimness. "All right?"

Mike took the card. It was too dark to read. The fellow turned and started to walk away.

"Just remember," he called over his shoulder, "Mr. Pastor's looking for somebody with *class*. And he's a sucker for anything patriotic."

Missing

T he intense light of late morning streamed through the tall windows of May's bedroom. Nervously, she eyed the clock on the corner of her rosewood writing table. She had checked it at least a dozen times in the last fifteen minutes. He should have arrived before now. It wasn't like him to be late.

It had been only a matter of hours since the last guests departed from the holiday ball. Long hours during which she had been unable to sleep, wondering why Mike had left last night without a word to her. Her mother had claimed he appeared ill, but May thought it unlikely. He was fine when she saw him in the gentlemen's dressing room, just before Teddy's inopportune arrival. The recollection of that kiss haunted her incessantly. She had always wondered what passion felt like. Now she knew.

She turned back to the poem she'd been writing in a futile effort to occupy her mind. It was the one she had intended as a gift for Mike, a declaration of sorts. A love poem. But now she was less certain than before how he would react to it. She simply *must* see him.

Frustrated, she closed the red tooled-leather cover of her journal, that repository of all the dreams and worldly ambitions she was not supposed to have. She used to feel there might never be anyone she could trust to understand them—to understand *her*.

But that was before Mike.

Admittedly, just that morning it had occurred to her that her obsession with him might be nothing more than a useless protest of her inevitable future as Mrs. Theodore Livingstone. But it couldn't be only that. From the first moment they met, she had been struck as surely as if Cupid himself let fly an arrow straight to her heart. Granted, he wasn't nearly as handsome as Teddy or, for that matter, as most of the other young men she knew. Neither did he always dress in the latest style. But he had one quality none of the others did, one attribute that, in her eyes, made him perfect.

He was an artist.

It had become almost a daily habit to lose herself in fantasies about him, imagining their life together—he pursuing his music, she her poetry. She knew from her reading of history that great artists were often lonely people. It seemed most of them led tragic lives. But it wouldn't be like that for the two of them, not if they had each other. What more would they ever need?

She considered again his disappearance from the ball. Had he left because of Edward MacDowell's unexpected performance, afraid of being compared to someone so lauded by the public and the press? But walking out without a word! He must have known how she would feel.

And now this—failing to show up for their lesson. She feared he hadn't forgotten. He had chosen not to come. Not to see her.

Unless he had left a message with someone . . . perhaps her mother *knew* the lesson was canceled and simply had neglected to mention it. Maybe he really *was* ill.

She rose from her desk, tossed her journal into the drawer of the commode, and hurried from the bedroom, making her way down the wide hall flanked by gold sconces and a gallery of somber old-master paintings. As she descended the sweeping marble staircase to the foyer, she spotted her mother in front of the carved walnut console to the right, studying her reflection in an eighteenth-century vermeil mirror, painstakingly adjusting the angle of what appeared to be yet another new hat. Bundled in a sumptuous ermine-trimmed cape, she was obviously on her way out. May was surprised to see six trunks lined up at the door.

"You didn't tell me you were leaving this morning," May said, coming up behind her.

"I thought you'd be sleeping."

Actually, whether her mother stayed or went was not in the least bit important to May. She had only one thing on her mind. "Did Mr. Bernard cancel the piano lessons for today?"

Appearing satisfied, finally, with the details of her ensemble, Mrs. Convery pivoted to address her eldest daughter. "No, he didn't. But I was planning to dismiss him anyway. I've never been impressed by that young man. I don't know why I let you convince me to have him perform at my ball—though as it turned out, I didn't need him."

"Dismiss him! But Mother, Emily and I are doing very well under Mr. Bernard's instruction."

"Nonsense! It was meant as a temporary position anyway. You know that. Miss Sidorov will be returning from Russia in a couple of months. And until then, I've found someone else to take over, someone I learned of just yesterday from my friend Mrs. Applegate, who recommends her highly. Mrs. Eagleton will make the arrangements."

"But I don't want a new teacher!"

"Hush now! And pay attention," her mother continued, blithely ignoring May's objection. "I'll be back in six or seven weeks. We have a lot of work to do in preparation for your coming-out ball. We must still go through the motions, you know. Even though you have a husband already waiting in the wings." She smiled at May as if the two of them were co-conspirators, though nothing could have been further from the truth. "Nevertheless, a coming-out ball marks your official entry into society, and everyone is anticipating a spectacular event. You are, after all, George Convery's daughter."

She hated the way her mother always referred to her that way, as if she herself took no responsibility for May's existence.

"But Mother, you make it sound like my future is already decided."

Isabelle Convery raised her brows.

"I mean, concerning Teddy—" May paused. Maybe this wasn't the ideal time to present her case, but better now than too late. "It seems to me that my own inclinations should be considered."

"Inclinations? Whatever are you talking about?"

"I'm talking about my *feelings*, Mother. My preferences in matters of the heart."

"My goodness, May! I can't think of a young woman who wouldn't be thrilled at the prospect of becoming Mrs. Theodore Livingstone. You couldn't wish for a more handsome husband. Or one with a more promising future."

"But Teddy and I have nothing in common. Nothing of importance anyway. He has no appreciation of the arts. No curiosity about the things that interest me."

"You and Teddy have *everything* in common! Why, you've grown up within a few blocks of one another. You've known each other since you were children. And your fathers are business partners. Someday soon Teddy will be a partner, too."

"I don't care! What could be more *boring* than being married to a banker?" May was sorry to insult her own father, but she had lost all patience. "The simple fact is that I'm not in love with Teddy."

"My dear girl, don't you know that love is fleeting? Far wiser to base a marriage on mutual advantage."

"You mean like your marriage to Father? How well has *that* worked out?"

Her mother's solicitous expression quickly changed to one of shocked indignation. "How dare you say such a thing to me!"

"I'm only stating the obvious, Mother."

"You should not suppose yourself so clever as to imagine what goes on between a husband and wife behind closed doors."

"Closed doors? The two of you for the most part live in different houses!"

"Your father and I have made sacrifices in order to do what's best for you and your sister. If you have no appreciation of that, then you are even less perceptive than I thought."

May bit her tongue, holding back what she really wanted to say—that a woman doesn't marry a man thirty years her senior except for money and position. And that, by the way, she had noticed the looks frequently exchanged between her mother and Pierre Durant, the handsome Frenchman who served as underbutler at the family's country estate in Connecticut. They were not the kind of glances typically passed between a mistress of the house and a servant.

"I'll have no more of this kind of talk from you, May. It's quite unbecoming of a young woman nearly ready to assume the responsibilities of adulthood." Her mother's tone was clearly meant to preclude further discussion. "Now pay attention. I've given Mrs. Eagleton precise instructions for your activities until my return from Connecticut. I've made sure that everyone knows you'll be staying in town for the entire season. Your social calendar is quite full. There's plenty to keep you busy—and out of trouble," she added pointedly.

It was too much, the way her mother simply brushed off every question and concern she raised. She would *not* be treated like a child! "Why should I spend my time with people who bore me to tears? And I won't be a slave to some ridiculous social calendar you've devised just so you can say you've done your duty without having to attend to Emily and me yourself."

Mrs. Convery seemed caught off guard by her daughter's belligerence but quickly recovered herself. "I wonder what your father would say if he were to hear you speaking to me like that."

"And I wonder what he would say about you and Mr. Durant," May spat out with a viciousness she hadn't known was in her. "That *is* why you're so anxious to return to Connecticut, isn't it?"

Isabelle Convery's face turned as scarlet as the silk roses atop her new hat.

"You see, Mother, I'm more perceptive than you give me credit for. And also shrewder. You force me to be. I will not study with a new piano teacher, and"—she paused, afraid now but determined not to lose her momentum—"and I will *not* marry Teddy Livingstone just because you and Father say I must."

The swift slap from her mother's hand fell hard across May's cheek. It was not the sting of it that stunned her but the mere fact of it; such a thing had never happened before.

"If you ever dare to threaten me again, young lady," Mrs. Convery said in a toxic whisper, "you will find out exactly how shrewd *I* can be. And I promise you will not like the result."

She swept her gloves off the console and headed for the door. "As I said, I'll be back in February." Mrs. Convery exited the foyer, leaving the door open for the footman, who immediately entered and began transporting her luggage to the waiting carriage.

"Mother—" May started to call after her but stopped. What was the point? Her mother would never listen. She had her own priorities, all of them more important than her daughter's happiness.

An aura of gloom settled over her as she contemplated what lay ahead. Her coming-out ball followed by the announcement of her engagement. Plans for a wedding that, as her mother predicted, was certain to be one of the most talked-about social events of the year.

How could she summon excitement for any of it when all she wanted was to be with Mike Bernard? By now, she'd imagined it so many times: the two of them traveling the world, mingling with artists and intellectuals—people who would appreciate her poetry, regard it seriously. She would be so happy, and he would be proud of her. They'd be proud of each other.

Inseparable.

Why shouldn't she have the kind of life she wanted—a life that only *he* could give her? That is, if he wanted her. And if he did—if they were smart enough, determined enough—how could her parents stop them?

Especially if they were to find out when it was already too late.

Path of Least Resistance

I studied at the Stern Conservatory, sir. My certificate—" Anxiously, Mike extracted a folded paper from his coat pocket and handed it to Tony Pastor.

Pastor, perched on the edge of a massive oak desk covered with stacks of sheet music, was stout, darkly mustachioed, and impeccably dressed, imparting an image that befitted his reputation as one of New York's most successful impresarios. He unfolded the document and looked at it, appearing puzzled. "But this says *Michael Brown.*"

"Mike Bernard is my stage name," Mike replied, hoping Pastor would be impressed.

"Stage name, you say." Pastor returned the certificate. "I understand these days you're playing at the Eloise."

Mike reddened. He wished that fellow, Jimmy, had been a little more discreet. "Played there once, sir. Just for fun," he added sheepishly.

"Needless to say, Tony Pastor's theater is a far cry from anyplace like that." Pastor looked at him askance. "But go ahead, have a seat."

Unable to think of anything he might say to mitigate the disgrace of having been discovered at the Eloise, Mike busied himself with removing his coat. He draped it over the back of the chair Pastor had offered him, placed his hat on a side table, and sat down. So far things didn't seem to be going particularly well.

"I assume you've been to my theater."

"Not yet, sir."

Pastor's lips tightened. "Then let me explain a few things. Tony Pastor's is a family theater, a place to enjoy clean, wholesome entertainment. Ladies and children are welcome. I take pride in the quality of the acts we present to our audience."

"Highly commendable, sir."

"We offer two shows a day, a matinee and an evening performance. I bring in some of the biggest headliners in the country. What I need is a musical director who can manage the pit orchestra. And I need a first-rate accompanist."

Mike nodded matter-of-factly, as if he wasn't at all surprised to be considered for such a position. Musical director! It sounded important.

"I'll warn you, the boys in the pit are not always the easiest to work with," Pastor said. "Neither is some of the talent. The biggest names are usually the worst. But a good musical director knows how to handle them. I don't like anybody's feathers ruffled. Especially the peacocks, if you know what I mean."

"Absolutely, sir."

Pastor reached behind him on the desk for his cigar box. He opened the lid. "Care to indulge?"

Mike declined with a shake of his head. Pastor selected a cigar, bit off one end, spit it out, and lit up. "I can see you're a young lad. Maybe well trained, but I'm guessing new to the business. Otherwise, you'd not be playing the Eloise." He winked and continued amiably, seeming to have forgiven Mike's former sins, at least for the time being. "You know, I came up through the ranks myself. Started out when I was just a kid, singing at P. T. Barnum's American Museum. Played the circus, minstrel shows, variety shows, you name it. I know what it takes to inspire a crowd. I know the thrill of holding an audience in the palm of your hand. As a matter of fact, I still like to take the stage for a song from time to time." He beamed at Mike, obviously enjoying the opportunity to talk about himself. "Guess you could say it's one of the benefits of having my own theater."

"When you're born with music in your blood, sir, it's impossible to live without it."

Pastor flicked the ashes from his cigar. "So, tell me, Mr. Bernard, what are your musical aspirations?" he asked, suddenly back to business.

Mike toyed with the idea of honesty, but quickly decided against it. What good would it do to tell Pastor that his passion was serious music? That he would need this job for only a short time, as a stopgap and nothing more. That playing a vaudeville house was among the last things he would choose to do with his talent.

"In Berlin, when I played my command performance for the Kaiser"—he paused to allow Pastor time to absorb the significance of this new and perhaps redemptive revelation—"I can remember thinking there could never be any greater moment. Not ever. But now I understand. When it comes to music, there's always more to experience." He looked Pastor square in the eyes. He would give it his best shot, just for the hell of it. "And, Mr. Pastor, there's nothing I'd rather do than be the *classiest* musical director you've ever had."

Saying nothing, Pastor stood up and walked behind his desk. He lowered himself into the big leather chair and leaned back, scrutinizing Mike as he puffed on his cigar.

"All right, young man, let's hear you play," he finally said. "Because if you're not first-rate, if you can't play the kind of music the people who come to my theater want to hear, there's no point in either of us wasting our time with conversation." He gestured toward the brightly polished upright piano in the corner, next to a tall window looking out on Fourteenth Street.

His heart flip-flopping, Mike rose from the chair.

"I'd be delighted, sir."

He strolled over to the instrument, trying to appear confident, just as a disturbing image flashed through his mind— Edward MacDowell embracing Isabelle Convery under the brilliant chandeliers of the Converys' Fifth Avenue ballroom.

He pulled out the bench and sat down, recalling the second tip Jimmy had given him: Pastor was a sucker for anything patriotic.

He gave a quick shake to his wrists, then set about making the piano sound as crisp and bright as a military band. In his mind, he could hear the roll of the drums, the bright burst of trumpets, the trill of flutes, feet marching, and the whip of flags fluttering in the wind. Miraculously, he was able to re-create it all, with the same bold energy and reckless passion he'd discovered in himself the night before at the Eloise.

He must have played for at least five minutes. When he was done, he looked up to see Tony Pastor still seated behind his desk, looking no less skeptical than before.

"I dare say they didn't teach you that number at the conservatory."

Mike wasn't sure what to make of Pastor's comment. Maybe he had miscalculated. Maybe what sold at the Eloise didn't sell at Tony Pastor's theater.

"I assume you've studied composition, orchestration. You know your way around a musical score?" Pastor asked.

"I do, sir."

"Hmm." He thought for a moment. "My trumpet player, Jimmy, seems to like you, but I'm not sure how the rest of the fellows in the pit would feel about taking orders from a kid. How old are you, anyway?"

"Twenty-one, sir," Mike replied, deciding an extra couple of years couldn't hurt. "Believe me, Mr. Pastor, I know how to handle myself. It won't be a problem. Remember, I learned about discipline from the Germans."

"Hmm."

Mike could hear Pastor absently tapping his fingers on the desktop in the rhythm of a marching drum.

"All right, young man," he finally said. With a low grunt, he pushed back his chair and stood up. "I'll pay you fifty dollars a week. You'll start right away."

Mike was caught off guard by the suddenness of Pastor's offer. In fact, now that the position of musical director was actually within reach, he wasn't sure he wanted it. This was vaudeville—acrobats and jugglers, dog acts, tap dancers, second-rate crooners. He imagined himself standing at the door to Tony Pastor's theater, barking out come-ons to the crowd. *Step right up and see the greatest show on earth. Mike Bernard, musical director extraordinaire, will amaze you with his superhuman feats. Watch him soar through the air as he plays the piano with one hand tied behind his back.*

But it was a job. And the money . . .

"I thought it would be more." Though the words unquestionably came from his mouth, Mike could hardly believe he'd said them. Fifty dollars a week, two hundred a month—that was nearly as much as his father made in a year, more than he'd ever seen at one time in his entire life. But hadn't he read somewhere that vaudeville stars were paid hundreds for a single engagement at a top theater like Tony Pastor's?

Pastor sat down abruptly. "What exactly did you have in mind?" he said, his tone reserved.

Mike knew little of the art of negotiation, but double seemed like a good place to start. "One hundred a week."

Maybe it was unreasonable, all things considered, but Pastor undoubtedly expected him to drive a hard bargain. Not to do so would make him seem a rank amateur. "With all due respect, Mr. Pastor, I'm sure you'd agree that a skilled musical director is a theater's most important asset."

Pastor glared at him. "I don't need a lecture from you on the theater business. I'm doing you a huge favor offering you this position, you know. You can count yourself lucky that my current director gave short notice that he's going on tour, and I'm in a hurry to find a replacement. Nevertheless, there are far more experienced people out there looking for a job like this, and they'd take it for less."

Mike arose from the bench. This was the tricky part, he told himself. The rest would be easy. Silently, he walked over to the chair where he'd left his coat, retrieved it, and picked up his hat from the table. Then, turning to Pastor, he managed what he hoped would pass for a self-assured smile. "Thank you very much for your time, sir."

He had done it! He'd called Tony Pastor's bluff. He felt a sudden surge of pride at his own cleverness. Pastor was only waiting for the perfect moment to deliver his next offer. He was sure of it. Mike started counting in his head, with each step that he took toward the door. One, two, three—

"Mr. Bernard!"

He swung around, his mouth watering. He wouldn't be greedy. He wanted this over with.

"Sorry we couldn't reach an agreement," Pastor said.

Mike waited, expecting the compromise any second.

"I wish you the best of luck. You've got talent." With a curt nod, Pastor started thumbing through a tall stack of sheet music.

Mike was too stunned to move. Was it over? Had Pastor dismissed him? He wanted to say something, but he had no idea what—unless it was to beg Mr. Pastor for forgiveness.

Pastor looked up from his work. "You're still here?"

"I—I'm sorry, sir." Embarrassed, Mike turned on his heel and scooted out the door. It was then that the enormity of his mistake hit him full force. Fifty dollars a week! He would have been practically rich. What had he been thinking to refuse a salary like that?

He looked over his shoulder. The door to Pastor's office was still open. Slowly, he retraced his steps, waited a moment, then poked his head around the corner. "Excuse me, sir?"

Pastor looked up for the second time. "Yes?"

"I'll take the fifty."

Pastor paused. The slight twitch at the corners of his mouth suggested he was pleased, maybe amused, but all he said was, "We'll see how you do."

Fancy Man

Jessie Boyce lounged in bed in a pink silk chemise, smoking a cigarette. She was exhausted from the trip to New York. Worse, she was impatient and bored. Seemed she was always waiting for Ben.

On her back, twisting a lock of long, black hair around her finger, she watched the smoke spiral toward the ceiling. So easily distracted, Ben was. He should have met her at the hotel with a big bouquet of roses, her coming all the way from Louisville and after so much time they'd been apart.

But then she ought to know by now what to expect out of Ben Harney. And, after all, wasn't she just as crazy about him as ever? Her *fancy man*, she liked to call him. Wildly charming, unpredictable, never played a song the same way twice.

She smiled dreamily. He was that way with lovemaking, too.

She wondered if he'd thought to get her a Christmas present. She supposed just finding him in one piece would be enough of one. As far as she knew, he'd managed to stay out of trouble lately. Still, she was always worrying about him. A white musician traveling with an all-Negro band was bound to attract attention, and sometimes not the best kind. But then, this time Ben wasn't with the band. He said he wouldn't need them at Tony Pastor's theater.

She sat up suddenly, listening. She could hear brisk footsteps in the hallway, coming closer. The next second, Ben broke through the door, breathless.

"Baby!"

He tossed his bowler onto the dresser and shrugged off his coat, letting it drop to the floor.

"Got here just as fast as I could," he said, diving onto the bed next to her and rolling her into his arms. He pulled the cigarette from her lips and dangled it mischievously, just out of her reach.

"Give that back!" she demanded, laughing.

"Nope. I want your full attention."

She ran her fingers through Ben's soft reddish hair, marveling at how she never could stay mad at him for long. "It's all yours."

Ben dumped Jessie's cigarette into an ashtray by the bed and climbed on top of her, planting a trail of kisses up the side of her neck to her ear. "I've missed you something awful."

"You mean that?"

"'Course I mean it."

"I hear there's lots of pretty girls in New York."

"Not a one of 'em as pretty as you. Besides, I only been here four days myself."

"Oh, I see!" She tried to wriggle away from him. "You haven't had time to look around much. Is that what you're saying?"

He pushed up on his arms, smiling down at her. "Now, you know I didn't mean to say *that.*"

She laughed. "Well, I'm here now, so you don't need to look any further. Besides, you and Strap must be real busy rehearsing for opening night at Tony Pastor's."

Ben shook his head, frowning. "Haven't seen hide or hair of Strap, and I'm starting to get nervous. We open in just over a week. I told him it wasn't a good idea to go off traveling by himself. He doesn't know anything about Missouri. No telling what kind of people he might have run into."

Jessie knew that Ben's concern wasn't just because he needed his sideman for opening night. He considered Strap a good friend.

"Just before he left for there, he was saying how he heard white people in Sedalia were real friendly and all," Ben went on, "but I just read a story in the paper last week about some lynching in another town not too far from there. A black man accused of trying to rape a white woman. That's usually how it starts. Maybe he just happened accidentally to brush by her on the street or something. It can be like that. Seems the innocent ones get scooped up more often than the guilty, and people don't seem to care. They call it justice, but it's not like any justice I know."

News of a lynching always made Ben think about his old friend Tom Strong and what happened to him back in Louisville. Jessie knew he still blamed himself.

"But Ben—honey, there's no sense worrying about Strap. There's not a thing you can do except wait for him to show up. I'm sure he will."

"Can't figure what would keep him from getting here when he said he would. He was looking forward to playing New York, I know he was."

"You just keep your mind on getting ready for opening night. If we have to, we can handle it fine without Strap. Why, this is the kind of break we've been hoping for since the beginning."

"You're right about that."

"What did Mr. Pastor say when you told him about me?"

"About you?"

"Uh-huh. That you've got the best white-lady coon shouter in the business."

"Fact is I haven't told him yet."

"What?" She gave Ben a hard shove. "Why not?"

"I will, honey, but after opening night. Soon as I can. Look, he doesn't even know about Strap—not exactly, anyway. I figured there was no sense complicating our negotiations. He'll find out everything soon enough. By then, I'll be in a position to get even more money out of him."

Jessie felt her insides tightening, the way they always did when Ben tried to skirt around something that was important to her. Before he could stop her, she'd slithered out of bed.

"Hey, where you going?"

She marched over to the window and parted the blinds. Snowflakes were swirling in front of the glass, the sinking sun partially hidden behind tall, big-city buildings in the distance. Soon it would be dark. For a moment, she forgot about herself, thinking of Strap out there alone, making his way to New York. Ben was right. A lot of things could happen. Terrible things. But she had a feeling he was all right, and she trusted her feelings. She'd always had a sixth sense, and it was seldom wrong.

Neither was it wrong right now about Ben. He didn't want her with him on opening night. It was going to be him and Strap. Or, if Strap didn't show, he'd go it alone.

"What's wrong with you, Jessie?" Ben rolled out of bed, sidled over to her, and spun her around. "You got something clouding up your mind, so why don't you just go ahead and spill it?"

Jessie hesitated, then let him have it. "You think Strap is good enough for Tony Pastor's, but I'm not?" She pushed him out of her way and stomped over to the nightstand, where she lit another cigarette, extinguishing the match with a sharp flick of her wrist. "You know, lots of people think I have it in me to be a big star. But what's it to you? Long as I follow you around and tell you how wonderful you are, that's *all* you care about."

By accident, she caught a glimpse of herself in the mirror above the dresser—the angry pull of her brows, the heated glow of her cheeks, the way she drew on her cigarette with such ferocity. This wasn't the first time Ben had seen her like this. In fact, sometimes she wondered if he didn't somehow enjoy it.

"Why is it women always have to give up everything for love?" She took another long pull on her cigarette. "I figured we'd be different. Or at least *I'd* be different."

"Jessie, honey! Don't you worry about a thing, baby." Ben's words were slick as butter on his tongue. "We're a team, just like I always said we'd be." He came up to her again and pulled her close, gently stroking her hair.

Jessie tried to work up the steam to push him away again, but his touch was like a magnet, too powerful to resist.

"Tony Pastor may not know it yet"—she felt the softness of his lips on her ear, the warmth of his breath—"but he's getting himself one heck of a deal. Ben Harney, Strap Hill, plus the unbelievably beautiful and talented Miss Jessie Boyce—all come to take New York City by storm."

The Awakening

W hat do you think of the new headliner?"
Jimmy, trumpet in hand, leaned across the
piano. It was January and the first matinee of 1896
at Tony Pastor's theater. With only ten minutes until showtime,
Mike was busy making last-minute notations on the opening
score.

"Actually, I haven't heard him." He hurriedly scribbled
something in the margin. With his debut as the theater's new
musical director only minutes away, he had plenty on his mind
and no time for small talk.

"Some people say Ben Harney's a Negro passing himself
off as white."

Mike didn't look up. "Doesn't matter to me what he is."

"Well, me neither, I guess. 'Cept I hear Pastor's paying him
a whole bunch of money. More than he's paid any other first-
time headliner without a New York reputation."

Mike stopped writing. "How much is Harney making?"

"Don't know exactly. But Pastor must think he's something
pretty special. I don't get it. A fellow from Kentucky singing
colored songs?"

Mike knew that Harney played the piano and sang. Beyond that, nothing. "I guess we'll find out for ourselves this afternoon." He went back to working on his score.

"Rehearsal was kind of tough today, huh?"

"It was nothing."

"Those Jemm sisters, they can be a real pain in the butt." Jimmy chuckled. "Heard they said you were stepping on their vocals with your fancy piano work."

"Not my fault if they don't know what sounds good."

"What did Pastor say? He doesn't like trouble, you know."

"Like I said, it was nothing."

"Well, that's good." Jimmy straightened up. "Listen, kid, take it easy this afternoon. There's plenty of time later to show what you've got." He patted Mike on the shoulder. "Just do things Mr. Pastor's way," he advised before lumbering off to take his seat with the other players.

Mike caught a glimpse of Pastor standing in the corner of the orchestra pit. He knew his boss was already irritated with him because of what happened at rehearsal. The singing Jemm sisters were identical twins with the shrillest, most annoying voices he'd ever heard. He figured anything he could do to drown them out would have been a favor to the audience.

He pulled out his pocket watch, checked the time. Only five minutes to go. Ensconced behind the piano, he took a private moment to absorb the atmosphere of the theater that was to be his new home, at least for a while. The interior of Tony Pastor's was designed to inspire awe. The elaborate carvings of the proscenium arch were framed in cream and gold, the drop curtain decorated with allegorical figures, and the oval fresco above the auditorium painted with cupids, roses, and clouds. The walls were a pale shade of blue, while the seats on the main floor, in the boxes, and on the two levels of galleries were upholstered in dark-blue velvet. Clusters of electric lights attached to the gallery balustrades twinkled like bouquets of stars.

Tonight, nearly all of the theater's twelve hundred seats were filled, the patrons reputed to be an egalitarian mix of working, middle, and upper classes. Mike breathed deep, inhaling their various scents—perfume, sweat, stale tobacco—mingled with the warm, salty aroma of freshly roasted peanuts from the lobby concession stand. He detected, too, the faint odor of cloves, a common way to mask the smell of liquor on the breath. Though Tony Pastor maintained the family-friendly atmosphere of his theater by banning alcohol, a bar was conveniently located next door. Undoubtedly, some of the men had already been there, including a fair number of the musicians now warming up in the pit.

Mike had never played before such a large audience, yet he felt fairly calm about his debut, assuming what he did this afternoon was unlikely to be judged with a critic's ear. He imagined there was little room for seriousness at Tony Pastor's vaudeville theater, little expectation of the sublime. This crowd was here to be amused and amazed by the lineup of a dozen separate acts ranging from singers and dancers to a jump-roping dog and a shark-swallowing regurgitator.

And, of course, the headliner, Ben Harney.

Pastor gave him the nod that meant it was time to begin. Mike signaled the orchestra, the house lights went black, and, with appropriate musical fanfare, the curtain rose.

The first attraction was a waltzing monkey. The little beast, dressed like a harem girl, was ordered about by a bare-chested man in billowing silk pants and a flowing headdress. For background, Mike led the orchestra in its rendition of "The Blue Danube," punctuated periodically by strains of an oboe meant to sound like a snake charmer's pungi.

Next were the singing Jemm sisters, followed by a comedy dialogue between two bums on a park bench that garnered plenty of laughs despite having been scrubbed clean of its funniest but marginally off-color material during the morning rehearsal. For the audience's further delight were the all-male Liberty Quartet, a professional regurgitator—who started by swallowing a goldfish and worked his way up to a small shark—a dog and donkey act, and, last before intermission, the British-born singer and dancer Pauline Markham. She had once been a popular favorite but was rumored to be on a downward slide. Still, this afternoon she earned a standing ovation and returned for two encores.

Mike accompanied all of them, sometimes with the pit orchestra, sometimes solo. While he took special care not to step on the Jemm sisters' vocals, for which he received an approving nod from Pastor, he was not so timid with some of the other numbers, diverging from the score just enough to wow the audience with a few bars of grandiose intro or a fast and flashy finale. As a classical musician, he had been bound to the printed page. His job was to interpret, and that was all. Indeed, to alter a single note of the masters would be blasphemy. But here at Tony Pastor's, nothing was sacred. Here, he was free to be his own master.

Already, to his surprise, he was starting to like it.

It was past four o'clock when the headliner, Ben Harney, finally strutted across the stage to the polite applause of an audience with absolutely no inkling of what they were about to see and hear. At first glance, Mike was unimpressed. Though Harney smiled and waved to the crowd, he appeared uncomfortable and rather insignificant, alone on that huge stage after all the colorful antics that had preceded him. Behind his piano was a serene backdrop of a country road winding through fields of cotton. Yet his attire would have been more suitable for the ballroom—a black tailcoat, stiff-collared shirt, white bow tie, top hat. In his right hand, he carried a shiny black cane. As soon as he sat down at the piano, he leaned it against the frame, pulled down the tail of his jacket.

And then he began to play.

Right away, the driving rhythm of his music, with its unusual syncopated accents, set itself apart from all that had preceded it. What came out of Ben Harney's mouth made it all the more curious—a raw voice that scraped like gravel, and streetwise lyrics sung in a dialect so out of character with the way he looked as to be jarring to the senses. He wore no burnt cork to blacken his skin and exaggerate his lips in the manner that was expected of Negroes or those who impersonated them on stage. Yet this lanky young man hunched over the keys, a shock of fine red hair obscuring his face, sounded as black as could be.

> *Standin' on the corner, didn't mean no harm*
> *This mawnin'*
> *The copper grabbed me by the arm*
> *Without warnin',*
> *Took me down to the jail house door,*
> *Place I had never been before*
> *This mawnin'.*
> *Put me on board a Frankfort train,*
> *Loaded me down with a ball and chain.*
> *Every station that I passed by*
> *I could imagine my baby cry.*

A shout rang out from somewhere in the back of the theater. Harney's head snapped up. A smile spread across his face.

A short, wiry Negro in blackface, costumed in a red-and-white-striped jacket and a silver top hat, started to make his way down the theater's center aisle, shuffling his feet in a circle and clapping his hands as he went. Every time Harney sang out a phrase, he echoed it.

Bye-bye, my honey, if you call it gone, O Babe,
Bye-bye, my honey, if you call it gone, O
    Babe,
Bye-bye, my honey, if you call it gone.
Bye-bye, my honey, if you call it gone.

The back-and-forth continued on and on, the effect hypnotic. Finally, the black man reached the front of the theater, hopping onto the stage with the grace of a panther. Harney stopped playing, swiveled around on the bench, and grabbed his cane. Then, without missing a beat, he started doing what had been billed as "Ben Harney's Famous Stick Dance"—really nothing more than a tap dance that he performed sitting down. His feet and his cane kept the rhythm while his sideman resumed the ring shout, circling and shuffling his feet, stomping and clapping, working himself into a righteous frenzy. Every now and then, Harney would stop for a beat or two, an extended pause, and then start up again with the cane and his feet and an exuberant shout from his partner. Finally, he tossed the stick in the air, deftly catching it with one hand.

"Ladies and gentlemen, Mr. Strap Hill!" Harney cried, pointing the cane at Strap, who spun around, sprung into the air in a wide scissors leap and landed in a split, providing Harney enough time to reposition himself at the keyboard for the final chorus.

You've been a good old wagon but you done
    broke down.
You've been a good old wagon but you done
    broke down.
You've been a good old wagon but you done
    broke down
This mawnin'.

62

Harney struck the last chord and, with a shout, jumped to his feet. Both performers turned to the crowd, raising their arms in an exuberant gesture of triumph. Then, in sync, they swept into a low bow.

For a few seconds, uncertainty hovered in the air, as if no one was quite sure what to do. Then, suddenly, the whole theater erupted in applause. Men, women, and children abandoned their comfortable seats, everybody on their feet, clapping and cheering. Ben Harney and Strap Hill wore smiles a mile wide. Harney slapped Hill on the back, Hill slapped Harney. As the delirium continued, they linked arms and broke into a lively jig, which set the crowd off even more.

Amid the chaos, Mike sat quietly behind his grand piano, hands folded in his lap. He could feel the dampness beneath his shirt, tiny beads of sweat sprouting on his forehead. What was going through his mind was treasonous, a betrayal of all he'd believed in for as long as he could remember. The years of study, the expectations of so many. But would it really be so terrible if he wanted something different, something *more*? Why had he worked so hard if not to win the kind of adulation he was witnessing right now?

He wondered how much Tony Pastor was paying Harney. Jimmy had suggested it was a lot. His own salary, which only a few days ago had seemed like a small fortune, now felt insultingly paltry. The more he thought about it, the hotter under the collar he got. He was a classically trained pianist! He'd performed for the Kaiser! He could play rings around Ben Harney!

But would he ever have the nerve to try something as daring, as brilliant as what Harney had just done? It wasn't only a matter of spicing up some popular tune with a bit of bravado, like he'd done at the Eloise. No, this was brand-new territory. Jimmy said there was talk of ragtime being nothing more than *colored folks' music*. But no one seemed too sure. Maybe that was Ben Harney's biggest stroke of genius—claiming to be its originator with nobody in a position to dispute it.

Mike's mind raced ahead, imagining his own name, his smiling face on the marquee in front of Tony Pastor's. Making ten times the money he was earning now. Maybe more.

It was just an idea, maybe a crazy one. But if he really *wanted* to, could he do it?

Could he?

Café Showdown

A horse-drawn hansom cab pulled up in front of Tony Pastor's. The driver quickly jumped down to open the door for his sole passenger.

A slender young woman emerged from the windowed interior. She wore a fine wool cape with mink trim, a matching hat mounted atop her coiffure. Her expression was serious, not at all like someone out for an entertaining time at the matinee.

She glided past the tall marquees on either side of the main entrance, stopping at the booth to purchase her fifty-cent ticket. Then through the lobby, through the double doors to the auditorium, and down the center aisle, claiming her seat in one of the front rows.

Throughout the entire show, she spoke to no one, nor did she take much notice of the cavalcade of acts. Even the headliner, Ben Harney, now finishing his second week of a three-week engagement.

Her eyes rarely left the orchestra pit.

When the matinee was over, the crowd rapidly thinned. The musicians made a hasty exit, while the musical director remained in the pit, sorting through his stack of scores.

"Congratulations."

Mike looked up with a start. "Miss Convery! What are you doing here?"

May observed with a sinking feeling that he appeared not at all pleased to see her.

"I bought a ticket for the show, just like everybody else. Is that all right with you?"

"How did you find out I was here?"

"I do read the newspaper, you know. I saw the write-up in the *Times*, extolling the virtues of Tony Pastor's brilliant new musical director. I'm sure you can't have thought your whereabouts would remain secret forever. Though apparently you had no intention of letting me know what had become of you."

Mike looked down at his hands. "I meant to talk with you, to explain—"

"Then why didn't you?"

"Look, I've only been working here a couple of weeks. There's been a lot to do. I've been very busy."

"Busy? Too busy to tell me why you ran out on my mother's party with a hundred people waiting to hear you play? Too busy to tell me you wouldn't be coming anymore for our lessons?"

He seemed annoyed. "Your mother didn't want me to play at her party. She dismissed me, sent me upstairs to twiddle my thumbs so Edward MacDowell could steal all the glory. She couldn't have been surprised that I walked out. As a matter of fact, I'm sure she was relieved."

"And what about me? And my sister? We were expecting you for our lessons." It was painful to be discussing piano lessons when what she wanted was to ask him how he could bear to have left her that way. Didn't he know how desperately she longed to see him? Didn't he feel the same?

May glanced around the theater, the rows and rows of empty seats, and was suddenly afraid. Perhaps it had been a mistake to come. Was her life really so vacant that she had nothing better to do than seek out someone who clearly had forgotten she even existed? Her gaze lingered on the open doors to the lobby. Maybe she should leave, before she humiliated herself further.

She was startled to feel Mike's hand on her wrist.

"Come on, let's go," he said. "It's no good here."

She hesitated, but not long, before offering her assent with a nod. He moved his hand to her elbow and rapidly propelled her up the aisle, through the double doors into the lobby, and out the theater's main entrance to Fourteenth Street. The burst of frigid air brought her back to her senses. He'd not bothered with either a coat or hat. Was he impervious to the cold? Impervious to all feeling?

"How far is it, wherever it is you're taking me?" she demanded.

"Not far."

They walked without speaking, stiffly side by side, until they arrived at a tiny café still within sight of the theater.

"This is it." Mike opened the door, letting her pass before he followed her inside. The place smelled of coffee, fresh bagels, and smoked fish. They found a small table tucked away in the corner and sat down across from each other, as much distance as possible between them—though that was not at all what May wanted.

A gawky young waiter with a pockmarked face lost no time in rushing over to recite the menu. Mike cut him short, telling him just to bring tea. As soon as he was gone, an uncomfortable silence settled over the table.

"I'm very sorry if I offended you," he began.

Offended her? Her heart sank. He must realize she was here for something more than an apology! Surely he knew how much she missed him, how special their time together had been to her. She'd never shown her writing to anyone else. And that kiss—he had wanted it as much as she did. He had barely been able to tear himself away, even with Teddy pounding on the door. She'd been so certain they were meant to be together. But now, seeing him like this—the way he was acting . . .

"You really don't care if you ever see me again, do you," she declared, quaking inside. "You seem to have found it quite easy to put me out of your mind completely."

"That's not so. You mustn't think that."

The urgency of his tone gave her some slight comfort.

"If you really want to know, I've thought about you a lot since I took the position at Tony Pastor's. I thought about writing to you, trying to explain, but—"

"You could have called. We have a telephone, you know."

"I suppose."

"Or you could have come in person."

"I thought about that, too. But, in the end, I didn't because—because I knew it wouldn't do any good."

"Why not?"

"Because nothing would change the facts of the situation."

"What *facts* are you talking about?"

Mike looked away. "You can't think of me as you're doing now—as you did on the night of your mother's ball. I told you then it wasn't right. You and I can't have feelings for each other. Not *those* kinds of feelings."

"But why not?"

"For lots of reasons."

"But why?"

"I can't explain. It's too complicated."

"Complicated?" She leaned toward him, her body tense with anticipation. Was now the moment he would finally open up to her? "You're always so secretive. You always listen, but you never say what you're feeling. It's like there's a wall around you. I tried to find a way through it. You wouldn't let me. Except for that night—that kiss—"

She stopped speaking. The waiter was back. He deposited their order on the table like it was hardly worth his trouble and wordlessly departed.

Mike poured a heaping spoonful of sugar into his tea and slowly stirred, his eyes locked on the murky liquid spinning in the cup. "About *that*—I'm sure you must realize I was taken completely by surprise. I had no idea *what* was happening between us. Or even what I *wanted* to happen. For God's sake, I was your piano teacher!"

For the first time all afternoon, May smiled. It was almost silly, the way she had to coax it out of him. But the agonized look on his face said it all. Soon he would admit to his feelings, to everything she had waited and hoped for.

"None of that matters now. You don't answer to my parents anymore. They can't stop us from being together."

Mike looked up from his tea. "Have you lost your mind? What do you think your father would say if he knew you were here right now?"

"I don't know, and I don't care."

"Well, you should. As far as your parents are concerned, my position as musical director in a vaudeville house isn't much to brag about."

"But what about your concert tour? It's bound to be a big success."

Mike dropped his gaze. "The tour—it's been delayed again."

"For how long?"

He hesitated. "Until spring."

"All right. But in the meantime, you're obviously doing very well at Tony Pastor's."

"You don't understand, May. What I'm earning at Tony Pastor's—it's not bad, but it isn't the kind of money that would impress your father." He paused again. "Speaking of your father, I-I've heard that he's got quite a temper. That he's even been known to—"

"Won't you please stop talking about my father?" She caught hold of his hand, clinging to it tightly. "There's only one thing that matters—that we were meant to be together."

"*Meant* to be together?" He gave her a long, dark look before decisively pulling away. "Haven't you got me confused with your golden boy, Teddy Livingstone?"

Her stomach tightened.

"Come on now, you can't think me that stupid. I know enough about you and that Livingstone fellow to know that if he isn't your fiancé already, he will be soon."

"So that's why you stayed away?"

Mike made no reply.

"All right, maybe I should have told you about Teddy."

"Told me what? That your parents have decided you make a good pair? Why should it have mattered to me? I had no designs on you then—and I haven't now either."

She hated seeing him like this, sullen and withdrawn, when less than a minute ago they had been on the verge of a breakthrough.

"I'm *not* in love with Teddy."

"I'm sorry, but there's no point to this conversation." With a scowl, Mike pulled a few coins from his pocket and tossed them on the table.

"Come on, let's go," he said, leaving his tea untouched, barely looking at her as he rose from his chair. Speechless, May followed him, desperate for a way to convince him of her determination *not* to become Mrs. Theodore Livingstone.

The sinking sun was nearly blinding as they stepped outside onto the crowded sidewalk. Everyone seemed in a hurry to get somewhere. The brakes of elevated cars squealed in the background, cable cars clanged their bells. A line of horse cars rolled past, prancing steeds blowing smoky breath from their wide nostrils. Squinting, May could see the arched entrance to Pastor's theater down the street, the freestanding marquees on either side announcing the week's attractions. She wondered if Mike planned to leave her now. To say goodbye right there on the street. Maybe forever.

"Where do you live? You know, you've never told me."

"What difference does it make?"

"But I want to know."

He sighed, seeming anxious to be over with all this. "The Hotel Chelsea on West Twenty-Third. I just moved in."

Resolutely, she linked her arm through his. "All right then, let's go. We can walk there."

He regarded her warily. "Why would we do that?"

"You're not afraid, are you?" She flashed an impish smile, trying to make it all seem not so terribly serious.

"What are you talking about? We can't—"

"Shhh." She placed her finger lightly on his lips, her heart pounding. This chance might not come again. "We can do anything we please."

Digging for Gold

N ew song?"

Ben Harney stopped playing and looked up. "Hey, snuck up on me, didn't you!" He grinned. "Hope you don't mind me borrowing your piano. I kind of like it down here in the pit."

Mike tossed his coat over a chair and set his leather briefcase on top of the piano. He opened the latch, spreading the jaws wide. "Something new?" he asked again, rummaging through the sheet music inside, just to be doing something.

"It's called 'I Love One Sweet Black Man.' Jessie's going to sing it."

"Jessie?"

"Ah, that's right. You haven't seen her yet. Jessie's my girl. It took some doing, but I convinced Mr. Pastor she'd be a real fine addition to the act. She's been badgering me something awful, but I wanted to wait till near the end of my run. Give everybody a surprise. Keep 'em talking. She's the best damn coon shouter you'll ever hear. 'Course she'll have to black up, singing a number like that, and Strap with her. But I think she's going to kill 'em."

Mike wasn't terribly interested in hearing about Jessie or the new number. He'd been hoping to run into Harney when he could ask him a few questions. Up to now, the two of them had barely exchanged a word.

"So"—Mike assumed his friendliest face—"where'd you learn ragging, anyway?"

"Invented it myself."

Mike closed his briefcase with a loud snap. "Some people say it's colored folks' music. In that case, I guess you couldn't have invented it."

"Those people are just wrong." Ben stood up, stretched his long frame, and yawned loudly before plunking himself back down on the bench.

"But there must have been something, or someone, that gave you the idea."

"Not saying I didn't get some inspiration here and there. Was a fellow I heard once playing on a long-neck fiddle, up in the Cumberland Mountains. Had a real interesting way of breaking up the rhythm. I liked it, so I experimented on the piano till I put together something kind of the same, but different. My own style."

"How about your lyrics? How'd you come up with them?"

Ben chuckled. "You might say I've got a real good imagination."

"But the dialect—"

"It fits with my music, so I use it. No law against it, is there?" His eyes swept over Mike as if he were taking quick measure of him. "You're a pretty good player yourself. You studied in Europe somewhere—where'd they say?"

"Berlin."

"Never been there." Ben looked down at his hands, pulled at a hangnail. "But I sure do like New York. I plan to stick around here for a while. Least until I finish writing my book."

"You're writing a book?" He never would have imagined Harney as the book-writing type.

"Yup, *Ben Harney's Ragtime Instructor.*" Ben recited the title as if it were poetry. "Going to show people how easy it is to rag just about any popular song. Probably even you could do it!" He laughed. "I just explain it real simple, so anybody could understand. Start out saying that the first thing you need is a good, strong left hand. That's important, 'cause the bass is what draws the listener in, makes him feel that powerful rhythm all the way down in his bones."

Harney demonstrated, playing slowly at first. "See how I'm using my left hand, the bass, to play single notes on the odd-numbered beats and chords on the even-numbered beats? So that in the right hand, the melody accents fall between the beats."

After just a few bars he stopped, then wiped his hands on his pants. "That's about all there is to it."

Harney wasn't saying a thing that Mike hadn't already figured out.

"But then, of course, you got to add what I call *soul*," Ben went on. "And that's the tricky part. Not too many can take it that far. Technique is one thing, feeling is another."

Mike didn't say a word, but he was thinking just the opposite. Technique was everything. Why, he could pair that syncopated rhythm with the fastest, slickest technique imaginable and transform Ben Harney's fake colored ragtime into something pure New York City.

He asked Ben a few more questions; it was clear Harney loved to hear himself talk. Then, not wanting his interest to appear anything more than casual, Mike changed the subject.

"Nice," he said, pointing to Ben's right hand and a big gold ring in the shape of a lion's head.

"My ring? Oh, this here is something mighty special." Ben stretched out his hand so Mike could get a better look.

75

"Belonged to a colored man, name was Tom Strong. Don't know how he came by it, 'cept he swore he didn't steal it."

"Nice," Mike said again. The thought crossed his mind that maybe he ought to get himself something flashy like that.

Ben slipped off the ring and handed it to Mike. "Take a closer look. Those eyes are real rubies."

Mike ran his finger over the finely crafted face. "Must have cost you."

"Tom used to come hear me every night when I played over at the Red Rooster in Louisville. Said I was the only whitey he ever knew who could play music to stir a black man's soul. Called this ring his lucky charm. Jessie calls it a *talisman*. You know what that is, don't you?"

Mike gave a slight chuckle. "Sure. Supposed to have magical powers, ward off evil spirits or something." He dropped the ring into Ben's open palm. "Don't tell me you believe in that kind of mumbo jumbo?"

"I sure do." Ben slid the lion's head back onto his finger. "One night, between sets, Tom and me were slugging down a couple of whiskeys and he was telling me about this ring and how it was full of magic. I just laughed. Then he hands me the ring, says I should wear it. Says if I do, something really good is bound to happen. Thought he was joking with me. Still, I figure it's a fancy-looking ring, why not wear it for the night? Can't do any harm. Sure enough, that very same night a fellow named Bruner Greenup comes in and hears me play. Offers to help me publish my first big hit, 'Good Old Wagon.'"

"You can't think it had anything to do with that ring."

"I don't *think* it did—I *know* it. But that's not all." Suddenly, Ben's clear blue eyes clouded over. "Didn't give the ring back to Tom that night. Was too busy talking to Greenup, and by the time I finished, Tom was gone. Any rate, figured it didn't matter. I'd run across Tom soon enough and, in the meantime, I sure would take good care of that ring. Next night, I was on my way to the saloon—that's when I saw him. Up in a big old hickory tree, hands tied behind his back, half naked, deprived of his manhood. That's how they left him, swinging back and forth in the wind. Like there wasn't any more to him than that. Just something you could leave to rot." He gave a slow shake to his head. "Haunts me so bad. I keep thinking, if Tom had been wearing the ring 'stead of me that night, maybe he'd be alive right now. Maybe I'd still be playing my rags at the Red Rooster instead of here at Tony Pastor's. Doesn't seem right, does it? I just don't understand how it can be that one day you're sitting in some saloon, drinking whiskey, laughing and carrying on, and the next day—next day you're just a shadow swinging in the breeze."

Mike didn't know what to say. He had no desire to get personal with Harney but, after a story like that, he probably ought to come up with something at least mildly comforting. "Listen, sometimes things happen for no reason except somebody being in the wrong place at the wrong time."

"Thing is, more often than not it's an innocent black man on the end of the rope. I'm telling you, it burns me the way Negroes are treated, even up north where it's supposed to be so much better for 'em. I've traveled with colored all over, and I know what they're up against. When me and my boys were on the road, used to have a heck of a time finding any place decent would put all of us up for the night. Sometimes we never did, ended up camping out somewhere. I wouldn't take a room if they wouldn't take my boys, too. A lot of white folks thought I was strange that way. Or they thought maybe I was colored, too, even if I look white as a sheep's fleece. 'Cause why else would I care?"

Ben pushed an unruly shock of rusty-colored hair from his face. Noticing the smattering of light freckles across his fine-tipped nose, Mike wondered how anyone could imagine he was anything but white.

"Never thought about it much when I was growing up in Kentucky. We had lots of colored working for us. Used to play my banjo with 'em down by the river." He smiled wistfully. "Those were good times all right, even though I got into some trouble every now and then. My grandfather, he was a lawyer and real strict. Me and him didn't always see eye to eye, 'specially when it came to my music. And them pretty colored girls, too. I tell you, I had me some sweet ones back then, but I paid dearly for it. My grandfather saw to that."

The more Harney went on, the more Mike realized just how little the two of them had in common. Harney obviously came from a family of some means. Yet here he was, playing his Negro songs, acting like it was his own life he was singing about. Sure, it was a shame about his buddy Tom Strong. It was a shame about a lot of things that happen to people who don't deserve it. Maybe Ben Harney didn't know, but there was plenty of misery in this world, more than enough to go around. If he had a mind to, he could tell a story or two about *his* old stomping grounds, the tenement slums on the Lower East Side—stories that would make a country boy's hair stand on end.

"Hope I haven't bored you," Ben said suddenly. "I do tend to go on and on sometimes. My fiancée tells me I should have been a preacher."

"Fiancée?"

"My girl, Jessie. Popped the question just a few days ago, right here in New York." Ben stood up, buttoning his jacket like he was ready to leave. "Of course, it's not official—"

The click-clack of heels on tile cut Ben's disclaimer short. "Must be Jessie now. Strap and her are supposed to meet me to go over the new number."

A striking blonde in a purple-and-black walking dress, tightly cinched at the waist, sashayed past them down the center aisle. Ben, appearing pleasantly surprised, called after her, "Good morning to you, miss!"

The young woman shrieked and spun around, her hand flying to her bosom. Seeing the two of them, she started to giggle. "Lord Almighty! I'm sure sorry, but you scared me nearly to death. I didn't know anybody else would be here at this hour. Why, good morning, Mr. Bernard!" She tipped her head in Mike's direction.

Ben leaped out of the pit. "I don't believe we've met. I'm Ben Harney."

She caught her breath. "Oh, my goodness! Why, I just love your music, Mr. Harney!"

"Thank you. And who am I so fortunate to be addressing?"

"Hattie Conroy. I'm one of the dancers. Maybe you've seen my act—the big production number, just before you come on?"

"Enchanting."

"You're too kind. I'll bet you don't even remember it."

"No, really. Silver chiffon. I remember it well. I especially remember you," he added with a wink. "Do I detect the hint of a Southern accent, Miss Conroy?"

The young woman's cheeks turned bright pink. "Born and raised in Georgia."

"Charming."

Mike cleared his throat, as if he were about to say something. No one noticed.

"Now let's see," she said, still appearing flustered. "Didn't someone tell me that you're booked at Keith and Albee's after you leave here?"

Mike's ears perked up. This was something he didn't know. Keith and Albee's theater was Pastor's biggest competitor. So they were after Harney, too!

"That's right. First of February. For a month."

"Then you'll be in New York for a while," she observed coyly.

"Plan to be here for quite some time." Ben smiled. "Sure do hope we run into each other again. Maybe backstage?"

"The pleasure would be mine." Then, glancing at Mike, she added, "I'm so glad to see you, Mr. Bernard."

Mike sprang to attention.

"I wanted to ask about that second number—could you please slow it down just a little? It's kind of hard to keep up with the music. The girls were talking about it last night."

Mike bristled. After treating Harney like royalty, all she had for him was a complaint? "I'll see what I can do," he replied tersely.

"Thank you." Hattie Conroy turned her adoring gaze back to Ben. "Well, I'll leave you two gentlemen alone. I'm sure you have work to do."

"Very nice meeting you." Ben lifted her gloved hand to his lips. "I'll be paying extra-special attention to your dancing tonight."

With obvious reluctance, she continued on her way to the backstage dressing rooms. Mike's eyes were on Ben, whose eyes were unquestionably on the sway of the attractive young woman's gait from behind. Odd behavior from a man who had just announced his engagement to be married, he thought.

But then, a lot about Harney had turned out to be not what Mike expected.

Dreams Past and Present

I t was three o'clock on a frigid morning in mid-February, and Mike was sound asleep. He'd been up late. The Biddle Piano Company had delivered his new piano only a couple of days ago. It was a popular upright model, nothing fancy, but it had a nice-enough tone and the action was the weight he liked, not too heavy. Already he'd been hard at work writing his first rag—the one that was bound to establish him as a force to be reckoned with on every vaudeville stage in the city. He knew it was coming, the day when his name would appear as the featured attraction on the marquee, as big and bold as Ben Harney's was right now.

He'd finally called it a night around two thirty. Exhausted, he climbed into bed and immediately was dead to the world. He was usually a sound sleeper and slow to wake. But not now.

Someone was banging on the door to his apartment.

Startled, he jumped out of bed, slipped on his robe, and hurried into the parlor. Could it be a fire? Maybe they were evacuating the building. He tossed a worried glance at his new piano. He'd only paid the first installment and would still owe the rest even if everything went up in flames.

"Coming, coming!" he called, padding across the wood floor in bare feet.

He flung open the door and was astonished to find his father standing in the hallway, his workman's cap and canvas coat dripping with melted snow.

"Sorry, boy, but this can't wait."

Julius Brown had always been a man of few words and fewer displays of emotion. But tonight there was an unhinged look about him, something close to panic in his eyes. Not waiting for an invitation, he stepped across the threshold.

"It's Mutter. She might not make it through the night."

"What are you talking about?"

The last time Mike had seen his parents was just after his debut at Tony Pastor's, a month and a half ago. He'd stopped by only briefly, feeling an obligation to tell them that he'd soon be moving. He never explained how he was able to afford his new apartment, and, fortunately, they'd not asked, assuming he was still employed by the Converys and having no idea what kind of money he was making. His mother seemed well enough then, except for a winter cough, but everybody in the tenements had one. It was the coal soot and lack of ventilation that helped make the five-story ratholes a perfect breeding ground for respiratory problems.

His father's eyes scanned the small apartment. He'd never been here before, and Mike could guess what he was thinking. The Chelsea was a residential hotel, not the fanciest place but a world away from the tenements.

"She's been coughing up blood," his father resumed, "and now the fever's took her bad."

"What do you mean, *now*?" Mike shut the door, already filled with foreboding. And anger. "How long has she been sick? And why didn't you tell me?"

"I knew you'd be trying to blame me, boy. But it's Mutter wouldn't let me come. Didn't want you to worry."

"You've never listened to her about anything before," Mike shot back, knowing the outrage he felt toward his father was largely guilt. Here he was, living more comfortably than he had a right to, while he ignored his responsibilities. He should have found a way to move them out of that place. He'd meant to.

"I'll call for a doctor." Mike's tone was gentler now. No point in trying to blame anyone. "Just let me get dressed. I'll be ready in a minute."

He turned toward the bedroom, but his father grabbed his arm.

"All she wants is to see you before she goes. Too late for doctors."

Mike yanked his arm away, his temper again rising. Why was his father always so ready to say nothing was any use? He'd been the same way about Mike's music. Never believed it would come to anything. *A boy needs a useful trade,* he'd said, never failing to add in a disparaging tone, *What is he, a fagala?*

He tried to calm himself. "Now listen to me, Pa. She may need to be moved to a hospital."

"You know Mutter. She won't go."

Mike set his jaw. It didn't matter what his father said, what either of them thought. "The doctor will decide."

Mike followed his father in darkness up the narrow wooden stairs in the tenement off Orchard Street where his parents had lived for more than seventeen years. An icy wind slithered through every crack and crevice, making it uncomfortably cold but doing little to dilute the heavy, oily smell of burning coal. Behind Mike, Dr. Franz Jacobs brought up the rear. A kindly gentleman in his seventies, slight of build and stooped in the shoulders, Dr. Jacobs was retired from medical practice but maintained a continuing charitable interest in public health.

He occupied the apartment just down the hall from Mike, who had told him tonight, as bluntly as possible, of his desire to keep family affairs confidential.

As the three men entered the Browns' tiny flat, Mike drew a sharp breath. The light of two oil lamps on the kitchen table laid bare the disarray—dirty dishes piled everywhere, iron pots and pans crusty with scorched potatoes and cabbage and beans. The stench of garbage overwhelmed the small space. A couple of well-fed rats scurried along the wall behind the stove, going about their filthy business apparently without the slightest fear of reprisal.

Mike turned to his father in disgust.

"How long have you been living like this?"

"She wasn't up to doing the housework," his father replied with a shrug, kicking aside an empty can.

"You couldn't manage to do any better than *this*?"

"What do I know about cooking and cleaning?"

"Let me take a look at her, please," interrupted Dr. Jacobs.

"In there." Mike's father nodded toward a dark cubbyhole just off the kitchen.

The doctor picked up one of the oil lamps. "Why don't you both wait here for a few minutes?"

"Going out for some air," Mike's father muttered, slinking away like a dog with his tail between his legs. After a few seconds, Mike heard the dull clomp of boots on the wooden stairs.

"I'm sorry about all this," he said, turning back to Dr. Jacobs.

"What matters is our patient," the doctor replied gently. "I'm going to examine her now," he said, heading into the next room.

Mike sat down at the kitchen table. He covered his face with his hands. How miserably he had failed them. He should have come by. Brought money. But he'd been so preoccupied with his work—his position at Tony Pastor's, his bold, new plans for the future.

And, of course, now there was May.

Taking her to bed, from the start, had been wrong. She claimed she loved him, but that didn't justify it. Their behavior was reckless, dangerous. He should never have listened to her. He should have resisted. Over the past month, he'd questioned so many times why he had allowed himself to be talked into it.

But he knew the answer, and it was not that difficult to understand. She made him feel like he was someone special. As if he was worth being loved. No one else had ever done that.

No one except Ma.

With a sigh, he raised his head. From where he sat, he could see directly into the adjacent sitting room, where another lantern burned. Oddly, it was in perfect order, as if nothing had been touched since the day he left for Berlin over five years ago. The lace curtains at the window, the corner shelf with his mother's favorite knickknacks: a cobalt glass pitcher, a porcelain figure of a little girl carrying a basket, a tiny Chinese dragon, a cup and saucer painted with pink flowers.

In the center of the room was a worn rug, unraveling at the edges, with a muted floral pattern in the center. To the right, his mother's sewing machine, the table next to it piled high with piecework still to be assembled—strips of elastic, safety pins, buckles, and button-and-metal-loop fasteners. A large round basket on the floor stood ready to receive the finished items.

On the left, the narrow, high-backed sofa on which he had slept as a young boy still occupied the same spot against the wall. Above it, his mother had hung a cheaply framed lithograph, an idyllic scene of sheep grazing in a meadow, the blue sky dotted with impossibly perfect clouds.

As impossibly perfect as his mother's dream for him. A concert pianist! But that's what she believed in, what she'd worked so hard for, what had given her life purpose. That hope was all she ever had.

Too quickly, Dr. Jacobs appeared in the doorway of the bedroom, his leather bag in his hand.

Mike jumped to his feet. "How is she?"

"I'm sorry not to have better news for you, but there's really nothing that can be done for her at this stage. She has very little time left."

"But how could it happen so fast?" Mike protested, as if the doctor had no right to make such a pronouncement. "I saw her not long ago. Not so terribly long," he added, averting his eyes, hoping Dr. Jacobs wouldn't sense the depth of his culpability.

"She's got tuberculosis, pneumonia on top of it. That's what's doing her in. I've seen it over and over in these tenement houses." He peered into the sitting room, perhaps trying to get a sense of who Eva Brown might have been. "Your mother work in the clothing trade?"

"Yes."

"Any other children?"

"I had a brother. He died when he was four. Influenza."

"Son . . ." His mother's voice from the bedroom was a hoarse whisper.

"Go to her," Dr. Jacobs said with a somber nod, "while you still can."

Overwhelmed by a sense of impending doom, Mike entered the bedroom. His mother lay wrapped in blankets on the iron-frame bed. He was stunned by how she looked— cheeks sunken, eyes ringed with purple, lips pale and cracked. She labored visibly for every breath.

He perched on the edge of the bed. Gently, he took her hand; it felt bony and cold, the skin papery.

"I'm sorry, Ma. I didn't know. I didn't know—"

He felt like he was going to cry, but he didn't. For some reason, he couldn't.

"You come to say goodbye?" she said.

"Not goodbye. You'll get better. The doctor said so."

"No, son."

"You have to. I've already reserved a front-row seat for you at my first concert. You don't want to miss that, do you?"

She attempted a smile. "Concert?"

"Yes, just like you always wanted. I was going to come by tomorrow and tell you."

She gave her head a tiny shake. "You just think of me, all right?"

Think of her? Of how utterly he had failed her—in every possible way that a son can fail his mother?

"Listen, Ma. I'm going to send a carriage with white horses to pick you up that night. Buy you a fancy new dress, too. Your favorite color, blue. It'll be the greatest time ever. You'll see."

It was a shameless lie, but what difference did it make now? In his mind and heart, a new dream had already supplanted the one she held so dear. It had been difficult enough for him to accept it. Maybe it was a blessing that she'd never have to.

"Tell me again, son."

He leaned forward. "What, Ma?"

"That you'll make me proud."

"Yes, Ma. I'll make you proud. I promise."

The Forbidden

May stood in the narrow hallway in front of Number 233. It was around eleven, an uncommonly cold morning in the first week of March. She was bundled up in her gray wool cape with the mink trim and matching hat. Her cheeks stung from walking headlong into an icy wind. She had told the hansom driver to drop her off a few blocks south of the Hotel Chelsea. It seemed safer that way.

She opened her handbag, pulled out the key, and unlocked the door. Seeing Mike slumped on the sofa fast asleep, she smiled. Probably he'd been working late again. Music paper, covered with his scrawled notations, was strewn all over the piano and the floor. She wondered if he'd finished writing his first song. He was onto something big, he said, something that would make a great deal of money—the possibility of which always seemed so terribly important to him. Besides, he'd reminded her, a concert tour would have taken him far away and for a very long time.

She could have said right then how much she'd been looking forward to that tour, how desperately she wanted to go with him. Did he really imagine for a minute that she wouldn't?

But maybe it was better, for now, to let him follow his muse. He seemed excited about this new music called *ragtime*. If it was really as important as he said, then he was sure to become famous. And that would be good—for both of them.

"Mike, wake up!"

His eyes flew open.

She was ready for him. Again. Seductively, she slipped the long cape from her shoulders. It dropped to the floor in a heap. She removed her hat, her gloves, gaily tossing them on top. Resting her back against the door, she beckoned him with a curl of her finger.

"We only have an hour this time."

He approached her, tentative as always. Sometimes it bothered her how he seemed almost hesitant to touch her. Other times, like now, his shyness made her feel deliciously powerful. Wasting no time, she led him by the hand into the bedroom. Beside the bed, she stopped.

"Undress me."

Wordlessly following her command, he helped her out of her day dress of printed cotton and silk twill. Between her desperate kisses, she shed several layers of petticoats and then her camisole. She unhooked her corset in front; he unlaced it from behind. Then she lay down, leaning back on her elbows to watch as he first removed her boots, then detached her black stockings from their garters and gently rolled them down her slender legs.

"Your hands—they're shaking. What's wrong?"

He withdrew from her sharply, taking a step back. "Nothing's wrong."

"But you're shaking," she repeated.

"It's just that I'm tired. I was up late. And I don't like being rushed," he added testily.

She sat up, worried that she'd offended him. "I know, darling. I wish you'd let me tell Mother and Father what we've done—all of it—so we don't have to sneak around anymore."

"You'll do no such thing." Her suggestion seemed to unnerve him even more. "Haven't we been through this already? We agreed to wait, remember? At least until I've got a publishing deal. Or I'm headlining somewhere. So they don't think—"

"Why does it matter what they think? They can't do anything to us anymore."

"You don't know what they can do. Not really."

How she hated hearing him talk this way! She'd been looking forward to their time together, and now he was ruining it. "You're not sorry, are you? You know I love you very much." She smiled, holding out her hand to him. "Please, don't stand there like that, so far away from me."

He came forward and sat down on the edge of the bed. Half his face was illuminated by the light from the window, the other half in shadow. The thought came into her mind that perhaps she'd never really seen him whole. When he wasn't hiding some part of himself.

She scooted closer to him, taking his hand. "And I can tell that you love me, too," she said.

He sniffed slightly as if disbelieving of her or wanting to seem that way. "And how is it you know so much about love?"

"Well—" She faltered. What *did* she know of love? She had never observed it between her parents, seldom felt it from her mother. Her father, though he'd always provided her with security, most of the time was too preoccupied to notice her. The only one who'd ever truly taught her about love was Evie, the colored woman who had taken care of her since she was little. It was Evie's soft bosom she'd snuggled against, Evie's words of wisdom and compassion that always brought her comfort when all else failed.

"Listen to me, May." Mike's eyes clung to her, deadly serious. "It may be hard to understand, but all this, what's happened with us—it's very different for me than it is for you. I don't know how to explain it, except to say—" He let out a sigh that sounded so full of frustration it frightened her. "The fact is, I've never known anybody like you. I never would have thought—well, like I said, it's different. *We're* different, in ways you couldn't imagine. I'm grateful that you think you love me, but—"

"*Think* I love you?" She drew his hand to her naked breast. By now, she knew its power. "Don't you *feel* how much I want you?"

He hesitated, but she could sense his resistance caving, just like that night in the gentlemen's dressing room, when she'd kissed him for the very first time.

"Yes, I suppose."

"And you want me, too—don't you?"

"Yes." His expression softened. With his finger, he traced the curve of her cheek as if it were something immensely fragile. "Of course."

His acquiescence brought a smile to her lips. She had not made a mistake. Everything would be all right. Releasing him, she pulled the pins from her hair, letting the soft waves cascade all the way down her back.

"In that case, my darling, you must prove it."

Unmasked

A carriage lurched around the corner of Seventh Avenue and West Twenty-Third Street, the driver reining in his horse in front of the Hotel Chelsea. A tall, handsome young man, who had been pacing the sidewalk in front for the last fifteen minutes, quickly opened the cab door and offered his arm to the older gentleman inside.

George Cornelius Convery, suffering from gout, leaned heavily on his ebony cane as he lowered himself to the ground.

"Thank goodness you're here," Teddy said. "I thought about trying to handle the situation myself but decided it's too delicate a matter."

"That is, if your suspicions are correct."

"I wish it weren't true, sir, but I'm certain that it is."

"We shall see."

The two men made their way through the hotel's sparsely furnished lobby and then, very slowly, climbed the stairs to the second floor, Mr. Convery stopping every few steps to catch his breath. Finally reaching the top, they headed down the narrow black-and-white-tiled hallway. At Number 233, Convery tapped the door with his cane.

"Mr. Bernard!"

There was no answer.

"We know you're in there!" Teddy yelled. Mr. Convery scowled, signaling him to be quiet.

There was a noise from inside. A thump. Muffled voices.

"Mr. Bernard! This is George Convery. I'd like to speak with you."

He waited only a few seconds more before reaching for the handle, turning it, and giving the door a push. The two men stepped across the threshold into a small parlor. The simple furnishings consisted of a brocade-covered sofa, a couple of wingback chairs, and a low table with a black marble top on which sat a half-drunk bottle of soda and a folded newspaper. The only remarkable item of furnishing was the upright piano in front of the window, its rosewood cabinet polished to a fine luster. All around it, sheets of white music paper were scattered over the floor like patches of snow.

"Can I help you with something?" Mike appeared in the doorway from the next room. His hair was disheveled, his shirt wrinkled and loose. He was barefoot.

"That depends," said Mr. Convery. "Is my daughter here?"

"Miss Convery? Here?"

"Mr. Bernard, let's not play games. I have information that my daughter has been spending time with you here in this apartment. Is that correct?"

Before Mike could reply, May pushed her way past him. She had put herself back together reasonably well, except that her long hair hung loose and in a tangle.

"Yes, Father, I'm here."

"And what exactly are you doing here?"

She stared at her boots. "I really don't think that's any of your business, Father."

"What did you say?" He banged the floor with his ebony cane. "I'll not have you talk to me like that, young lady!"

94

"It's pretty obvious what's going on here," Teddy said contemptuously, glaring at Mike. "I knew you were a gold digger from the start. But you didn't have to drag May through the dirt."

"It's not his fault." May, ignoring Teddy, dared to lock eyes with her father. "I invited myself. It was all my idea."

"I find that difficult to believe, May. Your upbringing would not permit such a thing."

"But it's true. I'm not ashamed. I'm in love with him." She glanced over her shoulder at Mike. He was fidgeting with a button on his shirt, pale and visibly shaken. She turned back to her father. "And we're married."

Mr. Convery staggered, his knees crumbling. He would have fallen if Teddy hadn't caught him firmly by the arm. Instinctively, May rushed to his other side. Together, she and Teddy helped him into one of the blue-velvet wingback chairs.

May fell to her knees beside her father, tears welling up in her eyes. What had she done? Might the shock of it be enough to kill him? "I'm sorry. I didn't mean to upset you. I wanted to tell you. It's just that I knew you wouldn't approve. You and Mother have such old-fashioned ideas about certain things."

"You're being used, May, and you don't even see it," Teddy said caustically, eyeing Mike like he was about to go after him.

"The only one planning to use her is you," Mike retorted.

"I'm not the one who's sullied her."

"All right, that's enough!" Mr. Convery roared. "I'm not here to referee a shouting match between the two of you. I'm here for my daughter." He turned to May. She'd never seen him look so old. Was it that she'd simply not noticed it before? Or had *she* done this to him? "You couldn't be married. It's impossible."

"But we are."

"How? And why would you do such a foolish thing?"

She bit her lip. "As I said, Father—I love him."

95

He shook his head. "Love!" He leaned close to his daughter, so close that his sour breath, tempered by the sweetness of scotch, was hot on her cheek. "Do you know how ridiculous you sound? You don't know anything about this man."

"Everything he's told you about himself is a lie," Teddy interjected.

"That's not so! Mike has never lied to me about anything." She glared at Teddy. He was behind it all. Her father never would have discovered her here without his interference.

Teddy's mouth settled into a hateful smirk. "Remember how you said his parents were dead? He was raised by his uncle in Chicago, owned a publishing house? Well, I've got news for you. There was never any uncle, no publishing house in Chicago." His eyes were blazing as he addressed Mike directly. "And maybe you'd be so good as to tell May about that wonderfully picturesque place off Orchard Street that you've had occasion to visit from time to time?"

Mike lunged at Teddy, grabbing him by his shirt collar, red-faced and sputtering. "You—you bastard! You've been spying on me."

"Stop it! Are you both crazy?" May screamed, scrambling to her feet.

Again, her father pounded his cane on the floor. "Bernard, I'll have you arrested!" he shouted.

Mike backed off, breathing hard.

"What is Teddy talking about?" May demanded.

He stared at the floor. "There are a few things you don't know about me, that's all."

"What kind of things?"

"It doesn't matter now."

"I think we've heard enough." Mr. Convery rose from his chair with obvious difficulty. "Get your things, May. We're going home. As for you, Bernard—" He gave Mike a piercing look. "I haven't decided yet how I'm going to deal with you."

But May was not ready to surrender. Hadn't she told herself from the beginning that she was willing to sacrifice everything for the life she wanted? Let her parents disown her! Let Teddy gloat over a few unimportant details of Mike's history, as if any of it mattered. She had declared her independence. She would not give it up.

"Tell my father, Mike. Tell him that you love me. That we're going to be together—forever."

"May, stop dillydallying." Convery held out his arm for his daughter.

"Mike?"

What was wrong with him? Why didn't he speak up?

His eyes still lowered, Mike shoved his hands deep into his trouser pockets. "Look, Mr. Convery. I—I hope you can understand. I hope—" It was as if the words were being dragged out of him. Nervously, he licked his lips, not looking at May, not at anyone. "I—I'm just a kid, and well—I thought I was helping your daughter. Saving her from—from *him*." His eyes darted to Teddy, then away. "I sincerely apologize, sir. I—I never meant for things to go this far."

May's blood was pounding in her ears. Could this really be happening? Had he just *apologized* to her father? Renounced his feelings? Denied his intentions?

I never meant for things to go this far.

For God's sake, he was her husband! She had laid down for him, naked and trusting. She had given him everything.

"Let's go." Her father prodded her boot heel with the tip of his cane.

"Mike?" She gave him one last pleading look. His shoulders were slumped in deference. Defeat. Was this the same person who had vowed to love her for better or worse? The one she had even promised to obey?

She had the feral urge to rush at him, claw at his eyes, gnash her teeth, and spit in his face. But that impulse was quickly superseded by despair beyond hopelessness. He didn't love her. He never had. He was abandoning her, leaving her to fend for herself. She was more alone than ever.

In a daze, she bent to pick up her leather gloves, her mink-trimmed hat, her fine wool cape, which she allowed Teddy to slip over her shoulders. She took her father's arm, the bitterness welling up inside her, like floodwater pushing against a dike that would not hold.

Tables Turned

Jessie had been looking forward to their special after-the-show dinner at Leo's, one of Manhattan's fanciest restaurants. For her and Ben, tonight was a celebration of so many things—his record-breaking ticket sales at Keith and Albee's, his latest publishing deal, all the money suddenly rolling in. Two weeks from now, at the beginning of April, he'd be appearing at yet another of the top theaters. They all wanted him.

As for her own success, it could hardly compare. But still, it was quite something to have completed two New York City engagements alongside "one of the most popular vaudeville headliners to emerge in years." That's what all the newspapers had written about Ben. Maybe her two little numbers, one of them the song she sang with Strap, were only the icing on the cake. But she'd decided, after all, the icing was plenty sweet enough for her. She'd never seen Ben so happy.

And when Ben was happy, so was she.

They were seated at a prime table; already Ben had gained sufficient notoriety to merit the best the house had to offer. Oh, if her mama could see her now! There sure wasn't anything like Leo's back in Louisville. The main dining room was royal-blue velvet—the walls, draperies, upholstery, everything. Throughout the room, big black marble columns, each one embellished at the top with a golden bull's head, rose up like giant totems. From where they sat, she could see the sweeping marble stairway guarded by two colossal winged lions carved in stone. It all looked delightfully pagan, certainly lavish enough for the elite of Broadway to feel in their element. Jessie recognized a number of notables among the guests tonight, including Lillian Russell accompanied by a man with astonishing good looks, who leaned in so close whenever she spoke that his chin appeared to rest on her voluptuous bosom.

Jessie was about to point her out to Ben when she happened to notice another man, this one sitting alone in the farthest corner of the restaurant, his back to the crowded room. Though she couldn't see his face, there was something familiar about him. She watched as a waiter approached the table, and the guest turned slightly.

"Ben, isn't that Mike Bernard over there in the corner?"

Ben peered across the room, squinting. "You know, I think it is."

"Looks like he's dining alone. There's only one place setting."

"Yup, I guess so."

"That can't be very much fun."

Ben threw her a quizzical look. "You're not suggesting we should invite him to join us, are you?"

Jessie laughed. "You sound worried. Would it really be so terrible to get to know him a little better? Everyone says he's brilliant. Aren't you the least bit curious about him?"

"I've talked to him before. Besides, he's the one who's always been standoffish, not me."

"Maybe he's just shy. Besides, he *is* Tony Pastor's musical director. It never hurts to have friends in high places."

"Honey, *I'm* the one looking down on *him*, and don't you forget it. Hell, he's just a kid." Ben motioned for a waiter, who came running. "See that gentleman in the corner? Go tell him Ben Harney wants him over here for supper."

"Yes sir, Mr. Harney."

Jessie watched as the waiter delivered Ben's message. Mike swiveled in his chair and looked over at them, as if to make sure it wasn't some mistake. He hesitated, then nodded and stood up, approaching them with an attitude that appeared more resigned than eager.

Ben shot out of his chair and greeted him with one of his extra-firm handshakes. "Evenin' to you, Mike." He steered him over to Jessie. "You've seen my fiancée on stage with me, but I don't think you two ever got formally introduced. This here is Jessie Boyce."

"So nice to meet you finally, Mr. Bernard," she said, wondering if he was surprised at how she looked without burnt cork smeared all over her face. Then, too, her new evening gown of brocaded chiffon over black silk boasted a neckline lower than most would dare. He might even be slightly shocked. Looking at him up close, he did seem like a kid, though he probably wasn't that much younger than Ben.

Mike offered a slight bow. "The pleasure is mine, Miss Boyce."

"Have a seat. And let's dispense with all this *Mister* and *Miss* nonsense. We're all theater folks here," Ben said, summoning the waiter with a snap of his fingers before sitting down himself. "Bring my friend a drink."

"Actually, I've already had one."

"You'll have another."

Jessie noticed Mike's nostrils flare just a touch. Ben really shouldn't be so pushy.

"If you'd rather not—" she began, but Mike had already turned to the waiter.

"Gin, three olives."

Ben reached for Jessie's hand. "Mike, you remember I told you a little while back that I'd popped the question to Jessie? Well, tonight we're finally getting around to celebrating. I'm happy to announce that my gal and I have actually set a date. Decided to make the big leap next year, on New Year's Day, since Jessie here, she has this idea I'm about to make a resolution or two, turn over a new leaf, just as soon as she gets that ring on her finger. Isn't that right, honey?"

"If one believes in miracles," she said, smiling.

"Promised I'd try to cut down a little on my drinking. Maybe the gambling, too. But then, no sense in taking all the fun out of life."

"Well, congratulations to you both," Mike replied, though without much enthusiasm. The waiter, returning in what must have been record time, set a drink in front of him. Jessie watched with some surprise as he picked it up and downed nearly half in one swallow, the rest almost as quickly.

"You eat here often?" Ben asked.

"This is my first time."

"How come you're by yourself?"

Jessie gave Ben a sharp kick under the table.

"Was supposed to have dinner with Mr. Pastor, but something came up at the last minute and he couldn't make it."

"You could at least have brought a young lady with you. Why, you must have girls lined up every night hoping for an invitation from Tony Pastor's flashy young music director. Some of those dancers are real lookers. What's the matter—didn't see any you liked?"

"Ben, really!" Jessie was starting to wish she hadn't suggested bringing Mike over to their table. Clearly, he was not enjoying himself, and Ben wasn't making it any easier.

Ben scratched his head. "Come to think of it, didn't I see you with somebody one afternoon after the matinee? Was quite a while back, but I still remember she was awful pretty. Classy looking."

"You must be mistaken." Mike motioned to the waiter for another gin.

Ben took a gulp of straight whiskey and turned to Jessie. "Honey, we'll have to see what we can do about finding some cute little thing for Mike."

"I don't need any help, thanks."

"Maybe you're just too picky, old boy." Ben set down his glass and leaned back in his chair, surveying Mike with a curious eye. "Or maybe you need a few lessons in how to have a good time. The most important thing is not to take any of it too seriously. By golly, I could tell you some stories—"

Jessie cut him off. "Ben said he's been teaching you how to rag," she said sweetly, giving Ben one of her you'd-better-hush-up looks. When would that man learn proper conversation for company?

Ben jumped in before Mike could say a word. "Gave him a few of the basics, that's all. 'Course I don't say so in my book, but the most important part of ragging can't be taught. You got to feel it—right in here," he said, pounding his fist over his heart. "No disrespect meant, but that's where all the fancy training gets in the way."

Mike fished an olive out of his glass and popped it into his mouth. "I'd expect you to say something like that. After all, *your* musical influences remain somewhat of a mystery. But I have to disagree with your basic premise. When it comes to the piano, classical training is what separates the artist from the hack. Without it, a player runs the risk of being nothing more than a one-trick pony."

Ben looked surprised and a bit offended. "Folks seem to think I do a pretty fair job of ragging the classics. 'Course the only way to make it really big in ragtime is to write your own songs. Matter of fact, just signed a deal with Witmark to publish my new rag, 'Mister Johnson Turn Me Loose.' Going to be a killer hit."

Mike smiled, now with a devil-may-care ease that seemed out of character. Jessie surmised it must be the gin loosening him up. "Just happens that I signed with Howley, Haviland and Company this week to publish *my* new rag, 'The Belle of Hogan's Alley.' Got Jimmy Blake to write the lyrics for me."

"You're publishing a rag?" Ben sounded incredulous.

"Yup."

"Why, I think that's just great! Didn't I tell you, Jessie? Everybody's going to be trying their hand at ragging soon, even Tony Pastor's illustrious music director!" He leaned over to give Mike a friendly pat on the shoulder. "Anxious to hear what you've come up with as a first effort."

"Excuse me, sir." The same waiter who had earlier delivered Ben's invitation to Mike leaned over to whisper something in Harney's ear. Ben whipped the napkin from his lap, threw it down, and scooted back his chair.

"You two will have to excuse me for just a minute."

He got up, nodded to the tuxedoed messenger, and followed him across the room. A moment later, he was shaking hands with two well-dressed gentlemen seated at another of the best tables.

Jessie quietly observed as Mike called for another waiter and ordered his fourth drink of the night. She had always prided herself on having extraordinary intuition and considered *reading people*, as she liked to call it, her special gift. She was convinced there was something troubling Mike Bernard tonight—probably something to do with love.

"I'm sorry if Ben embarrassed you with his questions about a certain young lady. I could see from your reaction that the subject was painful. Look, I don't mean to intrude, but is there anything I could do to help? Maybe if you talked about it—"

Mike's latest drink arrived. Jessie watched as he proceeded to polish off most of it within seconds.

"I know you're probably thinking that it's none of my business, and you're right," she went on. "It's just that I was blessed with a natural gift for these things. I don't know where it comes from, or why, but I have this sixth sense about people. I seem to be able to look into their hearts, to actually feel their pain. It can be a burden at times, but I figure God gave it to me for a reason."

"Poppycock," Mike said abruptly, shoving his empty glass aside.

Poppycock? She could barely keep from laughing. Did he suddenly fancy himself an Englishman? She hoped he was finished drinking; he certainly didn't need any more of that gin! "You know, sometimes it helps to talk to someone."

"I talk to people all the time."

"I mean about what's troubling you." She ran a finger around the rim of her wineglass before looking up at him with a gentle smile. "Is it a girl? Because if you want to tell me what happened, I can probably venture a good guess as to what she's thinking. And maybe even how the two of you can make things right again."

"What's it to you?" His attitude seemed to have taken a sharp turn, his tone becoming slightly nasty. Still she forged ahead. She could feel that ache inside him, almost as if it were her own.

"Let me tell you, my Ben hurts me awful bad at times, but I always manage to forgive him. Forgiveness, you know, is one of God's greatest lessons."

"Forgiveness?" Mike practically spat the word.

"Yes, it's not the easiest thing to learn. But it can be the most rewarding."

"Is that what you do? Forgive Ben?"

"I've done it many a time. It took me a while to realize that even when Ben hurts me, he doesn't really mean to. I guess he just doesn't know any better."

Mike snickered.

"The important thing is that I know he loves me."

"He's got a funny way of showing it."

She brushed off his remark with a shake of her head. "He shows me all the time. If you knew him better, you'd know that Ben Harney is as true and loyal as they come."

"Ben Harney is one of the biggest skirt chasers I've ever met. Everybody knows it, even with him being new in town." Mike's eyes narrowed, his mouth twisting into a drunken sneer. "But you'll have to forgive *me*, Miss Jessie Boyce. I don't mean to burst your beautiful bubble."

He turned away and whistled for the waiter.

"Don't you think maybe you've had enough to drink?"

Mike swayed in his chair, his eyes half closed. "No, I don't. You know why? 'Cause it doesn't matter."

"*What* doesn't matter?"

"None of it." His head dropped forward and, for a moment, Jessie thought he'd fallen asleep. But the next second he was upright again—though he seemed to be having trouble focusing. "Ever hear somebody play the piano with broken fingers?" he said, his words slurred.

"Hey, sorry to take so long." Ben was back, smiling down at them.

Jessie was glad to see him. Mike's behavior was starting to worry her. What if he passed out at the table? Ben would know how to handle him. For better or worse, he had plenty of experience with drunks. "Business again? I swear, honey, they find you wherever you are!"

"I'm not complaining. Another deal in the works! I'll tell you about it later." Ben slid into his chair, announcing loudly, "I'm so hungry I could eat a horse! How about you, Mike?"

Mike opened his mouth like he was about to say something, then bent over the edge of the table and vomited.

Ruined

M ay sat rigid in the wooden chair, hands clasped in her lap so tightly they ached. Why must they keep this place so cold? Her eyes scanned the tiny room. Bare walls painted a putrid green, a single window with the shade pulled all the way down, metal sink and chest, long narrow table spread with a sheet.

Everything so cold.

Her gaze lingered on the rolling cart with its frightening array of sharp instruments as she recalled again the stories she'd heard. Horrible stories of young girls slowly bleeding to death as they writhed in agony. A just reward for their crimes, some would say. Maybe they were right.

She had tried her best to do the math, to figure how far along she was. She could only guess. Whether conception had taken place in the days before or after the ceremony was a technicality that seemed unimportant now. The marriage had been a sham from the beginning. Mike had proven that. Her father had arranged for a hasty annulment. She didn't put up a fight. Why should she? Mike wasn't willing to fight for *her*.

Her so-called husband had no compunction whatsoever about throwing her to the wolves.

But a baby . . .

She fought back tears. If only *he* wasn't the father! If only she didn't despise him so.

A bald-headed man entered the room, perhaps a doctor or someone calling himself that. His long white apron was stained with what undoubtedly was some other young woman's blood. "I assume you are Miss *Smith*?" he said, barely glancing at her.

"Yes. Madelaine Smith." Her voice sounded faint, as if it came from somewhere else. Somewhere she would rather be.

"I trust that everything has been explained to you." Distractedly, he rifled through the contents of a plain manila folder. "Here you are," he said, stopping for a moment to scan the page. "You say it's about ten weeks?"

"I'm not sure."

"And how old are you?" he asked, still not bothering to look at her.

"Seventeen. Almost eighteen."

"All right." He closed the folder and tossed it on top of the metal cabinet. "I'll examine you briefly, and then we'll get started." He paused. "Oh, the money—"

She was trembling as she opened her purse, pulled out the wad of cash, and handed it to him. He counted it quickly and then stuffed it into a long pocket in the front of his butcher's apron. He turned, opened the top drawer of the cabinet, and removed a white cotton gown.

"Everything off. Put this on with the opening in the front."

Meekly, she took it from him. Her eyes on the floor, she waited.

"Miss Smith? Did you hear me? Disrobe and put on the gown."

"I—I thought I'd have some privacy."

"Please, young lady, let's not be silly. We haven't much time. There are others besides you needing to be seen."

All of a sudden, the door opened. An elderly woman— the same one who had admitted May through the anonymous-looking locked door in front—poked her head around the corner.

"There's a gentleman outside. Says he needs to see *her*"— she nodded toward May—"and right away. He's very insistent."

The man in the apron eyed May threateningly. "Young lady, I thought we made it clear that you were to come alone and tell no one. The last thing we need around here is trouble."

"But I did come alone. And I didn't tell a soul."

"Well, obviously someone knows you're here." He turned back to the deliverer of this unwelcome news. "Did he give his name?"

"No, he was too busy swearing at me," she replied indignantly. "I'll try to find out. But he's causing an awful commotion. We've got to get rid of him." She ducked out, closing the door behind her.

"You understand, Miss Smith, that I will deny having had any intention of performing a procedure today."

May barely heard him. She was too busy retracing every step she'd taken that morning. She had told Mrs. Eagleton that she was visiting with a friend for the day. She had the coachman drop her off in front of Rebecca Simmons's house, and then, once he'd disappeared, she took a hansom cab directly here. There would have been no reason for anyone to suspect a thing.

Then it occurred to her—what if it was *him*? But no, he would be the unlikeliest of all. The last time she'd seen him was that awful morning when they were discovered together in his apartment. They'd not communicated since. He surely had no interest in her comings and goings. And there was no way he could have figured out the situation she was in—even if he cared to know, which he clearly did not.

The woman appeared again. "He says he's George Cornelius Convery, he owns half of Manhattan, and if I don't take him to his daughter he's going to have all of us thrown in jail."

Oh, God! How had he known?

"*The* George Convery? *He's* your father?" The man grabbed the file from on top of the cabinet and extracted a sheet of paper, which he tore into small pieces and discarded in a nearby trash bucket. He retrieved the cash he'd stuffed in his pocket and threw it into May's lap. "Put it back in your purse. And hurry up about it."

He turned to the woman still hovering anxiously in the doorway. "Go tell him that we haven't touched his daughter. We never had any intention of doing so. As a matter of fact, we were about to send her away and contact the family."

But there was no time to deliver his hurriedly contrived message. The next moment, George Convery burst into the room, wielding his ebony cane like a weapon, spewing more expletives than May ever could have imagined strung together in one sentence. There was no reasoning with him, nothing to do but allow herself to be dragged from the tiny room into the hall and out to the waiting carriage. Nothing to say but *I'm sorry, Father.* No one to offer a single word or gesture of comfort as they rode along in silence, headed back to the Converys' Fifth Avenue mansion.

May slumped in the leather seat, afraid that any minute she might be sick to her stomach. It was clear that her father couldn't stand the sight of her, and she didn't blame him. What she had intended to do was despicable. Still, she wished she'd had the courage to swallow a handful of pills and be done with it. If she had ended up dead, it would have been better than this. And if she had lived, no one would have been any the wiser. Eventually her father would have forgiven her for the fiasco with Mike Bernard. Someday things would have returned to normal.

But now, her precious freedom—what little there ever had been of it—was gone for good. Father would never let her out of his sight again. Or if he did, it would be to send her away to have the baby, someplace where they would consider her a criminal best kept under lock and key. A sinner with no hope of redemption.

She stared out the window, wondering whether she ought to try to run away. Open the carriage door and jump out, dodge through the maze of traffic, disappear without a trace. But they would find her. Sooner or later she'd reach a dead end, with nowhere to turn.

The thought occurred to her again that maybe she deserved all this misery. She had planned to destroy her own baby! She'd been taught all her life that such an act condemned one to eternal damnation. But she wasn't evil; she was scared. She hadn't wanted a baby, but she would have kept it—if only Mike had been willing to stand by her. How could she be expected to manage it alone? How could she possibly endure the humiliation, the whispers and cruel comments? As fond as she had always been of saying she didn't care what other people thought, she was suddenly afraid of precisely that.

It was inevitable now. Bitter penance lay ahead. She had no choice but to accept the consequences of her actions. No longer was there any hope of a quick remedy. No chance of winning back the trust of her family—or even salvaging her self-respect.

There was a word for girls like her.

Ruined.

ACT II
1900

—

Deep in my heart that aches with the repression,
And strives with plenitude of bitter pain,
There lives a thought that clamors for expression,
And spends its undelivered force in vain.

—From "Unexpressed," Paul Laurence Dunbar

A Matter of Conscience

JANUARY 1900
NEW YORK CITY

Strap Hill made his way down Thirty-fourth Street, slogging through the slush left over from the first big snowstorm of 1900 and thinking about how much had changed since he last saw Otis Saunders four years ago in Sedalia. Back then, he could never have guessed how big ragtime was going to get. So big that it wasn't just Ben Harney making a name for himself in New York City. Now there were all those songwriters down on Tin Pan Alley wanting a piece of the pie. Maybe it had taken him longer than it should, but he was finally starting to understand what Otis meant about colored players not getting their due. That's why he was on his way to see Will Marion Cook.

Even the thought of it, though, gave him the willies. He'd heard about Cook's temper, that there was no telling what might set him off. He was just hoping not to get on his bad side. Especially since he was coming to ask for a favor.

He located the run-down building with the address someone had told him was the right one and went inside. As he
climbed the three narrow flights to Cook's studio, again he
fretted about having waited to the last minute. It was the six-
teenth of January, only a week until the big contest. He should
have come sooner. Now it was down to the wire.

He arrived at the top landing and found Number 310.
Surprisingly, the door was wide open. Thinking he shouldn't
just walk in, he stood there awhile, peering inside. It was a
small, plain room painted a pale shade of gold, without much
furniture or decoration—only a pine writing desk with a bunch
of newspaper clippings taped to the wall behind it, a couple of
simple side chairs, and an old, beat-up piano. What he guessed
must be Cook's violin and bow sat on top, like they were ready
to spring into action.

After a few minutes, Strap decided he should try to stir
somebody inside.

"Mr. Cook? Hey there, Mr. Cook?"

Almost immediately, he heard footsteps, and a man
appeared in the doorway from the next room. He was tall and
lean, Negro, wearing a black suit that made him look like an
undertaker. Or maybe it was his somber expression. As soon as
he saw Strap hovering in the hall, the two deep lines between
his eyebrows pulled together into a sharp peak. "And who are
you?"

Strap whipped off his wool cap. "Sorry, don't mean to
bother you, Mr. Cook."

"Who *are* you?"

"Name's Strap Hill, sir."

Cook kept staring at him, not moving an inch. "You sing
with Ben Harney, don't you?"

Strap was surprised to be recognized. "Uh-huh, that's me.
Mind if I come in?"

"I'm on my way out but—well, all right."

Just three or four long strides carried Cook halfway across the room to his desk. Behind it, he lowered himself into a worn leather chair, nodding toward the cane-back one in front.

Strap sat down without taking off his heavy overcoat. He could sense Cook was impatient; he'd best make short work of his business there. But he figured first he ought to butter him up a bit.

"Seen you seven years ago in Chicago, Mr. Cook, at the Columbian Exposition. And I know you done played the violin at Carnegie Hall. I know what they say about you afterward in the newspaper, too. They say, *Will Marion Cook is the world's greatest Negro violinist.*"

Cook leaned across his desk, a strange glint in his eyes. "And you know what I did when I read that, Mr. Hill?"

Strap shook his head. "No, sir."

"Well then, let me tell you. First thing was to pay a visit to that oh-so-magnanimous music critic and politely thank him for his review. And then"—he smiled dangerously—"I took my violin out of the case, dangled it in front of his overfed face, and I smashed it." He slammed his fist down on the desktop, nearly sending Strap through the roof. "Splintered it into pieces right there on his big, fancy desk."

Strap swallowed nervously. Had he said the wrong thing? Or was this Cook's idea of a joke? "Mind if I ask why you'd do a thing like that?"

"Exactly what that fellow said! *Why on earth did you do that, Mr. Cook?* And I looked him in the eye, and I told him. I said, 'Because I'm *not* the world's greatest *Negro* violinist.'"

"Ah, I get it. You was just being humble."

"I said, I'm *not* the world's greatest *Negro* violinist," Cook repeated, ignoring Strap's attempt. "No, indeed, I said. Next time you better write the truth—that Will Marion Cook is the greatest violinist *in the world!*"

Strap broke into a grin, relieved that the story had an ending that made some kind of sense. "Ha! Guess you teach that fella a lesson he won't forget."

"Oh, I doubt it, my friend. I doubt that he learned anything at all. Or if he did, it's long since forgotten." Cook's gaze shifted to the piano in front of the studio's only window. "Same with my *Clorindy*. They swore nobody would give two hoots for an authentic ragtime operetta, wouldn't pay to hear a bunch of colored folks sing, watch them strut the cakewalk. My *Clorindy*, it's Negro music through and through. I don't apologize for it, I celebrate it. After every finale, the whole audience—most of them white—would stand up and cheer for ten minutes straight. But people forget. Each time, everything we come up with, it's like starting over again, having to convince the ones with the money that it's worth taking a chance. That we're good at what we do. Maybe even the best." Cook shook his head, that same sharp frown popping up between his brows. Then, abruptly, he turned his attention back to Strap. "But you have something on your mind, Mr. Hill. Your reason for coming here?"

Strap fidgeted with his cap. Now that he had the opportunity to speak, the words weren't coming easily. Will Marion Cook was an important man. He might not take kindly to being asked for favors, especially from a stranger.

"Was just hoping you might be able to help out my friend, Otis Saunders. He's one hell of a rag piano player."

"What kind of help are you looking for? I've already got my own musicians."

"I know that, sir. But they's holding a big rag contest next week at Tony Pastor's theater. Hear they ain't allowing no Negroes, but I got a feeling my man Otis, he just might have a chance at winning. I figure if anybody has the connections to get the rules changed, it must be you—what with you being so respectable in the music world and all."

"Well, I thank you for your confidence. We've made some progress, I guess, but it's still hard getting our foot in the door." He eyed Strap with a half-suspicious look. "Maybe it's been easier for you, though—teaming up with Ben Harney. If you don't mind me asking, how come you're going out of your way to help this fellow Saunders? What about your partner? I doubt Harney would appreciate the competition."

Strap cracked his knuckles, glad he had a ready answer. "Ben's pretty good at watching out for hisself. I ain't worried about him. Besides, he ain't competing in the contest. Too busy getting ready for his performance at the Met."

"The Met?" Cook looked impressed. "Well, I can see why he'd want to save his energy for that."

Strap took a deep breath, hoping he could say what was on his mind without making a mess of it. "Been thinking lately, for a while now, that this ragtime thing—it ain't right the way colored players been cut out of the picture. Most folks in New York, they don't know nothing about ragging till Ben Harney come along. And them Tin Pan Alley types, they grab onto it and make it into something else. Don't get me wrong—I love Ben, he's like a brother to me. It's more some of them other folks. You know the ones I mean."

"Believe me, I know what you're saying." Cook paused. "As for this contest, though—well, I'll give some thought to your request, but I doubt there's anything I can do." With a sigh, he started to rise from his chair. "Sorry to rush you, but—"

Strap jumped up, anxious not to overstay his welcome. He'd done the best he could for Otis. "Got to be on my way anyhow. Thanks for your time, Mr. Cook—and good luck."

Cook shook a finger at Strap, softly clicking his tongue. "I'm sure you must know better than that, Mr. Hill. No black man ever got what he got on account of luck."

The Entertainer

Mike's arrival at the theater was timed for maximum impact. Dressed in a black tailcoat and tall silk hat, he swept through the packed crowd like a general rallying his troops, shaking hands, acknowledging familiar faces with a nod, every now and then receiving a slap on the back from a loyal fan. It was a routine he knew well.

Sometimes it was hard to believe that he'd been at this business of celebrity for almost four years now. Not only had he gained unprecedented notoriety as Tony Pastor's musical director, but his slick brand of ragtime had made him a smash-hit headliner all over New York City. On the nights he played Tony Pastor's, Mike's ritual before each show was to step out of the orchestra pit and strut up the center aisle, smiling and waving to the crowd, stopping halfway to make a full turn so that even those hanging over the upper and lower galleries could get a good look at him. But this was no ordinary Tuesday night. The usual evening performance had been canceled. Instead, there was a full-fledged party going on, a once-a-year event hosted on behalf of the employees. At the end of the evening, they'd split the till among themselves. When Mike arrived, it was already nearly one a.m., but the main attraction was still to come.

The contest for Ragtime King of the World was sponsored by the *National Police Gazette*, a seamy New York tabloid that covered sports, crime, theater, and scandal of all varieties. Tonight's competition had been billed as the ultimate challenge for the top ragtime players in the country. Anyone with the requisite talent, the paper said, had an equal chance at taking home the huge diamond-studded medal. And just so no one could claim he had missed out because he was otherwise engaged at the appointed hour, the contest would not commence until virtually every theater and reputable saloon in town had shut down for the night.

Through the smoke-heavy haze, Mike spied Richard Fox, *Gazette* chief, talking to one of the seven contest judges, all of whom worked as demo players in the publishing houses along Tin Pan Alley. Fox was a shrewd man, having become wealthy through a variety of quasi-legitimate enterprises. Contests of one sort or another, the more outlandish the better, were his specialty. Thanks to Fox, there were proud bearers of championship titles for hog butchering, water drinking, watermelon eating, and teeth weight-lifting, to name a few. He staged all his competitions like boxing matches, and that's what the crowd was expecting tonight—a no-holds-barred brawl as each player tried to outdo the rest, not only with his music but with whatever other tactics he could legally employ.

The chief had seen Mike and was fast approaching.

"There you are!" Fox had to shout to be heard over the hubbub. He locked Mike into a tight handshake as he vigorously pumped his arm. "Ready to go get 'em?"

Mike pried his treasured appendage from Fox's grip. "I'm going to need this, you know," he said drily, rubbing where the chief's fingers had left their imprint.

"Sorry, pal." Fox glanced around the room with a look of satisfaction. "We've got ourselves a packed house!"

This was not the usual relatively genteel crowd that frequented Tony Pastor's. Tonight, women and children were nowhere to be found. Contrary to the usual ban on liquor at the theater, booze was running freely. Wherever space allowed, makeshift bars had been erected, with patrons now lined up three deep. By this hour, many of those who remained upright did so with difficulty.

Fox turned his attention back to Mike. "Hey, what do you think about that bordello hack—that Jake Schaefer! A lot of nerve he's got questioning your bona fides!"

"I couldn't care less about Schaefer." Fox should know he didn't concern himself with that kind of cheap grandstanding. Schaefer, a player of reputed skill but with a lackluster resume, had recently gone on record accusing the contest judges of bias and challenging Mike's status as frontrunner.

"Always a few braggers around, think they can boost their chances just by mouthing off," said Fox, who had been more than happy to publish Schaefer's scathing diatribe in the *Gazette*. It was just the kind of controversy that spurred ticket sales.

"Don't worry about Schaefer. By the time this night is over, he'll be ashamed to show his face in public."

Fox nodded his agreement. "Sure do wish I could have convinced Ben Harney to make it. A match between you and him—now that would be something!"

Mike smiled, serenely confident that a showdown with Harney, this night or any other, was not imminent. He was not eager for one and surely neither was Ben. Not that they had ever discussed it. In fact, they'd exchanged very few words over the past several years. Mike had decided long ago there was no advantage to cultivating a friendship with his biggest rival.

"By the way, I made sure you're last on the program tonight." Fox flashed a conspiratorial smile. "You know I'm watching your back, old buddy!"

As if his back needed watching!

Tired of listening to Fox, Mike excused himself and headed backstage. He checked his watch. Still five minutes until the curtain went up. Enough time for a few puffs. He ducked through the exit to the alley. Outside, he leaned against the side of the building. His breath hanging in the chilly air, he searched his pockets for a cigarette but came up empty.

"Damn it," he muttered.

"Need a smoke?"

Mike looked up, startled. A tall, slender black man, well dressed in a fine wool overcoat, stood just a few feet away. He held a pack of cigarettes in his hand. He stepped closer, offering it to Mike.

"Go ahead," he said.

Mike hesitated, then took the pack, removed a single cigarette, and handed back the rest. "Thanks."

The stranger lit a match and held it for him. "I know who you are." He smiled. "Mike Bernard, ragtime player extraordinaire."

"That's right." Mike inhaled deeply, letting the smoke fill his lungs.

"I'm Will Marion Cook."

Mike immediately recognized the name. He recollected something of Cook's reputation, too. Brilliant. Difficult. He recalled that Cook studied the violin in Berlin and with the great Czech composer Dvořák at the National Academy. "You had a musical on Broadway somewhere, didn't you?" he said, just to make conversation.

"Played at one of the rooftop gardens. *Clorindy*, it was called."

"The reviews were decent, if I remember right."

"They were good." Cook lit his own cigarette. "Working on something new. Got a good feeling about this one."

"Well, best of luck." Mike took another deep drag and tossed the cigarette down, killing it with the heel of his boot. "Thanks for the smoke," he said as he turned toward the door.

"Mr. Bernard!"

Mike swung around, though he was anxious to be on his way. The first contestant would soon take the stage.

"Seems you'll have an easy win tonight."

"I imagine so." Mike pulled out his pocket watch and glanced distractedly at the dial.

Cook ignored the hint. It was clear that he had something else on his mind. "I'm sure you have a lot of pull with Richard Fox, being the *Gazette's* favorite and all," he said. "Maybe you'd ask him to reconsider opening the competition to colored players. It's not too late. I heard one of the contestants was a no-show. Schaefer, is it? Must have gotten a case of cold feet. But I know just the one to take his place. Guarantee you, the crowd won't be disappointed. Not that he could match your abilities and showmanship, of course."

So, this seemingly chance encounter was nothing more than a setup. Everybody always had an angle! "Sorry, but I don't run the contest," Mike replied, wondering if Cook was right about Schaefer. Fox hadn't said anything about him being a no-show.

"Otis Saunders, he's a Missouri boy. Folks out there, they've been ragging for a long time. Saunders is good. Like I say, no match for you. Still, he deserves a chance."

Mike was starting to wish he'd skipped that cigarette. He didn't like being ambushed in the alley like this, especially not tonight. "I've got nothing against Negroes performing on any stage or competing for any prize they want to. But like I said, it's not my contest."

He turned to go.

"But you'll talk with Mr. Fox?"

Mike pivoted back on his heel, irritated. "I'm a musician, Mr. Cook—an entertainer. I'm not out to change the world. I'm afraid that's your job."

A slow smile crept over Cook's face. "I understand. Well, good luck to you tonight anyway." He tipped his hat like he was about to leave, then paused. "It's a shame Ben Harney isn't competing. But then, I guess he's busy brushing up for his big performance at the Met."

Mike froze. Harney playing the Met? "Must be," he said lightly, not wanting Cook to sense he'd been caught by surprise.

"Oh, so you've heard about it then."

"Hasn't everyone?"

"You're right. Everyone has."

Cook nodded amiably, turned, and took off down the alley, whistling an upbeat tune. The melody assaulted Mike's ear like the buzz of an annoying fly.

Ben Harney's "Good Old Wagon."

The Coin Toss

A ll right, everybody! Your attention please!"
Fox stood at the front of the stage, waiting for the
last of the restless throng to quiet down. They seemed
more than anxious for the big contest to begin.

"First, I want to welcome all of you tonight. This is a
momentous occasion, an event the whole city will be talking
about for a very long time to come. As promised, we have
twelve highly qualified contestants, the finest ragtime players
to be found anywhere. They'll compete for the title of Ragtime
King of the World."

The crowd cheered, a few high-pitched whistles sailing
over the top. "One of them, and only one, will leave the stage
in possession of the top prize, this one-hundred-percent-certi-
fied diamond-studded medal!"

He held up the octagon-shaped gold-and-diamond medallion. Suspended from a wide red-white-and-blue-striped ribbon, it glittered impressively in the lights, setting off another
round of whoops and whistles. Fox waited until the noise died
down.

"When I say that these twelve individuals are the top players of ragtime piano in the entire country—excuse me, the entire *world*—I assure you it's no exaggeration. The *National Police Gazette*, of which I am proud to be the chief, has spared no trouble or expense in making sure that only the best of the best are represented in this contest tonight. No one will be able to challenge our claim that the winner deserves the title Ragtime King of the World!"

"Get on with it, why don't you!" somebody yelled from the back. He was joined by a similarly inebriated chorus demanding that the show begin.

Fox signaled the orchestra pit. The crash of a tam-tam reverberated throughout the theater, startling everyone into silence. He reached into his pocket and pulled out a slip of paper. "Earlier, the judges drew names out of a hat to determine the order of the contestants." He consulted the list. "Let me see . . . ah, whaddaya know! It's ladies first! Let's hear it for the lovely Ragtime Mame, all the way from Pittsburgh!"

From the stage wings, Mike observed with mild curiosity as the first contestant, the only female in the group, made her entrance. She was a petite, shapely blonde, decked out in a flouncy red-and-white dress that made her look like a strawberry ice-cream sundae. A swell of cheers, hoots, and catcalls greeted her.

A young stagehand had come up behind Mike and was watching with hungry eyes. "If she can play half as good as she looks, she just might win this thing."

"Never heard of her," Mike said dismissively.

The young woman sat down at one of the two upright pianos arranged back-to-back on the stage, adjusting the ruffles of her skirt before she began to play. She was clearly nervous and fumbled her first few notes. Besides that, her prim demeanor was better suited for a tea party than one of Richard Fox's rowdy extravaganzas. In spite of himself, Mike felt a touch of sympathy. Five minutes later, she left the stage, garnering only lukewarm applause.

The next contestant, a fat German from Ohio, proved himself a decent player with good moves, and he had the crowd excited. Three-quarters of the way through his rendition of Joplin's popular "Maple Leaf Rag," a man dressed in the same striped waistcoat and straw boater, an identical twin, leaped onto the stage. Standing side by side at the piano, they finished the number as a duet. It was certain the whole fiasco had been prearranged with Richard Fox as a device to drive the house wild, which it did, and also to create a bit of drama when the judges summarily disqualified the original contestant from the competition.

"Idiot," Mike muttered, smiling to himself.

Eight more hopefuls followed, all of whom employed the standard devices—jacking up the tempo, gyrations, acrobatics, thumping out the bass with elbows and knees. Their antics were nothing new, seen hundreds of times in countless saloons and music halls. But these were supposedly the best of the best, at least according to Richard Fox.

Fox mounted the stage again, presumably to introduce the next contestant. Instead, he made an unexpected announcement.

"The judges have informed me of a stunning new development in tonight's competition." He cleared his throat. "Mr. Jack Schaefer apparently has recanted the outlandish claims made in his previously published letter to the *Gazette* and has decided not to make an appearance. The only other player available on such short notice to take his spot has, unfortunately, just now been disqualified. As posted in our official rules and regulations, members of the colored race are *not* eligible to compete in this contest. Therefore—"

A swell of protest erupted from the now thoroughly soused crowd.

"Bring him on!"

"Let's hear the nigger!"

"Let him play!"

Fox seemed surprised. So did the seven judges, who, perhaps fearing some kind of drunken insurrection, quickly formed a huddle. After conferring for only a matter of seconds, one of them rushed onto the stage and whispered in Fox's ear.

Fox wagged a finger in the direction of the orchestra pit. Again, the gong sounded, partially drowning out the hisses, boos, and jeers, after which the chief made a show of setting the record straight.

"Sorry, seems I was misinformed. We promised twelve contestants and, true to our word, we've got twelve!" An empty liquor bottle flew past his ear, no doubt encouraging an abbreviated version of the next introduction. "Here he is, Otis Saunders from Sedalia, Missouri!"

So Cook had gotten his way after all! For the first time all night, Mike felt a hint of concern—only because he imagined Cook wouldn't be eager to endorse a loser. But then, it would take nothing short of a miracle for some fellow out of nowhere to come along and snatch the title from under his nose.

Otis, perhaps caught off guard by the sudden turn of events, was hustled onto the stage amid raucous cheers. He wore a dark-blue jacket with gold epaulets and a red sash, and what looked like a military kepi on his head. It soon became apparent that if his outfit wasn't enough to make an impression, his playing was. He had a deadly left hand—strong and steady— and he played his ragtime without gimmicks. He didn't need them. He seemed to know exactly how to connect with his listeners, how to pull them into the music like they had no choice but to come along. Maybe it was his easy toe-tapping and the sway of his lean body in the blue jacket that so perfectly animated the lively ragtime beat. Or how the droplets of sweat on his brown skin, glistening under the lights, gave him an almost messianic radiance. Or maybe it was because that million-dollar smile on his face made it all look so effortless.

Saunders's five minutes raced by. Before Mike could think of anything to criticize about his performance, he had risen from the bench and turned to the crowd. A substantial portion of the audience was already clapping, stomping, whistling, demonstrating by whatever means at their disposal that they approved of the nattily dressed young man who, grinning broadly, bowed and then bowed again. There were, of course, naysayers whose angry boos occasionally surfaced above the rest of the commotion. Probably they'd placed their bets on Mike Bernard and now weren't quite so certain.

Even Mike was forced to admit that Otis Saunders had breathed life into the competition. Now it was up to him to breathe fire.

"It's been a great night so far, but I'm willing to wager it's about to get even better." Fox glanced at Mike in the wings and gave him a thumbs-up. "You know him from his countless appearances at Tony Pastor's and his fame throughout the great city of New York. Friends, you've been waiting all night for this, but wait no longer! Our last contestant, purely by the luck of the draw—the one, the only, Mike Bernard!"

Mike shot out of the wings, and the audience went wild.

"Tear it to pieces!"

"Knock the ivories off o' the box, Mikey!"

"You're the best, Mike!"

There hadn't been another contestant all night greeted with this kind of adulation. He'd been foolish to waste even a second worrying about Saunders. It was clear from this reception that the title of Ragtime King of the World was already his.

He made a sweeping bow, sending the crowd into a renewed frenzy. Then, in a surprise move, he proceeded to lift the protective wooden case off the front of one of the pianos, exposing its innermost parts—the *guts* of the instrument. Not only would everyone hear how amazingly fast he could play, they would be able to see the flurry of hammers striking strings.

Immediate cries of foul emanated from the ranks of the other contestants. The judges were challenged to make a ruling. Earnestly, they bent their heads together, seemingly engaged in a heated debate. It didn't take long to reach a decision.

"The judges have ruled that removing the case does not alter the mechanics of the piano and therefore does not violate the rules of this contest. Mr. Bernard is free to proceed."

Mike let the crowd cheer fully a minute before he sat down at the piano with a flourish of tails. He started with a few bars of Rubinstein's Melody in F, what Tony Pastor would have called a *classy* selection, the purpose of which was to remind the crowd, in case they had forgotten, that Mike Bernard was no bordello hack. He followed this taste of the legitimate classics with his own ragged version of the same, then on to an exhibition of artistry and speed that could not fail to leave listeners breathless.

Over the last four years, Mike Bernard's style had become almost a genre unto itself. It had none of the grittiness of Ben Harney, none of the quirkiness. If it was short on authenticity, as some had claimed, there was plenty else about it to please the crowd. And it wasn't only his technical mastery. From the first note to the last, Mike was in a love affair with sound, enchanted with a language he understood far better than the spoken word. Bound to it by a connection that, for him, had always been stronger than a human touch. This extraordinary magic was not something left to the imagination of his audience. Anyone paying attention—and that was everyone—could clearly see it, hear it. Feel it.

But tonight, he wasn't taking any chances. With only a couple of minutes left, it was time to uncork the showstopper.

From his earliest days at Tony Pastor's, Mike had learned the power of summoning the patriotic spirit. Americans love to be reminded of their wars, their heroism, their sacrifice. Nothing can trump love of country, and that's what Mike was counting on now. Though he had never served in the military, never even fired a gun, he had an uncanny ability to recreate the sounds of war—bugles calling, boots marching, cannons booming. In the midst of a ragtime melody, he could move a crowd to tears with a subtly inserted phrase from "The Star Spangled Banner" or take them back in time with a jaunty strain of "Yankee Doodle." He was a master at leaving them awestruck, the haunting melody of "Taps" gently fading into the distance.

Tonight, he lived up to expectations and then some, his reward an ovation, complete with stomping feet and chants of "Bernard! Bernard! Bernard!" It appeared that popular sentiment was in his favor. Refreshed and exuberant, Mike exited to the wings and readied himself for his return to center stage as soon as Fox announced the winner.

It took less than a minute for the judges to reach a decision. Mike straightened his jacket, moistened his lips. Fox unfolded the paper.

"Ladies and gentlemen"—he paused—"we have a tie!"

Mike's anticipatory smile faded abruptly.

"Looks like maybe it's you and me," said Otis, who had quietly come up behind him.

Fox continued. "Two contestants will face off—Mike Bernard and the Missouri boy, Otis Saunders. Could both of you please come out here?"

Mike was surprised—but not really. With Richard Fox, there always had to be a twist, some sort of shocker.

The two men walked onto the stage in single file, standing side by side next to Fox as he explained that each would have two minutes to perform his own rendition of a song already selected by the judges.

"That song is—" Fox consulted his latest official document. "Oh, this is a good one. The song the judges have chosen is"— he chuckled—"'All Coons Look Alike to Me.'"

A murmur rippled through the crowd, along with some low-pitched laughter. Fox grinned amiably at the contestants. "You both ready?"

The perpetual smile on Otis's face had disappeared. He raised his hand slightly, as if he wanted to say something.

"Is there a problem, Saunders?"

"I don't know that one," Otis said, his eyes mercilessly dissecting Fox.

Fox translated loudly for the audience, clearly enjoying the drama. "The boy from Missouri says he's not familiar with that particular song."

Fox knew. Mike knew. Probably everyone in the theater knew. There wasn't a ragtime player or enthusiast anywhere who was unfamiliar with that song. So-called coon songs, like the cakewalk, had become ubiquitous in minstrel shows, vaudeville, even Broadway. This particular one was written by the well-known composer Ernest Hogan, a Negro. Besides having been made famous by a popular white singer, it had been sung by plenty of colored entertainers in blackface, too. Some might even call it the granddaddy of all coon songs. But obviously that didn't matter to Otis Saunders. There was no denying the racial slur implicit in the selection. He was refusing to go along.

Fox eyed the judges. Several of them shook their heads.

"Well, Saunders, the judges have informed me that they really have no other choice but to consider Mike Bernard the winner. But thank you for your participation in the *Gazette*'s—"

"We'll each choose our own song."

Fox turned to Mike, a befuddled expression on his face. "Did you say something, Mr. Bernard?"

"I said we'll each choose our own song," Mike repeated, this time loud enough so the judges and everyone in the packed theater could hear him. "That is, if the judges agree."

"Well, I don't know—"

Mike took a certain pleasure in watching Fox squirm. Getting rid of Saunders by default would have been the perfect solution to a potentially sticky situation. Saunders had been more popular with the crowd than anyone expected, forcing the judges to go out of their way to appear fair by calling the contest a tie. But when all was said and done, Fox had the reputation of the *Gazette* to think about. A Negro as the *Gazette*'s Ragtime King of the World? The chief would never live it down.

But Fox's concerns were not Mike's. If at first he had resented the idea of a playoff, by now he'd decided it was to his benefit. There was no glory in too easy a win. Saunders was good, but there was no way he would come out on top tonight.

One of the judges stood up. "If Mr. Bernard has no objection to each player choosing his own song, then the playoff can continue."

With the look of someone who'd just been smacked in the face with a pie, Fox announced that he would flip a coin to determine the order in which the contestants would play. It was understood, at least by those well studied in such matters, that whoever went last always enjoyed the advantage.

"Heads, Mike Bernard will go first. Tails, Otis Saunders."

He flipped the coin high in the air. It was a bad toss. Instead of falling at his feet, it fell directly in front of Otis. Fox quickly stamped his foot on top, then slid the coin to neutral territory. He bent down and picked it up.

"Tails it is!" he cried, holding it up between his thumb and index finger as proof of the call. "Mr. Saunders goes first!"

Mike headed for the wings while Otis, hesitating as if he wasn't sure what to do, finally went to take his place at the same piano Mike had played earlier. The case remained off, the inner workings of the instrument still exposed. As Otis began to play, everyone could see precisely how fast the hammers were hitting string—and it was fast. He was tapping his foot, the sweat shining on his face, everything just as before—except there was no trace of that million-dollar smile.

For the second time tonight, Mike had a brief episode of doubt. What if he was wrong? What if the crowd was out to humiliate Fox or just shake things up for the fun of it? What if the loyalty of his fans couldn't be counted on? Coming in second to a no-name player from Missouri?

Jake Schaefer might have the last laugh after all.

Otis chose a piece written by his friend Scott Joplin but, near the end, added a surprise, a series of spectacular chromatic runs up and down the keyboard—something for which Mike was well known. By the time Saunders finished his fireworks display, nearly everyone was on their feet cheering. It was a response that would have given any performer cause to rejoice, perhaps to imagine victory was within reach. Yet, after what seemed a perfunctory bow, Otis hurried off to the wings, brushing past Mike without a glance.

It was nearly four in the morning. Most of the crowd was gone, the cleanup crew starting to disassemble the makeshift bars, a not-so-subtle hint to the remaining patrons that it was well beyond last call. Mike had accepted too many free drinks to count, shaken so many hands that his fingers were sore. All he wanted now was to pack up his medal and go home to bed. He was relieved when he managed to slip past Richard Fox, who was entertaining a group of big-bellied City Hall bureaucrats. The last thing he needed was for Fox to drag him over for another round of besotted congratulations on his new title, Ragtime King of the World.

Mike hurried along, looking forward to finally enjoying some peace and quiet in the privacy of his backstage dressing room. He threw open the door.

"Hope you don't mind, Mr. Bernard." Otis Saunders stood in the center of the room, his hands stuck deep in the pockets of his trousers. "Wanted to congratulate you on your big win, but it wasn't so comfortable for me out there with the rest of 'em. Decided just to wait for you here."

Mike might have told Saunders he had no business back there. He hadn't been invited. But something stopped him. He entered the room and headed straight for his padded armchair. Wearily, he sank into it, stretching his legs out in front. "You did well tonight," he said amiably. "Just not well enough."

Otis remained standing, though there was an empty chair next to Mike. "You and I both know, no matter what, I didn't have a chance in hell."

"I wouldn't say that."

"Look, I didn't come here to bellyache about the contest. I'm grateful at least I got to show what I could do. Even if the whole thing was rigged."

"You're sounding more and more like a poor loser." Mike was surprised to hear Saunders complain. For some reason, he'd thought him bigger than that.

"Come on, first the judges pick that coon song and want me to play it. Then Fox does his phony coin toss. Heads you go first, tails me. The thing landed right at my feet. I seen what it was. Heads! When I heard him call tails, that's when I knew for sure it wasn't no use. I was never going to win."

"You weren't the best player, simple as that."

"I'm not saying that I was. But Fox and them judges wasn't about to let no colored *boy* win the title. That's just the way it is."

Mike thought for a moment. Saunders was right, of course. But the contest was over now. The title was his, and he deserved it. "There are lots of players who've tried to beat me. So far none of them has. Whether they were colored or white didn't make any difference in the end."

"Maybe so. But you can't deny the cards was stacked against me tonight. Fox didn't even want me in the contest. And he cheated—just to make sure I didn't get to play last."

Mike stood up. This conversation was pointless. "Sorry, but it's late. I need to be on my way." He walked over to where his greatcoat lay across the chair. His back to Otis, he pulled the wide ribbon with the medal over his head and dropped it into his hidden grouch bag.

"Mr. Bernard—" It appeared Otis wasn't finished. Mike turned around, his patience wearing thin. It had been a long night. "Maybe the reason I showed up back here wasn't so much to congratulate you—or to bellyache. Maybe it was 'cause I wanted to thank you. After all, you was the only one who even thought about giving me a fair chance. That was decent of you, letting me pick my own song."

Silently, Mike shrugged on his heavy coat. He didn't want gratitude. He didn't need it. What he'd done had only served to ensure his undisputed victory. There was nothing more to it than that.

He headed toward the door, Otis's words still hanging in the air. Suddenly, he stopped, turned around. "You know, Saunders, between you and me—those judges are a pack of fools. I know all of them. Not a single one could play his way out of a paper bag."

Otis's face relaxed. "Amen." Chuckling, he slapped on his hat and wrapped a long woolen scarf around his neck. "Hey, maybe I'll see you around."

"Sure—maybe . . ."

Otis hurried past Mike and out the door, his step surprisingly lively. He seemed, in fact, like a different man than a minute before, one who maybe could see the world for what it was and laugh.

Déjà Vu

T he occasion was a private affair organized by Mrs. Angela Wellington, a beacon of New York society and benefactor of numerous charities benefiting what the upper classes liked to call the *worthy poor.* Tonight's musicale at her home in the exclusive Murray Hill neighborhood was to raise funds for the Industrial School for Homeless Children, an institution with the mission of reducing crime, vagrancy, and prostitution among the city's growing population of orphans and abandoned children. Mrs. Wellington was fond of saying that every child funneled into the school made it safer for decent people to walk the streets of New York.

The April evening was stormy, heavy rain pounding an angry rhythm on roofs all over the city. Guests arrived under the shelter of wide umbrellas held by drivers and doormen paid to suffer the elements on their behalf.

"Hello, madam. Good evening, sir. May I take your wraps?" One of several attendants rushed over to assist May and her escort as they entered the slate-tiled foyer. Several other guests arrived on their heels, the ladies complaining loudly about the unbearable hardships of protecting their elaborate hairdos from the driving wind and rain.

"Can you direct me to the ladies' powder room, please?" May asked, as a footman deftly slipped the brushed-velvet cape from her shoulders. She was dressed in an elegant gown of lavender silk, her hair pulled into a French twist and secured with an amethyst-studded comb.

"Upstairs, first door on the right, signorina." The handsome Italian, well schooled in furtive glances and strategic brushes of the hand, was trying to catch her eye, but she quickly looked away. She had no interest in flirtation, even the harmless variety.

"Excuse me while I freshen up a bit," she said to the older gentleman who had arrived with her. "If you like, I can join you inside," she added, nodding toward Mrs. Wellington's front parlor, where many of the guests were already milling about.

"Are you sure, dear? I'd be happy to wait for you here."

"No, please. I caught a glimpse of your old friend Mr. Ferrell, and he appears to be alone. I'm sure he would enjoy your company for a minute or two."

"Very well. I'll see you inside."

May watched as her uncle passed through the double doors and was greeted by the stout Mrs. Wellington and her daughter, a large and awkward young woman who appeared conspicuously ill at ease sharing host duties with her gregarious mother. She quickly turned to make her way upstairs to the ladies' room, inadvertently colliding with a gentleman who was standing close behind her, facing the other way. When he looked over his shoulder, it took her a second or two to realize who he was.

"Mr. Bernard," she breathed, barely able to speak his name—something she had hoped never to do again for as long as she lived.

It had been more than four years since she'd seen him—to be precise, the morning of the fifth of March, 1896, when they made love at his apartment for the very last time. In the interim, he'd become one of vaudeville's biggest celebrities. There was a different look about him now; perhaps it was the glow of success. Nevertheless, it was shocking to realize she almost didn't recognize him. She had noticed his sharp intake of breath when he saw her; he was clearly as disconcerted as she was.

"Well, it's been a long time," he said, stating the obvious as if it were such a terribly clever thing to say. "You look lovely—as always." His smile struck her as painfully wooden. "And Mr. Livingstone? Is he here tonight?"

So he knew, and he'd wasted no time in telling her! The hastily arranged nuptial had taken place two months after Mike disappeared from her life. He must have read about it in one of the society columns. At the time, the marriage of George and Isabelle Convery's daughter to the son of William and Phedora Livingstone was big news.

"I'm afraid not. He's away—in London." The moment the words escaped her lips she wished she could take them back. It was no business of his to know that Teddy was gone. Or anything else about her. And the way he was looking at her—she felt naked, exposed. She could not, in fact, recall ever being so ill at ease in someone's company, almost to the point of nausea. How embarrassing if she should actually become sick right there in Mrs. Wellington's foyer!

She was about to hastily excuse herself, though such politeness was more than he deserved, when an exotic-looking young woman, her lips darkened with an excess of rouge, slithered up beside Mike, grabbing his arm with an attitude of possession.

145

"Ah, there you are." Mike smiled briefly at the new arrival and then addressed May. "Mrs. Livingstone, allow me to introduce Miss Sophia Ferrari."

Miss Ferrari's almond eyes scanned May from head to toe before the young woman formally acknowledged her. "It's a pleasure to make your acquaintance, Mrs. Livingstone."

May nodded stiffly.

Mike jumped in to fill the awkward silence. "Mrs. Livingstone and I haven't seen each other in years. It was quite a surprise to bump into her tonight—though I'm wondering if maybe she was aware of my scheduled performance. If I'm not mistaken, the program was included with the invitation."

"I hadn't noticed," May responded quickly. What conceit to imagine she had come tonight because she wanted to see *him*!

Miss Ferrari was again eyeing May, this time like a fox about to spring on a rabbit. "If I might ask, how is it that the two of you are acquainted?"

It was none of her business, of course. But then, what difference did it make? "Mr. Bernard used to be my piano teacher—in the days before his great celebrity. When he still preferred *Cho*pin to *show* business."

"Oh, how funny!" Miss Ferrari laughed, leaning in closer to Mike as she did so. "Well, thank goodness he changed his mind about all that! Otherwise, who would have become the Ragtime King?"

"Oh, I'm sure they would have found *someone*." May glanced into the parlor with an air of distraction. "Forgive me, but my uncle is saving me a seat in the next room. I should find him before the concert begins."

"Of course, if you must. But I do hope we'll have a chance to talk again sometime. I'd love to hear more about what Mr. Bernard was like before he became a star."

Without so much as a parting look at Mike, May made a beeline for the entrance to the parlor. She hurried inside, managing to slip by Mrs. Wellington and her daughter unnoticed. All she wanted was to find her uncle and sit down before she collapsed. But where was he?

In her unsettled state of mind, Mrs. Wellington's parlor seemed a veritable maze. The priceless antiques usually showcased there had been moved to accommodate row upon row of folding wooden chairs. Against the walls, narrow tables displayed a variety of edible delicacies—raw oysters, escargot, duck-liver pate, Danish cheeses, French pastries. Platters that, by now, had been worked over rather thoroughly. She finally spotted her uncle, relieved to see that he had selected seats near the back of the room and on the aisle. Keeping her head down, she wove her way across the crowded floor, the other guests occupied with convivial conversation over champagne and canapés.

"There you are, dear," he said, as she slid into the chair next to him. "Wasn't that Mike Bernard you were talking to, in the foyer?"

She was surprised that he recognized Mike. Her uncle wasn't fond of popular music, having become a belated devotee of the Met after the Academy of Music stopped presenting opera.

"Yes, I was wishing him luck with his performance tonight."

He nodded and, obviously suspecting nothing, turned back to reading the evening's program. Glancing around the room from her well-hidden vantage point, May saw that Mike had taken a seat in the front row. Miss Ferrari was on one side of him, hands in her lap, looking bored or simply vacant. Mrs. Wellington was on his other side. He paid no attention to either of them, seeming lost in his own thoughts. May wondered if he might be going back over every detail of their brief conversation in the foyer, just as she was. Might he be thinking how drastically she had changed? She was well aware of the subtle weariness to her face, the slight downward pull to the corners of her mouth. And she had become thin—too thin, those who knew her often remarked.

She tried to get another look at Mike's companion, but by now the young woman had turned her face away. May imagined she must be someone from the theater, an actress, maybe a singer or dancer. A free spirit, doing as she pleased, living the bohemian life. The kind of life May had dreamed about once, before everything changed.

She watched Mrs. Wellington lean over and whisper something in Mike's ear, in response to which he nodded and smiled. The hostess pointed to the printed program on her lap, Mike laughing with a dismissive wave of his hand. He turned to the side, and his eyes roamed the crowd. She moved slightly to the left, so her face would be concealed by the gentleman sitting in front of her.

She wondered if he really thought she had come tonight because of him. In truth, if she had known he would be here, she most certainly would have refused Mrs. Wellington's invitation, no matter how worthy the charity. That Teddy was out of town only made matters worse. Might he even suppose that she had gone out of her way to bump into him at a time when she was unaccompanied by her husband? She wouldn't put it past him to entertain a notion so preposterous! In fact, hadn't he already implied it when he insisted she must have known he was appearing in tonight's program?

But one thing was undeniable. Seeing him, speaking with him, being so close that she could smell the tart citrus of his cologne—it had felt dangerous.

She had the sudden urge to leave before the concert began, to tell her uncle she was suffering from another of her periodic headaches. But then, certainly, he would insist on accompanying her, and she knew he had been looking forward to the evening's entertainment. So instead she remained where she was, resigned to wait.

After what seemed an eternity, the program began. Two others played before Mike, both offering predictable selections from Chopin, Bach, and Mozart, the usual fare for events of this nature. Each was glowingly introduced by Andrew Hastings, the portly editor of *Arpeggio*, a magazine featuring musical scores and commentary appealing to serious music aficionados. At the end of their performances, each received politely appreciative applause.

Now Hastings again made his way to the lectern installed to the right of a grand piano. Once ensconced behind it, he adjusted his spectacles, peering above the wire rims with a professorial air.

"Our last performance this evening is a bit of a departure," he began, sounding unmistakably apologetic. "There is no doubt that Mr. Mike Bernard, the venerable musical director of Tony Pastor's theater, is a pianist of consummate skill. By all accounts, he has greatly elevated the quality of musical entertainment at the theater and has been heard at various venues around New York. Mr. Bernard was trained at the Stern Conservatory in Berlin and, I am told, has played before Kaiser Wilhelm II, among other European royalty. He is known these days by the unassuming moniker Ragtime King of the World. I'm sure Mr. Bernard will take no personal offense if I express my views on this popular phenomenon of ragtime."

Hastings looked over his glasses at Mike in the front row, smiled condescendingly, and continued. "As I have been discussing this evening in my earlier comments, music has always been a reflection of the society in which it exists. But more than reflecting society, music also influences it. That is what alarms me, and many others, about the sudden surge in popularity of a musical form that, by its very nature, appeals to the basest human instincts, thwarts the intellect, and literally poisons the ear of the listener."

Hastings pushed his spectacles higher on his nose. "The rhythmic basis for ragtime—that is, syncopation—has its origins in primitive Negro music. That in itself should elevate our concerns regarding the effect of this music on the moral fiber of American society and particularly our youth. How many God-fearing Christian parents would truly wish for their children to adopt the loose, devil-may-care attitudes propagated by the vulgar, titillating rhythms of ragtime? I daresay none!"

May noticed some of the guests casting sidelong glances at Mike in the front row. For the first time all evening, she was enjoying herself, imagining how angry he must be to receive such an insulting introduction. Didn't it serve him right, for assuming he was the star attraction?

"Now, lest I be misunderstood," Hastings continued, "and as I believe I said before, Mr. Bernard is a player of consummate skill. His stylized versions of many of the classics are, on occasion, quite interesting. And, while it is not within his power to change the essential nature of this unfortunate music which is so popularly in demand, he has perfected its technical performance, and for this is deserving of our admiration."

Hastings now looked directly at Mike, like a judge about to deliver his sentence. "So, without further ado, it is my pleasure to introduce Mr. Mike Bernard. I ask that you give him a warm welcome."

Mike rose to only a smattering of applause. Who, after all, would dare to admit being a fan of ragtime music after what they'd just heard from Andrew Hastings? When he reached the piano, he stopped short of sitting down at the bench. He cleared his throat, obviously preparing to speak. None of the other players had felt it necessary to augment Hastings's introduction, but it appeared that he planned to be the exception.

"Mr. Hastings has spoken eloquently of his disdain for ragtime," he began. "As a musical scholar, he must know that syncopation has been employed for its unique effect by many of our most revered composers—Bach, Beethoven, Mozart, and Schubert, to name a few. Of course, it was only a minor feature of their compositions. I suppose Mr. Hastings would agree, then, that the corrupting influence of this insidious rhythmic device on the whole of Western civilization has, to this point, been minor as well."

He paused until the light ripple of laughter subsided.

"There are those who would summarily reject all music that doesn't meet their criteria for so-called seriousness. Many are commentators, like Mr. Hastings, who believe that their own scholarly critiques are essential, that ordinary people can't possibly appreciate music simply by listening to it and letting it naturally touch their hearts. Music critics can't bear the idea that, when it comes to the popular music of ragtime, no one is interested in their opinions.

"Now, I myself am no admirer of music that is crude and inelegant, which is why I've devoted myself to refining the elements of ragtime so as to charm even the most sophisticated listener, such as each and every one of the guests gathered here this evening." He made a slight bow to the audience. "I could certainly play for you a program of Mozart or Beethoven, selections I've performed hundreds of times in concerts all over Europe. But I prefer to entertain you tonight with what can arguably be called the only true American musical form— ragtime. I'll begin with one of my own compositions, appropriately titled 'The Ragtime King.'"

Lifting the black tails of his coat, Mike settled himself at the piano. Then with a wave of his arms, he lowered his hands to the keys.

Having already sat through a long program of the classics, not to mention endured the monotonous musings of Andrew Hastings, the crowd was clearly grateful for a change of pace. Perhaps reassured by Mike's counterinterpretation of syncopation's history, more than a few of New York's leading citizens

151

could be seen tapping their feet and bobbing their heads in time to the music. Mike's style tonight was well suited to his audience. No gimmicks, no acrobatics, a dignified rendering that might as easily have been presented on the stage of Carnegie Hall.

May forced herself to listen for a minute or two. Then, unable to stand it any longer, she leaned over to whisper in her uncle's ear. He started up from his chair, but she firmly placed her hand on his arm. After planting a swift kiss on his cheek, she rose from her aisle seat, traversed the short distance to the half-closed door at the back of the parlor, and made her escape into the foyer.

She gathered her cape and umbrella from one of the attendants and asked that a cab be summoned. The moment it pulled up in front, she hurried outside. As the footman assisted her up the step, she could feel him staring at her. Perhaps, she thought, he noticed the drops glistening on her pale cheeks— and realized the rain had long ago ceased.

Gesture of Kindness

The headaches had started almost immediately after Melvin was born. Since then, they had only grown worse. May was quite imaginative in coming up with excuses—too much champagne, too little sleep, the heat, the cold, the help complaining, relatives meddling, friends gossiping. Anything could set her off.

For a long while, she had resisted the idea of consulting a neurologist. It could have been she was concerned there might be something seriously wrong—or, maybe worse, that it was all her imagination. But Dr. Joseph Adams had been very reassuring. He'd said he could help, but it would take time. This would be her eighth visit.

Usually when she sat in the comfortable waiting area of his office, drenched in its soft, soothing shades of blue, she felt a predictable mixture of anticipation and guilt. The anticipation was for a welcome break from the monotony of everyday life, for the brief comfort of having a disinterested party with whom to talk about some of the pressing things on her mind. The guilt was because she had never been totally honest with Dr. Adams about what weighed so heavily upon her. After all, what would he think of her if she were to express ambivalent feelings about motherhood?

She didn't *resent* the children. Of course not! How could she look at those dear little faces—Melvin, going on four now, and two-year-old Anna—and not fall in love? It wasn't their fault. They weren't responsible for the death of her dreams, the loss of freedom she'd never really had. She had made her own mistakes. The first, believing in what she thought was love. The second, allowing herself to settle for so much less. But it was too late to change any of that now. All she wanted was for Dr. Adams to find a way to relieve the pain.

Today she must be on her guard even more than usual. She wished she could confide in Dr. Adams about what had happened at Mrs. Wellington's musicale—tell him how deeply shaken she was by it, and why. It was not that she cared anymore for Mike. Far from it. She hated him—almost as much as she feared even the thought of him. No, she could not talk with Dr. Adams about their chance meeting; it would not be wise. Perhaps, in a weak moment, she might blurt out something that she would later regret. It was fine to speak to the doctor of her lonely childhood, her manipulating mother, her distant father. Her former dream of becoming a poet, an artist. These were acceptable disappointments, harmless longings. Not a scandal so grave that, if she ever admitted to it, not only her family's respectability but her son's entire future would be destroyed.

She had again started worrying that Mike might have sensed she was hiding something when the door from outside swung open, offering her a welcome distraction. The young Negro woman who entered was of average stature, though on the plump side, with pleasant but not striking features. She was nicely dressed in a pink day frock with a velvet collar and cuffs and a matching wide-brimmed hat decorated with silk peonies. She crossed the room to the secretary's desk, where May heard her introduce herself as Abbie Mitchell.

"I don't see that you have an appointment with Dr. Adams," the secretary replied curtly.

"I'm afraid I don't. I was only passing by, and I saw the doctor's sign, and I hoped—"

"It doesn't work like that, missy. You need an appointment."

"But I thought perhaps—"

"I don't care what you thought. Dr. Adams does not see patients coming in off the street."

May was listening intently. She surmised that the brusque manner in which Dr. Adams's secretary was treating this newcomer was because the young lady was colored.

"It's just that I'm in an awful situation, and I was hoping— well, the truth is—" The would-be patient dabbed at her eyes with a lace handkerchief. "I don't know where to turn. I'm so afraid. Is there no time today when the doctor could see me?"

"None at all."

"Maybe tomorrow, then?"

"Dr. Adams is a very busy man."

"But if you told him it's urgent. My husband—I think there might be something dangerously wrong with him. Something— something mental."

"Didn't I tell you already, missy? Dr. Adams has no appointments."

"Wait." May rose from her chair. "Forgive me, but I couldn't help overhearing. My appointment with Dr. Adams is next. You're welcome to have it, if you like."

The young woman turned toward May, who was surprised to see that she seemed not much older than a girl. "That is so very kind of you, ma'am. But I couldn't do that. I couldn't take *your* appointment with the doctor."

"But I insist. I see Dr. Adams regularly. It's nothing if I should miss a visit." In truth, May found the prospect of skipping today's session to be somewhat of a relief.

"Mrs. Livingstone," the secretary interjected in a shrill voice, "Dr. Adams reserves the right to select his own patients. I'm sure you understand."

May swung around, furious. She had imagined for an instant that it was her treasured Evie, the woman who had raised her, standing before the appointment desk, suffering the humiliation of being treated like someone unworthy of common courtesy. "This young lady clearly has some kind of crisis on her hands. Surely, Dr. Adams would not refuse to meet with her this once if there's a possibility he can be of assistance. And I doubt that he would approve of you treating anyone who walks into this office with such impertinence."

The secretary's mouth dropped open for a moment before she clamped it shut. Stonily, she turned back to Abbie Mitchell. "What exactly *is* your problem, miss?"

"Like I said, it's my husband. He's had some disappointments lately. He doesn't handle such things well. He's a musician, a temperamental one, I'm afraid. Sometimes he sinks into such a state of melancholy, he just climbs into his bed and won't rise up out of it. When he gets like that, all he wants to do, day in and day out, is lie around the house, smoking his pipe, reading old write-ups in the paper, reviews of his performances. It's the ones that aren't so good that he reads over and over again. And that just makes him madder until—" She choked back sobs, holding the handkerchief tight to her mouth. "I just don't know what to do. I don't know how to get him to stop. I'm afraid he might—I hate to think he's capable but—sometimes I wonder if he might actually kill somebody."

She glanced at May, her face stricken. "I know I shouldn't be talking like this, not to strangers. It isn't right. My husband, he's a proud man. But then, he's aired his dirty laundry in public a time or two himself. Everybody who knows Will Marion Cook knows he's not a man to hide his feelings, especially when he's angry."

May felt awful for her. As alienated from one another as she and Teddy were, at least she'd never been afraid of him in the physical sense. Though perhaps she owed that to her father. Teddy wouldn't dare displease him. "I do hope Dr. Adams can help you," she said.

"I only wish it was me who needed the cure, not him. He's stubborn as a mule, that man. And ornerier." Miss Mitchell tried to smile, but the failed attempt only made her appear more despondent. "Just last week he got so mad that he sneaked into my dressing room right before a show and took a scissors to my costume. Cut it all to shreds. I barely had time to run out and find something to replace it. I was so upset I could barely sing that night."

"You're a singer?" May instantly forgot all the rest, latching onto this interesting tidbit of information. This unassuming young girl was an artist? May felt a twinge of jealousy.

The door to Dr. Adams's private office opened. An elderly woman dressed in black swept past them and out the door. Dr. Adams, a kind-looking gentleman with silver hair and wizened eyes, appeared a few seconds later.

"Good day, Mrs. Livingstone. I'm ready for you now."

"Dr. Adams—" The secretary hurried over to him and whispered in his ear. He glanced once at Abbie Mitchell and nodded.

"Mrs. Livingstone?" he prompted, gesturing toward his office.

May remained where she stood. "I hope you've agreed to see this young lady in consultation, Dr. Adams."

He raised his brows, appearing surprised. "Is she an acquaintance of yours?"

"Yes, she is. And I would be most grateful if you'd meet with her. I'd be happy to give her my appointment. I could see you another day."

"That's not necessary, Mrs. Livingstone." He turned to Abbie Mitchell. "Have a seat in the waiting room, please. I'll see you when Mrs. Livingstone and I are finished."

May smiled at Miss Mitchell. "Good luck to you," she said, pleased that she had gotten her way and rather proud of herself as well. It seemed so seldom these days that she had the courage to speak her mind.

A New Friend

———

May stepped outside into the bright midmorning sunshine, escaping the confines of Dr. Adams's office with her usual sense of relief. Again, she had managed to avoid telling him the truth of her situation. She was beginning to wonder why she even bothered to come. Maybe she was only wasting his time—and hers.

"Mrs. Livingstone?"

May twirled around, startled. "Oh—hello!"

The girl she'd met in the office waiting room approached her. "Sorry if I scared you. I only wanted to thank you again for your kindness back in the doctor's office. It's not often that someone goes out of her way like that for a stranger."

"It was nothing. But what are you doing out here? Why aren't you in with Dr. Adams?" May had been so eager to leave the office she'd not noticed the young lady was absent from the waiting area.

Miss Mitchell was obviously embarrassed. "I thought better of it at the last minute. I hate to imagine what would happen if my husband found out. I hope you're not angry—I mean, after the trouble you went to, speaking up for me and all."

"No, I'm not angry. But why are you afraid? What do you think your husband would do?" Maybe it wasn't her place to be so inquisitive, but May sensed a troubled soul who needed to talk to someone. If not Dr. Adams, then anyone who might lend a sympathetic ear. She was more than happy to do so; listening to someone else's troubles might be the best antidote to her own.

"I don't know what he would do. That's the problem."

She flashed back to what the young woman had said about being a singer. In that moment, May had felt an instant affinity with her. A curiosity to know more. "Tell me about your singing. How long have you been a performer?"

"A couple of years now. Actually, that's how I met Mr. Cook—auditioning for his musical, *Clorindy*. I remember what he said when he first saw me: 'What do *you* want, little girl?'" She laughed. "Guess he couldn't quite believe that a proper little girl in pigtails, who didn't know a thing about ragtime and mostly sang Ave Marias on the fire escape, could possibly be suited for a role in his Broadway production."

"But did he give you a part?"

"Yes, a small one—but the song he gave me to sing turned out to be a hit. I stayed with the show for a while and could have kept on with it, but instead I decided to go back to school. Pretty soon, though, Mr. Cook offered to bring me back as the leading lady. How could I refuse? I was so proud to be making twenty dollars a week! And then, eventually—the two of us, we ended up getting married. It hasn't been long."

"If you don't mind me asking, how old *are* you?"

"Almost sixteen."

So young and already on the stage. And married. "And your husband is supportive of you continuing with your career?"

"Oh yes! If it wasn't for our music, I guess Mr. Cook and I wouldn't have much to talk about, or to argue about either. He always knows exactly how he wants something to sound, and if it isn't *just so*, he can be very difficult. Sometimes he'll have me sing one phrase over and over, maybe two or three hundred times, until I get it perfect—or at least the way *he* wants it." She sighed. "But then, he *is* the composer, so I suppose he has a right to be fussy."

"You only sing *his* music?"

"Lately I've been branching out. You see, Mr. Cook's endeavors don't always bring in a lot of money. That's why I got this idea to start singing at some private events. Last week, I was booked for a party at the home of Mr. and Mrs. Vanderbilt. Mr. Cook accompanied me on the piano, and it was a big success. Brought him out of his melancholy for a little while, too. My agents, Brooks and Denton, they've been very helpful in booking appearances at the homes of several notable families."

"How enterprising of you!" She liked this young woman and admired her, too—an actress and singer, someone unafraid to make her way in the world and at such a tender age. In a way, though, her story made May feel old and, worse than that, shamefully unaccomplished. She thought of her precious journals full of poems, now reduced to lonely relics gathering cobwebs in the attic, and it made her ache with an emptiness that felt like bereavement. "I'm glad that we met, Mrs. Cook. And I do wish you the best."

"Likewise. But—I'm sorry, Mrs. Livingstone—I generally go by the name Abbie Mitchell."

"Oh yes, forgive me. I should have remembered. That was how you introduced yourself."

"I use my maiden name for most things. Though you might be surprised, considering how I behaved this morning in Dr. Adams's office, I usually prefer to keep my personal life personal."

May nodded her approval. How wonderful to be in a position to make those kinds of decisions for oneself! "By the way, are any of Mr. Cook's musicals currently playing?"

"Not at the moment. His new operetta opens at the New York Theater Roof Garden in a few months—the fifteenth of August."

"Oh really? What's the name of it?"

Miss Mitchell hesitated. "It's called *Jes Lak White Fo'ks*. It's a satire," she added hastily. "Understandably, not everyone appreciates that kind of thing."

"Oh, but I love satire."

Miss Mitchell bit her lip, still appearing uncertain. "Then perhaps you *would* find it entertaining."

"The fifteenth of August, you say? I'll definitely attend." May thought for a moment. It would, of course, depend on whether Teddy happened to be away. Everything always did. "That is, if I can."

Original Sin

Jessie clung tightly to Ben's arm as they hurried past the Marble Collegiate Church on Fifth Avenue, its spire glistening like silver in the clear morning light. They were going to be late, as usual. Ben would have slept through the appointment altogether if she hadn't dumped that pitcher of cold water on his head at seven o'clock sharp. She guessed marriage hadn't changed Ben as much as she had hoped it would. He was still a Kentucky boy through and through. Still loved to drink, loved to gamble, stay out late, and flirt with any pretty girl who came his way. Not to mention spread his money around like it was fertilizer.

But since his meteoric rise to fame, at least he had plenty of it to spread.

They headed up the publishers' row on Twenty-Eighth Street. A tinny cacophony leached from the demo rooms all along this portion of the street, each publisher determined to churn out new tunes faster than anybody else, all of them in a rush to discover that next huge hit. A great song could easily sell half a million copies, maybe a lot more. A song with a big name attached to it was always a sure winner.

And there was no bigger name than Ben Harney.

"Now Ben, don't get too greedy with Mr. Paull. Nobody does sheet music as good as him. And you know a snappy-looking cover is what sells."

"What sells is a popular composer writing smash hits. Without that, Mr. Paull would have to find himself another line of work."

Ben broke loose from Jessie's grip, taking the steps two at a time all the way up to the entrance of E.T. Paull Music Company. Edward Taylor Paull must have seen them through the window, because it was he who held open the door as they passed into the tiled foyer.

"Good to see you, Mr. Harney. And—"

"This here is Jessie Boyce. That's her stage name. She's actually Mrs. Ben Harney."

"Ah, of course! I should have recognized you. What a pleasure it is to meet you in person, Mrs. Harney."

Paull ushered them into his office, guiding them to a comfortable sofa. A tea service and a selection of pastries sat within reach on a low coffee table. Ben plopped down unceremoniously in the middle, his long legs splayed out in front of him.

"Can you move over, honey?" Jessie stood looking down at him, hands on her hips. She'd done her best to teach him, but manners were not one of Ben's strong points.

"Oh, sure. Sorry." He scooted to one side, and she sat down, carefully smoothing the skirt of her new blue-and-white pinstriped day dress.

Paull settled into a chair directly opposite them. "I was delighted that you accepted my invitation to meet this morning."

"Truth is, I've long admired your publications," Ben replied, helping himself to an apricot Danish. "Thought it might be about time we considered working together. As a matter of fact, got a song I think you'll want to get your hands on pretty quick."

"Impossible that I wouldn't!" Paull offered the plate of pastries to Jessie, who smiled as she gave a little shake of her head.

"It's called 'I'd Give a Hundred if the Gal Was Mine.' I'm sure you know it. It's already a killer hit on Broadway. When it's ready for the printed page, I want it done real classy."

Paull bobbed his head up and down, leaving no question as to his enthusiasm. "Classy is our specialty."

"The other thing is"—Ben bit into the Danish—"on the cover—"

Paull interrupted with a solicitous smile. "Be assured I will personally oversee the artwork. Of course, if there's a particular theme you have in mind, I'd be more than happy to have our artists work directly with you as well."

"That's all fine. But there's something else, and this is important. I want the cover to say—in big, bold letters after my name—*Originator of Ragtime*."

"Why yes, of course, that would be entirely appropriate."

Jessie decided now was the time for her to speak up, before Mr. Paull got to thinking Ben was a little too full of himself. "It's not that Ben wants to boast, but there's so many others these days who are trying to copy him. I think the public gets confused by it all, don't you?"

Paull didn't hesitate even a second. "Thanks to Mr. Harney, ragtime has literally swept the country. There are bound to be copycats, but certainly none can hold a candle to the man who started it all. I have no doubt the public quite clearly recognizes that fact."

"Well, thank you," Ben said. "By the way, I see that you're publishing Mike Bernard now." He tried to sound offhand, but Jessie knew better. Though he'd never admitted it, Ben resented Mike's success as a ragtime headliner, success that seemed to follow on his own heels a little too closely. He didn't mind claiming credit for having taught Tony Pastor's musical director how to rag, but he didn't appreciate having to compete with him for bookings at the top spots in town.

"Yes, we've got a couple of Bernard's pieces that are doing pretty well," Paull replied eagerly, oblivious to the danger. "You'll be interested to know that he and I are in discussions now about the possibility of him managing our professional bureau. I expect he'd do a great job promoting the best of our new music. What songwriter wouldn't want Mike Bernard playing one of his numbers around town? Maybe even you, Mr. Harney?"

The look on Ben's face required no interpretation. "Mike Bernard won't be playing any of my songs, I can tell you that much. First of all, there's no way he could play any Ben Harney composition and make it sound the way it's supposed to. Second, I've got a name ten times bigger than his."

Jessie laid a restraining hand on Ben's knee. "Ben doesn't mean to belittle Mr. Bernard's talent or his reputation. But we all know that Mike Bernard's style of ragtime is a world away from Ben's."

"Of course! Why would I ever dream of looking beyond Mr. Harney to promote his own music?" Paull gushed, suddenly appearing to find his earlier suggestion appalling. "It would be inconceivable that anyone else could do it justice."

Jessie was relieved to see Ben reach for a chocolate croissant.

"Then let's get down to brass tacks, Mr. Paull. What exactly do you propose to offer me for my latest song? And it'd better be a whole lot more than you paid Bernard for his," Ben added with a wink.

"Oh yes, Mr. Harney. That goes without saying."

Cat and Mouse

Mike hurried past the two giant marquees that guarded the entrance to Tony Pastor's theater, trying to avoid Ben Harney's smiling face plastered just below the announcement trumpeting the young Kentuckian as the undisputed originator of ragtime. He knew it shouldn't bother him. These days, between regular stints as Pastor's musical director, he was headlining at all the big theaters nearly as often as Harney. Still, everybody knew Ben Harney was paid more than anybody else in town. He was vaudeville's top draw. His songs were always instant hits. Harney had published six rags just last year. Six to Mike's one! How could anyone be so prolific?

Mike tried the theater's front door. Not surprisingly, it was locked. He had come early thinking he'd work on his new rag, the one he had promised his publisher would be ready three weeks ago.

He set down his briefcase, opened it, and rummaged around inside until he found the key to the back entrance. He'd walk around and let himself in, maybe stop for a minute at his backstage dressing room. He kept a pack of cigarettes there.

Though it was not his habit to indulge before evening, for some reason this morning he craved a smoke.

As he headed around back, his thoughts turned again to May Livingstone. Over the past month or so, he'd often found himself thinking about her—the way she looked that night at Mrs. Wellington's. Still beautiful but with a weariness that was impossible not to notice. Their encounter had been so stilted; the way it had ended felt incomplete—as if there were something more that should have been said.

Without wanting to, he went back still further—to that awful morning in his apartment at the Hotel Chelsea when he was ambushed by George Convery and Teddy Livingstone. Sometimes he felt ashamed of the way he'd crumbled in front of them—in front of *her*. He remembered how she'd begged him to say he loved her. And the excuses he'd made.

Had he really felt sorry for May, as he claimed? Did he marry her so she wouldn't be forced to marry someone she didn't love?

Or maybe he'd done it just to enjoy the look of helpless outrage on Teddy Livingstone's face when he found out that May hadn't *saved* herself for him after all. Hadn't he wanted to get back at Teddy for unnerving him so badly on the night of Isabelle Convery's ball, just before he was to have played for a hundred of New York City's wealthiest patrons? Instead he'd lost his nerve and given up the opportunity of a lifetime after Teddy threatened him in the name of George Convery.

But no, he doubted that revenge was his motive for marrying May. At nineteen he hadn't been clever enough to be so Machiavellian. Besides, hadn't Teddy gotten the last laugh after all? When Mike finally stood face to face with George Convery, it was Teddy's words that echoed ominously in his head: *I don't suppose it would be so easy to play the piano with broken fingers.*

Thank God it had never come to that! Perhaps miraculously, May's father had decided to ignore him, to let him off, totally unscathed.

Whether he deserved it or not.

Mike used his key to open the heavy metal door of the theater's back entrance. He passed through, pulling it closed behind him before heading down the hall toward his private dressing room, trying to shake off the feeling of guilt that had settled over him again. It was foolish to dwell on the past, even more foolish not to see it for what it was. The marriage had been all her idea and a childish one at that, a way to escape the future her parents had decided was best for her. He should feel no responsibility for what happened, or almost none. Hadn't she brought most of it on herself?

And yet, she said she *loved* him. Was it possible he had loved her, too? But if he loved her, wouldn't he have refused to give her up? Wouldn't he have found the courage?

"Oh yes, baby, yes! That's so good . . ."

Mike ground to a halt in front of the headliner's dressing room, occupied this week by Ben Harney. He had heard someone inside, a woman's voice, soft and breathy. He leaned forward, listening intently. There it was again. First, gentle moaning, and next a thumping sound that rapidly picked up speed. As it continued, Mike started to feel embarrassed about eavesdropping. Still, he couldn't tear himself away.

He leaned in a little closer. All he could hear now were grunts and groans, decidedly male in origin. He was surprised Ben and Jessie couldn't find a better place to carry on than Harney's dressing room at the theater. It seemed so déclassé, as his old professor at the conservatory used to say whenever he or one of the other scholarship students from America let slip some of their low-class vernacular. Mike had tried hard to rid himself of all that, to speak like someone who'd grown up having the best of everything—like the story he'd told May.

Mike wrenched himself away from the door and hurried down the hall, suddenly anxious to escape the sound of Jessie and Ben's lovemaking. He skirted around the bucket and mop that someone had left in the middle of the hallway and then rounded the corner at high speed, his own dressing room now only a few yards away.

"Whoa! Slow down there!"

"Jessie!" He had very nearly crashed into her. But what was *she* doing *here*? "Sorry, I wasn't expecting anybody else to be around this early."

"I'm supposed to meet Ben. We're going over a new number with Strap. I'm half an hour early, though." She held up a folded newspaper. "Going to do a little reading. Good to keep up with what's going on in the world, you know."

Mike hesitated, considering the crisis that he knew was in the making. A crisis he could choose to avert—or not.

It was an odd dilemma. Part of him wanted nothing more than for Ben to get caught with his pants down, literally. But then, there was Jessie. He recalled that night at Leo's restaurant, the sweet way she talked about her fiancé. She'd insisted he was as loyal as they come. It had been obvious that she believed it.

A sudden cynicism welled up inside him. Why should Harney have it all—more money than anyone plus a woman like Jessie who adored him? He didn't deserve her. Or the rest of it either! But, somehow, he'd managed to pull the wool over everybody's eyes.

"Actually, I think Ben may be in his dressing room. I didn't bother to stop. Got here early so I could do some work of my own at the piano. Just felt like getting out of the apartment. You know how it is."

"You'll be working in the pit?"

"Yes, but don't worry about it. You go ahead. I'll wait until you three are finished with your rehearsal. If it won't take too long, that is."

Jessie seemed surprised by his generosity. "Thanks. If you say Ben is here, then we can get started right away. Hopefully, Strap will show up a little early, too."

"You just hurry along then," Mike said, starting to get nervous that Ben might soon finish with his hanky-panky.

"I will. And thanks." She proceeded to turn the corner, heading toward Ben's dressing room.

Mike waited a moment, then took a couple of steps back and peered around the corner. He felt bad about Jessie. But wasn't it worth it to see Ben exposed for what he really was? A pretender.

She was almost there, a few yards more. He licked his lips, ready for the fireworks.

Suddenly, Ben's door opened. A colored woman exited the room. She wore a plain black dress with a white apron, the standard uniform of the theater's cleaning staff. That explained the bucket and mop that had been left in the middle of the hall.

"Mornin', ma'am," she said, slipping past Jessie and continuing down the hall.

Why hadn't Jessie confronted her? Asked her what she was doing in Ben's room? Or had she assumed she'd only been cleaning?

"Jessie, what you doing here?"

Strap Hill appeared in the doorway of Ben's dressing room, pulling up his suspenders. "Thought we was meeting up in half an hour."

"We are. Hope I didn't interrupt anything."

Mike couldn't see Jessie's face, but he had a feeling she was giving Strap one of her all-knowing smiles. Like she'd given Mike that night at Leo's, before he got drunk and made a fool of himself.

Strap looked at the floor, shuffled his feet for a second, and then glanced down the hall where his lady friend had resumed her mopping.

That was that!

Mike turned toward his dressing room, expecting to feel disappointed; strangely, he felt almost relieved. Yes, Ben was a fraud. Jessie was bound to get hurt someday.

But after all, maybe it was better some *other* day.

Laughter to Tears

May disembarked from the hansom cab with a rush of childlike elation. How wonderful it was to be here on this lovely summer evening, alone and with such an adventure ahead!

These days, a theater outing was a rare treat. She spent most of her evenings at home with the children. And, of course, a houseful of servants at her beck and call, more of them than she knew what to do with. But she'd not forgotten her promise to the young lady she'd met at Dr. Adams's office, Abbie Mitchell, nor her curiosity about Miss Mitchell's husband, Will Marion Cook. Tonight, she'd come to the New York Theater Rooftop Garden to witness the premiere of Cook's one-act operetta, *Jes Lak White Fo'ks*.

In front of the theater, she paused a moment for a breath of night air. A multitude of stars shimmered in a sky of black velvet, the nearly full moon a mother-of-pearl white. It was almost eleven thirty; in order to attract an after-theater crowd, rooftop performances often started quite late. That was fine with May. She had been able to put Melvin and Anna to bed herself, tucking them in with the usual hugs and kisses. Unless they awoke during the night, which they seldom did, they wouldn't even know she was gone.

She proceeded to the box office and bought her ticket, then passed into the Grand Lobby with its mirrored walls, high ceiling, and low-hanging crystal chandeliers; it was packed and buzzing with the chatter of excited theatergoers. Most were on their way out, having already attended the top-billed attraction playing in the main auditorium. She slipped through the crowd, paying no mind to the occasional curious glances that always attend to a woman out alone at night. She found the elevator empty, the operator waiting.

As she ascended to the rooftop, in spite of herself she thought of Teddy—so often absent, never missed. He spent at least half his time in London, where the bank held many of its most valuable assets, his frequent sojourns away from New York a godsend allowing her a certain measure of peace and independence. But it was never enough; his inevitable return seemed always to loom dark and heavy in her mind.

She had, on occasion, resolved to try harder to make their marriage work, if only for the sake of the children. But her good intentions invariably came to nothing. She told herself the fault wasn't only hers. Neither of them had married for love. For her, it was not a matter of choice but of necessity. For him, somewhat the same—a business deal, assurance of his future controlling interest in their fathers' firm. In his eyes, she was a commodity.

Still, she could appreciate that it must be difficult for Teddy when people remarked, as they frequently did, that Melvin bore not the slightest resemblance to him. Of course, the reason had never been discussed with anyone, not even between the two of them. Whatever Teddy thought, he'd chosen to keep it to himself, and she'd chosen to let him. In fact, her father was still the only one who knew, unequivocally, who Melvin was. From the beginning, he had insisted on absolute secrecy.

George Convery had decided first against abortion, then adoption. May was surprised by her father's stubborn assertion that no child with Convery blood in his veins would grow up among strangers. A hasty wedding, he said, was the best remedy for May's predicament. As it happened, fate intervened to provide the perfect cover. Teddy's mother was dying. The doctors had given her only a couple of months more. What kinder parting gift than the joy of seeing her only son walk down the aisle? And so that chapter of May's life—marriage and motherhood—had commenced beneath a cloud of deception.

The elevator lurched to a stop and she stepped out onto the rooftop, glad to again have the stars and moon overhead. A light breeze from the harbor brushed over her face, refreshing as a mist of cool water. She smiled. It felt good to be free, even if only for a little while.

She surveyed her surroundings with eager curiosity. The rooftop was a fantasyland, with little café tables set among gaily lit arches and greenery, and a duck pond with a wooden bridge where people stood to make wishes and throw coins into the water. A narrow promenade circled the entire garden. She'd read somewhere that at various points along the walkway one could see beyond Central Park or all the way to New Jersey. Maybe some other evening she would have time for a leisurely stroll, but not tonight.

Arriving at the theater area, she was led to her seat by a handsome young usher dressed in a blue-and-gold uniform. He was Negro, as was almost everybody she saw. Women in stylish evening gowns and men in black suits and white bow ties stood in the aisles, talking and laughing as they waited for the show to begin. Picking up snippets of conversation, May gathered that tonight's premiere performance was a source of great pride to those gathered on the rooftop, their own Will Marion Cook now tuning up his orchestra in preparation for the overture. For a moment, she worried that she might be sorely out of place, perhaps unwelcome. But she quickly brushed off those feelings, remembering that she had been invited, more or less, by none other than Abbie Mitchell, the composer's wife and, as it turned out, one of the operetta's stars.

A drum roll sent everyone scurrying to their seats. The chatter subsided, and an anticipatory hush fell over the crowd. The tuxedoed man in front of the orchestra, whom she assumed to be Mr. Cook, raised his baton, paused a moment, and the music began.

The operetta's overture, from beginning to end, was brilliantly orchestrated, leaving May with the impression that Will Marion Cook's music was worthy of any theater in the city, not just the less prestigious venue of a rooftop garden. As for the libretto, it was only a few minutes into the story when she began to understand what Abbie Mitchell had meant when she intimated *not everyone* was likely to appreciate its satirical humor. The operetta's central character was Pompous Johnson, a Negro attempting to arrange a marriage between his daughter and a European prince through an array of absurd and elaborate deceptions. None of the story's cast of characters escaped ridicule. Those portrayed as white and wealthy were mercilessly skewered for their Victorian manners and morality, while the Negroes who sought their favor by parroting such supposedly *respectable* behaviors were similarly mocked. May saw how it would be possible to take offense, though she certainly did not. In fact, she enjoyed seeing the upper-class society toward which she had always felt a decided contempt exposed for its foolish pretensions.

Abbie Mitchell, cast as Pompous Johnson's daughter, displayed a stage presence every bit as commanding as that of her older and presumably more experienced costars. Her singing voice was a joy, astoundingly clear and pure, its impressive range more than compensating for what was perhaps a slight deficit in volume. May could easily imagine Abbie as a little girl singing Ave Marias on the fire escape; it seemed not at all surprising that Will Marion Cook would want to personally nurture her talent. A shame that, as his wife, she had come to fear him.

Throughout the evening, she laughed more than she'd expected to—more, in fact, than in a very long time. But most of all, it was the music she loved. Though ragtime had always been associated with the worst of her memories, tonight she managed to open herself to its boundless energy, bobbing and swaying to the infectious beat right along with everyone else in the theater, marveling at how the power of music can bring people together and make them forget the differences that at other times seem so difficult to bridge.

The evening flew by until suddenly it was the finale, a chorus of vibrant, triumphant voices rising from the open-air theater all the way to the stars. How she wished that sweet, heartfelt music could go on forever! Instead, the curtain came down, ending her journey into a world that before tonight she barely knew existed. The world of Negro musical theater. She clapped so hard that her hands stung as the velvet drape rose and fell half a dozen times more, cast and orchestra taking bow after bow. That was when she got her best look at Will Marion Cook. An elegant man, she thought, but so very stiff. Despite the crowd's overwhelming approval of the evening's performance, he wasn't smiling.

She stayed in her seat as long as she could, not anxious to leave, watching everyone around her stream into the aisles until only a few stragglers remained. Most had migrated to the café or the promenade or had taken the stairs or the elevator down to the main floor. She ought to have been tired, but she wasn't. She briefly considered going somewhere for a nightcap. Undoubtedly, there were any number of places close by, night spots that she might have enjoyed were she in the company of a gentleman. But a woman alone? At this time of night?

Reluctantly, she took the elevator to the lobby and hailed a hansom cab outside. She climbed in and gave the driver his instructions through the rear hatch. She was going home.

They had traveled not more than two blocks when she noticed some sort of commotion on the sidewalk. It took only seconds to realize that something catastrophic must have happened—or was unfolding at that very moment. Men and women were running in all directions, shouting and screaming. Some cowered in the doorways of shops that were closed for the night. It seemed that all were Negroes, dressed in fancy gowns and black tailcoats. With a growing sense of horror, she realized they must have been part of the audience with whom she had sat on the rooftop, enjoying an evening of laughter and song under the stars.

People began to spill into the street, suddenly appearing out of the shadows, darting in front of her cab and others. Her driver sharply reined in his horse, the hansom jerking to an abrupt halt. In the glow of the streetlamps, she saw men sprawled on the sidewalk. Some lay motionless, others scrambled to get up and away from a small group wielding wooden bats and boards. White men.

May watched as the gang knocked a Negro man to the ground, then viciously kicked and beat him amid the shrieks and wails of a tiny colored woman who valiantly tried to fight them off. Several black men came to her aid. A skirmish ensued, a tangle of flailing arms and fists. A white man collapsed to the sidewalk, clutching his stomach.

Terrified, May wanted only to avoid being further caught up in the chaos. She was about to open the rear hatch and shout her instructions to turn around and head the other way when she stopped.

Was that Abbie Mitchell?

She pressed her nose to the window. It was difficult to see the woman's face. She was running along the street, now only a few yards from where the hansom was stalled, followed closely by a black man, the upper part of his white shirt stained with blood.

May was quaking as she opened the door and leaned out. "Miss Mitchell! Abbie!"

The woman slowed, peering through the dimness.

"It's May Livingstone! Abbie, please! Get in the cab with me!"

Abbie Mitchell turned to the man at her heels, grabbed his hand, and pulled him along with her to the cab. May scrambled to the other side as they jumped in, the man slamming the door behind him.

May screamed through the rear hatch, "Get us out of here!" The driver laid his whip to the horse's rump, and the hansom made a sudden U-turn and sped off toward the east.

"My God, are you all right?" May focused first on Abbie, her eyes searching for any sign of physical trauma.

"I think so."

The young woman was breathless and extremely frightened but didn't appear to be hurt. Her companion, though, had a bloody gash above his left eye. May pulled a handkerchief from her purse and handed it to him.

"Thank you, ma'am. I'm sure it looks awful, but actually they didn't get me too bad."

Abbie turned and buried her face in his chest, dissolving into tears. May noticed the tender way he stroked her hair as he tried to calm her. This was not Will Marion Cook. She was sure of it. Having just seen the composer leading his orchestra, she would have recognized him.

"Do you know what started the trouble?" May asked, directing her question to the stranger.

"I guess you didn't hear about what happened a couple of days ago. The policeman who got stabbed."

May shook her head, slightly embarrassed to admit how oblivious she'd become to everything around her, how insulated from the world outside her own small sphere. "I'm afraid I haven't been reading the paper much lately."

"Seems there was some sort of misunderstanding between a colored man and a plainclothes police officer. The officer saw the fellow's lady friend standing alone on the street and assumed she was soliciting. Colored fellow comes out of a store, sees what's going on, and gets into a fight with the officer. Cop gets stabbed, colored man runs away, and next thing there's a riot. Started on the west side two days ago, and that was bad enough. But now this—" He shook his head. "Just gave them an excuse to go after decent folks out for an evening of entertainment. And it won't end here, I'm afraid."

"But attacking innocent people like that—what good can it possibly do?"

"Men like that aren't out to do good, ma'am."

Abbie raised her head and turned to look at May through her tears. "I'm sorry, Mrs. Livingstone. I should have introduced you to Mr. Johnson, but I was too upset even to think of it."

"J. Rosamond Johnson, ma'am."

He was a handsome man, probably no older than thirty, with deep, sensitive eyes and full lips that seemed to naturally curve into a smile. Even now.

"I'm sorry we have to meet like *this*," May said, "but I'm certainly glad to have come across the two of you when I did."

"Our sincere thanks, Mrs. Livingstone," he replied.

"But Miss Mitchell—where is Mr. Cook?" May asked. It had just occurred to her that he could have been among those attacked by the angry gang of whites. Might he still be embroiled in the conflict? Could he be in mortal danger?

"Honestly, I don't know where he is right now. He was mad about something and stormed out of the theater right after the last curtain call. I sure hope he was well on his way to Mrs. Lamprey's before the trouble started."

"Mrs. Lamprey's?"

Abbie and Rosamond Johnson exchanged a quick glance. "Mr. Cook stays with Mrs. Lamprey sometimes. They're good friends." Abbie must have sensed May's confusion. "I like her, too. She's a white lady, a widow. She loves Mr. Cook's music."

"I see," May said, though she didn't really. Did Abbie mean to imply that her husband was having an affair—and that it didn't bother her? "Well, I hope he's safe. As for the two of you, you'll come home with me tonight. No sense in taking any chances."

Mr. Johnson appeared surprised and reluctant. "That's very kind of you, but we couldn't impose like that. We'll be fine." He peered out the window. "In fact, you can drop us off anywhere now. Seems perfectly quiet around here."

"But I insist. You and Miss Mitchell will come with me. I've got plenty of room, and my Evie is as good as any doctor. She was with my family for years, and now she's with me. As a matter of fact, I can't imagine ever being without her. She'll take care of that cut in nothing flat. And after a good night's rest, you'll both feel better. This whole night will seem like just a bad dream."

Spiritual Connection

The tall windows of the limestone mansion on Fifth Avenue, just a few blocks from where May grew up, were dark when they arrived. May led Abbie Mitchell and Rosamond Johnson through the iron gates and up the semicircular steps leading to a curved central bay with four fluted stone columns. A hanging lantern cast a golden light on the arched doorway of bronze and glass.

She unlocked the door. They entered quietly, not wanting to disturb either the sleeping children or the house staff, all of whom had retired for the night. May turned a switch to light the huge crystal chandelier, illuminating a marble foyer with a vaulted ceiling.

"Your home is magnificent," Abbie whispered, her wide eyes roaming the spacious interior.

"Thank you," May replied, painfully aware that the opulence of her home perfectly exemplified the excesses of wealth critiqued in Will Marion Cook's brilliant operetta. "Let's go into the kitchen. It will be easier to tend to Mr. Johnson there."

She led them down the wide gallery, lighting each area as they went. They passed through stained-glass doors into a wood-paneled dining room and then, at the far end, through a small door leading to the butler's pantry and, finally, the kitchen.

May twisted a key on a mounted porcelain base, and the room was instantly bathed in light. Glass-front cabinets spanned an entire wall, displaying row after row of carefully arranged china and goblets. Opposite were two gigantic iron stoves recessed beneath a marble arch. In the middle of the room, a long wooden table for preparing food appeared ready for the following day, with various tools for weighing, chopping, and mixing already assembled.

May settled her guests at a smaller round table in front of the kitchen's eight-foot-high brick fireplace. Tonight, of course, there was no need for the warmth of a fire, though she would have welcomed the friendly crackle of a blaze.

She excused herself and went to find Evie. Roused from sleep, Evie hurriedly threw on a robe and slippers and came down to assess Mr. Johnson's head wound.

"Seems like it ain't too deep," she said after she'd finished cleaning the gash with hot, soapy water, "but it'll make a big lump for a while."

"Long as I didn't lose too many of my brains, I think I'll be all right," Mr. Johnson joked.

Evie chuckled. "I can bandage it up, if you want. The bleeding's stopped, but it's good to keep something tight on it."

"Thank you, ma'am."

Meanwhile, May had been looking around to see what she could offer her guests in the way of food. A freshly baked chocolate cake on a glass-domed platter caught her eye. She cut several slices, placing them on gold-rimmed dessert plates. She thought about moving everyone into the drawing room but decided against it. The kitchen seemed comfortably homey, the aroma of roast beef and potatoes hovering in the air. A bottle of Madeira sat on the counter. She asked Mr. Johnson if he would mind opening it for them.

"Evie, would you care to join us?" May asked, knowing that she would refuse. Evie was from the Old South, where certain boundaries were never crossed, and she remained set in her ways—even knowing how May despised those kinds of rules.

"Oh, no. I'm headed back to bed."

"All right, but thank you again for your help. I'm sorry we had to wake you in the middle of the night."

Mr. Johnson echoed May's apology. Evie brushed it off with a wave of her hand. "Wasn't nothing to it. Glad it wasn't worse."

"Excuse me, but—" Abbie had remained quiet ever since they arrived at the kitchen. "I wonder if I might go with Miss Evie. I'm not feeling terribly well. Just tired, I'm sure. But if I could lie down somewhere . . ."

"Certainly." May glanced at her with a look of concern. "You're positive there's nothing wrong? You weren't harmed by anyone?"

"No, it's nothing like that."

"Why don't you come on with me, honey," Evie said gently. "I'll get you settled in for the night in my room."

"Evie, wait." May hesitated. Of course, she could count on Evie not to say a word about any of this to Teddy. There was no love lost between them and, besides, she would trust Evie with her life. "I thought Miss Mitchell and Mr. Johnson could stay in the two guest suites on the second floor."

Evie smiled and nodded. "I'll see to it."

"Thank you so much, Mrs. Livingstone."

Abbie rose from her chair, suddenly pressing a hand to her stomach with a sharp intake of breath.

May sat up in alarm. "What's wrong?"

"Nothing."

"You're sure?"

"Yes, I'll be fine."

May paused a moment. "All right, but my bedroom is close to yours, at the very end of the hall. Come and find me if you should need anything later."

Evie led Abbie away and their footsteps quickly faded, leaving May and Rosamond Johnson alone. May noticed the look of sadness that had come over his face. Was he remembering again all that had happened that night? Reliving the terror?

"I keep thinking about that magnificent finale of the show tonight," she said, hoping to distract him with pleasanter memories of the evening.

Mr. Johnson shook his head. "A pity, isn't it?"

"A pity?"

"Yes—that a show like that has to close down so quickly, almost before it's off the ground."

"The show is closing? But tonight was the premiere."

Mr. Johnson stared moodily into his wine. "After what happened out there in the street, I doubt it will stay open long. There's too much tension between colored and whites right now. *Jes Lak White Fo'ks* was stepping on toes enough as it was, but now it's going to seem even worse. People are going to say it's too provocative." He looked up, meeting her inquisitive gaze. "That includes the owners of the roof garden. And there's no place else for a show like that to go."

"But it's not fair to blame the trouble on Mr. Cook's operetta. It had nothing to do with that."

"'Course it didn't. But that won't matter. Those fellows figured they were taking a big chance anyway, putting on a show with Negro music and a Negro cast. I suppose they thought of it as a grand experiment—one that now they'll chalk up as a failure. Or worse."

She recalled what Abbie had told her about her husband's moods, his erratic behaviors. Might all this be enough to push him over the edge? "And how will Mr. Cook handle that?"

"Not well," Mr. Johnson replied. "And the timing couldn't be worse, what with Abbie expecting a baby and all."

"A baby?" She should have known! "Maybe we ought to take her to the hospital to be gone over by a doctor. She appeared to be in some distress just now. Did you notice?"

"She's not very far along. I expect she'll be fine, like she said."

May wasn't entirely convinced, but she had told Abbie to fetch her in the night if anything was wrong; hopefully the young woman would have enough sense to do so.

Mr. Johnson took a couple of swallows of Madeira and set down his glass. "Thank you for inviting us into your home— but I really must be going." He scooted back his chair, at the same time reaching into his pocket and pulling out several coins. He laid them on the table. "If you don't mind, would you please give this to Miss Mitchell in the morning? She might need money for a cab."

"But I invited both of you to spend the night here."

"I know you did, but it's not at all necessary for me to stay. It's enough for me to know that Abbie is safe."

"You've suffered an injury. I insist that you should stay until morning."

"I really couldn't. But thank you."

"I simply won't take no for an answer."

Impulsively, May reached for the bottle of wine and filled his glass to the top. She did the same with hers.

Mr. Johnson leaned back with a sigh. "You're making it very difficult to refuse."

"I mean to," she replied, surprised by her determination not to let him go. "But tell me—if I'm not being too nosy. Miss Mitchell mentioned that Mr. Cook might be staying tonight at the home of another woman. An admirer of his music, she said. Does Mr. Cook often leave his wife alone at night?"

Mr. Johnson appeared to stifle a smile. "Will Cook would be the first to admit he's not the marrying kind. We were all surprised when he made the announcement about him and Abbie. I'm afraid he got used to having his pick of women—every size, shape, and color—when he was a student in Europe. Things are different for us over there, you know. Anyway, he likes to call it *the lure of the Negro genius*. He claims there's nothing more fascinating to a woman."

"Are you saying he's having an affair with her, this Mrs.—"

"Mrs. Lamprey. I wouldn't call it an affair. It's more of an *arrangement*. She's actually a very nice lady. And she's fond of Abbie as well."

"I see." May supposed it was odd how protective she felt toward Abbie, whom she barely knew. Of course, it was none of her business. "And you, Mr. Johnson—tell me about yourself."

"Not much to tell really. I studied music at the New England Conservatory in Boston and, for a time, in Europe. Taught school in Florida for a while, until I moved to New York. That was just over a year ago. Lately, I've been doing some composing with my brother and with Bob Cole. I don't know whether you've heard of Mr. Cole, but he's a substantial figure in Negro musical theater. I'm greatly encouraged by our work together so far."

"So you're a composer. And what kind of music do you write? Is it similar to Mr. Cook's compositions?"

"Our styles are somewhat different, but we do share a belief in the uplifting power of music. There should be great opportunity for Negroes to excel in the musical arts. But, if I may be frank, Negro music is too often misrepresented, or stolen from us, by people who really don't care about where we come from or who we are."

"You mean white people?" she asked, wondering how deep his resentment toward the white race might run. Perhaps even toward her.

"Unfortunately, there are people of all races who resist progress."

"I'm sure that's true." She hesitated. "Though I don't profess to be greatly knowledgeable about music, I do love it. I've studied piano a bit. The classics mostly. For a while, my sister and I took our lessons with Mike Bernard. You've heard of him, haven't you?"

Mr. Johnson raised his brows. "Ah, yes. Mike Bernard. Well then, you must have learned how to rag, at least a little bit."

"No, I'm afraid not. This was before his great fame. When he was just starting out, with aspirations to be a concert player."

"A lot of us have had those aspirations at one time or another."

"But, Mr. Johnson, you never told me what it is that you compose. Is it ragtime music?"

"I write for the theater and, yes, frequently ragtime. But being classically trained, I let a bit of that come through as well."

May nodded and took a sip of her wine. She was starting to feel its relaxing effect, starting to feel quite comfortable in the company of Mr. Johnson. "Too bad it's so late, or I'd ask you to play something for me."

"Of course, I'd be happy to—but you're right. It's late."

They were quiet for a moment. "What is it that you like to do with yourself, Mrs. Livingstone?"

"Well, I have two children. They keep me very busy. And my husband—" She stopped. "Actually, he's gone quite often. On business overseas. So I do have a lot of time to myself. I fear that I waste much of it, but I like to read. Poetry mostly. I used to fancy myself a poet," she added with a laugh. "Back in the days when I thought I had something important to say."

"And don't you?" His gaze was deep and steady.

"No, I've come to see that I don't. Not really."

"Hmm. *Not really?*" He scooted his chair closer to the table. "In that simple little comment, I sense a dream that is not entirely lost."

May felt the color rush to her cheeks. "A dream too impractical ever to come true."

"Says who?"

"Mr. Johnson, you're very nice to humor me. But I'm smart enough to know that I'm *not* smart enough. What I mean is, there are people with far greater writing talent than mine. Besides, I don't know that I'd be very good anymore at being a romantic. Although I must say that living on wine and chocolate doesn't sound so terrible."

"Maybe you underestimate yourself. Granted, I don't know anything about your poetry, whether it's good or not so good. But as far as being a romantic, I'm not sure one ever can completely lose a quality like that. Maybe you've only misplaced your inspiration. But there's always more, if you look hard enough. It might be just around the corner."

"I'd like to think you're right. But the fact is, my life is no longer my own. I haven't the freedom to look around corners."

"Freedom? Now, that's a subject I know a thing or two about." Mr. Johnson rapped twice on the wooden tabletop. "What I know is this: Freedom is something you've got to fight for. It doesn't get handed to you, no matter what they say. It's not yours until you make it yours. Until you decide there's simply no other way to live."

She surmised he was talking about something much bigger than himself. Certainly bigger than her silly problems. Still, she asked, "But what if it's too late?"

He regarded her with a quizzical smile. "I can only guess your age, but I guarantee you're far too young to be thinking it's too late for *anything.*"

"But I've made so many mistakes."

He pressed his palms together, looking thoughtful. "You know what I love about mistakes?" he said finally.

She shook her head.

"By the time you recognize them, they're already in the past. And if you want to badly enough, that's where you can leave them." He sat back, crossing his arms over his chest. "May I hear some of your poetry?"

May squirmed in her chair. "I—well, I don't have any of it handy."

"And you can recite none of it from memory?"

"I suppose I could. But really, I wouldn't want to bore you."

"I wouldn't be bored. I'd like very much to hear it."

Why was her heart suddenly beating so fast?

"I'm flattered by your interest, but perhaps a reading of my poetry is something we should also save for another time."

Again, he smiled at her in that gently curious way. "I understand. It can be difficult to share something so personal, especially with a stranger."

Funny, she thought, but Rosamond Johnson already seemed more like a friend. "I've never shared my poetry with anyone," she said. Then, remembering it wasn't true, she added, "Actually, there *was* someone. Once." Why was it that she couldn't bear the thought of misleading him, as she did everyone else?

"And there will be someone again. You must learn not to be afraid of what other people think of your work, Mrs. Livingstone. That is, if you want to be an artist."

"Of course, you're correct."

"But if you're not ready to share your poetry with me, then I'll share some with you instead."

"You write poetry?"

"Not exactly. I'd like to share someone else's poetry with you, if that's all right. Someone whose work I greatly admire. You may have heard of him—Paul Laurence Dunbar? He's a

Negro poet, a friend of mine and of my brother's. Anyway, probably my favorite of his poems is this one. You don't mind if I recite it for you, do you?"

"I would be thrilled to hear it."

"All right then. It's called 'Sympathy.'"

He sat up, filled his chest, and began to recite in a rich, resonant baritone.

> *I know what the caged bird feels, alas!*
> *When the sun is bright on the upland slopes;*
> *When the wind stirs soft through the spring-*
> *ing grass,*
> *And the river flows like a stream of glass;*
> *When the first bird sings and the first bud*
> *opes,*
> *And the faint perfume from its chalice*
> *steals—*
> *I know what the caged bird feels!*

> *I know why the caged bird beats his wing*
> *Till its blood is red on the cruel bars;*
> *For he must fly back to his perch and cling*
> *When he fain would be on the bough*
> *a-swing;*
> *And a pain still throbs in the old, old scars*
> *And they pulse again with a keener sting—*
> *I know why he beats his wing!*

> *I know why the caged bird sings, ah me,*
> *When his wing is bruised and his bosom*
> *sore,—*
> *When he beats his bars and he would be*
> *free;*
> *It is not a carol of joy or glee,*

*But a prayer that he sends from his heart's
   deep core,
But a plea, that upward to Heaven he
   flings—
I know why the caged bird sings!*

The silence that followed seemed to have a resonance of its own. And in the midst of that silence, she wondered how a poem so deeply tragic could at the same time fill her with such delirious hope.

Mr. Johnson pulled a gold watch from his pocket. "My, my! Did you know it's after three in the morning? I'm sure you must be tired."

Perhaps she was, but May didn't want this night to be over. She sensed there was still so much more to learn about Rosamond Johnson. And from him. But he must be exhausted after all he'd been through.

"If you like, I can show you to your room now. I hope you'll be comfortable."

Mr. Johnson glanced down at his bloodstained shirt. "I'm sorry—"

"Please don't apologize. I'll have Evie find another shirt for you in the morning. One of my husband's should fit you well enough."

"If you're sure it's no trouble . . ."

"No trouble at all, Mr. Johnson." Their eyes met, and she was suddenly close to tears, thinking of that caged bird, the blood from his beating wings upon the bars. "Thank you for sharing your friend's poem with me. I'll never forget it."

"Tell you what—I'll send you one of Mr. Dunbar's books."

"Oh no, please. Don't."

His disappointment was obvious. "I only thought you might enjoy reading some of his other poems."

"But I would," she replied quickly, realizing he'd misunderstood. Did she dare tell him what she really meant? Would he think her too forward? Might he even imagine her as just another rich white woman drawn to him out of curiosity? *The lure of the Negro genius,* he had called it. But this wasn't anything of the sort. She wondered if there was a chance he was experiencing the same surprising attraction that she was. A spiritual connection. Something that felt genuine and rare.

The possibility filled her with a sudden boldness.

"What I meant to say, Mr. Johnson, was that I'd rather you gave it to me in person—when we see each other next."

The Apology

I t was late on a Wednesday afternoon when Mike hired a horse-drawn hansom to take him to Fifth Avenue and Forty-Ninth Street, at the last minute asking the driver to drop him off a couple of blocks shy of his destination. He needed a few minutes to think. A short walk and a touch of air, cooler now that it was near the end of September, should help to clear his head. And afford one final opportunity to change his mind.

He had learned where May lived from Mrs. Wellington. It hadn't been difficult. He merely told her that he'd run into his former student at the charity concert last April. Mr. and Mrs. Livingstone, he said, were in the process of redesigning their music room, and Mrs. Livingstone had asked whether he might be willing to consult with them on the particulars. Though it was not his usual line of work, he consented to help but then promptly misplaced Mrs. Livingstone's card. He felt terrible, he said, for waiting five months to get in touch.

That part, at least, was true.

Ever since the night he and May saw each other at Mrs. Wellington's, he'd been unable to put her out of his mind. Funny how, lately, he could remember only the good. How, from the beginning, May had a knack for making him feel important. Making him imagine himself better than he was. How she had given herself to him in a way no one else ever had—completely, without reservation. Thinking about it after all this time he had come to the conclusion that, in her naïve way, May had genuinely loved him. What astonished him most was that she loved him *then*—when he was nothing, nobody.

He had *wanted* to love her in return. Or he thought so now. But when it came to the important people in his life, there had always been an uncomfortable disparity between what he wanted to feel and what he actually felt—which often seemed like not enough. Sometimes he wondered if he simply had no capacity for love. Maybe there was something missing, some basic component of a human being that he was born without. Or maybe it was simply that there could be no room in his life for any love but music, an explanation he found far easier to accept.

Now, he asked himself again whether it was possible he really *had* loved her. It was too late, of course, to matter. But wouldn't it be better if he knew?

Before he felt entirely ready, he found himself in front of the massive limestone mansion where May and Teddy lived, a residence almost as palatial as the home in which May had grown up, where he used to give the Convery daughters their piano lessons. His self-confidence took a precipitous dive. Seen through the eyes of people like the Converys and the Livingstones, his accomplishments must seem little more than child's play. What did they understand about musicianship and what it takes to become great? The talent, the dedication, the inspiration. To them, it was all small time, and he would never be anything more than a cheap music-hall entertainer.

He hesitated at the edge of the driveway, pulling his hat low over his eyes. He had done fine without May's forgiveness up to now. Why was he suddenly so in need of it? Could it be, despite his success, that he really hadn't changed? That he still felt as insecure, as unworthy, as before?

But that was ridiculous. Everything had changed, especially him. He was the Ragtime King of the World. The one nobody could beat.

He marched through the iron gates and up the driveway, then mounted the steps of the curved central bay. Standing before the arched doorway of bronze and glass, he raised the heavy knocker and let it fall.

"Yes, sir?" A colored maid in a black dress and white apron stood before him, squinting against the sun.

"I'm here to see Mrs. Livingstone."

"I'm sorry, but she's not accepting visitors. Would you like to leave your card?"

He hesitated. Was this meant to be his deliverance? It must, after all, be for the best. "No, that won't be necessary. Thank you anyway."

He turned to leave but then heard a woman's voice from somewhere behind the half-closed door. "It's all right, Thelma. You can let Mr. Bernard in."

She must have been looking out a window. Maybe she'd seen him at the end of the driveway and expected him to simply pass by. But she *wanted* to see him.

Resolutely, he pivoted and stepped over the threshold, handing the maid his hat.

"If you'll come this way please." She guided him across the marble foyer. A short way down a wide gallery, she pushed open a door on the left. "You can wait in here, sir."

As he entered the room, a sobering thought occurred to him, one he should have considered before. "By the way, Mr. Livingstone doesn't happen to be in—is he?"

"No, sir. But Mrs. Livingstone will be with you shortly."

He smiled. "Thank you."

ELIZABETH HUTCHISON BERNARD

Alone in the room, he took a moment to catch his breath. He felt as if he'd been running, his heart was beating so fast. His wandering gaze fell upon the exquisite grand piano in front of a wide leaded-glass window. It was an outrageously expensive instrument with a carved Louis XV cabinet, nearly every inch of it custom painted in an ornate design of gold on cream. He wondered how often it was played, if at all.

He glanced around some more, searching for anything that might tell him more about the woman May had become. But there was little of a personal nature on display—an antique Persian rug, a blue damask sofa, and several matching chairs arranged at precise angles in front of an empty fireplace. Above the mantel was a huge oil portrait of George Cornelius Convery, stern and unflinching, just as he looked that day when he and Teddy Livingstone invited themselves into Mike's tiny apartment in the Hotel Chelsea. Unnerved, he turned back to the piano, now noticing a small stack of sheet music on the bench. He went over to take a closer look. Bending down, he began to rifle through it: Chopin, Bach, Mozart—

"Good afternoon."

May stood in the open threshold to the music room. She looked healthier than when he'd seen her at Mrs. Wellington's. There was some color to her complexion now, and she appeared less gaunt. She was dressed simply in a cream-colored shirtwaist and an ankle-length tan skirt decorated with brown embroidery. He noticed that she held a book in her hand, her finger marking the page, as if she'd been interrupted while reading.

"Won't you have a seat?" she said, entering the room and quietly closing the door behind her.

"Thank you."

With measured steps, trying not to appear overanxious, Mike went to the sofa and sat down, again unsettled to find himself facing the portrait of George Convery. May chose an armchair directly across from him. Between them was a low, round table. A tall vase of long-stemmed pink roses sat in the middle, partially obscuring their view of each other. No one moved it aside.

"Forgive me for coming by like this, unannounced, but I happened to be in the neighborhood, and—oh, by the way, I got your address from Mrs. Wellington, in case you're wondering." He cleared his throat. "Anyway, it was quite something running into you at the musicale. Very pleasant, of course. But I felt as if we couldn't talk freely. Miss Ferrari—and let me assure you, she and I are nothing to each other—" He stopped again, realizing how terribly nervous he sounded, how nervous he *was*. "I regretted that you left before we could—"

"Before we could *what*, Mr. Bernard?" The interruption might have been merciful if not for the impatience in her tone.

"Before we could catch up on what had transpired in each other's lives over the past four years." If only he could know what she was thinking. He should have moved those flowers! "I was wondering how you've been. Are you still writing your poetry?"

"Is that what you came here to ask me? About my poetry?"

"Not only that, of course. But I know how much it meant to you. Back then."

"Yes, it did. But now I read other people's poetry." She glanced at the book in her hand, a tiny smile forming at the edges of her lips. "Have you ever wondered why the caged bird sings?"

He had no idea what she was talking about, but this whole business already felt incredibly awkward. Not at all as he had imagined. Maybe it was best just to get it over with. "I might as well get straight to the point of why I'm here."

"Please do."

"The fact is—well, it should come as no surprise that I've always regretted what happened."

"What happened *when*?"

"I mean, at the end."

"The *end*?"

"Of course, not *just* the end. I suppose I didn't handle things well from the beginning. But when I think about what happened to us, I can't help but feel—"

"Happened to *us*?"

A bead of sweat rolled down from his temple. He brushed it away, hoping she hadn't noticed. Why must she repeat everything he said?

"Look, I've come here to say that I'm sorry for what happened. The last thing I wanted to do was hurt you. If that's what I did—like I said, I'm sorry."

His apology did not sound quite as sincere as he'd intended. He made another attempt. "Maybe you imagined all this time that I'd forgotten you. I see now that I should have told you. I should have let you know how much I regretted what happened, how things ended. But you understand I had no chance against your father. There was nothing I could have done. If there had been something, anything, I would gladly have tried."

"Really?"

"Yes." He thought for a moment before adding, "I knew you didn't want to marry Teddy. I tried to save you."

She touched her forehead. "Yes, I remember that's what you said at the time. What you told my father."

"I said quite a few things—except maybe what I should have."

She seemed to be waiting, expecting him to finish. To say what he had just admitted he should have said before. He was sweating profusely. He licked his lips, swallowed. But the words would not come. They would not, just as they hadn't the first time.

"Well then." She gave a little sniff—a prelude, it appeared, to a change of subject. "You certainly are a big celebrity now. I see your name in the papers all the time. You must be enjoying the notoriety—the money, the *women*." She paused. "Are you?"

Her question embarrassed him. No doubt she could guess there had been many women since her. None that meant anything. But, as he had learned, the public loves gossip. And a celebrity needs headlines. "Well, it's nice to be appreciated. But then again, I suppose fame isn't everything."

She raised her brows. "Oh?"

Of course, he didn't believe anything of the sort. Why was it so hard to be honest with her, even now? "Look, May, we can't change the past. What's done is done. I only wanted you to know that, back then—under the circumstances—I tried my best."

"Of course." May leaned forward, moving aside the vase of flowers. "I understand perfectly."

He began to breathe a little easier. Now that he could see her clearly—now that she could see him—maybe it was time to tell her about Teddy's threat, the terror that had haunted him for months afterward. The paralyzing fear that her father would seek revenge, that he'd be left a cripple with broken fingers, useless hands.

"I'll be honest. Apologies don't come easily to me. But when I saw you that night at Mrs. Wellington's, it made me start thinking. Made me realize that maybe I should explain the reason why I—"

"Mr. Bernard—*Mike*."

She placed her book on the table between them, slowly running her finger along the bottom edge, like she was counting the beads of a rosary.

"It's nice to hear you call me *Mike* again," he said, fighting the sudden urge to reach for her hand, wrap his fingers around it. "I'm glad we have this opportunity to talk. To clear the air. What I should have told you before is that—"

"Please—don't."

She lifted her hand from the book, *The Poetry of Paul Laurence Dunbar*, and leaned back in her chair, her eyes steady on his face. "This may come as a shock to you, but nothing you could do or say matters in the least to me."

She paused but not long enough for him to react. "If it makes you feel better to have finally said the words *I'm sorry*, it shouldn't. As a matter of fact, you only show your arrogance all the more by intruding into my life again, as if you have a right. You talk about what happened to *us*. It was *me* it happened to. You never even cared to know about it. You were free to go about your business, becoming famous, doing as you pleased. I was the one who lost everything. So it doesn't matter now what you say. The only reason I allowed you into my home this afternoon is because I wanted to tell you how much I despise you. I wanted to say all the things I've kept inside for so long. Things I've allowed to literally make me ill. But I'm finished with that now. I've finally realized that you were never, ever worth it."

Mike had been listening in stunned silence, his earlier remorse—the beginnings of a long-forgotten tenderness— quickly turning to anger. He'd not imagined her capable of such vitriol. She had invited him in, pretended to listen. She said she understood. She had meant to trick him, to lay a trap, when all he had tried to do was say he was sorry! Clearly, she had become like the rest of her family. Worse even than her mother.

There was a tap on the door. It opened, and Thelma peeked around the corner. "Excuse me, Mrs. Livingstone, but you asked me to let you know when it was five o'clock. Your appointment?"

May stood up abruptly. "Yes, thank you, Thelma. You may bring Mr. Bernard's hat."

"I have it right here."

The two women had precisely choreographed everything, leaving him no opportunity to utter even a word in his own defense. Now that he was thinking with a clearer head, he questioned whether he had owed May an apology at all. Wasn't *she* the one who had started the trouble? The one who lured him into becoming her confidant, invited herself to his apartment, and then encouraged him to violate every rule of decent behavior? She was perfectly willing to place him in danger, possibly mortal danger, with no regard for what her father might do, how easily George Convery could destroy him. It was a miracle that he hadn't, in one way or another.

Without waiting for him to stand or respond to her outrageous accusations, May snatched her book from the table and sailed across the room, her nose in the air, past Thelma and into the gallery. Mike heard the sharp click of her heels on the marble tiles as she hurried down the hall. He could have shouted something after her, something to make her seem as small as she had tried to make him feel. To bluntly inform her that *she* ought to be the one apologizing to *him*.

But what would be the point?

He took his time getting up, letting his anger cool before he finally strolled over to Thelma and, without looking at her, accepted his hat. By the time they reached the front door, a calm numbness had settled in. He had been a fool to imagine this could turn out well.

But he had delivered his apology. His conscience was clear.

And he would never again waste a single precious thought on May Convery Livingstone.

ACT III
1912–1913

Love is the light of the world, my dear,
Heigho, but the world is gloomy;
The light has failed and the lamp down hurled,
Leaves only darkness to me.

　　　　　—From "Lyrics of Love and Sorrow," Paul Laurence Dunbar

The Proposal

S trap, why do we have to go see this Ben Harney fellow? Can't you take me shopping? I told you before, I need me a new hat."

It seemed that Lucinda Jones wasn't about to budge from her spot in front of the lit-up Macy's department store window with all the ladies' hats lined up in a row. The way Strap saw it, though, there wasn't a thing wrong with the hat she had on. In fact, he was just thinking he'd never seen her looking finer than she did right then. Underneath her knitted shawl, she was wearing that blue dress he liked, the one that showed the pretty curve of her collarbone. Her felt hat with the ostrich feather matched it just right. Maybe she thought it wasn't fancy enough, he didn't know. But in his eyes, she didn't need anything else to make her beautiful.

Lucinda was something special. Not just pretty, but sweet. A nice girl, not part of the theater crowd. She worked as a maid in one of the fanciest houses on Fifth Avenue. The pay was decent, and she told Strap they treated her like one of the family. But the fact was, Lucinda already had a family of her own. She and her mother lived in an apartment down in Harlem, along with Lucinda's three children. In the year they'd been seeing each other, Strap had never asked about the fathers, except he knew there was more than one and Lucinda had never been married. Still, she was a nice girl—maybe a little too trusting was all. She was only twenty-four. Strap figured she needed an older fellow, somebody like him, to take care of her properly.

It was the fall of 1912, and Strap was pushing forty-three. He'd done all right for himself, he guessed. He hadn't made a fortune, and he wasn't famous either. But he couldn't complain. Back in the beginning, he sang off and on with Ben. After that, he spent a few years on the road, touring the vaudeville circuit. Now he took whatever small opportunities came his way. He'd met a lot of girls, never had anything too serious with any of them. But Lucinda was different.

This morning, he'd dressed up in his green plaid suit and his straw boater, something special on his mind. Something that scared him nearly to death, but he'd decided it was now or never.

Of course, Lucinda had to pick *now* to get fussy!

He took her by the arm, gently but firmly pulling her away from the store window and toward the curb. Meanwhile she kept jabbering about how there was a big sale going on, and there were all kinds of bargains, and it was her only day off, and why couldn't they do what *she* wanted for once. He signaled for a cab. A few went by; some were full, others empty, the drivers likely on the lookout for clientele presumed to have deeper pockets than a colored man in a cheap plaid suit. Finally, one of them pulled over. Strap hustled Lucinda inside and jumped in after her.

"Sunnyside Hotel in Greenwich Village!"

It was a last-minute thing, this idea of paying a visit to Ben and Jessie. Strap heard they'd been halfway around the world to Australia, there and back on a steamer. He couldn't even imagine how far away Australia might be. All he knew was he wouldn't want to be out there in the middle of the ocean, waves churning, sharks circling, not a speck of land in sight. It was just last April that the *Titanic* went down after everybody swore it couldn't. No sir, he told Lucinda, he'd rather have his feet planted solid on the streets of New York City, where the worst that could happen was getting run over by a trolley or a speeding Model T.

But the main reason they were headed for the Sunnyside Hotel wasn't to hear about Australia or even to see Ben. It was Jessie. Strap always said she was about as close to being a witch as anybody he'd ever come across. One look at a person, she could tell what was on his mind, if he meant to do good or harm, if you could trust him. Strap was going to ask her about Lucinda, whether she was really the right girl for him. Jessie would figure it right away. He knew she would.

He shoved his hand into his jacket pocket, just to make sure the ring was still there. He hadn't said a word to Lucinda— just in case. But today would settle it. If Jessie had the right feeling about Lucinda, he just might ask her to marry him right then and there.

The cab pulled up in front of the Sunnyside Hotel, a plain wooden building, four stories high, painted a bright yellow. There was a sign in the window. Lucinda read it out loud: "*Rooms by the Day, Week, Month, or Hour.* You sure this is the right place, Strap?"

Strap pushed his hat to one side, scratching his head. Ben and Jessie used to stay at all the best hotels in town. "We about to find out."

He helped Lucinda out of the cab, and the two of them went inside to the lobby, Strap steering her around a wet stain on the threadbare carpet that looked suspiciously like blood.

"Don't take no niggers here," said a gnarly-looking clerk at the front desk.

"Looking for Mr. Ben Harney. Got a delivery for him."

"Delivery?"

"Just send somebody up, would you? Tell him Strap Hill is here."

The clerk glared at Strap a moment longer before he turned to a kid sitting in the corner playing dice. "Go up to Number 124 and tell 'em a nigger named Hill is here asking for 'em."

The boy jumped up, dusted off his pants, and darted off. In less than a minute, he was back, looking up at Strap. "Mr. Harney says for you to go on up."

Strap nodded, slipping him a nickel. Then he and Lucinda headed up the stairs. Strap could feel the clerk's eyes on his back until they rounded the curve.

Ben and Jessie were standing in the open doorway. Ben wore a faded smoking jacket, Jessie a long white robe. She looked like she'd just gotten out of bed, her thick hair piled on top of her head and stuck full of pins.

She engulfed Strap in a big hug. "How'd you find us?"

"Wasn't hard. Just got to know who to ask, that's all."

"And who is *this* delectable creature?" Ben was eyeing Lucinda like a starving man gazing on a feast.

Strap put his arm around her and pulled her close. "This here is Lucinda Jones."

"Mighty fine to meet you," Ben said. "But let's not stand out here in the hall. Come on inside, both of you."

They were led into a dim room devoid of cheer, its only window facing a brick wall and framed by tired lace curtains hanging lopsided on their rod. The air felt compressed, with a dank, musty smell like socks that needed washing. The four of them sat down, Jessie and Lucinda on the bed, Strap and Ben in wooden chairs around a small table. Strap could tell already that Lucinda wasn't impressed by his friends.

"I hear you two been touring the world," Strap began, though he was anxious to get on with the real purpose of the visit.

"Yup, lot of places we never expected to see," Ben said, smiling at Lucinda. "Everywhere we went, seemed like they couldn't stop talking about us, writing us up in the papers and all. Folks in Australia, they're a little behind America when it comes to music. We both blacked up for the shows, and everybody seemed to like that. My rags caught on like wildfire."

"In a way, it was like a new beginning," Jessie said. "All that excitement we used to feel when we first started out, it was just like that again."

"Them was good times all right," Strap agreed. "But where you headed next? Or you playing New York for a while?"

Jessie jumped in before Ben could take a breath. "We're taking a few weeks off, just to rest up a bit. The trip, wonderful as it was, took a lot out of us. By the way"—she turned to Lucinda—"I apologize for this place. It's not our usual style, but we thought it might be a good idea to lay low for a while. Maybe even economize a bit—right, honey?" she added, turning to Ben.

Ben rolled his eyes. "Sure, babe."

It was no secret. Jessie had been trying to curb Ben's wild spending for as long as Strap had known them, even in the best of days. Until Al Jolson came along, Ben Harney was making more money than anybody, but he was letting it go faster than anybody, too. Strap wondered if all that had finally caught up with them.

"Anyway, it's good to be back," Ben said. "Hey, Strap— what'd you think about those Boston Red Sox beating out the New York Giants for the World Series? I hope you weren't betting on the Giants, my friend. If I'd been here, I probably would have lost my shirt. Jessie would have been madder 'n hell at me, too."

"No, I didn't put no money on 'em. Matter of fact, I stopped betting a long time ago. Stopped drinking, too." Strap looked over at Lucinda, her hands folded in her lap like a proper lady. "I got my mind on other things these days. Looking to the future. Saved up enough cash to maybe get myself a piece of land somewhere. You know—settle down."

"Settle down? You?"

"I think that's wonderful, Strap," Jessie chimed in. "There comes a time when home is a pretty nice place to be. Sometimes I wish Ben and me had a little house somewhere, back in Kentucky or maybe Tennessee. Pretty country out there, greenest grass I ever saw. I used to love to ride a horse up into those hills, look out over miles and miles of rolling pasture. Used to pretend it all belonged to me." She let out a long sigh. "We could have done that, honey," she said, turning again to Ben. "We could have scooped up a bunch of cash and bought us a farm, raised horses and pigs and whatever else we wanted. We could have done that."

Strap wondered if Jessie was only talking that way because she knew what it was he wanted for himself and Lucinda.

"Jessie's starting to get soft on me, Strap."

"Oh, Ben! Why don't we be honest about it? Good lord, if we can't speak the truth to our old friend Strap, who on earth *can* we talk to?"

"What y'all talking about?"

"It's just that I'm feeling a change on the way, Strap. The bookings aren't coming in quite so fast as they used to. And we've heard the talk. Some of the theater owners even told Ben outright that he ought to update his style, that you can't do the same thing for fifteen years and not have people get tired of it. Music is slicker these days, I guess. Oh, we've still got our fans, the ones who'll love Ben Harney till the day they die. But we're starting to slip. And I hate to say we're not prepared for it. We were having so much fun we forgot to think about the future. Let that be a lesson to you. You, too, Lucinda. The future will be here before you know it."

"Come on now, Jessie. These two don't want to hear you talking like that. Besides, you're exaggerating something awful. We got plenty of bookings ahead of us. Good ones, too."

Ben was out to change the subject, and that was fine with Strap. He figured it wouldn't do any good to start fretting over his old friends now. They would be all right.

"But we want to hear about you," Jessie said, smiling at Lucinda. "How long have you and Strap known each other?"

Lucinda looked at Strap, as if she expected him to answer for her. He didn't.

"Just about a year now," she said. "Ain't that so, Strap?"

"Why, Ben and I hadn't been together even that long before we started talking about marriage."

Strap smiled. He'd been right about Jessie. She knew why he was here.

Lucinda dipped her head. "Oh, I don't think much about things like that. See, I got three children, and there ain't no man going to want that burden. Besides, I got me a real good job. I can take care of myself."

Jessie reached over to give Lucinda's hand a motherly pat. "There's not a woman alive more independent than I am, dear. But there's the matter of the heart. When your heart tells you it's time, this is the one, then you'd best listen. You know what I mean, don't you?"

That's when Strap stared straight at Lucinda and wouldn't take his eyes off her. His heart was pumping fast. He would have given anything if he could have read that girl's mind, but he hoped Jessie was doing it for him. It was all he could do to keep himself from pulling out the ring that very second and telling

Lucinda—telling everybody—what was on his mind. That by the time you hit forty-three, or close to it, you've learned a few things. That he knew he wasn't an important man. Not like Ben, not like Will Cook. He wouldn't ever be any richer than he was right then. Still, if he could find a little piece of heaven, have a real home and somebody to share it with, he figured that should be enough.

Slowly, he moved his hand to his pocket. He reached inside. His fingers tightened around the ring. He was thinking about what he'd say and how he'd say it and how Lucinda would look afterward—surprised, happy. Knowing she'd found a man who loved her and wanted to take care of her, even with all those little mouths to feed.

Lucinda hadn't said anything yet. Her head was still bent over so nobody could see her face. But when she looked up, it was straight into Jessie's eyes. Strap was so sure of what she was about to say, he almost didn't need to hear it. She knew what Jessie meant. She felt it herself. She felt it right now— more than ever.

"Yes, ma'am, you're right." And then she gave Jessie a little smile—sort of sad, it seemed. "I guess my heart just ain't told me nothing yet."

If Strap hadn't been taught a long time ago that a man doesn't cry, that's what he would have done, right there in front of everybody. The truth had slapped him in the face, and there wasn't any way he could pretend it hadn't. Lucinda turned her eyes to the floor. Jessie was looking at Ben, Ben at Lucinda. Nobody wanted to look at Strap.

Inside his pocket, he opened his hand and let the little band of gold slip through his fingers.

The Penthouse

Mike had suggested his penthouse apartment for this afternoon's interview. The panoramic views of Manhattan were breathtaking, the lavishly decorated interior further testament to the enormity of his success. On the telephone, the reporter from the *Chatterbox* had a nice voice. She sounded young. He thought he detected a hint of flirtation. It occurred to him at the time, *This could be interesting*. Now, gazing across the Hepplewhite coffee table at the slender blonde in a simple black skirt and ruffled white blouse designed to accentuate her rather significant curves, he congratulated himself on his intuition.

"So, Mr. Bernard," she said, extracting a pen and notebook from her leather satchel, "I can't tell you how thrilling it is to meet you in person. I've been a fan of yours for as long as I can remember."

Mike leaned back in his favorite French bergère chair with a self-satisfied smile, his confidence honed by well over a decade as one of vaudeville's top stars. These days, there wasn't a big house in New York he didn't play regularly. On the road, he was always at the top of the bill. "Maybe your article won't beat me up too badly then," he bantered amiably.

"I assure you, I plan to be most complimentary. May we begin?" She positioned her pen over the page. "I'm sure my readers would like to know how you feel about being among the first ragtime pianists signed to Columbia Records."

Mike drummed his fingers on the arm of his chair. This would never do! "Let me clarify something for you, Miss—I'm sorry, what did you say your name is?"

"Redmond. Layla Redmond."

"Miss Redmond, I am not *among* the first. I *am* the first."

Her lips formed a silent *oh* as she bent over her notepad, presumably amending her spurious *facts*. "Thank you for pointing that out, Mr. Bernard. Accuracy is a journalist's most important responsibility."

Mike bestowed a generously forgiving smile. "As to how I feel about my transition to recording artist—actually, I'm awestruck by this technology of the phonographic disc, which allows one to achieve, dare I say, a certain measure of immortality. It's gratifying to realize that, many years from now, even centuries in the future, people will still be listening to me play—long after I've departed this worldly life."

"How poetic!" Miss Redmond continued to scribble on her pad, faster now. Finally, she stopped. Flipping back to an earlier page, her finger slid down the paper until she apparently found what she was looking for.

"Mr. Bernard, you've been called the Paderewski of ragtime as well as vaudeville's greatest pianist. At the same time, as you know, there are many who have questioned the value of ragtime as a musical genre, even its moral integrity." She seemed to be reading this little introduction from her notes, but now she looked directly at him, eye to eye. "Do you ever regret having devoted your career to what the American Federation of Musicians once officially labeled *unmusical rot*?"

Mike stifled his first urge, which was to order Layla Redmond to pack up her precious notebook and get out. The truth was, it unsettled him to hear this young woman, a perfect stranger, articulate the very question he'd asked himself from his earliest days at Tony Pastor's theater. It wasn't that he shared the outlandish concerns about ragtime's corrupting influence on youth or any such nonsense as that. For him, the issue had always been personal. Did he sacrifice a more distinguished legacy merely for the sake of expediency?

But that was mere speculation, something that he ordinarily disdained.

Earnestly, he leaned forward in his chair. "It's true that my original intention was to become a concert pianist, but then I gradually drifted into the line of work I'm doing now. And perhaps I *am* better off." He smiled complacently. "Financially, at any rate."

"Well, yes—just look at this apartment! It's beautiful, and the views of New York are extraordinary."

"Why, thank you. If you like, I'd be happy to give you a tour of the place. I have mementos of various highlights of my career all over. Even in the bedroom."

The reporter blushed, quickly consulting her notes again. "Let's talk about marriage."

"I hope that's a proposal!"

She laughed self-consciously. "I mean, have you ever been married?"

Mike hesitated. This was territory in which he felt decidedly uncomfortable. "The life of a musician isn't exactly conducive to settling down. But that's not so terrible, is it?"

"But surely there's been someone special in your life. Someone you cared for deeply—or perhaps still do."

"I'm afraid the story of my life doesn't exactly read like a Victorian romance," he quipped. "You might say I've had my share of flings."

217

"Of course, there was the matter concerning Blossom Seeley."

Mike had figured his recent involvement in the Seeley-Curtin child custody case might come up sooner or later. There had been a lot of publicity—the kind he could do without.

"Miss Seeley's husband accused the two of you of having an affair when you were touring together out West. Was there any truth to his allegations?"

He sniffed contemptuously. "Not a smidgen."

"But the *Oakland Tribune* reported that Miss Seeley's suicide attempt in San Francisco was the direct result of an argument between the two of you. What happened that would cause her to drink an entire bottle of Lysol?"

Mike shifted in his chair. Miss Redmond had certainly changed her tune. She sounded more like a prosecutor than a reporter.

"I don't know what the papers said, and I don't care. Blossom Seeley is a marvelous singer and comedienne. I enjoyed working with her. But we were professional colleagues, nothing more. While we may have occasionally disagreed about one thing or another, I can assure you it was never serious. And never *personal*."

"Some might say her behavior sounds like that of a woman scorned."

Abruptly, he stood up. This was too much! He should have known better than to agree to an interview for a gossip tabloid like the *Chatterbox*. Who reads that kind of garbage, anyway?

"Miss Redmond, I'm afraid you'll have to excuse me. I have some important matters to attend to."

Layla Redmond's head popped up from her notebook, her expression contrite. "I—I hope I didn't say something to offend you. If so, Mr. Bernard, you really must forgive me. It's just that readers of the *Chatterbox* really love getting the inside scoop on the lives of their favorite celebrities. I guess you could say they like to live vicariously."

Mike stood for a moment looking down at her, mesmerized by the provocative rise and fall of her bosom beneath the ruffles of her white shirtwaist. She *did* appear genuinely distressed.

"Calm yourself, Miss Redmond," he said, gentler now. "Tell you what, why don't we finish our little interview over a drink? It might make us both feel better."

A look of relief washed over her face. "Thank you so much. I don't drink, but you go ahead."

"No, I insist. Just a small one. Both of us."

"I really couldn't." She glanced down at the nearly empty page in her notebook, a tiny crease appearing between her brows. "Well, perhaps just a drop of brandy—to soothe my throat."

"Good."

Mike headed for the liquor cabinet, already planning his next move. A serious-minded woman like Layla Redmond would not be an easy conquest. He would need to make her feel special, as if he'd chosen her above all others, selected her for his most precious gift.

And what did Layla Redmond want more than anything?

A bombshell of a story.

He turned around. "Once we're nice and relaxed, I'm going to tell you something I've never talked about before. Not to anyone, Miss Redmond. On or off the record."

"Oh my, really? That would be wonderful! Whatever it is, as long as it's *new*, the paper can play it up really big."

He hesitated, nudged ever so slightly by a touch of uncertainty. Did he really want to venture so close to the truth?

He flashed back to that painful afternoon when May tossed him out of her sumptuous Fifth Avenue mansion as if he were some obnoxious door-to-door salesman. Though he had always told himself it didn't matter, it did. That apology, after all, was the closest he had ever come to declaring his feelings. Or to imagining he understood them.

Besides, what he had in mind now was only good fun, a bit of a tease for Miss Redmond's readers. Of course, he wouldn't take it too far. He was still a gentleman. But he couldn't help picturing the look on May's face when she read it, as she undoubtedly would. Someone would mention, probably in an offhand way, the surprising article in the *Chatterbox* about her old piano teacher. Her curiosity would get the better of her. She'd be furious! Or maybe not. Maybe, after all these years, she'd be genuinely sorry for having acted the way she did, insulting him like that when he was only trying to tell her that he cared.

"Mr. Bernard?" Miss Redmond prompted, looking up at him with bright, hopeful eyes. "You were saying something about an exclusive? Just for me?"

She certainly was lovely! And a devoted fan.

"Yes, for you, Miss Redmond. I'm going to tell you, on the record, about the *only* woman I've ever really loved."

Recognition

Ay's eyes scanned the crowd gathered in a small room at the New York Public Library. He said he would come, and he always did. But the program was about to begin, and there was no sign of Rosamond Johnson.

"Miss Convery, we'll start in two minutes."

Sarah Allen, the young woman in her early twenties delivering this ultimatum as she hurried toward the lectern, reminded May of herself when she was that age. Restless, frustrated, wishing things to change faster than they possibly could. Not that May was so terribly different now. She was older, of course, and hopefully wiser. At thirty-four, she liked to think she had largely overcome the self-doubt that constrained her earlier years. And while she hadn't changed everything in her life as she might have wished, she *had* changed quite a bit.

The name May Convery was well known in New York literary circles. Almost as important, her work as an activist for women's equality had earned her both praise and scorn. She had always admired the suffragettes, believed wholeheartedly in the struggle. Now she was one of them and not at all bothered that some might condemn her for it—even her own husband.

For the sake of the children, she and Teddy remained married but in fact had little to do with one another. Teddy's primary interest was the same as always—expanding the robust banking empire established in partnership by their fathers. He'd been very successful at it.

She had to admit, to his credit, he'd done his part for the children. He had never held anything back from Melvin, at least not anything material. As far as his affections, they had always been lavished primarily on their daughter, Anna. But then, aren't little girls always their fathers' pride and joy? Teddy knew, of course, about May's history with Mike Bernard. But, all these years, if he had suspicions that Melvin was not really a so-called miracle baby—a tenacious survivor of premature birth, as everyone had been told—he had continued to keep his own counsel.

Her first book of poetry, penned under her maiden name, May Convery, was published in 1904. Entitled *Reflections on the Moon*, it had as its theme the often-fragile reconciliation between motherhood and the longing for personal freedom. Profits of that book as well as the six others that followed had been donated in their entirety to the National American Woman Suffrage Association. Sales of tickets from tonight's reading from her latest volume, published in October, were also to benefit the NAWSA and to help finance the Washington, DC, protest parade planned for next March.

"Ladies and gentlemen, if you would please take your seats, our program is about to begin."

Standing behind the lectern, Sarah brought down the gavel with an authoritative crack. May glanced around the room once more, hoping she had simply not noticed Rosamond's arrival. Disappointed, she took her designated seat in the front row, waiting for Sarah to introduce her. She had asked to reserve the seat next to her for Rosamond. Apparently, it was to remain empty.

"With the publishing of her very first collection eight years ago," Sarah began, "poet May Convery became an instant favorite, not only among women involved in the suffrage movement but women everywhere who were searching for a voice, for a kindred spirit who could so beautifully articulate their deepest longings, their most fervent hopes, and their rejection of outdated moral edicts that only serve to keep members of our sex in bondage. May Convery is a wife, a mother, an activist, and an artist. She has shown women everywhere that we do not have to sit idly by while others make decisions for us. She has proven that a woman with something to say and the determination to say it *will* be heard. She is an example to us all, especially younger women such as myself who will carry the torch for women's equality into the future. That is why it is such a thrill for me to again introduce to you—those who have followed her writings throughout the years and those who may have only recently discovered them—the esteemed poet May Convery."

The small audience, probably no more than a hundred, broke into enthusiastic applause as May rose from her chair and turned to acknowledge the warm reception with a smile. It was then that Rosamond entered from the rear door. Her spirits lifted at the sight of him. She was pleased to see that he had brought Abbie Mitchell with him. And there was someone else, a very pretty and well-dressed colored woman. May noted, with a faint sense of foreboding, how she clung tightly to Rosamond's arm as they hurried down the aisle.

May took her place behind the podium, distracted. Aware of a strong desire to again search the crowd for Rosamond's face and that of the unknown woman at his side.

She opened her book.

"I'd like to begin with a poem I composed last year in honor of my dear friend, the amazing vocal artist Abbie Mitchell, who I'm delighted to see is here with us tonight."

"The reading was beautiful, as always!" Abbie said, giving May a warm hug.

"Thank you, dear. Sorry to keep all of you waiting."

May had been forced to linger at the lectern for a few minutes after the program ended, engaged in conversation with several organizers of the Washington, DC, women's suffrage parade, who offered her a position at the front of the march. She was uncertain, however, that she would be able to attend. Her father's health had taken a dramatic turn for the worse. For now, she was needed here.

May's gaze shifted to Rosamond and again she felt uneasy. Over the years, she had learned to read his expressions so well. Sometimes it was uncanny the way the two of them could communicate with only a look. But what she saw in his eyes tonight was impossible to fathom.

"Rosamond, it's wonderful to see you." She turned to the woman by his side. "I don't believe we've met. I'm May Convery."

"I was about to do the honors myself," Rosamond said. "May, this is Miss Nora Floyd. Miss Floyd has recently joined James Europe's all-Negro Clef Club Orchestra. She's a former student of mine."

"A pleasure to meet you, Miss Convery," Miss Floyd said, smiling warmly. "Mr. Johnson has told me so much about you."

"Oh—well, I hope nothing too terrible."

Miss Floyd laughed. "Oh my, no! I'm sure you know, Rosamond is one of your biggest fans. He has nothing but wonderful things to say about you."

So she called him Rosamond . . . "I'm awfully relieved to hear it," May replied, trying to sound light.

"Miss Floyd is a very talented artist herself," Rosamond said, with a look of pride May thought far exceeded that of a teacher for his former pupil. "But then, James Europe wouldn't give the time of day to anyone who wasn't strictly first class. He was bowled over by her audition. Guess he didn't expect anybody who looks like Nora to tickle the keys of a piano like she does. She can rag every bit as well as she plays the classics. He hired her on the spot."

May forced a smile. "How impressive."

"You've heard that the Clef Club is to perform at Carnegie Hall, haven't you, May?" Abbie asked. "Will has been asked to conduct a portion of the program."

At least this news was cause for May to muster some genuine enthusiasm. "That's fantastic! I hadn't heard, but it doesn't surprise me. It's long overdue that he took another bow at Carnegie Hall."

"Yes, it *is* time." Though Abbie and Will had been divorced for more than four years now, they remained attached in many ways and still collaborated frequently. May admired the way Abbie had taken control of her life after the split. It hadn't been easy, especially with two children.

"If you're not already committed for the rest of the evening," Rosamond said, "we wondered if you'd like to join us for a light supper at the home of Miss Floyd's parents. Nora is a wonderful cook. One of her many talents." He beamed at Miss Floyd, who again looped her arm through his.

May decided instantly to decline, though she felt ashamed of herself. She had no other plans. She was only being petty. Why should she be upset over whatever kind of relationship might be developing between Rosamond and Nora Floyd?

In the twelve years she'd known Rosamond, they'd become close friends. At first, it surprised her that she would be so drawn to him. It was embarrassing to admit that, despite the intimacy of her relationship with Evie, she'd never really known a colored man. Yet from that very first night, she felt there was something special between her and Rosamond—a rare kind of understanding. Neither had ever suggested, in word or deed, anything beyond that. But there *was* something else, an unspoken connection, perhaps a higher kind of love that didn't require the ordinary forms of expression. Love in which intimacy was achieved by a touch of the hand, a gentle smile.

Rosamond had managed to achieve substantial fame as a composer and performer, his struggles for recognition in some ways mirroring her own. When others belittled her talent, Rosamond had been there telling her not to give up, filling her goblet with wine and her heart with cheer. Their periodic nighttime rendezvous were always clandestine. Only when Teddy was in London and only in places where a black man in the company of a white woman wouldn't raise too many eyebrows. Places where the Negro musical theater crowd gathered and where the two of them could be found tucked away in some dimly lit corner, sipping Bordeaux, discussing the finer points of musical composition or possible themes for her next volume of verse. Comparing the challenges of being a woman, albeit white and privileged, with those of a man of color, in a world controlled by those intent on preserving the status quo. Or just laughing about some silly thing that had happened to one or the other, or maybe someone they both knew. They had confided so many of their disappointments of the past, their hopes for the future.

Except for those few that were better left unspoken.

There was no doubt that she loved Rosamond. But she had always told herself she was not *in love* with him. And she had believed it—until tonight.

"Thank you for the invitation, but I'm afraid I can't."

"Of course, we understand," Rosamond replied, telegraphing his disappointment. May hoped he didn't sense her reason for not joining them. If there was ever a time she wished to hide her feelings, it was now.

"But you will mark it on your calendar to come with me to the concert at Carnegie Hall on the twelfth of December," Rosamond said matter-of-factly, leaving no possibility that she might refuse. "Abbie will be singing, and Miss Floyd playing in the orchestra. Which leaves the two of us to cheer them on."

"Yes, the two of us," May repeated, wondering if that auspicious event might be the last time she would ever have Rosamond all to herself.

All That Glitters

M ike, what brings you to our neck of the woods?"
From behind his desk at the music publishing
firm Waterson, Berlin and Snyder, Henry Waterson
raised his ample derriere a few inches off the chair and offered
an uninspired handshake.

"As usual, Henry—business." Mike wasn't good at hiding
his disdain for Waterson. He much preferred dealing with his
partner, Irving Berlin. At least Berlin could recognize a good
song when he heard one. But it appeared that if there was a
deal to be made today, it would have to be with Henry.

"Please, have a seat." Waterson nodded toward a chair
opposite him. "But before we get started, you've got to see
this!" He opened his desk drawer and pulled out a small scrap
of black velvet, which he laid on the desktop. Carefully, he
unfolded it and picked up the gem inside—a huge, radiant-cut
diamond. Wedging it firmly between his thumb and index finger, he held it up to the light, a smile spreading across his face.
"What do you think of this baby?"

Mike leaned forward to get a better look. "How many
carats?"

"Five. Perfect color and clarity."

"Gift for your wife—or a friend?" Mike smiled conspiratorially, though he was thinking that Waterson surely would need the lure of an expensive bauble like that for any halfway attractive woman to give him the time of day.

"No, I plan to turn it over quickly. Shouldn't be difficult, not with this kind of quality. Just need the right buyer. Would make a fabulous ring, wouldn't it? Flashy as they come."

"Yes, it certainly would."

Waterson eyed him cagily. "What about you, Mike? You've always had a penchant for flash."

"Me?" Mike chuckled. "No, I'm afraid I wouldn't know what to do with a diamond that big."

"Big enough so even folks in the last row would see it sparkling under the lights," Waterson said enticingly.

Mike sat back, contemplating what Waterson had just suggested. It was true he'd always admired Ben Harney's ring—the lion's head with the ruby eyes. A ring with this gem would outflash Harney's any day of the week.

"Tell you what. I've got a couple of rags that I'm looking to sell for a good price. I came here first. Make that diamond part of the deal, and maybe I won't have to look further."

"Ha! Part of the deal? Do you have any idea what this stone is worth? Give me the rags with a big wad of cash on top, and we might be able to talk business."

Mike laughed. Waterson was bluffing. He was obviously in over his head on that diamond and wanted to get rid of it fast. And regardless of what he might say, he wanted Mike's latest rags—as cheaply as he could get them, of course. But Mike had never played the game Waterson's way.

He wasn't about to start now.

◆ ◆ ◆

Mike closed the door to Waterson's office behind him. With a self-satisfied smile, he patted his left jacket pocket, enjoying the feel of the huge stone inside its wrapper of black velvet. Admittedly, the ring he was already imagining for himself could only be described as ostentatious. But at this stage of his career, wasn't he entitled? In fact, wasn't that what his fans expected? Modesty had never been his trademark.

"Mike! Hey, buddy, it's been a long time."

Mike tried to look pleased as his old rival approached him, hand outstretched. He couldn't even remember when they'd run into each other last, it was so long ago. Seemed Harney wasn't around New York much anymore.

"You're looking well," Mike said, though arguably Harney had never looked worse. His jacket was the outdated boxy style, his shirt wrinkled, his shoes in need of a shine. Mike sneaked a glance at Ben's hand, the lion's head ring. He was surprised to still feel a touch of jealousy. That ring had always fascinated him, much more than it should.

But soon he'd have something far better.

Ben patted the pocket of his baggy jacket. "Got a new rag here. Thought I'd give Waterson and Berlin a chance at it."

"By all means."

"'Course, on the telephone Waterson told me they weren't so interested in rags right now. You think that's true?"

"I just sold him two of mine." Mike couldn't help gloating. Obviously, it was Ben Harney's rags they didn't want, Ben who had precipitously fallen out of fashion.

"Hmm. I must have misunderstood him. Well, doesn't matter—he's going to love this one. And if not, there are plenty of other publishers who will."

"No doubt. Anyway, nice seeing you." Mike swiveled on his heel, anxious to be on his way.

"Hey, hold on," Ben said, grabbing Mike's arm. "How about us getting together for dinner sometime, before Jessie and I go back out on the road?"

Mike glanced away, trying to think of a tactful way to refuse. He came up blank. "Sure, give me a call. And good luck with Waterson." Again, he started to leave.

"Mike, wait a minute!"

Reluctantly, he turned around.

"I got this brilliant idea the other day. Something that can't help but make both of us a lot of money. I'm pretty sure you're not opposed to *that*, right?"

Mike smiled. Occasionally, Harney had a way with words. "I'm a firm believer that when it comes to money, there's always room for more."

"And I agree with you. That's why I figure it's about time for us to have a playoff. A contest. You and me. It's never happened in all these years. I guess we've both been too busy with other things. But think of it, Mike!" He swept the air with his hand, like a magician about to pull a rabbit out of a hat. "Madison Square Garden! *The Originator of Ragtime Ben Harney versus Mike Bernard, Ragtime King of the World, in a head-to-head battle to the death.*" He grinned. "How does that sound, my friend? Can't you almost hear the cash registers ringing?"

Mike was both amused and slightly annoyed. He had made a point of avoiding a head-to-head with Harney for nearly fifteen years. Why would he be interested now? Of course, it was obvious why Ben would want to do it. It was no secret that Harney wasn't the draw he used to be. He'd like nothing better than to capitalize on Mike's name.

"I'm telling you, Mike, this would be the biggest thing ever to happen in the world of ragtime. Think of the publicity. Folks would be clamoring for tickets, and there wouldn't be enough to go around. Who knows, maybe they'd end up begging us to stage a rematch! Double the profit."

"It's an intriguing idea, Ben, but—well, I'm afraid I'm not interested."

"But why not? It'd be good for both of us. Look, I know you think you can beat me, and maybe you can. Either way, each of us makes a bundle of dough. I can accept being the loser, if that's what it comes to. Not that I think it would," he added hastily. "I got enough fans here in New York to start my own country. But I say let the best man win—whoever that may be!"

Harney was right about one thing: if they were able to stage a contest at Madison Square Garden, they ought to make a small fortune. And it was true—Harney might not be as big as he used to be, but people hadn't forgotten him. The hint of a comeback might spark enough interest for a onetime event. Besides, hadn't he always wanted to take Ben down a notch or two? If he'd been afraid to try before, he wasn't anymore.

"Tell you what. I'll think about it."

Ben's face lit up. "I knew you'd come around. You've always had a good business sense about you. Even the way you latched onto ragtime. Why, you were one of my very first disciples, if you don't mind me calling you that. And look where it got you. Fame, fortune, and more women than you know what to do with!" Ben laughed, giving Mike a firm punch in the arm. "Listen, I'll give you a call in a few days so we can discuss the details and get this thing rolling." He pulled a pen and a scrap of paper from his pocket. "What's your number?"

Mike hesitated. Did he really want Harney badgering him with calls?

"You know, I'm pretty hard to reach. Why don't you give me your number instead?"

"My number?" Ben reddened slightly. "Tell you what. I know you're playing at the Orpheum this week and next. How about I stop by one night after the show? We can go out for a drink or two, talk things over some more."

"Fine. Hopefully, you'll make it a night that I don't have other plans," he said, just to give himself an out. The more he thought about staging a contest with Ben, the less sense it made. He had his reputation as a top-tier headliner to consider. He didn't need a stunt like this to boost his popularity.

Even if it was tempting to imagine the pleasure of publicly bringing Ben Harney to his knees.

Flash of Green

M ay took her place at the end of a line of ticket holders that stretched all the way down the block. Despite the biting cold, she didn't mind waiting. It was a wonderful turnout for the much-anticipated performance of the Clef Club Orchestra, an orchestra like no other ever to take the stage of Carnegie Hall.

According to what Rosamond had told her, tonight's performance would feature no fewer than fourteen upright pianos, commandeered by some of the best ragtime players in the city. That plus sixty mandolins, fifteen guitars, and sections of violins, cellos, double basses, brass, and woodwinds. As he had explained, this odd assemblage of instruments and musicians, many of whom couldn't read music, was perfectly suited to the unique harmonies and syncopated rhythms of ragtime.

But it was not the orchestra on May's mind as much as it was Rosamond.

She had gone to extra lengths with her appearance tonight. Her chestnut locks were tucked beneath a stylish silk turban, an exotic creation like those the French fashion designer Paul Peirot had recently shown in Paris to rave reviews. Her new look was dramatic—her hazel eyes rimmed with smoky gray, the sharp angle of her Cupid's bow accentuated by dark-red lipstick. A sequined evening dress, for now hidden beneath a winter cape, conformed to her slender figure in a manner that left little to the imagination. Even the luxurious fox boa around her neck was intended to lend an air of provocative glamour.

She had at first tried to convince herself it was just for fun. Why shouldn't she try something a little bit daring? It wasn't a sin to want to be attractive in a modern sort of way. But now, as she watched Rosamond cross the street and hurry toward her, she felt nervous. Would he think that she was trying to compete with Nora Floyd for his attention? And, after all, wouldn't he be right?

"May, good to see you!" Rosamond took her leather-gloved hands in his and gave them a gentle squeeze. "I hope you haven't been waiting long."

"No, and I guess it wouldn't have helped to get here early anyway. They don't seem terribly anxious to let us in."

He assessed the line and their position near the end. "It shouldn't be too much longer. I hope you're not chilly." He touched her fur boa. "Something new?"

"Yes—I mean, no. I've had it for some time. It's just that I seldom wear it."

"It looks warm," he said, smiling his approval. "I'm awfully glad you were free tonight. Timing was on our side."

"Yes, it was. Teddy will be coming back from London any day now."

"In time for Christmas, I assume."

"Oh yes. He wouldn't miss that. He's bringing back some special gifts for the children this year. Of course, they're not really children anymore! But they still get excited when they see packages under the tree with their names on them."

"Christmas is a special time, isn't it. A time for family. It's always been my favorite holiday."

"What are your plans this year, Rosamond? I know you often visit your mother in Florida."

"Yes, I'll be going to see her." He hesitated. "Miss Floyd will be coming with me."

May tried not to appear ruffled. "Oh, really?"

"I'm anxious to introduce her to Mother. You see—well, I imagine you may have sensed something when we were all together at your last reading. I mean, about Nora and me?"

May looked away, embarrassed. What a fool she was to have thought there was any way she could keep things from changing between her and Rosamond. Or that she could alter their course, turn them in a new and insanely reckless direction. Begin a journey that, for so many reasons, would be doomed from the start.

"Yes, I noticed the two of you seemed quite taken with one another. But I had no idea it was so serious. That's wonderful, Rosamond. I'm very happy for you."

"I knew you would be," he said, though May was certain she had failed to convince him. "If all goes well, I'm hoping Nora and I might tie the knot next year."

"Marriage?" May felt as if he had cut off her air. "Isn't that kind of sudden? How long have you known each other?"

"I think I mentioned to you that she was a student of mine, so we've actually known each other for quite some time. But it's only recently, when I saw her all grown up, that I realized— *we* realized we'd like to make a life together."

"I see."

They both fell silent.

"May—" Now it was Rosamond who failed to hide his agitation. "I could easily ignore what I'm reading in your eyes. We could pretend that you really are as happy for me as you say. And that would be all right, because I know someday you will be." He paused. "Is that what you want us to do?"

She forced a smile. "I guess I'm not as clever as I thought. Maybe I imagined I could hide behind my new makeup. Maybe distract you enough so you wouldn't notice," she said, attempting to make it sound like a joke.

"You should know better. When it comes to you, seems like I've always been able to see past the exterior. Maybe that's because you've never been afraid to show me your vulnerable side. From the first night we met, I could see in you that caged bird beating its wings against the bars."

Why did he have to be so dear, so eloquent? "I'm only being selfish. I know that. It's just that you've become so important in my life—" Frantically, she blinked back the tears that were starting to rise. "One of us being married all these years was bad enough. But both of us? I'm sure Miss Floyd wouldn't be too pleased about you staying out until the wee hours of the morning, especially with another woman—even a friend."

"I don't intend to let her put me on a leash, if that's what you're afraid of. Besides, Nora isn't like that. She knows the theater life." He stared straight into her eyes. Though she wanted to, she was powerless to break away. "Come on, May—we've been friends now for a long time. We're something special to each other. I know that. But we also know our limits. You understand what I mean."

May wrapped her boa tighter around her neck. "Forgive me, Rosamond. I honestly don't know what I was thinking. I went a little crazy, I guess, but I'm all right now. Really I am."

Rosamond patted her on the shoulder. "That's my girl." He glanced toward the front of the line. "Hey look, we're starting to move."

"Good, I can hardly wait to get out of this cold."

He took a step forward, then stopped, turning to her with a look like none she had ever seen from him before. "You understand, it's not that I haven't thought about it. About us. I *am* a man, you know. And you *are* a beautiful woman, one who's dear to me as well. But May—it could never be like that with us. Not in this world. You and I both know that, don't we? Don't *you*?"

May held her breath, wondering how long she could control herself, how long she could stand there next to him without taking his hand, without resting her head on his shoulder. Without kissing him the way she realized now she'd always wanted to—deeply, passionately. Without fear.

But, of course, there would always be fear. Perhaps most of those standing in line to hear the all-Negro Clef Club Orchestra were people of a liberal bent, but society as a whole would not be sympathetic toward a love affair between a white woman and a colored man. She wasn't so naïve as to think otherwise. Rosamond would be the one to suffer most. Down South, some were still inclined to lynch a Negro man for simply looking at a white woman. Things were better here, but even in New York racial hatred sometimes revealed itself in all its hideousness. Wasn't that how they had met?

She pictured Nora Floyd, remembering how beautiful she looked that night at the poetry reading, how satisfied and secure on Rosamond's arm. She didn't want to resent her the way she did. She *must* overcome these bitter feelings before they destroyed whatever relationship she and Rosamond might still have left.

"May?" Rosamond was waiting for her answer.

"Yes, Rosamond. I know. Not in this world."

The Romantic

The chamber orchestra played a hauntingly rapturous melody as the party of four entered the opulent interior of Jimmie Marshall's café, a popular spot catering to the Negro musical theater crowd along with a smattering of white artists and intellectuals. Glad to be out of the cold, May removed her fur boa but kept her cape draped over her shoulders, self-conscious about the seductive gown she had chosen for the evening, its intent embarrassingly obvious.

They were led to a table in front, near the small stage. May sat across from Rosamond, with Abbie and Miss Floyd on either side of him. A waiter in a black suit and white bow tie promptly took their drink orders, leaving four leather-bound menus that no one seemed in a hurry to open. Abbie and Nora—as she had insisted May should call her—were bubbling over about the phenomenal response to the concert and especially to Will Marion Cook's performance. When he finished conducting his hit song "Swing Along," the audience gave him a standing ovation and called for two encores. He had been moved to tears.

"What a night this has been!" Abbie said, as she had done at least a dozen times already. "I hope Will keeps the memory in his heart for a very long time. If he can manage to do that, maybe the next affront, whenever it comes, will slide off a bit easier."

Rosamond snickered good-naturedly. "I doubt it, but we can hope. Look, not many men are born to the kind of greatness Will enjoys, but there's a price to pay for it. We all know that." He smiled at Abbie with obvious affection. "And you, Abbie—you're not one to talk of your successes or your trials, but they're no less than Will's. Good God, woman! What you've achieved against all odds! Performances at Buckingham Palace. A concert for the Russian czar. Not to mention a starring role in *The Red Moon* opposite Broadway's most handsome and talented leading man."

Everyone laughed, knowing the leading man of whom Rosamond spoke was none other than himself. *The Red Moon*, staged a few years back, had been one of his biggest successes, as both a composer and an actor.

"Surely I've been blessed. But I wouldn't have been able to do it, Rosie, if it wasn't for Will. That man was hard on me, all right, but he sure did teach me how to sing."

"We've all learned a lot from Will. I only wish he wasn't so damn unpredictable. On any given day, you never know which Will Cook you're going to get—but then I suppose it keeps things interesting."

"I find Mr. Cook inspiring to work with," Nora interjected, "though I must admit I wouldn't want to be married to him. But then, I'm very particular in my taste when it comes to husbands," she added, beaming at Rosamond.

Rosamond reached over to rest his hand on top of hers. "We'll see about that," he said gently before turning to May. "Heard something about your old piano teacher the other day. You know—Mike Bernard?"

May tried to smile, wondering if the evening might be going from bad to worse. In all the years she'd known Rosamond, as close as they had become, she'd never told him what happened to her when she was seventeen.

"Oh really? What about him?"

"There's a fellow named Strap Hill comes to our jam sessions upstairs sometimes. Used to sing with Ben Harney. He says Harney is talking about a rag contest between him and Bernard. Says they're looking into having it at Madison Square Garden. Only thing is, Strap's not certain if the whole thing might just be a figment of Harney's imagination—wishful thinking, I guess. Says Harney isn't as well off as everybody might assume." Now Rosamond addressed Nora, who was listening with rapt attention. "Harney's wild spending is sort of a legend around New York. To his credit, though, I've heard he's awfully generous with folks. Generous to a fault, if there is such a thing."

"When is this contest supposed to happen?" Nora asked, taking a ladylike sip of her iced brandy with gingerette and raspberry syrup.

"Like I said, I don't know that it actually will. Would be interesting, though."

"Who do you think would win?"

"These days, probably Bernard. Unless Harney could manage to come up with something unexpected—something different than he's been doing all these years."

"But people must be getting awfully tired of Mike Bernard," May suggested, perhaps a bit too stridently.

"Bernard is a virtuoso. He *wears* better than Harney, I'd say. More adaptable, too. He can play just about anything and play it well. A musician like that tends to fare better over time. But then, Ben Harney might still be a formidable opponent. He was on top a long while, and people don't soon forget that."

"I would think not," May said.

There was a brief lull in the conversation, a vacant space into which Nora eagerly stepped. "May"—she flashed one of her incredibly charming smiles—"Rosamond tells me you have two children."

May pulled back uncomfortably. Nora's sudden inquisitiveness felt like an intrusion. Besides, she always found it difficult to talk about her children. Though she was terribly proud of them, she was also wary. Might someone sense that something wasn't quite right? Might she somehow slip up, accidentally reveal what must never be revealed? She knew it was irrational, but she couldn't get over the feeling that her past was always on the verge of being exposed.

"My son Melvin is sixteen now. And Anna is fourteen," she replied stiffly.

"My goodness, they're almost grown. Don't you dread the day they'll leave you to go out on their own?"

Now May was even more annoyed, for no reason other than Nora trying to be friendly. Or could it be that the younger woman was hoping to cast May in the role least threatening to her own ambitions, to remind Rosamond that his longtime friend was someone else's wife and the mother of two nearly grown children? With a burst of spitefulness, May slipped the heavy cape from her bare shoulders, her sequined gown sparkling wildly beneath the crystal chandeliers of Jimmie Marshall's.

"I'm not the hovering type, if that's what you mean. Anybody who's read my poetry—even a little bit of it—knows that much about me."

"Oh—I didn't mean to imply—"

"And what about you? Do you want children?" May knew it was rude to cut Nora off midsentence. But she couldn't help herself.

"I suppose I might. Abbie has managed to have children *and* a thriving career. So have you. I'd like to do the same, if I could."

May reached for her scotch. "I'm sure you'll find a way."

"I suppose your husband must be very proud of your success as a poet," Nora continued, perhaps trying to make amends for her earlier blunder. "You know, I just realized Rosamond has never mentioned Mr. Livingstone's line of work. Do you mind me asking?"

"He's a banker. An investor. And no, he's not proud of my success. Not in the least."

"Oh—" Nora glanced at Rosamond, clearly embarrassed. "Forgive me. I seem to be putting my foot in my mouth tonight. But I just assumed—"

"One should never assume, Miss Floyd. Not when it comes to relationships." Abruptly, May pushed back her chair and stood up. "I hate to spoil the party, but the truth is I developed a terrible headache at the concert. Nothing to do with the music, I assure you," she said, offering Abbie an apologetic smile. "It's been building all day, and I simply can't ignore it any longer. The only thing to do when it comes on like this is to lie down in a dark room with a cold compress. So that's what I must do, I'm afraid."

Rosamond's face reflected only concern. "I won't allow you to run off like this by yourself. I'll take you home in a cab." He rose, and then bent down to whisper something in Nora's ear— something that changed her worried frown to a smile. "Ladies, I will be back to join you shortly."

May was already up and putting on the cape she had discarded only moments ago. "Sit down, Rosamond. I'm perfectly capable of seeing myself home." Hearing how harsh she sounded, she added more gently, "But thank you. I appreciate the offer."

"You're sure you'll be all right?"

May nodded, avoiding his eyes. Turning to the two ladies, she again offered her apologies. Then, flinging the fox boa around her neck, she sailed through Jimmie Marshall's café, out the door and into the frigid night.

A cab had just pulled up to the curb when she felt a hand on her elbow.

"I'm not letting you go alone."

She turned to see Rosamond, his face half obscured in shadow.

"But what about Nora?"

"She'll wait."

Rosamond opened the cab door. She wanted to tell him she didn't need him, she would be fine alone—but that would have been a lie.

She slid onto the seat and over to the far side. He entered after her, then closed the door and gave the colored driver his orders.

"You've been a mess all night. I've never seen you like this."

She didn't answer, instead turning her face toward the window.

"Giving me the silent treatment?"

"No, of course not." With a sigh, she made herself look at him. The lights along the street illuminated the back of the cab enough for her to notice, not for the first time, how his hairline was starting to recede, and the deep, double-pronged crease between his brows. There was no question that if he wanted a family while he was still in his prime he had best not waste any more time. She, on the other hand, was finished with all that.

"You know, May, there's a saying I heard once. I don't know where it comes from. Something like *Happiness isn't having what you want; it's wanting what you have.* Does that make any sense to you?"

"A bit too fatalistic for you, isn't it?"

He laughed. "You're right, it is. I hoped you wouldn't notice." He reached for her gloved hand. "We have a lot in common, though I suppose most would find that surprising. I guess I did, too—at first. But we've always shared the same love of beauty, the same passion for freedom. You've told me more than once that you're attracted to the forbidden. I've admitted the same to you. I suppose both of us understood what that meant."

"Did we?" Her heart was beating fast.

"Even so, we never acted on it."

"No, we didn't."

"I think that was very wise. Because if we had, I'm not sure we would still be friends today."

May couldn't let him off so easily. "Perhaps we'd be much more than friends. Isn't that just as likely?"

He hesitated. "I don't know."

"But I imagine it's too late to find out." She held her breath, waiting. She knew it was wrong to even hint at such a thing. She was a married woman. He was in love with Nora Floyd. But what if he were to say, *No, it's not too late*? What if he were to tell the driver not to take her home, to take her to his place instead? What if—

"You know something, May?"

She gave up her thoughts reluctantly, sure that whatever he would say next was bound to be a disappointment.

"I've been caught up in the theater for so long, I wasn't sure I'd ever want a family. Seemed like a wife and children would only get in the way. I wouldn't be able to give them the attention they'd deserve. But now—suddenly I want it all. I want it very much. I guess that's because of Nora."

She could see a trace of sadness in his eyes. She knew it wasn't *his* sadness, only the reflection of hers.

"I envy you," she said softly. "No—I envy *her*."

"You shouldn't envy anyone, dear." He leaned over and placed a kiss on her cheek. "Not too many people find their calling in life. *You* have."

"But I'm lonely, Rosamond. And it appears I'm about to become lonelier still."

"We won't let that happen. I want you and Nora to become friends. You'll like her, I promise."

"I'm sure I would. That's not what I mean. It's just that—"
She turned away again. She sounded so pathetic, so childish.
What must he think of her? "It's just that I've never really loved
anyone—not really. Not until you came along. And even then,
I was too foolish to realize what it was. Until I was about to
lose it."

"You're not about to lose anything. But yes, things will be a
little different. I'd be lying if I said they won't."

She was surprised to find the cab already past Forty-Ninth
Street. A few moments later, they pulled up in front of her
home. The lights in the foyer burned brightly. She dreaded
having to talk to anyone, even Thelma or her dear Evie. What
she was feeling tonight, and for whom, was yet another secret
she must keep.

"Shall I walk you to the door?" Rosamond asked.

"No, best that you don't." They'd always been careful. There
was no reason to stop now.

He ran the back of his hand along her cheek. "We'll get
through this, May."

She nodded. "Thank you for seeing me home."

"No thanks necessary. Just make me a promise."

"A promise?"

"Yes."

If he was going to ask her to be happy for him, of course
she would say yes. But could she really do it? "If it's not too
difficult. At any rate, you know I'll try."

"Promise that you'll never give up on it."

"Give up on *what*?"

"On what you do best." He smiled. "On being a romantic."

The driver opened her door; she got out of the cab.

She had not answered Rosamond. What could she have
said? How could she possibly make him understand that it's no
good being a romantic by yourself?

Big Tipper

I t was after ten when Mike checked his overcoat at the Ziegfeld Moulin Rouge Theatre on Broadway and Forty-Fourth Street. He was dapper in a black evening suit, his starched white shirt embellished with monogrammed French cuffs, his black patent shoes like mirrors. But, as far as he was concerned, it was the ring that made the man.

Fourth finger, right hand. Five carats in a thick, heavily engraved white-gold setting.

Already it was January, two months since he cut a sweet deal with Henry Waterson for the diamond in exchange for a couple of his new rags. He recalled what he had thought then, and he'd been right. His new diamond ring made Harney's lion's head, with its tiny ruby eyes, seem like a mere trinket!

As he hurried through the brightly lit lobby, rich with red velvet and gold-gilded plaster, it occurred to him that Ben had never gotten in touch, never said another word about a contest between the two of them at Madison Square Garden. Not that it mattered to *him*. If anything, he was glad not to be bothered.

"Good evening, Mr. Bernard. Always nice to see you." With a flourish, the head usher, Edwardo, opened the golden doors to the main auditorium and then personally led him to a seat near the front, receiving a customarily generous tip. If there was one thing Mike had learned over the years, it was how to make himself welcome and the circumstances in which goodwill could be especially worthwhile.

He had been looking forward to tonight, to indulging what had increasingly become his habit—trolling for young beauties at the Follies. He relied heavily on Mr. Ziegfeld's reconnaissance. Why waste time scouring the city for nubile girls of extraordinary endowment when someone else had already done the work?

It was easy enough to justify his prurient interests. Any up-and-coming young woman in the theatrical profession would consider it a feather in her cap to be seen about town with a celebrity as big as he was. For his part, such affairs were a pleasant enough diversion, though he assiduously avoided any serious involvements. The other thing he had learned over the years, maybe the most important: commitment was not in his nature.

"Mike, is that you?"

Feeling a hand on his shoulder, he turned to see Charles Lennon, an acquaintance from the old days at Tony Pastor's theater, leaning forward from the seat behind.

"Why, it is!" Lennon exclaimed. "Good to see you. What do you think about Williams topping the bill? Times are changing, wouldn't you say?"

It was 1913, and Florenz Ziegfeld Jr. had created a stir in some circles by featuring the Negro comedian Bert Williams as a bona-fide headliner, along with the Australian-born comic Leon Errol. His daring had paid off. The duo was bringing down the house every night.

"Everything changes sooner or later, I suppose. Great to see you," Mike said, hurriedly turning back. He couldn't care less about Williams and Errol. He was here to see the chorus-line finale, sixty handpicked specimens of the all-American girl. And he was just in time.

Bedecked in pink feathers, pearls, and little else, the girls began making their entrance down a long, curved flight of stairs that shimmered like silver against a backdrop of azure sky. On either side of the staircase were massive pillars wrapped in pink chiffon, lighted from inside to create the effect of iridescent cotton candy. Mike fell into a state of rapt attention as the dancers—or *hoofers*, as they were often called—glided down the stairs like graceful birds in flight, their smiles never wavering. The music swelled as they assembled in formation. Each would have her moment to bathe in the spotlight, the audience feasting their eyes, before pivoting to ascend the staircase and, like a mirage, disappear into the painted clouds.

"Mr. Bernard." Edwardo hovered in the aisle to his left. He bent down to speak in a confidential whisper. "After the show, there's a girl you might want to meet. She's brand new. A real looker."

"Which one?"

"Third from the left."

Mike zeroed in. She wasn't as tall as some of the others; still, she had nice legs. Adequate curves. Face like a Kewpie doll.

He gave Edwardo a smile and a nod before shoving another five dollars into his ready palm.

"So, you're the famous Mike Bernard."

Tossing her feather boa over one shoulder, she leaned against the bar at just the right angle for her clingy silk gown to accentuate the smooth curve of her hip. Her stance was bold, her smile less so, as if she wasn't quite sure of herself.

"Edwardo said you wanted to meet me?" she said.

Mike looked her over with a practiced eye. She was even prettier up close. And very young.

"I told him I wanted to meet the new star of the Ziegfeld Follies."

Her laugh was melodious. "Well then, I'm afraid that wouldn't be me."

"A matter of opinion."

"Well, thank you."

She paused, again with that look of uncertainty. Mike didn't mind if she seemed nervous around him. He was used to having that effect on women, especially the younger ones.

"I'm Dolly Zuckerman. Pleasure to meet you."

She offered her hand. He lifted it to his lips, his eyes never leaving her face. "What do you drink, Miss Zuckerman?"

She shrugged. "Whatever you're having."

Mike motioned to the bartender. "Couple of gins, with olives," he said. "At the table."

He placed his hand on her elbow. "Shall we?"

As he guided her through the maze of candlelit tables, his ears were alert for the inevitable whispers. "Isn't that Mike Bernard? Who is that with him?" He selected a spot against the wall, beneath a bronze-and-crystal sconce with arms like glowing antlers. He helped her into a chair, settled himself in the one opposite her. The waiter appeared tableside and deposited their drinks. Immediately, she took a sip, crinkling her nose as it went down.

The encounter began with the usual small talk. He asked the questions, she answered them. She was originally from Syracuse, she said. Her mother died young. Her father remarried. A couple of years ago, after his furniture business went under, they moved to a place just east of Manhattan, in Queens, a two-story that her aunt owned. Her father ran a candy store downstairs; the family lived above.

"When I auditioned, I didn't give myself much chance of becoming a Ziegfeld girl. I mean, they're all so beautiful and talented. And I was just—well—I mean, I'd never been to New York City before. I didn't know much of anything about the way things work around here."

"At least you've figured out how to go up and down a staircase rather nicely."

She gave him an indignant look. "If you're implying that I'm stupid, I'm not. One has to start somewhere, you know."

He was surprised by her bristly response. He hadn't meant to insult her—not really.

"Actually, I'm a singer."

"A singer?" This was the part he always found difficult to endure. He had heard it so many times before. Yet he felt obliged to ask, "What do you sing? Opera?"

She blushed. "No, popular songs. Irving Berlin—that kind of thing."

"And where, may I ask, have you sung these popular songs?"

"Well, nowhere. Not yet."

"Oh, I see."

She played for a second with the little curl in front of her ear. "I love being a Ziegfeld girl, but I do aspire to greater things. As a matter of fact, tomorrow I'm auditioning for a part in a Broadway musical."

"Is that so?" Mike stifled a yawn.

"If only I could get it! I'd be so thrilled. Papa would be, too. He thinks the costumes Mr. Ziegfeld has us wear are way too skimpy. I told him he's just old-fashioned."

An unwelcome thought popped into Mike's mind. He and this naïve young woman's father could easily be close to the same age. After all, he was thirty-six now. He'd be surprised if she was even eighteen.

"So, I'm curious," she said, taking another sip of her drink, this time from a tiny straw. "Why, out of all the girls, was I the one you wanted to meet?"

He pretended to think for a moment. "Oh, I don't know. I liked your hair? I thought you had a pretty smile? Or maybe just because you're new."

Darts flew from Dolly Zuckerman's eyes. "Look, I know what you're thinking. What some men expect of a Ziegfeld girl, especially one who's a little green. Just so you understand, I'm not looking for a sugar daddy or anything like that. I'm serious about my career."

He stuck to the script, the one that had worked for him so many times before. "How serious *are* you?"

"Very. I know it will take some time, but eventually I'm going to be a Broadway star. Maybe even make a phonograph record. Like Sophie Tucker. She used to be with the Ziegfeld Follies, you know."

Mike was amused. Like Sophie Tucker? That was an interesting twist. Granted, this Dolly Zuckerman was unsophisticated—perhaps slightly delusional—but there was something sort of quaint about her. She had fire. And she liked to dream big.

"Somehow I don't see you as the Sophie Tucker type," he offered gently.

"Oh, but she and I have a lot in common."

"What exactly would that be?"

She hesitated. "For one thing, we're both Jewish."

Mike picked up his drink and took a swallow, studying her face. It was really quite pleasant.

"Maybe you'll sing for me sometime." He could almost feel her pulse quicken.

"You want to hear me sing?"

"Maybe I can even help you somehow."

"Help me? That would be wonderful."

"Of course, I can't promise anything."

"No, of course not."

"In the end, it all depends on you."

"I understand."

"I'm sure you already know, this is a tough business. You have to be willing to do whatever it takes to succeed. Are you?"

She gave him a wary look. "If you mean hard work—"

"Really, Miss Zuckerman," he interrupted, assuming his most innocuous expression, "would I be suggesting anything else?"

"I'm sure you wouldn't." She looked away, then back. "Please forgive me, but I've heard some of the girls talk about such awful things. It seems there are those in the business who would try to take advantage of inexperience."

"Despicable as it is, I'm afraid so."

"Actually"—she stared down at her drink—"I probably shouldn't tell you this. But it happened to me once. One of my first auditions. The director asked me to lift my skirt because he wanted to see my legs. I did it. I supposed it was necessary. And then he put his hand on me, where he shouldn't. And he put his other hand over my mouth—"

"Miss Zuckerman, please." Mike didn't want to hear the rest. Stories like that only reminded him of the seamier side of show business, the side he considered himself above. He had never forced a woman to do anything against her will; he didn't need to.

She bit her lip. "I never told Papa. If I had, he would have made me give up my career. He would have put me to work behind the counter at the candy store."

Sipping on her drink, she raised her eyes to look at him. They were beautiful. The color of cognac.

"Sometime maybe you'll tell me who that fellow was," Mike said. "I'll send somebody over to teach him a lesson."

She gave a little shake of her head. "Thank you, but I wouldn't want anybody to get hurt on my account. Besides, I taught him a lesson myself. I stomped on his foot and kicked him in the shin, and when he let go, I ran out and told all the other girls who were waiting for their turn that they better not go in there. Most of them stayed anyway."

Mike smiled. "You know how to take care of yourself, I guess. Where'd you learn that?"

"Back in Syracuse."

He decided not to question her further. There was nothing more he needed to know. Not right now. He'd already made up his mind.

"We'll talk more about all that some other time," he announced blithely, pushing back his chair and standing up.

Her face fell. "I knew I shouldn't have told you."

"Don't be silly."

"Then why are you leaving? Where are you going?"

"*I'm* not going anywhere," he said, coming around to coax her out of her chair. "*We* are."

Indiscretion

"O h, my goodness," Emily exclaimed, running her plump finger down the newspaper column, her lips silently forming words as she read. She looked up. "May, you'll never believe what's in this issue of the *Chatterbox*."

May reluctantly turned away from the lovely view through the back-parlor window of George Convery's Fifth Avenue mansion, the garden covered in a white mantle of fresh-fallen snow, not a single footprint sullying its purity. She had more important things on her mind than the latest celebrity gossip, but her younger sister had always been fond of that sort of harmless smut. Perhaps it was a substitute for what she lacked in her own life, having so far eschewed any serious relationship with a man—for reasons that, in her case, no one seemed compelled to question. But then, Emily had always been her father's favorite. Apparently, she could do as she pleased.

"Here, look at this article." Emily ripped out the page and slid it across the rosewood tea table.

May set down her cup, sighing as she retrieved what was undoubtedly just another poorly written account of the scandalous adventures of someone she cared nothing about. The next second, she caught her breath. The headline, in bold black letters, read, *Ragtime King Carries Torch for Mystery Woman.*

She pulled the paper close, raising the single sheet so it hid her face. The article filled the entire page. It detailed Mike Bernard's career, his latest theater engagements, tours, recordings. Her heart pounding, May skimmed line after line. Near the very end was the part meant to compel curious readers to slog through all that came before it. The part where Mike Bernard—*in a rare moment of candor,* reporter Layla Redmond wrote—admitted to being in love with a married woman, a woman who came from wealth. He claimed to have met her years ago, before she achieved fame as a writer. When pressed for a name, his response was obliquely transparent: *Let it suffice to say, she is well known among supporters of the women's suffrage movement.*

And then came the biggest bombshell, Redmond continued. *Once upon a time Mike Bernard and this mystery woman were actually married—but only for a little while. According to Mr. Bernard, her family put an abrupt end to their union. Though he has never recovered from the heartbreak, he was forced to move on with his life. This from a man who is known himself for having broken a few hearts along the way!*

Her hands starting to shake, May quickly lowered the page. "What some people will do for publicity!" she said, trying to keep her voice steady. "I suppose he wants to drum up sympathy from the public. Maybe so they won't think so badly of him after that sordid Blossom Seeley scandal."

"You're probably right," Emily agreed, taking a sip of tea, her eyes glued to her sister's face. "Still, if he really is in love with someone he can never have, it's kind of sad."

"I wouldn't waste my time feeling sorry for Mike Bernard."

"But he sounds lonely. Don't you think so?"

Why must she persist? "As I said, he's decided he needs to make himself appear less of a cad. I doubt the public will fall for it. Not after everything else that's been written about him over the years."

"Like that story about him being discovered with some other fellow's wife, each in half a pair of pajamas," Emily chortled, before her sister's stern look silenced her. "But May, you're acting as if you don't like him. He was always very nice to us when he came to the house for our piano lessons."

"Aren't you forgetting how he walked out on Mother's party when he was supposed to be the entertainment? And then he never showed up again?"

"Yes, I remember. But so what? He became famous. I don't blame him for not having time for us anymore." She eyed May again. "He said this woman is a suffragette. And a writer. If I didn't know better, I'd think he was talking about you."

May could feel the blood drain from her face. Yes, this was her sister. But Emily was a gossip, incapable of keeping a secret. That's why she'd never been told about the marriage, the baby. It was safer that way.

"You know, it's funny—I had the same thought! I was trying to think who it might be, but, really, I have no idea. There are so many women in the movement who are writers of one sort or another. My guess is the whole story is a fabrication. He wants sympathy. Or he wants to cultivate fans among liberal-minded women. Who knows?"

"Maybe."

"Anyway, I'm surprised you still enjoy trash like this," she scolded, glad at least that Emily hadn't asked to have the article back. She would dispose of it herself, at the first opportunity. "Don't you think you should spend your time on things of more literary value? Have you started that French novel I gave you last month, *La Vagabonde*? It's wonderful."

Emily shook her head. "No, I haven't had time. I'm still reading the one I found in Father's library. I told you, it's by Oscar Wilde." She picked up her knitting bag from the floor and withdrew a book from among the bundles of yarn. Handing it to May, she said, "You've read it, I think."

May set aside the page from the *Chatterbox*. "Oh yes, *The Picture of Dorian Gray*," she said, relieved to be talking about something other than Mike Bernard. "I remember it well. Brilliant."

The two women sat in silence, Emily continuing to read more of the *Chatterbox*, despite the lecture from her older sister, while May appeared to reacquaint herself with the Oscar Wilde book, thumbing through the pages with a look of intense interest. In truth, she was barely keeping pace with the flurry of frantic thoughts in her head.

She mustn't panic. It really wasn't so bad. At least he didn't say she was a *poet*. Being a *writer* could mean a lot of things. But perhaps what bothered her most was that he claimed to still carry a torch—unless the reporter had made that up herself, for the sake of a titillating headline. After all, sensationalism was the bread and butter of a scandal sheet like the *Chatterbox*.

But how dare he talk about her at all, even in the abstract! Hadn't she told him once how she despised him? And she still did, even after all these years. Expressing her bitterness had not lessened it. The facts remained as they were before. It was because of him that she had been forced to live with the most painful secret imaginable, one she couldn't share even with her closest friends. With her sister or her devoted Evie.

"Mother!"

Her son, Melvin, burst into the room, breathing heavily as if he'd been running. May swept up the newspaper article, hastily folding it and slipping it between the pages of the Oscar Wilde novel.

"What is it, dear? I thought you'd be visiting with Grandfather a bit longer."

"Something terrible has happened! I was in his room talking with him, and then he grabbed at his chest and he kind of twitched around for a minute and then stopped. I don't think he's breathing!"

May and Melvin halted just inside the doorway to George Convery's lavish bedroom suite, allowing Emily to push her way past them. May knew her sister wanted to be the first at their father's bedside, and that was all right with her. But she also knew that Emily's hope was futile. The moment May saw her father, lying perfectly still, his jaw slack, she understood they were too late.

"Father!" Emily held his wrist, feeling for a pulse. She turned to May with an expression of disbelief.

May stepped over to the bed and, saying nothing, lowered the lids over his eyes. Her calmness was not coldness. It was only that her father's demise was not unexpected. According to the doctor, it was long overdue.

Melvin lingered behind, clearly distraught. "Was there something I should have done? Could I have saved him?"

"No, sweetheart."

He came over to stand beside May. "You know what the last words he spoke to me were?" he said, staring at his grandfather's lifeless face.

May was gripped with a sudden fear. "What?"

"He asked me to pour him a scotch."

She couldn't help but smile, partly in relief, partly because George Convery always loved his scotch. "I hope he had a chance to enjoy it."

Melvin shook his head. "It was right after that when he grabbed at his chest. I never got a chance to get him that drink."

"It doesn't matter, dear."

"We'll have to telegraph Mother," Emily said bleakly.

"Oh—must we?" Of course, May knew they must. It was just that she had never forgiven her mother for moving to Paris years ago, leaving the family with little explanation except the obvious one. She had run off with the underbutler Pierre Durant—and a great deal of Convery money.

She laid a hand on Melvin's arm. "I'm glad you were with him, dear. He would have chosen you to be the one to see him off," she said, knowing it wasn't true but wishing it were. George Convery had never truly embraced Melvin as his grandson, though neither had he rejected him. May supposed he'd done the best he could to overcome his disappointment in her; he'd tried not to take it out on the child. Still, it was not in her father's nature to be forgiving. Perhaps, she thought suddenly, she was more like him than she wanted to admit.

May bent to kiss his forehead. It was still warm. "I'll call the doctor so he can arrange for the medical examiner."

Emily nodded, tears glistening in her eyes. "Dear, dear Father . . . we'll never forget, so many wonderful memories."

"Yes—" May's voice broke, but she was not remembering happy times. She was thinking of that morning in Mike Bernard's apartment, when her father told her she knew nothing about love. As it turned out, he was right. And he was right about Melvin. If he hadn't dragged her out of that abortionist's office, her darling boy wouldn't exist. It was her father who had guarded her secret all those years. Her father who had always been there for her. And yet she felt, in most ways, that she didn't really know him. When did they ever talk deeply about anything that mattered? She wasn't even sure that he believed in God. Or how he felt when her mother deserted him. Or what he thought of her notoriety as a poet. She wondered if he'd read a single one of her published books.

Maybe she was to blame. Maybe she didn't try hard enough to understand him. She was too sure he could never understand her.

Or she was still too ashamed of the past to let him try.

The Parade

Riding on horseback down Pennsylvania Avenue toward the White House, May kept her head erect, face forward. Atop several layers of her warmest undergarments, she wore a tailored black walking suit and black hat, as did the five other riders in her section. They were flanked on either side by women on foot. Some carried the American flag, others waved banners of purple, white, and gold emblazoned with the phrase *Votes for Women*.

It was the third of March, a day before the inauguration of Woodrow Wilson. An estimated five thousand marchers, maybe more, had gathered in the nation's capital, braving the cold to demand passage of a constitutional amendment granting women the right to vote. Many had walked all the way from New York City. Led by Rosalie Jones, who had earned the affectionate moniker *General* Jones, they were determined not to let anything, including the hardships of winter weather, keep them from descending on Washington, DC.

The women making their way down the avenue, cheeks glowing from the cold, eyes burning with conviction, came from every stratum of society, the wealthiest to the poorest. This was no picket line, no stubborn demonstration by a handful of militants hoping for a small headline in the morning paper. This was a force to be reckoned with, a force to which the politicians in Washington would have to answer, sooner or later. These women were betting on the numbers; there were too many of them to ignore.

But despite the impressive turnout, the suffragettes were clearly outnumbered. The street was lined with tens of thousands of onlookers, some only curious but others intent on undermining the women's morale. They included men of all descriptions, from common laborers in canvas and khaki to office types in overcoats and gray bowlers. Men presumably with loving mothers and sisters, devoted wives, obedient daughters. Men who no doubt considered themselves inarguably civilized but, in the blink of an eye, had changed into quite the opposite. Their relentless heckling was predictably rude, shockingly hateful.

The arrogance of these ill-mannered naysayers only served to harden May's resolve. But their vociferousness made her nervous. The policemen stationed along the parade route didn't seem to be taking their assignment too seriously. Rather than pushing back on the crowd, they appeared perfectly happy to let the worst of the rabble-rousers do whatever they wished. Already a few had crossed the line that separated spectators from protesters, the authorities either unaware or simply choosing to do nothing.

As she headed down the parade route, trying not to let her uneasiness get the best of her, May thought of what Rosamond had told her on the night they met, as they sat at her kitchen table sharing a fine bottle of Madeira. *Freedom isn't yours until you make it yours, until you decide there's simply no other way to live.* Back then, she had only the vaguest notion of what he meant. She was too caught up in her self-inflicted misery; the only way she knew to express herself was through suffering. Her headaches had nearly driven her mad. But she had stopped seeing Dr. Adams long ago. Her need for him disappeared once she resolved to channel her anger and frustration in more pro-ductive directions—her poetry and the suffrage movement, work as vital to her now as the air she breathed.

There were some who argued that today's parade, with its theatrical flag-waving, mounted brigades, marching bands, and floats, would only engender hostility. It would end up setting the movement back, they said, not moving it forward. May had sided with those who believed the time had come to stop begging and start demanding, and she felt honored to be among those selected to ride on horseback near the front of the parade. Granted, over the years, proceeds from sales of her books had provided substantial support to the cause. But she preferred to think she was singled out because of the voice she had given to the movement through her poetry, which had achieved a popularity far exceeding her expectations.

Still, in the midst of all the praise and notoriety, at times she couldn't help feeling like an imposter, the kind of person who preaches one kind of life while living another. After all, her marriage was, and always had been, a hoax. It had become even more unbearable since her father's death. Not surpris-ingly, Teddy seemed to believe that the passing of George Convery gave him license to treat her however he pleased. His disdain for her appeared no longer to have boundaries.

"Help! Please, somebody help!"

The screams came from behind her. Twisting in the saddle, she saw that a small group of men had stormed the proces-sion. She watched in disbelief and horror as several of them ripped signs and banners of protest from the suffragettes' hands. Others began snatching women's hats from their heads, pushing women to the ground, or grabbing them by the arms and attempting to drag them off the street.

Dear God, how could this be happening? Where were the police? The parade organizers had been assured by DC officials that crowds would be contained, the marchers would be protected. Why was no one in authority lifting a finger?

May signaled to the several other women on horseback who were close by, all of them now aware of the unfolding chaos. Without having to utter a word, everyone seemed to understand what must be done. May was the first to turn her horse around. She had never been more terrified; the last thing she had planned on was becoming a vigilante. But how could she simply stand by as her sisters were spit upon, brutalized, and literally kidnapped off the street?

She took a tremulous breath, then dug her heels into the animal's side. The horse broke into a canter. Tightly gripping the horsewhip, May told herself she would not hesitate to use it on anyone who might challenge her.

She heard one of the men yell to his comrades to look out. As she and the other riders barreled into their midst, the pack of marauders took flight, their victims gratefully running into the arms of fellow suffragettes. Those who had been shoved to the ground scrambled to their feet, shaken but appearing not to be seriously hurt.

May pulled back hard on the reins, her horse obliging with a quick stop. The rescue had been easier than she expected. In fact, at that moment, she felt rather invincible. Yet if more such incidents were to come, the next might not go as well.

From her high perch, she surveyed up and down the street, searching for further signs of trouble, praying she would find none. It appeared that the police—some of them anyway—were starting to push back the unruly crowd at various spots along the parade route. She was relieved to see several stick-wielding officers fast approaching where she and the other riders remained on guard. A bit late, she thought bitterly. But at least they were finally on the scene.

"Hey, missy!"

Startled, she looked down. A heavyset man in a shabby canvas coat stood only a few feet from her horse. He was unshaven, unkempt—and he looked angry. May readied her horsewhip but held back. He'd not done anything yet, only asked for her attention. But he was unsavory looking, and he seemed agitated.

"Did you want something?" she said, keeping the whip low and out of sight.

"You got no business here, lady!" Suddenly, he lunged at the reins as if he meant to wrest them from her.

"Stop! I'm warning you!" She raised the whip, but before she could summon the will to carry out her threat, the man reached with his other hand into the pocket of his coat. There was the quick flash of steel as his arm swung back and he plunged his knife deep into her horse's neck. The animal let out a terrified squeal, rearing up on its hind legs.

It happened so fast. May lost her hold on the reins, her grip on the saddle, and then she was in the air. When she hit the ground, it was within inches of the crazed animal as it reared up again and again, whinnying and snorting. Dazed, but realizing that at any instant she could be trampled to death, she began to half crawl, half drag herself away from her frenzied horse and what she judged as the trajectory of its flailing hooves. Several women rushed over to help, daring to approach the frantic animal and pull her the rest of the way to safety.

Within seconds, police were swarming around her. One of them yanked her to her feet.

"Come along with me." The cop tightened his grip on her arm as he steered her toward a police wagon that had just pulled up alongside them, sirens howling.

She could feel a deep soreness in her left hip, as if the bone was bruised. But she was able to walk; she was grateful for that. If they were taking her to the hospital, there was no need for it. She wanted to stay with the parade. And there was the matter of her horse.

"Thank you, officer, but I'll be fine. Really." He wasn't listening. She raised her voice. "Officer, I have to see to my horse. He's been injured."

The cop, his grip like a vise, propelled her to the back of the wagon. Another officer opened the doors. There were several women already inside.

Her arms were wrenched backward. She felt the cold metal of handcuffs, heard the snap of the lock.

"What are you doing?" But there was no need to ask. She understood now. The police were not there to help her.

"Get in."

"But why? I didn't do anything. That man—he attacked my horse. Didn't you see? He had a knife. He stabbed my horse in the neck—"

"You charged your animal into a group of innocent bystanders."

"Innocent! Those men were attacking women on the street."

"You can't just take the law into your own hands, Mrs. Livingstone."

May froze. "How do you know my name?"

"Just get in the wagon."

"I want to know who told you my name."

"Look, lady, just be grateful you're getting out of this mess before it gets any worse. Maybe your husband doesn't want you getting beat over the head with a baseball bat." He gave her a quick look up and down. "Can't say I blame him. You're a real looker, even if you got some crazy ideas."

May's heart was racing, blood pounding at her temples. Could it be that Teddy had arranged her removal from the parade? A few days ago, they'd argued about her participation in the march. He had threatened to stop her. At the time, she brushed it off as nothing more than bluster. They had disagreed before; in fact, they always did. Yet here she was, being carted off in a wagon, like a dog on its way to the pound! Despite what the officer had said, she didn't believe for a minute that her husband was concerned for her safety. No, this was just another way for Teddy to assert what he saw as his new and rightful power.

"Eddie, give me a hand." Two officers, one on each side of her, grabbed under her arms and lifted her up. Wordlessly, they threw her into the wagon and slammed the door shut.

"Have a seat," one of the women inside said calmly, nodding toward a wooden bench opposite where the others sat. "Don't worry. We're not dangerous. We're here for the same reason you are—we refused to shut up."

Absence Makes the Heart

Mike drummed the countertop with his fingertips, his irritation mounting. The show had been over for an hour. She should have been here by now.

He had been looking forward to tonight, the moment when he would pluck the little black box from his inside coat pocket and hand it to her. She would be shocked, of course. "For me?" she'd say. Her heart fluttering, she'd raise the lid and gasp. Gingerly, she'd lift the pendant from its velvet cushion, the ruby heart dangling from a slender gold chain. "Oh, Mike, how beautiful!" He would fasten it around her neck, admire the way it rested on her youthful décolletage. And then—

"Another gin, Mr. Bernard?"

"All right, sure."

Mike glanced around the room once more, hoping to see Dolly fast approaching with a look of apology on her face. Disappointed, he grudgingly succumbed to the myriad distractions of Antonio's Roman Gardens—the cascading multitiered fountains, gilt-framed mirrors, pergolas and painted landscape murals, the tiny lights under the tables that shone pink through white linen cloths. It was a popular place for the theater set and the after-theater crowd, always with plenty of attractive girls around. His gaze lingered on one of them now—a tall redhead with the lithe body of a dancer.

But it was no use pretending. Lately, his interest was in Dolly—and only Dolly.

It had been over two months since that January night when he hustled her off to his apartment on the pretext of wanting to hear her sing. Surprisingly, she wasn't bad. Even more surprising, he had sent her home in a cab without even a serious flirtation.

For the next two weeks, he had acted as her personal vocal coach. Their lessons took place in the late morning or early in the evening, well before he had to leave for the theater. With a musical director's ear, he worked with her on her timing and articulation, challenged her to emote, to lose herself in the music. "Put it all out there," he'd shout. "Don't hold anything back." Eagerly, she consumed every morsel of advice, visibly crushed when she failed to please him, elated when he acknowledged she'd done well.

All the while, he was aware that something quite out of the ordinary was happening. When he and Dolly were together, he hardly recognized himself. It was strange how he took pleasure in her small successes—finally hitting that elusive high note, adding a particularly clever twist to the end of a phrase, doing all the little things a confident vocalist does to make a song truly her own. As far as taking her to bed, he had held back to the point of agony. It might have been a game he was playing with himself just to prove he had the fortitude.

Or maybe it was something else.

But on a Sunday night at the beginning of the third week, everything changed. It was already late in the evening when Dolly called to ask if he'd help her prepare for a Monday audition. She apologized for waiting until the last minute but insisted it wouldn't take long. Though she sounded perfectly fine on the telephone, when she arrived at his apartment her demeanor was decidedly glum, as if something upsetting had happened in the interim. Mike finally coaxed it out of her.

"You know that part I tried out for on Friday—the one in *Hello, Paris*? To replace the girl who's leaving the show because she's too pregnant? Well, the part went to Margaret! You remember her from the Follies lineup, don't you—the one with the fake blond hair?" Dolly rolled her eyes with her usual excess of drama. "I just don't understand it. I was so much better than her. Everyone told me so. But all along she said she had it in the bag. And you know why?"

Mike shook his head. He was sorry to see her down in the dumps but fascinated, as always, just to observe everything about her. At that particular moment, it was the endearing pout of her tender young lips that captured his imagination.

"Because she slept with the director, that's why! She admitted it. I even think she was proud of it."

"Well, something like that might give her a leg up, so to speak."

"Of course, if she wasn't any good at—well, in *bed*—then maybe she wouldn't get the part. That's how it works, right?"

How was he supposed to answer a question like *that*? "But, Dolly, she got the part. It's probably best if you just put it out of your mind. *Hello, Paris* isn't the only show in town. You've got another audition tomorrow—remember?"

"I guess you're right." Dolly sighed. "Oh, by the way, Margaret *didn't* get the part."

"Huh?"

She burst out laughing, clapping her hands, jumping up and down. "*I* did! I got it! Can you believe it? I'm singing on *Broadway!*"

Mike let out a howl. Sweeping her into his arms, he twirled her around and around until both of them fell onto the sofa, dizzy and breathless, like a couple of silly kids. After that, Dolly couldn't stop talking—about the character she'd be playing, the two songs she'd sing, the costume she'd wear, how they would style her hair. Mike let her go on and on, never interrupting unless it was to ask another question, to feed her excitement with his own.

That night they celebrated with a bottle of French champagne, just the two of them in his apartment. Ordinarily, Dolly was not a drinker. But somehow her glass always seemed to be empty, and Mike found himself filling it again and again. Before long, she was sharing chapters of her life that she said she'd never talked about to anyone before. Some of it made him feel genuinely sorry for her. She told him how she lost her mother when she was only six, how her father had turned to drink for a while and taken out his grief on her and her sister. Mike couldn't help comparing her story to his own, though there was a world of difference between them. Still, he doubted she'd be too shocked were he to tell her about his early years in the slums of New York. All the times he was beaten up behind the five-story tenement where his family lived. How his mother sewed piecework late into the night to pay for his piano lessons while his father argued it would all come to nothing.

But Mike didn't speak to Dolly of his life before show business. In fact, he barely spoke at all that night. He listened and he watched and he waited—until it felt right.

It didn't happen in the usual way. There was no false sincerity, no plotting of the next seductive move. It came about as if it were the most natural thing in the world. The touch of his hand on hers, his arm around her shoulders, a gentle whisper in her ear. He could tell by her eyes, the way they melted into his, that she had stopped being afraid. She wanted him.

Every time since, Mike experienced the same rarefied feeling, a sense of wonder he vaguely remembered from what seemed another life. When he'd promised a beautiful girl with long chestnut hair that they'd be together forever—even if he didn't believe it himself.

"Good evening, Mr. Bernard."

Mike awoke from his daydream. Charles Berton, the musical director of *Hello, Paris*, stood next to him at the bar. It was only a coincidence. They had crossed paths before but weren't well acquainted.

"Congratulations on the show. I hear it's terrific," Mike said, just to break the ice. It was true the write-ups had been positive but mostly in praise of the revue's composer and conductor, J. Rosamond Johnson. It was the first time ever that a Negro had led a white orchestra and cast in a New York theater.

"Thanks."

The bartender delivered Mike's nearly forgotten gin. Berton placed an order for straight whiskey.

"Hey, was just wondering—did you happen to see Dolly Zuckerman after the show tonight?"

"Dolly?" Berton gave him a curious look. "As a matter of fact, I did see her. She was with a young man, nobody I recognized. Handsome fellow, though. Seemed to be enjoying herself—quite a bit." Berton raised his hand for the bartender's attention. "Have that drink sent over to my table." Then, turning back to Mike, he said, "Nice to see you," and moved on.

It took a few moments for Mike to thoroughly process what Berton had just told him. He downed half his gin, shoved the glass aside. There was no reason to hang around here. He threw a few coins on the counter, stood up, and began pushing his way through the crowd. He was annoyed by the weight of the little black box in his inside coat pocket and considered tossing it out. Or giving it to the first pretty girl he saw.

He did neither.

Outside, the clear night air was a welcome antidote to the smoky morass of Antonio's. Mike started walking, letting his feet, like his thoughts, wander where they would. Maybe she'd decided he was too old. He ran a hand through his thinning hair. Did a young woman her age notice such things? His mind took a cynical turn. Maybe it was that she had already gotten what she wanted out of him. She'd made it to Broadway. With one mediocre role under her belt, she thought she had it all figured out. She'd decided she didn't need him anymore.

But no, there had been more than that between them. He was sure of it. Unless he was just a fool—or worse yet, a sentimental fool. Might he be hoping to rewrite an old story, this time with a happy ending?

He blindly made his way down Broadway, eventually leaving his familiar haunts behind, turning west. Oblivious to everything around him, he kept going over all the possible explanations for why Dolly hadn't shown up for their date at Antonio's. The most disturbing was that she had been with someone else. A *young* man. Handsome. And *enjoying herself*. Why didn't he ask Berton what he meant? What exactly were the two of them doing?

He kept walking on and on, preoccupied with speculations about Dolly, no particular destination in mind—until he suddenly noticed that he was passing by the Eloise Hotel. He stopped. From outside, the place looked almost the same as that night seventeen years ago, when he'd fled the Converys' holiday ball and come here, unwittingly, to seek his fortune. The only difference was that the hotel's once-black awning had faded to a dull gray.

On impulse, he entered the old hotel, trudged across its seamy lobby. With a firm push to the swinging wooden doors, he stepped into the saloon. Tonight, it was deathly quiet.

"What can I get for you, mister? How about a cold one, maybe some pickles and eggs to go with it?"

Mike slid up to the carved mahogany bar. "Gin, three olives."

"Right away, sir."

"*A sheynem dank.*" The familiar Yiddish phrase caught Mike's attention. He glanced to his left. A few stools down, a young black man had just been served a beer.

"*Nishto farvos,*" the bartender replied.

Apparently sensing Mike's curiosity, the young man turned toward him with a smile. "No, you're not hearing things. You speak Yiddish?"

"Not really. Where'd you learn it?"

"Oh, here and there." The kid gave Mike a long look. "Wait a minute, I know you. I've seen your face before—" He snapped his fingers. "I got it! Mike Bernard. Am I right?"

Mike couldn't help smiling. It was nice, after all, to be famous.

"Very good."

The young fellow slid off his stool. Stepping up to Mike, he extended his hand. "Name's Willie Smith."

Mike gave Smith's hand a mild shake. "Where did you hear me play?"

"Can't say that I have, but I've heard plenty about you."

"All right. I'll take that as a compliment."

Smith laughed. "No disrespect, sir, but when it comes to ragging, Scott Joplin is my hero."

"Joplin, huh? A fine composer. Can't seem to make it here in New York, though. I hear he's still looking for a new publisher."

"That's because Joplin doesn't follow the herd. He's a real artist, not a copycat. Not like some of the others. Most of 'em don't really know what ragging is all about."

Mike drew back slightly. "I trust you're not implying that *I* am one of those *others*?"

Smith shrugged. "Don't get me wrong. But ragtime's gone downhill since Tin Pan Alley tried to take it over. For some of those folks, it's just a money game, all the feeling squeezed out of it. Not much about it authentic."

It was déjà vu, like listening to Ben Harney brag about the so-called purity of his hackneyed Negro imitations. This kid didn't understand the first thing about what makes music great. Authenticity? How about playing it your own way—and better than anybody else?

"I don't know who you spend your time talking to, young man, but I can tell you one thing. The public decides what they like and don't like. I happen to respect their taste."

"Like I said, it's nothing personal. Just that Joplin is the greatest ragtime composer ever lived. Never sold himself out, never will."

"Music is a business, kid—if you want to make a living at it, that is."

Willie Smith stroked his chin, looking thoughtful. "Just wondering—all those contests you won, how many of 'em allowed colored players?"

Mike could see where this conversation was going, and he didn't like it. Why should he try to justify himself to this young punk? "I didn't make the rules, son. I've never refused to play against anybody, but a hell of a lot of people—colored and white—haven't had the nerve to go up against me."

"I sure would. If there's one thing I've plenty of, it's nerve." Smith glanced toward the back room, its door half open. "Want to come on and listen to me for a while? Even if there's nobody here, I gotta look like I'm working."

So, they still had a piano back there, and this kid was the one banging the keys for chump change! He wouldn't have minded taking a listen. But not after the way he'd been insulted. Besides, this tired old dump wasn't raising his spirits; in fact, just the opposite. He didn't know why he'd come here in the first place.

"Maybe some other time."

"Hey, now I remember!" Smith exclaimed suddenly. "Didn't they used to call you the Ragtime King of the World?"

Mike stood up, disgusted with everything about this night. "They still do. I'm not dead, you know." For God's sake, he was only thirty-six! What was wrong with these young people?

Smith made a little bow. "A *gute nakht* to you, sir!"

"Yeah, sure." Mike couldn't wait to get out of there, go home and straight to bed. His feet were sore, his head throbbing.

And that kid—he ought to lay off the Yiddish.

Breaking Point

May sat at the dining-room table, distracted by the way the morning light cast lovely dappled patterns on the Belgian lace cloth. An intimidating pile of unopened envelopes awaited her attention. She was hopelessly behind in her correspondence. But in the three weeks since her return from Washington, DC, her mind had been occupied with more important things than obligatory invitations to tea. Things she wished she could forget.

That awful morning when she was arrested, Teddy was waiting for her at the police station. They handed her over to him as if she were a truant child. If she didn't go quietly, they said, she'd find herself in front of a judge. Afterward, she learned that more than a hundred marchers were taken to hospital emergency rooms. Secretary of War Henry Stimson had finally called in troops from Fort Myer to assist the police in controlling the crowd. But despite threats to their safety, many of the women completed their march to the White House. She should have been with them.

All the way back to New York, Teddy did nothing but berate her. She was naïve, selfish, belligerent, uneducated, irrational, irresponsible. Her ideas were treasonous. He was ashamed of her and everything she stood for. He would tolerate it no longer, he said.

She had spent every day since then buried in the final revisions to her latest book of poetry. But even that proved torturous. It was her *life*, not her poetry, that needed revision. She had never felt it more than now.

With a sigh, she turned back to the envelopes waiting to be opened. Flipping through a few of them, she discovered one from an old schoolmate who was hosting a charity event in May. Though it wasn't a cause of particular interest, she supposed she'd have to attend. She slit open a few more, scanning the contents and placing them in the pile to be answered later—before she came to the one that made her heart stop. She had been expecting it, though not so soon.

She hesitated, wondering what to do. Put off opening it until another time? Pretend she'd never received it at all? But what would either accomplish? Failing to acknowledge the truth would not change it. Hadn't she done enough of that already?

Reluctantly, she ripped open the envelope and withdrew the card inside. It took only a few seconds to read:

Capt. & Mrs. Jas. W. Floyd request your presence at the Marriage of their daughter Nora Ethel Floyd to Mr. J. Rosamond Johnson, July 3rd, 1913, at 2 o'clock in the afternoon, Bloomsbury Central Baptist Church, London, England

It was official. Nora was to become Mrs. J. Rosamond Johnson.

That the wedding was to take place in London was not much of a surprise. Rosamond had been invited by Oscar Hammerstein to become the musical director of his Grand

Opera House there. It was a great honor and a stunning achievement. When May learned of it, she was ecstatic for him, though she realized it meant that he'd be leaving New York. Perhaps she had even hoped, in her more selfish moments, that his relocation also meant he would leave Nora behind.

But clearly, Nora would not be left.

"Miss May!" Thelma rushed into the dining room. A handkerchief was pressed to her mouth, tears streaming down her cheeks. "You got to stop him!"

Alarmed, May jumped up from her chair. "What is it, Thelma? Stop who? What's going on?"

"It's Mr. Livingstone. Evie just told me. He dismissed her this morning, before he left for the bank."

"What? That's impossible!" Evie, the woman who had raised her? She and Teddy had agreed long ago that Evie would always be part of the family. She was sixty-four now. It was inconceivable he would order her to leave.

"Said he wants her gone by the time he gets home tonight. But where's she going to go, Miss May? After all these years—" Thelma sobbed into her handkerchief. "I just don't understand. I know she didn't do a thing wrong! Not Evie. Why would he make her go?"

May could barely speak. "I don't know," she said, though it was a lie. She knew exactly. This was to be the punishment for her disobedience. Teddy had done it for revenge. For power. With her father gone, and now Evie, he figured she would have no one left.

But he figured wrong.

"Tell Evie to continue packing her things. As quickly as she can. And you, too, Thelma."

"Me? But—"

"Don't worry. Everything is going to be fine. I'm taking the two of you with me. With me and the children. That is, if you want to come," she added, realizing that she had no right to take Thelma's acquiescence for granted or, for that matter, Evie's. But, for now, she must.

"But where are we going?"

"Please, just trust me. I'll explain later. What I want you to do now is go back to Evie. Tell her that I'm fixing everything. It's all going to be better than ever. Much better. And please— tell her that nothing, no one, will ever tear us apart. Not any of us."

Thelma gave her a tearful smile. "Yes, Miss May. I'll tell her."

May entered the library and closed the carved double doors behind her. Pausing, she inhaled the sweet, musty aroma of the several hundred books lining the walls, their leather covers patinated by age and wear. She and Melvin had already trans- ported some of her father's favorite volumes here from her childhood home. The first step, she had supposed, in preparing the venerable mansion, so beloved by George Convery, for sale.

She approached the huge library table, opened the long drawer in the center, and withdrew the notebook in which she kept important names, addresses, and telephone numbers. Flying through the pages, she found the name she was look- ing for: Mr. Robert Englewood. He had been George Convery's attorney for years and, in the months since her father's death, had helped her to settle the estate, half of which had gone to her, the other half to Emily.

She reached for the telephone, lifted the earpiece from the cradle. Her hand was shaking.

Why was she so afraid?

Closing her eyes, she pictured Melvin's face, then Anna's. She had always tried her best to protect them, to pretend their family was as normal as any other. She had planned to go on that way until the children were grown. A few more years were all that was left. It had seemed like her duty to endure whatever she must.

But might there be circumstances in which duty defeats its own purpose?

When she recalled her childhood—all the years of observing her mother and father live separate lives while they pretended it wasn't so—the memory was like a sore that would not heal. As a girl, she used to wonder why her parents never spent time together. She wondered if, somehow, it was her fault. How might everyone's life have been different if that cloud of discontent, unspoken but always felt, were to have been lifted sooner?

Nevertheless, there was no doubt in her mind that if her father were alive he would condemn her roundly for what she was about to do. But he was gone, and she would no longer endure what he had endured. A marriage without love.

Within a couple of minutes, she had Robert Englewood on the line.

"Yes, Mrs. Livingstone? How can I help you?"

"I'd like you to begin drawing up some papers for me."

"Let me guess! You've found a buyer for your father's house on Fifth Avenue?"

"No, I'm afraid it's not that. As a matter of fact, I've decided to keep the house."

There was a long silence. "You're keeping it?"

"Yes."

"I assume, then, that you and your sister have reached an agreement on how to settle your respective interests in the property?"

"No, not yet." She wished he would quit *assuming* things and let her get to the point. "First, there are some other papers I'll need. They are to be delivered to Mr. Livingstone."

"Mr. Livingstone!"

"Yes, that's right." There was a slight crackling on the line, just a bad connection. "I'm divorcing my husband, Mr. Englewood—as expeditiously as possible."

In the Act

"**M**rs. Harney!"

Jessie rolled over on the lumpy mattress, her eyes heavy with sleep. Had she heard someone calling for her, or was it just another bad dream?

The light she'd left on for Ben was still burning. She propped herself up on one elbow, squinting at the bedside clock. Four a.m. She sighed, wondering at which bar Ben was spending his last quarter.

She lay back down. It would be tough getting to sleep again. August in New York was hot as hell, especially in a third-rate hotel room with only one tiny window.

"Mrs. Harney!" There it was again.

She scrambled out of bed, as quickly as she could. Their last tour had been a while ago, but her back still ached from shoving around that big trunk with all their costumes. Used to be she didn't have to lift a finger. Somebody was always there to do everything for her.

"Mrs. Harney!" This time the voice was accompanied by an insistent pounding. She grabbed her chiffon wrapper from the foot of the bed and hurried toward the door, wriggling into the sleeves as she went, ready to lay into whoever was making such a racket.

The man standing in the hallway wore a policeman's uniform. Politely, he removed his hat, obviously trying to ignore that Jessie was standing before him in a flimsy nightdress, covered only with an equally flimsy robe.

"Sorry to wake you, Mrs. Harney."

"Yes?"

"It's about your husband."

Her breath stopped. "What's the matter? Is Ben hurt?" She imagined him lying dead in the street somewhere, maybe too drunk to have seen the motor coach bearing down on him.

"No, ma'am. Your husband is just fine. Maybe a little upset right now, but other than that—"

"Upset? What are you talking about? What happened?"

"I'm sorry—it's maybe a delicate matter. He ought to tell you about it himself. But he asked me to come get you. Seeing as how I'm a big fan of his, I consider it a privilege, ma'am. Anyway, he wants you to bail him out of jail."

"Ben's in jail?" Jessie sighed. She wasn't really all that surprised, though it had been a while since he got himself in trouble with the law. "What was it—a brawl?"

"No, not a brawl." It seemed he didn't want to look her in the eye. "Maybe I'd best let him explain. Just wanted you to know that he's down at the station, Twenty-Sixth Street Precinct. Bail's set at thirty dollars."

Thirty dollars! She doubted she had that much. And why was the police officer being so elusive?

"You're sure my husband is all right?"

The officer shifted on his feet, appearing even more uncomfortable than before. "He's fine. Only thing is—you might want to bring him a pair of pants."

◆ ◆ ◆

"Honey, I can explain."

Jessie walked at a brisk pace, a good five feet in front of Ben. He seemed to be trying his best to keep up with her, but every time he got close, she sped up a little more.

"Jessie, slow down! You're killing me."

It was still early, and Twenty-Sixth Street was only sparsely trafficked. A few workers hustled by on their way to a factory job, a few carousers from the night before stumbled toward home, a few cops headed for the station. None of that mattered to Jessie. She whirled around, hands on her hips and fire in her eyes, and, as soon as Ben was within arm-swinging range, unloaded her best shot to the jaw.

"Hey!" Ben took a step back, rubbing his chin with an aggrieved look. "What's got into you, anyway? I told you I could explain."

"What's to explain? You're at some brothel in the red-light district, in the wee hours of the morning—without your pants—and the police raid the joint. Seems pretty clear to me."

"You've got it all wrong. Yes, I was there. A couple of fellows I met at a bar insisted I come with 'em. But I wasn't engaged in—in the act. As a matter of fact, I'd indulged in a puff or two of opium—all right, I know you don't approve—but the stuff put me right to sleep. Where my pants went to, I just don't know. I guess one of them fellows thought it would be funny if I woke up without 'em. Come to think of it, I don't know what happened to those two, whether they managed to get out before the cops swooped in, or what." He brushed a wayward lock of hair from his face and, smiling sheepishly, reached for Jessie's arm. "Come on, honey. Can't we just go back to the hotel and climb into bed for a while?"

Jessie pulled away sharply. "You go on, Ben. I'd rather take a walk." She opened her purse and withdrew a key. "Here. Number 13. In case you've forgotten," she said, slapping it into his palm.

She took a few steps to the curb, checked up and down the street, and then hurried across. She didn't look back at Ben. Just then, she didn't think she could stand the sight of him. It would take a little time. It always did. But this was the worst in a long while.

Jessie marched along Twenty-Sixth Street, past the Municipal Lodging House for the homeless, past the city morgue. At least Ben hadn't ended up there. And thank God, the police had reduced bail to fifteen dollars. That still left her with less than ten. But even if they were nearly broke, she was getting a cup of coffee.

She deserved it.

She found a café just down the street. The door was open, inviting early morning business. Enticed by the smell of coffee brewing and the warm aroma of freshly baked bread, she sat down at a small table under the green-and-white-striped awning. Someone had left a newspaper. Yesterday's, but that was all right. Anything to take her mind off Ben.

She scanned the front page.

> New York's Governor William Sulzer
> impeached by the state Assembly . . .
> Churchill proposes plan to aid France in
> the war against Germany . . . The pas-
> senger ship State of California sinks off
> the coast of Alaska . . . Houdini stuns the
> world with his straitjacket escape . . . At
> a roulette wheel in Monte Carlo, the color
> black comes up twenty-six times in a row.

She sighed, shoving the paper aside. What difference did any of it make? Her life was in ruins, her husband out of control. It was bad enough that he'd spent every last dime they had on drinking, gambling, and handouts to anybody and everybody who asked for one. But now this—picked up in a police raid. In a brothel!

She might as well face it. Ben would never change. The problem was, everything around him already had.

"What are *you* doing out so early?"

Startled, Jessie looked up to see Mike Bernard standing on the sidewalk just a few yards away. She couldn't remember exactly where or when they'd last bumped into each other, but it had to be at least three or four years ago. He looked the same. She wished that she did.

"I'm usually an early riser," she said, managing a half-hearted smile. "What about you? Burning the candle at both ends these days?"

"Occasionally. Mind if I join you?" he asked, already approaching her with obvious intent. She had little choice but to welcome him.

"Don't expect the service to be quick," she said. "It's been five minutes, and no one has shown up to take my order."

"At this time of morning, you have to go inside and place your order at the counter."

"Oh, I didn't know."

"I'll take care of it. What would you like?"

At least she'd be able to preserve what little cash she had left. "Coffee, black. And I'll take a donut, if they have any." She hesitated. "Make it two," she said, thinking she'd take one back to the hotel for Ben—though there was no reason she shouldn't let him starve.

Mike disappeared inside, returning after a couple of minutes with their coffees and a basket of assorted pastries. He set everything down on the table and took a seat across from Jessie.

"You make an excellent waiter," she quipped. "But it looks like you brought enough food for an army."

"If you buy twelve, you get a thirteenth one free."

"Such a deal." Jessie took a sip of her coffee. It was strong—just what she needed this morning.

"Where's your other half?" Mike asked. "You notice I didn't call him your *better* half."

"Still asleep."

"Did he tell you that we ran into each other a while back at Waterson, Snyder and Berlin? Actually, it was quite a while now. Last fall, I think."

Jessie sprang to attention. She remembered Ben's account of their chance meeting. He had seemed awfully excited about the idea of a playoff. The ragtime contest of the century, he'd said. They'd stage it at Madison Square Garden. It would be a huge moneymaker. She wondered now why he'd let it drop. A contest like that would be just the thing to pull them out of the hole they'd dug themselves into.

"Yes, Ben mentioned it," she said, her smile warmer now. She picked out a donut and took a bite. "Delicious."

"To be blunt, I didn't think Ben looked his best. His health all right?"

"Oh yes, there's nothing wrong with Ben. When you saw him, we were taking a vacation from the road. He tends to let himself get sloppy when he's off work."

"I guess we all enjoy a break now and then."

"Yes, they're so few and far between," Jessie replied, hoping she sounded convincing. She didn't want Mike to sense her desperation. Not with what she was about to say next. "By the way, Ben told me the two of you were discussing the possibility of a contest. Madison Square Garden, he said. Wouldn't *that* be exciting!"

Mike rummaged around in the bakery basket before selecting a blueberry scone.

"Ben seemed to think it was a good idea. I can't say I was too enthused. But then I never heard from him about it anyway."

"Oh really? I'm surprised, because he's still very interested."

"Hmm."

"Why, I remember when rag contests were the talk of the town, bigger than boxing matches—like when you won your title, Ragtime King of the World. There wasn't a soul didn't know about that contest. Plenty who had a wager on it, too. You were already a big star, but that just made you even bigger."

"That's true." Mike bit into his scone, a few crumbs falling from his lips. "But then, a contest only works to your advantage if you end up the winner."

"And aren't you always the winner?" She smiled provocatively, forgetting for a moment that she must look a mess. She had been in such a hurry to rescue Ben from jail that she didn't bother to fix herself up. "I was thinking—I mean, Ben was thinking—a contest like that would give everybody a boost. Put ragtime back in the headlines. People need to be reminded of what they've always felt about our music. Why they'll never stop loving Mike Bernard—"

"You can stop trying to butter me up, Jessie. Don't you think I know Ben's career needs a shot in the arm? You don't have to tell me what I can see for myself."

Jessie felt the warmth spread over her cheeks.

"Come on now. Relax!" He leaned toward her with an air of intimacy. "You know, I've always been an admirer of yours, Jessie. From afar, of course. But then, I imagine you sensed that. I seem to recall you have a knack for reading minds."

She flashed back to that long-ago night at Leo's. She was surprised he would bring it up, considering how badly he'd behaved. "Let's just call it *intuition*," she said, wondering why he was being so solicitous.

"But are you as sharp as you were then?"

"Why wouldn't I be?"

"I don't know. But let's find out."

Jessie laughed. "Find out *how*?"

"See if you can guess what I'm thinking."

He wanted to challenge her? It was kind of silly, but why not play along? Especially if it might serve her purposes.

"All right, let me see . . ." She closed her eyes, clasping her hands in front of her bosom in a pose reminiscent of Sarah Bernhardt. "You're thinking about a contest between you and Ben. You're thinking of the money, the publicity. And you expect to win, definitely you do. Ha! You might even place a very large bet on yourself—just for the fun of it."

She opened her eyes, folding her hands on the table. "How did I do?"

"I'm impressed." Mike grinned.

"You're humoring me, I can tell."

"I think we're humoring each other, aren't we?"

Suddenly, he reached across the table and laid his hands over hers. "I'll tell you a secret. I've always been a little bit jealous of Ben. Not his talent, not his success. I've enough of that myself." He leaned closer. "But I've always thought, *That Jessie—what a gal! I'd sure like to have a woman like that. Even if it was only one time.*"

Jessie's breath stalled. Had he just suggested what she thought he had? Was that to be the price for giving Ben his chance at a comeback?

"Sorry, Mike," she replied caustically, "but I'm afraid *once* for me is never enough—and I doubt you've got the stamina for more."

"Don't be so sure."

She bit her tongue, her anger rising. But the contest—maybe if she left now, while they were on reasonably good terms, there still might be a chance.

"Obviously, you're a very attractive fellow. But I'm a one-man woman. I know it's an outdated concept in theater circles." Gently she withdrew her hand, scooted back her chair, and stood up. "Anyway, thanks for the coffee."

"Jessie, Jessie! Wait." He was laughing now, acting as if the whole thing had been nothing more than a joke. "You win! Tell Ben that if he can arrange a meeting about this contest with the right people, the ones who can actually make it happen, I'll be glad to talk. But he'd better get on it quick, not like the last time."

He picked up the bakery basket and held it out to her. She hesitated, then took it from him.

"By the way, about the contest"—Mike's look pierced her to the soul—"I just want you to know that if I agree to do it, it won't be for Ben's sake. Or mine either."

Until Proven Innocent

Y ou Mike Bernard?"

A gray-bearded man stood in the doorway of Mike's Manhattan penthouse, his appearance unremarkable except for the black yarmulke on his head and the angry scowl on his craggy face.

It was six thirty on a Wednesday evening. Mike had only an hour until he'd leave for the theater. He was headlining at the Orpheus, along with the popular singer Willie Weston, for the entire month of August. The maid had left his supper for him. He was just starting to eat, and he didn't like being interrupted.

"Who are you, and what do you want?" he asked impatiently.

Without answering, the stranger shoved him aside and stepped into the foyer. "Shut the door."

Mike drew himself up. "Hey, what do you think you're doing? Get out of here or I'll call the police."

"You try anything funny and I'll start shouting. Tell all your neighbors what kind of fellow lives in their building. The kind who lures young girls into his apartment so he can take advantage of them."

Mike paused. That was certainly a strange thing for a robber to say. "What the hell are you talking about?"

The man's thick, unruly brows lowered like a gathering storm. "I'm talking about my daughter—Dolly Zuckerman. The one you knocked up."

Mike froze. This lunatic was Dolly's father? He quickly closed the door. "Come in and have a seat."

With a hollow feeling in the pit of his stomach, he led Mr. Zuckerman across the foyer and into the spacious parlor with its panoramic views of the city. He steered him to the nearest armchair. "Make yourself comfortable," he said, trying to sound pleasant.

Dolly's father sat down and immediately started in again. "I know you're a big shot in the entertainment world, but that doesn't give you the right to trample over innocent young girls like my Dolly. Have your way with them and then—"

"Wait a minute now." Too nervous to sit, Mike positioned himself behind an armchair just opposite Zuckerman's, his hands tightly gripping the back. "You said you're Dolly Zuckerman's father?"

"You heard me. Eli Zuckerman."

"And you said—" Mike licked his dry lips. "You said that your daughter is pregnant?"

"That's what I said."

"And you think I'm responsible?"

"Feh! I don't *think*, I *know*. Dolly finally told me so, and she'd have no reason to lie. Looking at you now—why, I can believe it. You're a schmuck if I ever saw one."

Mike's head was spinning. Dolly pregnant? He hadn't seen her for more than five months. The last time was right before she stood him up for their date at Antonio's. The ruby heart pendant he had planned as a surprise was still in the top drawer of his dresser. He'd felt like a fool. She'd played him for a sucker.

At least that was how it seemed. Since then, he had put her out of his mind. Almost.

"Listen here, my daughter is going to have a baby, and you're the only one who could be responsible."

Mike didn't know what to make of Eli Zuckerman. Was he telling the truth or maybe just trying to see how much he might be able to con out of somebody with a big bank account? "I don't know anything about Dolly's situation, and you certainly have no proof that I'm involved."

Zuckerman jumped up. "You calling my daughter a liar?" he shouted, taking a menacing step toward Mike.

Mike glanced at the bottle of gin sitting on top of the liquor cabinet a few yards away. A good crack over the head would certainly stop old man Zuckerman in his tracks. He hoped it wouldn't come to that. "If you don't control yourself, I'm going to have to call the police. You don't want to wind up in jail, do you?"

He must have said the right thing, because all of a sudden Zuckerman's head and shoulders slumped, and he covered his face with his hands. When he looked up a few seconds later, his demeanor was drastically altered. Either he was an exceptionally good actor, or he was actually on the verge of tears.

"Believe it or not, I'm not used to barging into places like some kind of crackpot. For God's sake, I run a little store, I sell candy to kids. I'm only trying to take care of my daughter."

"Please, sit down. Let's talk this over rationally." Mike came out from behind the chair, relieved that his uninvited guest seemed to have lost his steam. At this point, it wasn't Zuckerman's behavior that had him on edge; it was the news about Dolly. If he was really the father, then she had to be pretty far along. He wondered how she was feeling, if she was doing all right.

Still, he wasn't about to be conned. If she was pregnant and he was the baby's father, why wouldn't she have told him? And what about that young man Charles Berton had mentioned, the one Dolly was with the night she failed to keep their date at Antonio's? He might just as easily be the guilty party. Or even someone else.

"You're interested in knowing who the father is, aren't you?"

Zuckerman sat bolt upright. "You're denying you slept with her?"

Mike didn't know what to say. How do you suggest to a father that his young daughter might be bedding down not only with you but untold others? It was probably best not to. Besides, he didn't really think that about Dolly. It had been obvious that he was the first. It surprised him that the thought of her pregnant with his child—though it was nothing he'd ever intended—wasn't altogether unpleasant.

"Look, I'm sure we can straighten this whole thing out. She and I will talk. We'll see if we can't get to the bottom of it."

"There's no *bottom* to get to. Dolly says she's not interested in marriage. Says you're too old, and she's right about that. Why, it's nothing short of criminal what you did to my little girl." Zuckerman's eyes narrowed. "Listen, I don't care what kind of life you've lived up to now, and it's none of my business. But you're going to do the right thing by Dolly. The decent thing. I won't have my grandchild coming into this world without a father's name—even if it has to be yours, by God."

Birthright

B ut why have they quit? It doesn't make sense." May handed a cup of steaming jasmine tea to her friend Abbie Mitchell. The two women were enjoying a respite from the heat of an August afternoon in the back parlor of the Convery family's Fifth Avenue mansion, May's childhood home—where she and the children had been living since late March.

"It's fear, plain and simple. They haven't the courage to go through with it."

"After you worked so hard on that film! And you've said all along how good it is. Besides, I've been looking forward to bragging about my friend, the silent-movie star."

"Sorry, but I'm afraid *Lime Kiln Field Day* is destined for the junk heap. Biograph Company will stick the footage in a big can and throw it in a dark closet, and that will be the last anyone hears of it."

"But I don't understand. What is everybody so afraid of?"

"They've decided, after all, the public isn't ready. It's not only that the cast is Negro. It's the story—the romance part of it. I guess some white people don't think colored folks ought to fall in love. They're shocked that we actually kiss each other from time to time."

"What a shame it is!"

"Oh—speaking of *shame*," Abbie said with a sardonic smile, "did I tell you what happened to Will and the Clef Club Orchestra a couple of months ago when they were touring in Ohio?"

Snatching her third chocolate cookie from the gilded Rockingham plate between them, May shook her head. "No, tell me."

"It was a fiasco. When the orchestra arrived in Columbus around noon, tired and hungry, they couldn't find a single hotel that would take them or a restaurant that would feed them. They ended up napping on top of their trunks and boxes backstage, with nothing to eat but sandwiches they made themselves. And yet later, after the performance that night, the audience clapped and cheered so loud you would have thought every one of those musicians was some sort of hero. That's when Will decided to speak his mind. Told everybody in that theater just what kind of hypocrites they were and that his orchestra didn't want their applause."

May blotted her lips with a napkin. "Oh my! I imagine that didn't go over too well."

"Surprisingly, it did. Those folks felt so ashamed they ended up finding beds for the entire orchestra, in some of the finest homes in the city—their own!"

"I suppose one should consider that progress after a sort."

Abbie shrugged. "I'm not one to complain, honey. Prejudice is something I'm pretty used to. Thank goodness I get a break from it every now and then, when I go to Europe on one of my singing tours. They're fascinated with black people over there. Treat us like royalty. But here—well, you know how it is."

"Yes, I'm afraid I—"

May stopped midsentence, thinking she had heard footsteps in the hall. A moment later, Melvin entered the parlor, halting just inside the door.

"Excuse me, I—I didn't realize you had company."

"That's all right, dear. You remember Miss Mitchell."

He nodded, offering an oddly vacant smile. "Nice to see you, ma'am."

"Have you finished sorting through the rest of Grandfather's books to decide which ones you'd like to keep?"

"No, not quite." Melvin hesitated. "I—I wanted to ask you something. But I guess now isn't the best time."

"Is it terribly important?"

"No. Well—yes, actually it is—maybe," he added, dropping his voice.

"Please then, ask me." May could see that he was agitated.

Melvin approached his mother and handed her a piece of paper. "It's about this."

It appeared to be a page torn from a newspaper. She unfolded it, her heart skittering. Already she suspected.

"This fellow, Mike Bernard," Melvin said. "Do you know him?"

May looked up at her son, hoping her face revealed nothing but sure that it must. "Where did you get this? You don't read the *Chatterbox*! At least, I certainly hope not. That paper is pure garbage."

"It was stuck in one of Grandfather's books, *The Picture of Dorian Gray*."

May recalled very well the afternoon when Emily showed her the article about Mike, how she'd hurriedly slipped it between the pages of the Oscar Wilde book, the one Emily had borrowed from their father's library. It was the same afternoon George Convery died. No wonder she'd forgotten all about it.

"I'm afraid I have to be on my way," Abbie said, rising. "I've a rehearsal to get to." She smiled again at Melvin. "Good to see you, young man."

May started to get up, but Abbie stopped her. "Please dear, don't bother. I know my way."

A few moments later, May and Melvin were alone.

"Why don't you sit down, sweetheart?"

"That's all right. I'll stand."

"Now, what was it you wanted to know?"

"Are you aware of what he said—this fellow Mike Bernard?"

"And why would I be?"

"In that article, he says something about a woman. A woman he's in love with. That he was married to. She sounds a lot like you, Mother."

May's mouth went dry. She knew she should have planned for a moment like this. She should have expected it would happen someday. But she wasn't prepared. Not today.

"Give me a minute to read it." She stared down at the page, stalling for time. She remembered precisely what the article said. And she didn't want to lie to her son. Yet how could she possibly do otherwise? He was only sixteen. He wasn't ready for that kind of revelation.

And what about Teddy? Even though they were in the process of a divorce, Melvin still regarded Teddy as his father. Would it be fair to jeopardize the bond that had been assumed between them since the beginning?

As for Mike Bernard, he was unworthy of a son like Melvin. A son who had become a fine young man—without any help from him. A young man entitled to think of himself as a Livingstone. What havoc it would wreak if now he were to learn otherwise!

She lifted her gaze from the paper in her hand and, difficult as it was, looked straight into her son's questioning eyes.

"It's very funny, isn't it? The woman he describes does seem to have a lot in common with me. But I assure you, it's only a coincidence. That description could apply to a lot of women I know. And I've never even met Mike Bernard."

She watched Melvin's face, measuring his reaction. She saw his jaw tighten and sensed there was more to come.

"But that's not true, Mother. Aunt Emily told me once. It was a long time ago, but I remember it. She said the Ragtime King of the World, Mike Bernard, used to teach piano. Both of you were his students." His eyes narrowed. "Why would Grandfather have kept this article in his book? And why did you lie to me? Why did you say you don't know him?"

May clutched her hands tightly in her lap, every fiber in her body taut. "Oh yes—of course. How could I have forgotten? But then, he wasn't our teacher for very long. He moved on to other things rather quickly."

Melvin stared at her a moment longer. "Give it back to me."

She was startled by his commanding tone. Reluctantly, she handed the paper to him. "You know, I recall when Aunt Emily was reading that Oscar Wilde book. She must have saved the article. She always liked Mr. Bernard. Much more than I did."

Melvin had moved to a spot next to the window. He seemed to be studying the paper in the light, examining it like a detective searching for clues. "What do you think of his photograph?"

"What do I think of it? If you mean, has he changed in appearance since he taught Emily and me—yes, absolutely he has. That's another reason I didn't remember him at first."

"That's *not* what I mean." Melvin's face was clouded with suspicion. "Do you think he looks like me?"

May caught her breath. Melvin's speculations had already gone deep into dangerous territory. "Does he look like *you*? Heavens no! You two look nothing alike. I don't know how you could even imagine such a thing. You look like your great-grandfather, Cornelius Convery. You've seen his picture. Remember what I told you before, that you were the spitting image of him?"

"Yes, I remember. Nobody else thought so."

May couldn't stand it another second. Abruptly, she stood up and began fussing with the tea service, stacking the porcelain plates and cups, gathering the teaspoons, the cream, the sugar.

"Do you know where your sister is?" she asked stiffly, only for the sake of filling the silence.

"No."

"I thought the three of us would go out for supper tonight. Would you like that?"

He took his time answering. "I suppose."

"Good. I'll make a reservation at Delmonico's. What time would suit you?"

"I don't care." Melvin still appeared to be fixated on the photograph of Mike Bernard.

"Melvin, why don't you throw away that silly article?"

He looked up, returning her reproachful look with one that was frighteningly hostile. Then, shoving the paper into his pocket, he stalked out of the room.

ACT IV
1928–1929

"Oh, circumscribe me not by rules
That serve to lead the minds of fools!
But give me pow'r to work my will,
And at my deeds the world shall thrill.
My words shall rouse the slumb'ring zest
That hardly stirs in manhood's breast;
And as the sun feeds lesser lights,
As planets have their satellites,
So round about me will I bind
The men who prize a master mind!"

He lived a silent life alone,
And laid him down when it was done;
And at his head was placed a stone
On which was carved a name unknown!

—From "A Career," Paul Laurence Dunbar

An Act of Mercy

NEW YORK CITY
JUNE 1928

S trap had been waiting outside the Sunshine Theater, a third-rate establishment on East Houston, for more than an hour, hanging around like a stray dog and drawing more than his share of suspicious looks. The minute his target came out the door, he was on his heels.

"Mr. Bernard! Hey, Mr. Bernard!"

Mike shot him a wary glance with no flash of recognition and kept walking.

"Mr. Bernard, wait! It's Strap Hill. Used to sing with Ben Harney."

Mike swung around. His eyes narrowed to a squint. "So it is! Guess we've both changed some."

Strap flashed a grin. "Reckon so. More than thirty years gone by since me and Ben first played Tony Pastor's."

"Don't remind me. I try not to count the years."

"Well, at least we ain't dead yet."

Mike didn't smile.

"Listen, don't mean to bother you, but all right if I walk with you a ways?" Sensing that Bernard wasn't eager for company, he added, "It's about Ben."

"What about him?" Mike started walking, Strap falling into step beside him.

"Don't know if you heard about the heart attack."

Mike stopped abruptly. "Heart attack! When?"

"Month or so ago. Wouldn't even know about it if me and Lucinda didn't come back to New York for a few days to visit her mama. Some of the boys at a joint down in Harlem was talking about it."

"A heart attack," Mike repeated, as if he couldn't quite believe it. He went on walking.

"I guess he getting better," Strap said, measuring his stride to match Mike's, "but word is he kinda hard up for cash. And he ain't in no shape to work."

"Haven't seen Harney's name around town in a long time. In New York these days it's all about *jazz*." He glanced sideways at Strap. "Where'd you say you moved to?"

"Missouri. Little town called Sedalia. Real pretty there. My wife, Lucinda—took me a while to convince her, but now she don't want to be nowhere else in the whole world."

"Well, congratulations then. Sounds like you did the right thing getting out of New York when you did, before things changed. I've thought about it at times myself, but I'm what they call a city rat. I'd be out of my element anywhere else. Likely bored out of my mind."

"Not if you have yourself a good woman, like I do. You married?"

Mike didn't answer right away. "Nine years now."

"Nine years? God bless!"

They fell silent. From the start, Strap had felt funny about tracking Bernard down. He'd never known him well. But it was on his mind that if he could just get him to go see Ben, maybe

Bernard would feel obliged to help him out. After all, the way Ben always told the story, he was the one who taught Bernard how to rag. That ought to count for something.

"Was wondering—well, thought maybe you want to come with me to see Ben. You know, just pay him a friendly visit. Bet it sure would mean a lot to him."

"I don't know that he'd especially want to see *me* . . ."

"Oh, he be real pleased to see you. I know he would."

"Jessie still with him?"

"Why, that woman wouldn't leave Ben's side for nothing. Not for nothing."

They walked another half a block without a word. Strap wasn't in a position to be pushy, but it didn't seem it ought to take Bernard so long to make up his mind. Not about something so simple as helping out an old buddy.

"Who else has been over to see him?" Mike asked. "He must have a lot of friends in New York."

"You know about friends. Sometimes they just ain't around when you need 'em."

"Harney's really down and out, huh?"

"I reckon so, what with his health failing now. Only so much a man can take before he break. Before he just give up." It was then that Strap remembered. "Hey, what ever happen to that big contest at Madison Square Garden? Seem like that was a long time ago Ben was talking about it. I never hear who won."

Mike snickered, slowing down, as if that particular story required a more leisurely gait. "Ben was talking about it, not me. I offered to do it just as a favor. Told him to get the backers together. He never did. I don't know if he tried or not. Chances are, by then, it was already too late. Nobody figured Harney would have a shot, and what good is a contest if everybody already knows the winner."

"I guess you right about that."

They fell silent. Strap had run out of conversation and, besides, Mike Bernard seemed like a busy man. If Strap wanted to get him over to Ben's place, he'd best not waste any time. Spying a cab headed their way, he leaped to the curb and flagged it down. The car pulled over.

He opened the door and turned around. "You coming?"

The Lion Roars

B y golly, I can't hardly believe it!"

"What is it, Ben?" Jessie called out from behind the half-closed door of their apartment's tiny bedroom. She had been trying to fix her hair for the last ten minutes; it seemed to have a mind of its own these days, now that it was going gray.

"Better come out here quick, Jess!"

Alarmed, she threw down her hairbrush and pins and rushed into the sitting room.

"Well, glory be!" She flew into Strap's arms, and the two of them exchanged a heartfelt hug. Then she turned to Mike, trying not to let her mixed emotions show. She supposed it was good of him to come, though she imagined what had brought him was more curiosity than concern. "Mike Bernard! What a surprise."

"You're looking well," he said.

He was an adept liar. Her hair was a mess. Her old green housecoat was badly stained, the shapeless contour hardly flattering. She was sure, too, that Mike must notice the fine lines on her face, the loose skin hooding her eyes, her crepey neck.

And she must try to remember not to smile.

"Let's not pretend. Ben and I have both seen better days."

"Now, stop all this silly talk," Ben scolded. "Aren't you going to invite our guests to sit down? Maybe make us some tea?"

"No need to go to any trouble," Mike said. "We're not staying long. At least, I'm not."

"It's no trouble," Ben insisted. "Go on and sit down."

Strap and Mike each took one of the worn, overstuffed chairs that filled nearly half the small sitting room. Jessie knew what they were thinking, how bad it all seemed. The two-room apartment was cramped and dingy, the small galley kitchen not much more than a sink, gas plate, and small icebox; but it was open to the sitting room, perfect for keeping an eye on Ben. Jessie watched now as he eased himself onto the sofa, resting his cane against the arm. The same cane he had always loved to tap and twirl when he did his famous stick dance. These days he needed it to walk. Looking at him, struggling to save face in front of his old rival, she felt as if her heart would break.

"So how you doing?" Strap asked gently. "Getting your strength back now?"

"Little by little, I guess. Got to admit, this whole heart attack thing—it sure took me by surprise. You're just going along one day as usual, and then bang. It's like an earthquake in your chest, you can't breathe, and next thing you know, you wake up in a hospital."

"I bet pretty soon you be back out there, singing and dancing like you always done."

"Afraid not, Strap. Doctors say I got to take it easier from now on."

Jessie set the teakettle onto the gas plate, trying to think of something cheerful to say. "Getting Ben to slow down is next to impossible. That man's wild as a june bug on a string, and I guess he always will be."

"This time I got no choice. I got to quit doing what I love. That's what hurts the most."

Jessie tried again. Maybe Strap would have some good news for them. "Tell us what you've been up to, Strap. Good Lord, it's been such a long time since we've seen you!"

"Sure has. Back when I bring Lucinda over to meet you, reckon you must have thought it wouldn't come to nothing between her and me. But I keep at her and finally she say yes to being my wife. Talk her into moving to Sedalia, too. Bought me a little business, a feed-and-grain store right in the center of town. Got us two boys of our own now, almost grown."

"You still singing and shouting?" Ben asked.

"Have me a good jam every now and then. Pipes ain't what they used to be, but they's good enough to get by."

So far, Mike hadn't said anything, but Jessie noticed he kept sneaking glances at her. It made her uncomfortable to imagine what he must be thinking—how much she'd changed. But then, what about him? His hair had always been thin, but now it was thinner. And there were deep grooves lining his forehead. He must have his share of worries, like all the other old-timers from vaudeville days, now that ragtime wasn't so big anymore. She wondered about his hands. Were they still as fast as they used to be?

"Look, Ben," Mike said suddenly, as if he was anxious to get the visit over with, "about your situation—"

Ben cut him off. "Jessie and me are just fine. Matter of fact, we're headed to Philadelphia pretty soon. Got us a nice place out there."

"You done socked away a little nest egg, huh?" Strap said, casting a hopeful glance at Jessie.

She gritted her teeth. Ben wouldn't like it, but she wasn't about to let him misrepresent the facts. This was no time for pride or pretense. "You'd think so, wouldn't you? There was plenty of opportunity, but when you're used to living high on the hog—"

"Jessie, that's enough. Our friends here don't need you to recount our whole life history," Ben said, brushing her off with a wave of his hand. "Hey, Mike, did you hear Albee's selling the Palace Theater? They're going to make it into a damn movie house. A shame, ain't it?"

Jessie saw Ben eyeing Mike's well-tailored suit, his polished boots, his diamond ring. "Anyway, seems *you're* keeping busy enough these days," he continued. "This newfangled jazz—why, that should be right down your alley."

"Should be." Mike sounded prickly. It wasn't difficult to read between the lines, at least for Jessie. He might present himself well, but it was hard to imagine he wasn't feeling the pinch. These days, the colored jazz bands had a monopoly on the dance halls, and that's where everybody went. "Look, Ben, I didn't come to talk about me. Just wanted to see if you were still breathing, that's all."

Abruptly, Jessie turned off the gas plate. She wasn't serving tea. It seemed everyone was on edge. Anyway, she could see that Ben was getting tired. And there wasn't much more to talk about. Nothing that wouldn't end up making him feel worse than he already did.

Empty-handed, she approached the seated guests. "It was so nice of you both to come, and I sure don't mean to rush you, but the doctor said Ben shouldn't—"

"You know, Ben," Mike said, steamrolling over Jessie's apology, "I still admire that ring of yours. The lion's head. Always meant to tell you, if you ever want to sell it . . ."

Jessie froze, watching Ben as he slowly reached up to scratch his head. She already knew what he would say. It was no secret what that ring meant to him. It was the last thing he would ever give up.

But that's where they were now—down to the last thing.

"Honey," she prompted delicately, "weren't you saying just the other day that you might want to trade in that ring for something a little less showy?"

"I don't remember saying anything of the sort."

Obviously impatient, Mike rose from his chair. But now she didn't want him to go. He couldn't. Not yet.

"Ben, if Mike really wants that ring you should let him buy it from you. After all, wouldn't it be better in the hands of a friend? Better than some pawnshop?"

"No way I'm parting with the lion's head. Not to anybody, at any price. And that's final." Ben reached for his cane.

"Stay where you are, Ben. I can let myself out," Mike said.

Strap got up and, seeming about ready to leave as well, went over to Ben. Mike took a step toward Jessie. He lowered his voice to a whisper. "If you two change your minds, you know where to find me."

"No, I'm afraid we don't." Her mind wasn't going to change. That ring was their ticket to Philadelphia. How else would they get there?

Mike reached into his jacket pocket, pulled out one of his cards and a pen, and scribbled something on the back. Discreetly, he dropped it into the pocket of her housecoat.

Finished with Ben, Strap came to say goodbye. He wrapped an arm around Jessie's shoulder and furtively pressed a wad of bills into her palm. "That's just something I owe Ben, from a long time back."

Jessie bit down on her lip, trying to stop it from trembling. For Ben's sake, she mustn't cry. Not now. "You're a good friend, Strap," she said softly, giving his hand a squeeze. "The best."

Charity Begins at Home

Mike reclined in his favorite chair, trying to read the newspaper without his glasses, which he'd misplaced again. It was eleven thirty on Sunday night, and his Queens apartment was blessedly quiet. Both his wife, Katherine, and his seven-year-old son, Jules, had been in bed since nine. This was Mike's favorite time—when he could finally be alone.

Giving up on his reading, he let his weary eyes roam the modest living room. As always, he was critical of everything he saw—the flowered upholstery, the lace doilies, the oil painting of three ladies with parasols strolling in the park that hung above a reproduction of a Louis XIV side cabinet. Katherine had insisted on decorating the place herself and, at the time, Mike hadn't minded indulging her. Something he seldom did anymore.

With a deep sigh, he folded the newspaper, lining up the corners before setting it down on the table next to him. He was too tired to read. He might as well turn in. But then, what would he do in bed besides lie awake in the dark? There was no excitement at the thought of slipping under the covers next to his wife, no desire for intimacy. The truth was, he'd lost interest soon after they were married, when he saw that already she had changed from that reckless young actress who caught every man's eye into someone far more calculating. But her calculations had been off. Apparently, she didn't realize that, even then, the die was cast. Ragtime was on its way out.

It was all because of jazz.

Not that he couldn't play jazz. As a matter of fact, he could play it better than anybody. Since his earliest days at Tony Pastor's, he never stuck purely to the printed page; he always improvised. Ragtime, at least the way he played it, was a tour de force of spontaneity. *Swing*—it was second nature to him. And he knew how to fit into any ensemble. He'd tried to convince them a few years back, when he sat in at Reisenweber's Café with what was, at the time, New York's most popular dance headliner, the Original Dixieland Jazz Band. He performed brilliantly at that audition, proving beyond a doubt his mastery of the jazz idiom. But he knew how people felt and what they said. They were enamored of labels. Mike Bernard belonged to "The Past." Nostalgia had become his specialty.

He thought again of Katherine, asleep in the next room. Sometimes he wondered why they stayed together, though he supposed he knew the answer. It was too much trouble to do anything else. And too expensive. His divorce from singer Florence Courtney had been messy. They were married only two years, hardly long enough to count. But in court, Florence had been out for blood. She seemed to enjoy portraying him as a villain, and the papers were more than happy to cover the explosive proceedings in every titillating detail.

Women! They had been his downfall from the beginning. Yet what was success for if not to celebrate it in the arms of one enchanting female after another?

Exhausted, he closed his eyes, resigned to what he ended up doing almost every night—falling asleep in his chair. He looked forward to that brief, hazy interlude between wake-fulness and slumber when he would welcome the cavalcade of young beauties from his past, whirling through his mind like figurines on a brightly colored carousel. How he loved to admire them, to remember how all those lovely creatures had once, for a moment in time, been his.

Tonight, he fell into that same familiar dream—the one at the carnival, riding the Ferris wheel. In the distance, he could hear the slightly off-pitch music of a calliope. The wheel circled to the top, his head nearly touching the clouds. He turned in his seat to view the car just behind his. Dolly's car. She was with someone. A young man. Handsome, he supposed, though he couldn't see his face. They were kissing. He smiled and turned away. He was still at the top. Then he looked down. The earth seemed miles away, yet he could observe her on the ground, clearly, as if she were almost within reach. She was looking up, one hand shading her eyes, the other holding a bouquet of pink roses. He leaned over the side of the passenger car, desperately waving his arms. She must see him! He called out her name.

"May!"

Mike awoke suddenly. He'd heard a noise, he was sure of it. Was there someone outside his door? Maybe trying to pick the lock? There had been a burglary in the building only a month ago. He had thought about buying a gun.

He stood up, pulled the belt of his robe a little tighter, and went to investigate, grabbing a heavy gold-plated trophy from the bookcase as he passed by. Just in case.

He stepped lightly to the door and, hesitating only a second, threw it open.

"Hope I'm not disturbing you."

Jessie stood in the dim hallway outside his apartment. Though it was a warm night, she wore a velvet cape. Her hair was arranged in an enormous chignon and decorated with a wide headband the same shade of green as her wrap. She had obviously gone to some trouble to make herself presentable.

Mike knew immediately why she was there. Nearly a week had gone by since he and Strap dropped in for a visit. Time enough, he guessed, for Jessie to persuade Ben to change his mind.

"You do know what time it is," he chided, moving aside to let her pass. As she swept by, he caught the subtle scent of rose petals, and again his memory stirred.

"I'm sorry. It's just that I had to wait until Ben was asleep. He won't let me out of his sight these days."

Mike closed the door, grateful that Katherine and Jules were sound sleepers.

"Well, it's good to see you anyway," he said, tossing the trophy onto a chair before reaching to help her off with her cape. She clutched at the wrap, obviously not wanting to part with it.

"I can only stay a minute or two."

"Don't be silly. Come on, I won't have you standing there like a stranger. Sit down, and I'll bring you a drink. I've managed to keep a bit of a stash going, Prohibition be damned! What'll you have?"

Jessie sighed. "All right then," she said, allowing Mike to lift the cape from her shoulders. "Whiskey, if you've got any."

Mike draped Jessie's cloak over the chair, then went to the cabinet and poured a whiskey for her, gin for himself. He came back and sat down next to her on the sofa. Without further prelude, she pulled the ring from her purse.

"You said you've always wanted it. I guess now is your chance." She handed it to him. "But you know that you don't have to do this, right? Ben and I will manage. We always do."

Mike ignored her protestation, relishing the weight of solid gold in his palm. "How did you convince Ben to part with it?"

"I didn't."

He looked at her in surprise. "You mean he doesn't know?"

"He'll find out tomorrow, but there won't be anything he can do about it then. We're leaving for Philadelphia in the morning, and not a moment too soon. Ben needs a change of scenery. Being around here reminds him too much of the way things used to be, and that's not healthy for him now. Once we get to Philadelphia, it'll be a whole lot easier. His sister lives there, and she's got a real nice place. Said we can stay as long as we like."

So, she was going behind Ben's back! For a moment, Mike was mildly conflicted. He knew he should refuse the ring. He should hand it back to Jessie, tell her it belongs to Ben and should stay with him. He should give her some money anyway, knowing how badly they needed it.

But he wanted that ring. She was right. He had always wanted it.

"Well, if it's any consolation, you can tell Ben that I'll take good care of it for him."

"Oh, I'm not going to tell Ben that you have the ring! Please, he mustn't know. Let him think I pawned it. That's bad enough."

"Are you saying that he'd rather for anyone to have it but me?" Harney was *that* jealous of him? He smiled to himself. He'd always suspected it.

"I don't know." Jessie looked away, obviously upset. "At any rate, it's yours."

"Look, you shouldn't feel guilty about this. Neither of us . . ." His voice trailed off, his attention back on the ring. He slipped it onto his finger, admiring the way it looked on his hand.

Jessie picked up where he'd left off. "Sure, I feel guilty. But I guess Ben is just going to have to forgive me. Lord knows, I've forgiven *him* enough over the years! The fact is, we need the money. And anyway, that ring is from another time, another era. Best we don't think too much about the past. Certain things anyway."

325

Mike was grateful she was able to justify it all so neatly, so he didn't have to. "Just tell me what you want for it. I'm sure you have a fair price in mind."

He stood up, leaving her to think while he went over to his desk and pulled out his checkbook and a pen.

"It's up to you," she said. "I've never been much good at bargaining."

He waited, pen poised over the check. "But you must have a figure in mind."

"Whatever the ring is worth to you."

He thought for a moment about what she had just said. Did she put it that way on purpose, understanding full well that what the ring was worth and what it was worth to *him* were two entirely different matters?

He glanced at her sitting quietly on the sofa, her head bent, hands folded in her lap. It was glaringly apparent why she hadn't wanted him to take her cloak. Her dress was outdated and shabby, like something out of a secondhand shop and not at all her style. It was pitiable to see her like this, sneaking around in the dead of night, desperate to scrape up enough cash so she and Ben would have something to live on when they got to Philadelphia.

With a sudden resolve, he scribbled an amount and his signature on the check and folded it in half. It wasn't a huge sum, but it was the most he could afford. Probably more than she expected.

"Here you go," he said, returning to hand it to Jessie. She was already standing. She seemed anxious to leave.

"Thanks." She started to slip it into her purse.

"You're not even going to look at it?"

"I wasn't—but, if you want me to, I will." Jessie unfolded the paper. Mike saw her head snap back in surprise. When she looked up, her eyes were glistening with tears. "You're too generous, Mike. I don't know how I can thank you."

"Not necessary. We each got what we wanted this time, right?"

"Right." She smiled for an instant, long enough for him to notice she was missing a tooth, near the front. Embarrassed for her, he turned away. Best to end this quickly. He lifted her cape from the back of the chair and placed it over her shoulders.

"You'll have to let me know how Ben is doing."

"It's nice of you to say that, but I'll bet you won't give either one of us another thought after tonight. Now that you've got the lion's head."

Mike knew what she meant and, in a way, she was right. For him, finally possessing Ben's ring seemed like the end of a quest.

"Well, take care," she said, patting his arm before she hurried out the door.

Mike barely noticed her leave. He was too busy admiring the lion's snarling mouth.

Death's Door

I'm May Convery, from the Actors Fund."

A young nurse, wearing a white cap and starched white apron over her gray dress, nodded her acknowledgment. "Yes, we've been expecting you. Please come this way."

May followed her down the wide hospital corridor. Along both sides, patients lay on rolling carts, some of them sleeping, others staring into space. A few thrashed around, loudly announcing their discomfort and demanding attention from the doctors and nurses who hurried by on their way somewhere else.

"Along this hall is where we keep many of the terminally ill patients," the nurse explained. "At least those who can't afford a private or semiprivate room, though we try to give them one when they're almost at the end. Like the woman you've come to see." She stopped in front of a door numbered 206. It was partially closed.

"She's in there, in the first bed. I was told there's someone else with her right now. But you can wait here, if you like. Or down the hall, at the very end, there are a few chairs."

"I might as well stay here."

"All right. If you need anything else, please come to the nurses' station. Someone there will be happy to help you, Mrs. Convery."

"*Miss* Convery."

"Oh—sorry, ma'am."

May nodded her thanks and assumed her post next to the door, leaning with her back against the wall. She was grateful to have a moment to collect herself. These visits were unquestionably her most difficult duty as a volunteer on the board of the Actors Fund. And yet probably the most important.

She had become active with the organization about eight years ago. With the ratification of the Nineteenth Amendment to the Constitution giving women the vote, she felt in need of a new cause. Many of her close friends were involved in the theater, which made the Actors Fund seem a logical choice. Rosamond and his wife, Nora, as well as Abbie Mitchell, had encouraged her to become a benefactor. They knew all too well the plight of actors, musicians, and others whose great talents often failed to provide security in old age or in the throes of ill health. Many couldn't even afford a decent burial. Benefit performances, fairs, and a variety of local and national events brought in money for the charity, supplementing generous donations from wealthy individuals—such as May Convery.

A struggling bit-part actress on Broadway was on the list for today. May had been told this could well be the one and only visit. Her condition, they said, was imminently terminal. Cancer.

May always found it awkward to intrude on some poor soul grappling with death, to insinuate herself into a stranger's life at a time of such personal grief and turmoil. But the goal of the Actors Fund and its volunteers was to offer a measure of peace, to relieve the strain of uncertainty, to let a fellow human being know that he or she was not alone in the final hours. It was that mission of mercy that had brought her here this afternoon.

Now, as she waited by the door to the hospital room, she couldn't help but overhear bits and pieces of the conversation taking place within. Not so much a conversation, it seemed, as a monologue, and the shrillness of the speaker's voice made it almost impossible *not* to listen.

"That's why I'm here, honey."

"Thank you." The response was so soft, May could barely make it out.

"So, how old is he—your boy?"

"Bert? Just fourteen. I—I'm awful worried about him."

"Well, don't you fret. The Actors Fund will take care of everything. Like I said, that's why I'm here."

May's head jerked back. This woman had been dispatched by the Actors Fund? Had there been some sort of mistake, two volunteers accidentally assigned to the same patient?

She inched closer to the door, now feeling an obligation to eavesdrop.

"Now listen, about this money you saved for the boy—to send him to Juilliard, right?"

"No, he thinks so. But the life of a musician . . . it . . . it's no good."

"All right, honey. But listen, I got just one more question for you. The boy's father—what's his name?"

There was a long pause. "Mike. Mike Bernard."

May gasped. Had she heard correctly? No, it was impossible! But then, really it wasn't. They both were in the theater business; their paths easily might have crossed. It was no secret that Mike had a reputation when it came to women. Might this have been another of his flings gone wrong?

"You're married to *Mike Bernard*, the Ragtime King?" Apparently, the other woman from the Actors Fund was just as incredulous as May was.

"We're not married."

"But he's the boy's father, right? Does he visit him? Does he keep in touch?"

"No. The boy—he lives with Papa, above the store. In Queens."

There was a sound like rustling paper. "I guess I can sort all that out later. In the meantime, we're going to appoint what they call a *trustee*, somebody who'll make sure your money goes to the boy and no place else. You see? These here are the documents from the Actors Fund. Here's where you sign your name."

May's initial shock was quickly superseded by puzzlement, then outrage. The Actors Fund was not in the business of writing wills or serving as an estate trustee. It was there to provide funds when none were available, not to take control of someone's savings. The woman in that room was an imposter! And a thief.

May's first thought was to race to the nurses' station, order someone to call the police. But by then it might be too late. The papers would be signed, the vile perpetrator gone. It seemed there was only one way to handle the situation.

Giving the door a push, May burst into the room. The heavyset woman hovering over Dolly Zuckerman's bed looked up, startled by the sudden intrusion.

"Who are you?" May demanded.

"Who am *I*? Who are *you*?"

"You have represented yourself to Miss Zuckerman as an agent of the Actors Fund."

"That's right. What's it to you?"

"I happen to be a director of that organization."

The woman's jaw dropped slightly. "Well, isn't that a coincidence!" She hastily swept the papers from Dolly's hand and would have stuffed them into her oversized purse if May hadn't snatched them from her first.

"Give those back to me! You got no right—"

May stood her ground. "I'm warning you, whoever you are. Get out of here this minute, or I'll summon hospital security to have you removed. And you can be sure the Actors Fund will file charges against you on behalf of Miss Zuckerman as well."

"You got no idea what you're talking about." In a fit of anger, the woman roughly shoved May aside. "If this poor girl dies without a will, it'll be on *you*," she shouted over her shoulder as she lumbered out the door, apparently deciding it was preferable to leave of her own volition while she still could.

May, breathing hard, her knees shaking, turned to Dolly. What an awful scene to have played out in front of a dying woman! "I'm so sorry that you had to be disturbed in this manner, Miss Zuckerman. I assure you that person was not from the Actors Fund. I'm afraid she was here to steal your money. The money apparently intended for your child's education."

Looking closely at Dolly, May understood with sobering clarity that she had arrived none too soon. How utterly wasted away the young woman appeared! According to Miss Zuckerman's file, she was only thirty-three.

"Miss Zuckerman, I'm here to inform you that the Actors Fund will assist with any expenses associated with your illness and your"—she hesitated—"your burial arrangements, should that become necessary. I want you to rest assured of that and to know there are those who appreciate all the joy you have brought to others through your work in the theater."

Dolly's eyes met May's for only an instant before they drifted closed. Clearly, the effort of her earlier conversation had left her drained.

"Did you hear me, Miss Zuckerman?"

"The boy . . . I should have . . ."

"Your son? Bert?"

"Mike . . . he has to . . ."

"Mike Bernard?" May leaned in closer.

Dolly's head moved, a nod.

"Does Mr. Bernard know you're ill?"

She didn't respond.

"Do you want him to come?"

Her eyes opened. "No."

"All right, you don't want to see him. I understand. But is there anything I can do for you, Miss Zuckerman? Anything at all?"

Dolly appeared to be struggling, her lips moving without making a sound. May wondered if she should call for the nurse.

"Tell the boy . . ."

May bent closer still, so close she was forced to inhale the sickly-sweet odor of impending death, a smell she had learned to recognize. "Tell your son? What is it you want me to tell him?"

"No, Mike must tell . . . the boy . . . not to . . ."

Silence.

"Miss Zuckerman? Dolly—can you hear me?"

Reluctant Reunion

May sat behind the huge desk in her father's study, the desk from which she had so often observed him conducting business. She had always been fascinated by the way he dealt with people. Gruff, unsympathetic, adamant when it came to getting his way. If only she were more like him, she would pick up the telephone right now, call the office of the Actors Fund, and insist that they assign someone else to Dolly Zuckerman's case.

She opened the folder that contained Dolly's file and stared at the Client Profile, onto which she had scribbled a few notes about the existence of a fourteen-year-old son, the possibility of an estate, the attempted embezzlement. She had scrupulously avoided any mention of Mike Bernard or the message Dolly asked her to deliver.

With a frustrated sigh, she tossed the folder aside. Unknowingly, Dolly had forced her into the most awkward situation imaginable. The most painful as well. She knew that she was being foolish—and selfish. This wasn't about her and Mike. It was about the last wish of a dying woman. A message that must be delivered and had been entrusted to no one but her.

The easiest thing would be to telephone him. It should be quick and to the point. She would tell him what Miss Zuckerman said, vague as it was, and never even have to see his face. Or she could send a telegram. In fact, that was probably the best solution. It could all be accomplished without any conversation between them whatsoever.

"Miss Convery, your one o'clock appointment is here." Willard, her father's longtime butler and now hers, stood in the doorway.

"Appointment? I'm not expecting anyone. Who is it?"

"He says his name is Mike Bernard."

May sprang from her chair. "What? Are you sure?"

"Yes, ma'am. I have his card right here." He approached the desk and handed it to her.

She tossed it down without so much as a glance. "Did he say what he wants?"

"He said he's here concerning Miss Zuckerman—I believe that's the name."

She turned away, not wanting Willard to see how shaken she was—though it was probably too late for that. It was twenty-eight years since their last meeting, an experience that had been unpleasant for both of them. Why would this be any different? In fact, hadn't he shown the same brazen disregard for her privacy by this uninvited visit, when she had quite clearly told him before that he was not welcome in her home? And how had he known to find her *here*? How could he possibly be aware that she and Teddy were divorced, that she now lived in her childhood home? A sudden chill went through her. If he knew all that about her, might he also know other things?

She could, of course, send him away. But she would have to deal with him somehow, and soon. It was her duty.

Willard was waiting for his instructions.

"All right, you may see him in."

"Very well, ma'am."

With Willard gone, she turned her attention to her father's study. Feverishly, she scanned the shelves for any family photographs on display. There were several, two of them fairly recent ones in which Melvin was prominent. There was no question his resemblance to Mike was uncanny. She snatched the photographs from the shelf and shoved them into a drawer. Having accomplished that, she returned to sit behind her father's desk. The massiveness of it somehow made her feel safe, or at least *safer*. She smoothed her hair, licked her lips, and folded her hands in front of her—waiting. It would be all right. Everything would be fine.

"Mr. Bernard, ma'am." The butler stepped aside for Mike to enter.

"Thank you, Willard. You may leave us."

Mike remained standing where he had been deposited, just inside the threshold, perhaps expecting an invitation to sit down. Or perhaps not. She looked him over with a critical eye. He wore an expensive-looking suit, a crisply starched shirt, and alligator shoes; clearly, he meant to give the impression things were going well for him. Maybe they were; she didn't know or care. She noticed he was as lean as ever, without that paunch so many men develop as they get older. But his hair was sparse in the front, his forehead creased, his deep-set eyes lined and puffy underneath. He was showing his age.

"Well, here we are," he said.

"Yes, here we are."

She motioned to the chair on the opposite side of the desk. "Please." She tried to take a breath, but her chest was suddenly tight. "I understand you've come about Miss Zuckerman. I wasn't aware that you'd been informed of her situation."

"I wasn't," he replied, taking a seat. "Not until yesterday evening. I was contacted by the hospital. Apparently, she listed me as next of kin."

"I would have thought she had named her father."

337

"All I know is they called me. They also told me that some-one from the Actors Fund had been with her when she—when she passed. They mentioned your name."

"They shouldn't have. But, yes, I was there yesterday. Technically she was still alive when I left, but she had slipped into a coma. The doctor said most likely it was irreversible. Obviously, he was correct."

"And why exactly did you go to see her?"

"I'm on the board of the Actors Fund and a volunteer. One of the most important things that we do is visit those in need and let them know that help is available. I happened to be assigned to Miss Zuckerman's case."

Mike's eyes narrowed. "I take it, then, that you know all about Dolly?"

"Very little, actually. I know she was a Ziegfeld girl, she's acted on Broadway. I know her age and her marital status—single. And I know that she has a fourteen-year-old son named Bert who lives with his grandfather in Queens."

"And I assume you were told that I'm the boy's father?"

May was careful to maintain her disinterested posture. "Indirectly, yes."

"What's that supposed to mean?"

"When I arrived, Miss Zuckerman had another visitor. A woman named"—she reached for Dolly's file and pulled out the false Last Will and Testament—"Ida Gallagher." She looked up. "I don't imagine you've ever heard of her?"

"Name sounds familiar. I can't quite place it. Maybe vaudeville."

"Well, if I hadn't walked in on her little meeting with Miss Zuckerman, I'm afraid Dolly would have signed away every penny she had. Ida Gallagher had already obtained her signa-ture on this Last Will and Testament naming her and"—she consulted the papers again—"Mr. Fred Gallagher, probably her husband, as the trustees of Miss Zuckerman's estate. I plan to turn this over to the lawyer for the Actors Fund and see whether there's enough evidence to bring charges. But, of course, that's not the main concern now. My primary interest is to make sure Miss Zuckerman has a decent burial."

"Of course. When I heard someone from the Actors Fund had visited Dolly, it occurred to me that maybe she was in need of money."

"Well, she seems to have some kind of an estate. Based on the information in our files, it can't be much—unless we were misinformed. We'll need to investigate. Certainly, if we find that her family can't afford to take care of her properly, we will see to it. Unless, of course, you—"

"Let me explain something about Dolly and me," Mike interrupted. "Though I'm sure you've already made your judgment."

"I'm not in the habit of judging things I know nothing about."

He unbuttoned his jacket, crossed his legs. He appeared extremely tense. Perhaps almost as tense as she was.

"I met Dolly when she was with the Follies. I did what I could to help her get ahead with her career. We—we had a relationship, relatively brief. But sincere. At least on my part. She became pregnant and apparently wasn't even going to tell me. I did the gentlemanly thing. I offered to marry her. She turned me down. Said that marriage would interfere with her career. That was her excuse anyway. I pointed out that raising a child on her own would interfere more, but I guess she thought she had it all figured out. I was essentially dismissed, told I wasn't needed. Not for anything except my name. Of course, the old man wanted money. I gave Dolly some in the beginning, but when I found out she was just handing it over to her father, I stopped. I didn't trust him. I doubt anything I gave him ever would have gone to the boy. Besides, he treated me like scum. Who needs *that*? Anyway, I found out later that Dolly had told everybody we were married and divorced, I guess to save face. Frankly, I didn't care what she said." He leaned back, looking somewhat relieved to have made it through his entire narrative. "Am I really the boy's father? Probably. Did I care about Dolly? Yes, I suppose I did. At least to begin with. I got over it." He looked down at his hands. "Still, I'm sorry that she had to die so young. She was a sweet girl, back when I knew her."

May had listened closely to every word, all the while thinking how it was probably the most honest he'd ever been with her. Assuming he *was* being honest. Did he really not know for sure if he was the boy's father, or did he mean to suggest that such uncertainty would be just cause for the neglect of which he was so obviously guilty?

"And you came here today because . . ."

"Because Dolly gave the hospital my name. She must have wanted me to do something for her—finally."

"Yes, she did." May fortified herself with the thought that this unwelcome meeting was almost over. One last thing, and she could again bid Mike Bernard farewell, this time forever. "At the very end, Miss Zuckerman asked that I request something of you—in her words, to *tell the boy*. Her son, I'm sure. But then she fell into a coma. She never finished saying what she wanted you to tell him." She hesitated. "Except that—if I might speculate—I heard her say earlier, to that Gallagher woman, that her boy wants to attend Juilliard. It seemed she was concerned about it—that she feared pursuing a career in music might not be in his best interests. It's possible that's what she wanted you to talk with him about, though, as I said, I don't know for certain."

Mike ran a hand through his thinning hair. "Truth is, I hardly know the kid. I'm not sure he'd be interested in anything I might say. I doubt there's much I could do for him now."

"That's between you and your conscience." It was just as she had thought. He hadn't changed. He took no responsibility.

"Look, about Dolly—I'll pay for the burial, but I don't want the family to know. How about if I write a check to the Actors Fund, give it to you, and you can pretend when you talk to old man Zuckerman that the money is coming from the organization. Would you be willing to do that?"

"I'm afraid that would be highly irregular."

"But would you?"

It was all she could do to stop herself from berating him for being such a coward. What right did he have to hide behind the good works and reputation of the Actors Fund?

"I'll see if it's possible," she replied curtly.

"I'll take that as a yes."

He pulled out his checkbook and a pen, then scribbled something, tore out the check, and handed it to her—folded.

"Very well then," she said, tucking it into Dolly's file. "I'll give this to the Actors Fund tomorrow. I imagine someone will be in touch with you."

She waited for him to take his cue. She assumed he would be as eager to leave as she was to have him go. But, surprisingly, he seemed in no particular hurry. Perhaps he enjoyed torturing her with his presence.

"Our business is concluded," she said, standing up with an unmistakable air of finality. "I'll ring for Willard to see you out."

Slowly, distractedly, Mike rose from his chair. He wasn't looking at May. His gaze appeared focused on something directly behind her.

"Can I ask you a question?" he said, still without meeting her eyes.

"A question?"

"That young man in the photograph—is he your son?"

His words were like a punch to her gut. She turned, following where his eyes led—to a framed photograph on the highest shelf of the bookcase in back of her father's desk. How could she have missed it before? There he was, Melvin with his sister,

Anna. The picture had been taken around the holidays, when the children were in their teens. Anna was singing Christmas carols while Melvin accompanied her on the piano.

May stared dumbly at the photograph. He had seen Melvin's face! Did he recognize himself in it? And the piano! What could possibly be more incriminating?

"Actually"—her voice sounded thin, frightened—"that boy was a schoolmate of my daughter's. We invited him to join us for Christmas one year. A very nice young man."

She turned back to Mike, who was still staring at the photograph. She could only guess what was going through his mind—but it terrified her. Dear God, was this to be the end of everything?

"Are you ready, sir?" Willard stood in the doorway. She wondered how long he'd been there, whether he was present when she lied about the boy in the photograph.

It seemed as if Mike had to literally tear his eyes from the image in the frame. "Yes, I suppose I am."

"Then goodbye, Mr. Bernard," May said.

"Yes—goodbye, Miss Convery."

Pivoting on his heel, his shoulders thrown back like a military man, he followed Willard out the door and down the hall. As soon as they had disappeared around the corner, May sank into her chair, one hand pressed to her stomach, the other to her forehead. She was shaking.

This was all her fault. Her carelessness would surely lead Melvin to ruin. He would be stripped of his name, his dignity. He would despise her forever.

And he had every right to.

Lesson of Love

———

May found it impossible to sleep, the afternoon's meeting with Mike playing over and over in her head until she felt on the verge of madness. It had been like one of those mystery novels in which the killer nearly commits the perfect crime except for one tiny mistake. One mistake that ultimately means the difference between a clean getaway and life behind bars. How could she have been so negligent?

She had tried to convince herself that Mike hadn't noticed the striking resemblance between himself and Melvin and, of course, there was a chance he had not. But then, why would he make a point of inquiring who the boy in the photograph was? He hadn't asked about Anna. And the look on his face, the tone of his voice. She could feel the undercurrent of cynicism, almost like a threat. Yes, she was certain of it. Mike knew.

The question was, What would he do now?

She took heart in the fact that he had shown absolutely no interest in his son Bert. Why would he feel any differently toward Melvin? Perhaps what she had sensed from him was merely surprise. *Shock* might be a better word for it. Maybe anger at having been deceived. But whatever his first reaction, once he had an opportunity to think it over . . .

Again, she panicked, wondering what might be going through his mind at this very moment. What devious plan for revenge. But, certainly, he could have no illusions about his rights in the matter. He had none. Melvin was a man, not a boy. He was thirty-one now and soon to marry. It wouldn't be long before he had a family of his own. Mike had nothing to gain from exposing the truth. Nothing could come of it but harm.

She chastised herself for not being more cordial toward him this time. Wouldn't she fear him less if there was not such animosity between them? But her feelings could not simply be switched on and off. She had cultivated her bitterness for too many years. For a while, it had been a sickness. Now it was just a part of her that she had grown used to, like a nerve that most of the time is only a dull ache but sometimes flares into something more acute. The possibility of forgiveness had never occurred to her. Not when it came to Mike Bernard. Twenty-eight years ago, she had told him outright that she despised him; she'd said it again, more or less, today.

Had things really changed so little in all that time? Had *she* changed so little?

She rolled over, sinking her head deeper into the pillow as her thoughts turned back to Melvin. For the last fifteen years, ever since that afternoon when he confronted her with the article from the *Chatterbox*, she had felt his suspicion as a wedge between them. Maybe it was only her paranoia, a way to punish herself for having become the worst kind of hypocrite. After all, at the same time as she had encouraged her son to be a seeker of truth, she had done everything in her power to hide it from him.

Wearily she closed her eyes, hoping that sleep would claim her quickly. Maybe in the morning, things would become clearer. She would know what to do about Mike, about everything.

The raw edges of her anguished thoughts had just started to blur when the ringing of the telephone next to her bed startled her back to consciousness.

"Hello?"

"May, I'm sorry to call you at this hour." It was Rosamond, and he sounded rattled. "Will Cook collapsed in the middle of a performance tonight. A couple of cast members helped me get him to the hospital. I need you to find Abbie and bring her over."

"Oh my God! Of course, I will. But do you have any idea where she is?"

"She's singing in that show at the Cosmopolitan. It should be over by the time you can get there."

"All right. I'll get dressed and head over right away. Where did you take him?"

"Harlem Hospital on Lenox Avenue."

"There they are!"

May pointed across the huge room that was the open ward of Harlem Hospital to where Rosamond and several others were standing around one of the narrow beds that lined the walls.

"Oh my," Abbie said, clutching her friend's arm a little tighter. May had never seen her so distraught. "I'm afraid to know how bad it is—but come on, let's go."

They headed down the center aisle, weaving their way through a steady stream of rolling gurneys bearing the sick and injured, before they finally reached Cook's bedside. He was fully conscious, propped up on a couple of pillows. The sheet covering his chest was splattered with blood.

He smiled weakly at Abbie. "You found me out," he said. "Don't I always?"

May watched as Abbie gently wiped the sweat from his forehead with her lace handkerchief. They had been divorced for twenty years but still had obvious affection for one another—despite that Abbie had once filed a complaint against him and told the judge, *He haunts my life with a gun.* But that was long ago. Tempers had cooled, better sense prevailed. They had two children to think of. Yet May knew it wasn't only the children that bonded them; it was their musical genius.

Or maybe, she thought now, it was simpler than that. Maybe it was pure love, the kind that rises above everything else.

"Roy! So good of you to come."

Hearing Rosamond's voice, May turned to see who he had spoken to. He was shaking hands with a man who had just joined the group. A white gentleman, rather professorial. Someone she didn't know.

"I was sitting near the back of the theater and didn't realize right away what had happened," May heard him say. "How is he doing?"

"We don't really know yet. He's had tuberculosis for years, but it hasn't bothered him too much. Guess he thought if he kept ignoring it, it might go away. Could be he's headed for a little vacation at Edgecombe Sanitarium."

"Ah, that's a shame." The man approached Cook's bed. "Will, my friend, I see that you've gotten yourself into some trouble."

Cook's answer was a hard, relentless cough that brought up more blood.

A young Negro doctor, wearing a mask over his nose and mouth, appeared bedside and asked that everyone move out of his way so he could conduct an examination. Abbie appeared reluctant to leave her ex-husband's side but nevertheless complied. The three colored men who had helped transport Cook to the hospital drew her into their circle. May joined Rosamond and the new arrival.

"I don't suppose the two of you are already acquainted?" Rosamond asked, looking from one to the other.

"I haven't had the pleasure," replied the unknown gentleman, inclining his head toward May with a friendly smile. He was older, maybe sixty, with silver hair, a neatly trimmed mustache, and a prominent cleft in his chin. His lively blue eyes regarded her from behind wire-rimmed spectacles.

"Miss Convery, this is Mr. Roy Baxter. You might also know him as David Griffin. He's used both names in the course of his illustrious writing career. And, Roy, I'm sure you know the name May Convery, being no stranger to literary circles."

"But I'm certainly aware of Mr. Baxter's name as well—*and* Mr. Griffin's," May asserted, viewing him with a newly inquisitive eye. He and his fellow journalists at the old *McClure's* magazine had earned themselves quite a reputation as muckrakers, their bold reports uncovering shocking corporate abuses and political corruption.

"Roy is an old friend," Rosamond said. "One who, unfortunately, we don't get to see often enough. He's been a tremendous help to Nora and me in winning support for our music school. His writing has helped raise awareness of the work we're doing to make music education available to the colored children of New York."

"It's nice for a change to have something uplifting to write about." Mr. Baxter turned to May. "Miss Convery, I've been an admirer of your poetry for years. I'm honored to finally make your acquaintance."

May felt a blush spread over her cheeks. She always found such praise humbling, especially coming from a fellow writer. "And I've read many of your daring exposés. I have great admiration for a writer who pursues his story wherever it leads, no matter the danger. I, on the other hand, do most of my writing in the comfort of my bedroom."

"Ah, but you have it all wrong. Adventure is not outside; it's within."

She smiled knowingly. "George Eliot?"

"Not word for word." He chuckled. "Actually, I was hoping I might get away with taking the credit."

"Finding the right moment for truth is also a talent, Mr. Baxter." She glanced at Rosamond, who was regarding the two of them with a contemplative smile.

"Listen, after we get Will squared away, how about us three going out for a late bite somewhere?" he said.

"Brilliant suggestion, Rosamond! That is, if Miss Convery is agreeable to a late-night snack with two gentlemen known to engage in rather heated debates every now and then. To which, I might add, a woman's perspective would be a welcome addition."

May had been about to beg off. She was tired. She had, after all, been in bed when she received Rosamond's telephone call. But Mr. Baxter's response to the invitation was so enthusiastic that she would have felt awkward refusing. Besides, he seemed like an interesting gentleman; she already knew his reputation as a progressive firebrand. Surely the conversation would be stimulating. Perhaps it would even take her mind off the disturbing events of the afternoon.

Tomorrow, she supposed, would be soon enough to think about the future.

The Promised Land

Through the partly closed curtain, Jessie watched the sun, cloaked in a winter haze, slowly creep downward. Ben was fast asleep. Since they'd settled into their place in Philadelphia, he often slept from morning until evening, and then most of the night. Jessie, on the other hand, felt like she was always wide awake, whether or not she wanted to be.

She rolled onto her side and propped herself up on one elbow, gazing down at her husband of more than thirty years. Her long hair, tinged with gray, fell down around his face. The brush of it against his skin was enough to stir him.

"Hey, baby. Are we on yet?" he murmured, as if still in a dream.

"We're going to kill 'em, honey."

"I wish." He opened his eyes halfway, showing a sliver of blue. "How come I'm always so tired? Been sleeping all day again, haven't I."

"I guess you need the rest. Besides, we're night owls. Too late to change our feathers now."

"Suppose you're right. What you got for supper?"

Jessie hesitated. The pantry was bare and, as far as Ben knew, their pockets nearly so. She thought it best not to tell him about the money from Strap and, of course, the check from Mike Bernard. All together it wasn't an awful lot, but at least she could take small comfort in knowing they had something in reserve, for whatever new disaster the future might bring. "Can you go out and get a can of something to heat up on the gas plate?" she said. "I don't care what. I'm not too hungry anyway. Are you?"

"Hell yes! Surprising what kind of appetite you can work up just by sleeping. But did the check come from the Actors Fund?"

That was the other thing Jessie had done. Ben was too proud to apply for assistance himself, but she figured if anyone deserved it, he did. The monthly check was only a pittance, but it was enough to pay for heat and lights and a few other necessities.

"It's not here yet, honey. But did I tell you we got a letter from Strap yesterday?"

"Strap! Somebody teach him how to write?"

"No, he got somebody to write it for him. Anyway, he just wanted to make sure we got settled all right. Says there's another new jazz band in Sedalia that's all the rage. He's afraid pretty soon everybody's going to forget all about ragging."

"It's a shame. A crying shame."

"We had our glory days, honey. Let's not forget."

Jessie's gaze roamed the tiny bedroom. There was little evidence of those days now, just a *Ben Harney, Originator of Ragtime* poster and some old theater bills taped to the wall, right above a cheap pine dresser with a missing handle that she kept reminding Ben to fix. Maybe he would get to it tomorrow.

The story they told everyone back in New York, about Ben's sister having a nice place for them in Philadelphia—turned out it was only half true. His sister had a nice place, but what she'd offered them was a decrepit two-room flat on North Gratz Street, dead center in the worst part of town.

"I'm sorry, baby," Ben whispered, barely loud enough for her to hear. He must have been watching her. She always tried to keep a smile on her face, but sometimes it slipped.

"Sorry? Whatever for, darlin'?"

"You know what for. Wasn't supposed to be like this. Not for us. We had everything. I should have looked after our money better. It's just that I never saw it coming. Thought I'd always be playing and singing. People would never stop wanting to see Ben Harney in action." He reached for Jessie's hand. "I let you down, sweetheart. Didn't take care of you like I should've. I just wish—"

She touched a finger to his lips, not wanting him to go on. She had decided, after she let the ring go, that she wouldn't nag at Ben anymore, no matter what. The past was the past. "Don't you think I knew what I was getting into with you? My fancy man, that's what you were. That's why I loved you then—and why I love you still."

"Come here." Ben pulled her down on top of him. "You know I can't do like I used to, but I swear the feeling's still there."

"Then let's pretend." Jessie swung her leg over him and pressed her body against his, moving in a slow grind. "How's that, mister?"

"You're the best, honey."

"You should know. You've tried 'em all."

"Come on now, Jessie! That just ain't so."

She gave a little laugh, rolling off to the side. Whatever mischief Ben had gotten into in the old days seemed unimportant now. She settled back into her own space, her head resting on

351

a feather pillow that was missing half its stuffing. "Had a dream last night about our time in Australia. You remember it, Ben. It was like we were starting all over, everybody so excited about ragtime. Of course, back here in America they were already moving on to something else. That's how it always is, I guess. Something ends in one place but then it begins somewhere else." She curled a strand of hair around her finger, her eyes following the trail of a long crack in the ceiling. "I wonder if it's like that when we die. We finish here, do everything we're supposed to do, and then we start all over in some other place. You think so, honey?"

"I doubt it."

"But why not? Isn't that what they preach all the time about? Going to heaven? Collecting your reward for being righteous down here on earth?"

"Just trying to make us behave. That's all it is."

"I'm not so sure."

Ben sighed. "All I know is we better get up or we're going sleep the rest of our lives away."

She waited for him to roll out of bed, light the stove to get the place warmed up. He seemed to be expecting her to make the first move.

"Isn't there anything around here to eat?" he asked, suddenly grumpy.

"I'll take another look, honey." But she wasn't thinking about food. She was looking sideways at Ben—the sharp angles of his face, the deep creases. He was thinner than ever. His skin looked dry, his coloring slightly yellow. Behind those lips that she still loved to kiss, his teeth were a wreck. He needed to see a dentist. They both did.

"I'll tell you, Jessie, if I had it to do over—"

"But you don't."

"First thing would be Tom Strong."

Jessie frowned. She knew all too well where this was going. "What about Tom?" she said with a sigh, as if she had no choice but to follow the familiar script.

"I reckon I'd give up just about anything if only I didn't have to see old Tom hanging from that tree."

"You know it wasn't your fault."

"Maybe not."

"No, it wasn't." It was almost dark now. Jessie sat up to light a candle on the bedside table. "Listen, Ben," she said, wishing this could be the last time she'd have to tell him. "You've beat yourself up over Tom Strong and that ring all these years, and for what? Besides, Tom would have wanted your success. He would have wanted Bruner Greenup to wander into the Red Rooster that night. He would have wanted him to publish your song 'Good Old Wagon.' And he would have wanted the whole world to fall in love with ragtime. It couldn't have happened any other way. You had to do it. You're the only one who could."

"You really think so, Jess? It had to come down the way it did?"

"No other way it could have."

"But the ring—" He shook his head. "After all Tom did for me, how could I let it get away?"

"You didn't. I did. And I'm sorry."

"I wonder a lot about who has it now. Or whether it's still sitting in the window of that pawnshop you took it to. Hasn't been that long. It might still be there. If I knew for sure that it was—why, I'd head back to New York right this minute. I wouldn't care if I had to walk all the way."

"Well, it's not there, I'm sure. And, these days, you can barely make it to the grocer on the corner. Let's just forget about it, all right?"

"You know what else I regret, Jess?" Ben was obviously in one of his moods. "That my idea about a showdown between me and Mike Bernard never got off the ground. Just couldn't pull it together, hard as I tried. Knocked on so many doors, I lost count of 'em all. That contest would have saved us, honey. We would have been sitting pretty right now."

"Maybe if you had asked Mike to talk to some of his people—"

"He wouldn't have done it. It was one thing if it got handed to him on a silver platter, another if he had to work for it."

"I don't know about that . . ."

"Look, Bernard didn't really want to come up against me. I never met anybody more scared of being a loser."

She hesitated. "And what about you? You weren't afraid of losing?"

Ben turned his head on the pillow to look at her. "Why are you asking me a question like that?"

"Why? Because it always seemed to me you gave up on that contest pretty quick. You did a lot of talking about it to people you knew couldn't help you, but not to the ones who could."

"Are you saying you think I didn't really want it? You think I was bluffing?" He sounded indignant.

"Oh, you wanted the money. But when it came down to it—the thought of losing to Mike . . ."

"Sounds like you figure he would have won."

She pretended to consider it for a moment, not too long. "No, honey. I don't think that at all."

Ben sniffed. "Maybe Bernard never lost a rag contest, I don't remember. But he sure was a loser when it came to women."

"Really? Seems to me I was always reading something in the gossip columns about him and one beautiful woman or another," she said, taking a curious pleasure in egging him on. Besides, she hadn't seen him this animated in a long while.

"That doesn't mean anything. I don't think those women even liked him that much. It was his money, his celebrity that attracted 'em. That's all."

"And I suppose in your case, it was your charm and good looks?"

He rolled over on his side, flashing a devilish grin. "Well, I'm sure that had something to do with it."

"Actually, Mike wasn't *bad* looking," she went on, still not through with him. "Dressed up in his black tailcoat, he cut a dapper figure on stage."

"You're saying you thought Bernard was good-looking?" Ben raised himself up, like a rattler ready to strike. "He never made any move on you, did he? 'Cause if I'd known about it, I would have—"

"You would have *what*?" she prompted, trying hard not to laugh.

"Well, I wouldn't have stood for it, that's what!" With a grunt, he lay back down. "Not *my* girl. No way."

Jessie scooted close, resting her head on Ben's bony shoulder. Wasn't it kind of wonderful that he could still be jealous over her, even now? "You know, Ben, sometimes you're the silliest creature."

Water over the Dam

NEW YORK CITY
APRIL 1929

B y the time Mike was within sight of RKO Keith's movie theater, it was nearly noon. He was exhausted and soaked to the bone. He hadn't planned to walk the entire way, but with rain coming down in buckets it was impossible to find an empty cab. One good thing about it, though—the overcast sky probably made the faint gray-blue pallor of his skin less noticeable.

It was around eight last night when he made the call. The telephone rang a dozen times. He was relieved that it was Bert, not Eli Zuckerman, who picked up. When Mike announced himself, there was silence on the other end.

"Hello? You still there?"

"Yes."

"Have we got a bad connection?"

"I can hear you."

Mike cleared his throat. "It's been quite a while since we've spoken. Everything all right with you?"

"I guess."

"Look, Bert. I'm sorry about what happened to your mother and, well—I've been thinking that I'd like to see you. Talk to you."

"What about?"

"I'd rather tell you in person. Could we get together tomorrow at noon in front of the new movie theater on Northern Boulevard? RKO Keith's? It's not too far for either of us. I can take you to lunch somewhere."

"I'm busy tomorrow."

"This is important, Bert. Even if you can't have lunch, just come by, would you? There's something—something I'd like to give you."

Another silence. "I'll see," was all Bert said before he hung up.

Mike ducked beneath the theater's marquee, grateful for the shelter, and set down his leather briefcase. Today, it felt heavy as a bag of stones. His arm ached, and so did his feet. He leaned his back against the theater's stone façade, closing his eyes. He wasn't resting, not really. He was thinking again about how fast everything can change.

When he saw the doctor a couple of months ago, the diagnosis was unequivocal. The burning, difficulty urinating, swollen testicles—the symptoms were indicative of gonorrhea, an advanced case. "You'll need to inform your wife," the doctor had said, looking away as he added, "Anyone else?"

As for the cure, Mike already knew there wasn't one. The best his doctor could offer was a medicine containing silver. "It has certain side effects, but it might help," he explained, careful to emphasize *might* and adding that Mike would likely notice, over time, a slight bluish cast to his skin. He wouldn't die from the disease. Not directly anyway. But there could be complications, serious ones.

Since then, he'd been obsessed with thinking about his illness. Strange how it seemed to have altered the entire landscape of his life. Maybe what bothered him wasn't the thought of his inevitable demise, however distant or near, as much as what he would leave behind. He'd never expected to feel this way, as if he had no legacy. In fact, he had always felt precisely the opposite, as if his mark on the world was destined to last a very long time. But lately he'd been asking himself, What did it amount to after all? A couple of scratched discs gathering dust on a library shelf? A scrapbook of old newspaper clippings most likely headed for the trash barrel the moment he expired?

All his accomplishments were meaningless if there was no one who remembered, no one who cared. No one . . .

Mike opened his eyes, startled to realize he had drifted off. He didn't know for how long, but long enough that the rain had dwindled to almost nothing. The borough of Queens was blanketed in a light mist, the sun starting to peek through in spots. He looked at his watch. Half past noon. Bert was late.

Unless maybe he had misunderstood. About the date, the time. The theater. Or he wasn't coming.

Mike waited fifteen minutes more before calling it quits. The kid had stood him up. But then, why should he be surprised? Had he thought he could just snap his fingers and Bert would come running? Of course, the boy *should* have come. If he'd been taught any manners, he would have.

There was nothing to do now but go home. This time, Mike didn't even attempt to flag down a cab. For some reason he wanted to walk, to feel again the immense weight of that briefcase.

He arrived back at his apartment house with every muscle in his body in revolt. The weather had put a nasty chill in him on top of his other ailments. He took the elevator to the second floor, trudged down the hallway to his unit. A note was taped to the door. He pulled it down and opened it, read it quickly, and then crumpled it in his hand. The nerve! He'd been living here for eight years. So what, once or twice he was a little late with the rent? They'd get their money when he was good and ready.

He unlocked the door and stepped inside. The rancid odor of decomposing garbage assailed his nostrils, a not-so-gentle reminder that now he was on his own. Katherine hadn't exactly taken the news of his illness in stride. The next day, she packed her bags and, Jules in tow, caught a train to Chicago. Before she departed, she made it abundantly clear they would not be returning. Mike had better send money every month, she said, or he'd be hearing from her lawyer.

Was it odd, maybe even disgraceful, that he didn't miss either of them?

He dropped his briefcase to the floor, giving it a sharp kick just to let off steam. Then he remembered. He bent down, opened the latch, and pulled out his scrapbook, gently rubbing his hand over the smooth leather cover as he straightened his aching back. He had kept up that scrapbook for thirty years, stashing away reviews, printed programs, publicity shots— anything and everything that constituted a record of his career. Then, one by one, he pasted them, in chronological order, onto the blank pages. Why he had suddenly thought about giving it to Bert, he wasn't exactly sure.

Maybe it was all because of Dolly, this feeling that had come over him lately. That death was just around the corner. That life was meaningless. But now, thinking about it, he resented Dolly saying she was worried the boy might actually follow in his father's footsteps. She probably never even bothered to tell the kid that his father was someone to be proud of. At any rate, he guessed whatever he wanted Bert to know about his life, he would have to tell the boy himself.

Someday.

Maybe he ought to have the same talk with all three of his sons—including the one he had never met even once. The one May had planned never to tell him about.

He hated thinking about that afternoon, and yet he often did. May so stiff and proper behind her gigantic desk, looking across at him as if he were some sort of supplicant, she his self-appointed judge. And the photograph—seeing that young man's face had been like looking in a mirror, and for a moment he'd felt ashamed not to know him. Then angry. Angry that she thought he wasn't good enough to be the boy's father. He was the skeleton in the Convery family's closet, the one who had polluted their impeccable pedigree. The Jew, the entertainer, the propagator of scandal.

He could, of course, have stirred things up, demanded that the truth be told, exposed everyone who'd tried to deny his natural right. But in the end, after his indignation cooled, he had decided to leave well enough alone. May's boy didn't need him. It was the same with Bert, even Jules.

None of them needed him.

He had planned to ask Bert about Juilliard. He'd even thought, if the boy was serious about music, he might see if he could find a way to help. If it seemed right—if the kid had any talent—he could try to pull a few strings, call in a few favors.

But why should he go out of his way for a kid who wouldn't even give him the time of day?

He looked down at his scrapbook. It felt like an old friend. Inside was the world he knew and loved, a world that had always revolved around him.

He opened the cover.

The carefully chronicled journey started with an article from 1896, praising Tony Pastor's talented young musical director. He remembered how he had felt when he read that review for the first time. How it seemed like he was finally on his way to becoming *somebody*.

A few dozen pages of memories, and he stopped. August 1908, the obituary of his mentor and longtime boss, Tony Pastor. It was the only clipping in the entire book about someone other than himself. "How you doing, old man?" he said, affectionately running his finger over Pastor's photo before moving on.

He came, finally, to one of his all-time favorites. Although it was only a few lines from the *Chicago Daily Journal*, he had assigned it a prominent spot on a right-hand page. He read it now, savoring every word as if it were the most brilliant passage ever penned:

> August 23, 1910—Mike Bernard, the well-known ragtime pianist who is currently playing the fascinating Witmark number "Temptation Rag," gives a piano-playing exhibition that looks like an acrobatic sideshow and sounds like a speeding pianola. Bernard plays "Temptation Rag" and Paderewski's masterpiece with the same elemental motive of force.

He had enjoyed many flattering commentaries over the years, but something about this one went straight to his sweet spot. The writer obviously understood what he was all about. There simply was no other player, not a single one, so versatile, so comfortable with diverse musical forms. He read the ending again: *"with the same elemental motive of force."*

How he loved that phrase!

Mike continued on, thumbing through page after page, review after review. He paused near the end to admire a recent photo of him shaking hands with New York's mayor, Jimmy Walker. That had been a grand evening! He had worn his custom-made suit, one of his fine linen shirts with the French cuffs, his alligator shoes.

With a sigh, he snapped the book shut. Tucking it under his arm, he headed for the liquor cabinet. He poured himself a gin, took a big gulp. It felt good going down, just like it always did. He had become too morbid lately! A slow season on the circuit, a few setbacks here and there, and he was ready to give up. But no!

He lay the scrapbook down on the cabinet, gave it an approving pat. He had no regrets. Whatever sacrifices he'd made along the way, whatever mistakes, it was the life he had chosen, the one he'd been meant for. And, by God, it wasn't over yet.

There were still a few empty pages to be filled.

The Passing

"Theodore R. Livingstone, Financier, Dead at 56."

May folded the newspaper slowly, carefully, and set it aside on her desk—her father's desk. She leaned back in the soft leather chair and closed her eyes. She had read the obituary several times, though there was nothing in it that she didn't already know. Teddy had passed away suddenly—something to do with his heart, the doctors said—the day before yesterday. Perhaps by tomorrow, at the funeral, she might manage to shed a few tears.

The children were coming home. They would arrive tonight. She had heard from Abbie. From Rosamond and Nora. From many of her other friends—some who knew her best when she and Teddy were married, others who had come to know her only after she legally became May Convery again. Though everyone realized she and Teddy had parted long ago, many assumed a certain connection remained. After all, they must be thinking, she and Teddy had two wonderful children together.

Teddy had remarried. She'd been glad of it then, and she was now. Tomorrow morning, her only responsibility would be to show up at the church with a veil over her face, bow her head for a moment at the coffin, and then listen to others expound on Teddy Livingstone's exemplary character and life.

She knew she should feel guilty for her lack of emotion. She didn't mean to be callous or cynical. It wasn't as if he was a monster. He simply was not anyone she had ever loved. Nor had she liked him very often either.

Yet he had been a decent enough father to both the children, especially Anna. And he had never confronted her with the truth about Melvin, though she was certain he knew. It was the one kindness he had shown her; perhaps she should have had the grace to acknowledge it.

Opening her eyes, she glanced around her father's study, wondering why she hadn't done more to make it her own. Why she hadn't sold the house on Fifth Avenue a long time ago and moved into an apartment on Park Avenue. She could afford to keep the house—it wasn't that. Between the trust fund established by Grandfather Convery and the inheritance from her father, she had no financial worries and never would. But the neighborhood was changing, its fine old mansions being torn down and replaced by big department stores. And besides, what was the point of staying in the home where she had spent a good deal of her youth, an often unhappy youth at that? Why remain here, a prisoner of the past, constantly reminded of the guilt and despair that had taken root in her as a girl of seventeen?

She had always blamed Mike Bernard. But was it really his fault? Was it possible she had hated him all these years with a passion out of proportion to his crimes? A few months ago, when he came to her about Dolly Zuckerman and discovered the photograph of Melvin, she felt certain he would betray her yet again. She was convinced her dear son would soon learn that his very existence was a mistake, his whole life story nothing more than a subterfuge for his mother's sins. But the days and weeks went by, and Mike neither said nor did anything to harm her. Nothing, thank God, to disrupt Melvin's life. Had it been generosity on his part, or did he simply not care? Or perhaps she was wrong, and he really hadn't figured it out.

"Excuse me, ma'am." Willard stood in the doorway to the study. It unnerved her how he always was able to approach without a sound. "Sorry to disturb you, but Mr. Baxter is here. Do you wish to receive him?"

"Mr. Baxter? Oh—yes, of course. Please see him into the drawing room. I'll be there in a minute."

"Right away, ma'am."

May had not been expecting a visit from Roy Baxter but was pleased at the prospect of seeing him. They had spent a great deal of time together since that night at Harlem Hospital, eight months ago, when Rosamond first introduced them. She was surprised at how easily they fell in with one another, how natural it felt to be with him. Roy was a man who cherished many of the same values that she did and had fought for them just as hard. She had gone to the trouble of looking up all his old articles from *McClure's*, hard-hitting journalistic investigations that had awakened the public to rampant vice and corruption. It was exciting to think of him that way—as a crusader for justice. It made him even more attractive.

More than anything, it was a joy to again have someone to talk with late into the night, over dinner and wine and coffee and more wine. While she didn't agree with him on everything— how dull that would be, they often quipped—their verbal sparring matches always ended in laughter. She hadn't had such exhilarating conversations with anyone since Rosamond.

Yet she wasn't without doubts. It frightened her that she was becoming so involved. Was she only imagining that he loved being with her the way she did with him? Was she reading too much into the looks he gave her every now and then? Looks that seemed to suggest he appreciated her as a woman and that he was every bit the man to thrill her in all the ways she had dreamed, through these long and lonely years.

May arose from the desk, shaking down the sleeves of her black-and-gray Chanel suit. With a sweep of her hand, she smoothed the straight skirt, did the same with the sleek outline of her bobbed hairdo, and then headed for the drawing room.

Roy stood as she entered, approaching her with open arms. They embraced lightly before sitting down together on the velvet loveseat. Thelma had already anticipated the need for refreshments. A tea service and a plate of molasses cookies Evie had baked that morning sat on the low table in front of them, next to a vase of fresh white roses.

"How are you holding up?" he asked.

"I'm fine, thank you." As she lifted the silver teapot, she could feel his eyes searching her face. Was he questioning whether she really was as well as she claimed? He knew her marriage to Teddy had not been a happy one. She had confided that much to him, saying they simply were not a good match. She'd not said more.

She handed him a steaming cup.

"Other than having missed you the past few days," Roy said with a smile, "I'm here to see if there's anything I can do to help. The funeral—well, such things are always a strain for the family."

"The children are taking it very hard. I've spoken to them several times by telephone."

"You know I'm available if you need me."

"Of course, I know. And thank you." She had filled her own cup, but it remained on the table, untouched. "After the funeral, Melvin and Anna will be here for a few days. Perhaps you'd like to join us for dinner one night—not tomorrow, but the night after? I'd love for them to meet you."

Roy appeared genuinely pleased. "I'd be delighted."

"Then it's settled. Eight o'clock, here at the house." She hoped the children wouldn't mind. But it felt right to introduce them to Roy. Perhaps even necessary. "I've been meaning to ask you, how is Will Cook doing? You said last week that you planned to visit him at the sanitarium."

Roy set down his cup next to hers. "As a matter of fact, I saw him yesterday. He's looking quite well. I think some time off was exactly what he needed. I have no doubt he'll be back to his cantankerous self before too much longer."

"He's a man of many faces, isn't he? There are those who quake in their boots when he approaches, and then others who feel such love for him that they insist on calling him *Dad*."

"A complicated man, yes. No doubt he'll be remembered as a genius."

Suddenly, Roy reached for her hands, pulling them toward him, holding them tightly. "Death always makes one think more carefully about life, doesn't it? Makes you realize that you only have one chance to get it right—or if you've made mistakes, to rectify them."

His gesture surprised her. Even more so his words, which so perfectly mirrored what she had been thinking only a short while before. Questioning how she'd lived her life, the choices she'd made. Yet, as always, she had failed to come up with any answers.

He brought her hands to his lips and kissed them, one at a time. He had never done such a thing before. "Maybe this isn't the perfect moment, but—well, there's something I need to tell you, May. Something I should have said before now."

"Oh? What is it?"

"I'm afraid it may upset you."

May's enjoyment of their intimacy instantly turned to dread. Why did he look so serious? They'd been talking about death. Was he going to tell her that he had some terrible illness and not much time left? That he was going away, never to return? It frightened her to realize how empty she would feel if he were to disappear from her life. She hadn't meant to need him. And yet, suddenly, it seemed she did.

"Please, go ahead," she said, wanting it to be over. Wanting to know how bad it was going to be.

He looked down at their hands, linked together. "I have a confession to make. I shouldn't have hidden it from you."

"Hidden *what*?" His uncertainty made her even more anxious.

"I've represented myself to you as a free man—maybe not explicitly, but certainly by omission. You never asked if I was married, though I'm sure you must have assumed I wasn't. But I am. I have a wife back in Maryland."

She felt her heart stop, just for a second.

"We haven't lived together for twelve years. I've asked for a divorce many times, but she refuses. She's a devout Catholic."

May withdrew her hands, not sharply, not angrily. It was true she hadn't asked him if he had a wife, now or ever. Marriage was a subject she always tried to avoid. He had not *lied* to her. "You have children?"

"No. My wife—her name is Maura—she wanted them badly. But I guess it just wasn't meant to be. Unfortunately, she allowed it to ruin her life. And, for a long while, mine as well."

"And why did you feel you must tell me this?"

"Why?" Roy seemed surprised by the question, as if she should already know the answer. "Because I'm in love with you, May."

She froze. Such a declaration was the last thing she had expected, especially today. And after what he'd just told her. He had a wife. He was not free. Yet she understood very well how it was possible to be married to one person, in love with another.

"When you love someone, you should have no secrets," he continued, with a sincerity that made her feel guilty. He could never begin to imagine what she was hiding. From him, from everyone.

"Don't you suppose we all have secrets?"

"I don't want to have any when it comes to you, May. You've never said whether marriage is important to you, but—"

"It's not." Perhaps it was selfish of her, but she felt relieved that Roy's confession was only *that*—a wife who was nothing more than a distant shadow. He was not dying. He was not going away. "The truth is, I never wanted to be married—"

She halted midsentence. That was *not* the truth. She was lying to Roy. Why couldn't she trust him, as he had dared to trust her?

She reached for her tea, raised the cup, took a swallow.

"But, of course, I *did* marry—twice, actually." She paused, trying to gauge his reaction to the first of her revelations. There was none that she could sense. "I was seventeen. I don't know if Melvin was conceived before or after the marriage was official. At any rate, my parents quickly had it annulled. My father was the only one who knew the baby wasn't Teddy's. I never told my first husband that he was a father. It's possible that he knows now. If he does, it's because of my carelessness. And Melvin—he doesn't know about any of it. The subject came up only once—it was a fluke, another careless mistake—and I lied to him. I lied straight to my own son's face about who he is, about the blood running through his veins. I thought it was the best thing to do. Or maybe I was simply too ashamed of myself to care what was right. Maybe I was afraid Melvin would hate me if he ever found out the truth—his mother was a tramp and a liar, and he wasn't really a Livingstone."

She flashed back for the millionth time to that afternoon when Melvin asked if she thought he looked like Mike Bernard. The way she'd brushed his question aside—it was unconscionable. But that's what she'd done. She had no right to forgiveness.

"I've carried around my secrets, and the bitterness, for so many years that I'm afraid I've lost the ability to be rational about them. Actually, I never *was* rational—or fair. I blamed other people for what really came about through my own selfishness. I wanted so much to be free. I wanted to be an artist. I thought maybe I could live my dream through someone else, even if it might end up harming others. I didn't give that possibility much thought, because I was too intent on what *I* wanted. And when I didn't get it, I was determined never to forgive the ones I decided were responsible for my unhappiness. What really happened, though, was that I never forgave myself. Even today, I'm not sure I can."

During most of her monologue, she had avoided looking at Roy, but now she did. "So that's the woman you're in love with. Perhaps you'll entertain second thoughts."

Roy let out his breath slowly. "Second thoughts? No, my dear. Not a chance."

"But how could you respect someone who—"

"May, please." He pulled her close. She didn't resist. He felt solid, safe. "You have no idea what it means to me that you would open up like that. I know it wasn't easy for you. Especially after what I told you about my own situation."

Tentatively, she lay her head on his chest. The sound of his steady heartbeat was somehow reassuring. Still, he couldn't feel the same about her as before. It was impossible. "But your sins aren't as terrible as mine. You haven't hurt anyone the way I have."

"Let's not call them *sins*. Neither of us deserves that."

"All right, *transgressions*."

"You mustn't be so hard on yourself. I can understand why these thoughts would surface again now, with Teddy gone and the children mourning the loss of their father. But maybe your instincts about Melvin were correct all along. Maybe telling him the truth would have done more harm than good. And maybe now isn't the right time either. Maybe it won't ever be the right time." He gently stroked her hair as if it was something he had always done. "Look, I don't profess to know what's correct in a situation like yours, but I do know one thing. You're not a tramp, May. You're a *seeker*. It comes with being a writer, I'm afraid. But it doesn't have to destroy you."

"Maybe it already has."

"I promise you, it hasn't."

"I'm not sure anymore who I am, what I've become."

"What you are, May, is a damn good woman."

May wiped away an errant tear before it could leave its trail on her cheek. It was amazing how, suddenly, the world seemed such a different place. No longer dangerous but insanely hopeful. She felt giddy with the realization, however obvious it should have been all along, that the secrets she'd allowed to weigh her down for decades also had the power to set her free. To help her see the possibility of a life without regrets.

It wasn't too late.

Slow Night

Mike walked carefully down the familiar four steps to the lower level of Bill's Gay Nineties on East Fifty-Fourth Street, passed through the heavy wood-and-stained-glass swinging doors, across the tile entry, and up to the main room with its fine mahogany bar. If it were a Friday or Saturday, booze would be flowing like there was no tomorrow, everyone confident that, with the pull of a lever, bottles could be quickly dispatched to a sandpit in the basement. Thanks to Prohibition, living dangerously had become routine. Those weekend nights, when he and the other entertainers rotated nonstop among three bustling floors sparked with gaiety and loose chatter, Mike could almost convince himself that nothing had really changed.

But this was Monday, and Mondays were different. Except for a few patrons, the bar was empty. Mike shrugged off his coat and draped it over a stool, then sat on the next in line.

"You're early." The bartender poured gin into a short glass and dropped in three olives.

"Thanks, Jack." Mike took a swallow, then another, wondering if Jack had ever noticed the subtle blue cast to his skin.

In the tinted light of the bar lanterns, was it more obvious, or less?

"Guess playing the slow nights ain't much fun."

"Nope."

"Hey, I saw in the paper you were hobnobbing again with Mayor Walker. Friars Club, wasn't it? Some kind of benefit?"

"Joe Howard and I did a couple of numbers."

"Heard the mayor called you the originator of ragtime, toasted you with fake champagne, the whole bit."

Mike couldn't help but smile. Harney would have been fuming. "Well, he exaggerated some. But he's the mayor." He set aside his gin, only half finished. It wasn't like him not to drain it all the way to the bottom. But tonight, he didn't feel quite himself.

He slid off the stool, grasping the rail. The swelling in his groin was getting worse. He took a moment to steady himself before heading for the stairs. Haltingly, he climbed to the top, then walked a straight line to the stage at the far end of the room, up two steps, and behind the red curtain. He went over to the piano, pulled out the bench, and eased himself down. Tonight, it felt good just to sit.

Charlie parted the curtain and peered inside. His charcoal face was shiny with sweat, his white chef's apron spotted with grease. "Why you back here? It ain't eight o'clock yet. You okay?"

"I'm fine, fine."

Charlie didn't look convinced. "How about I make you something tasty right now? You got time before the show."

"No, not now. Maybe afterward."

"All right, whatever you say. But you not going home tonight with no empty stomach, you hear?"

Mike didn't answer. Long after Charlie had disappeared, he remained just as he was, slumped on the bench, his hands resting on the keys. It surprised him how he still craved the feel of ivory under his fingertips. Yet sometimes lately, he found himself missing the silkiness of a woman's skin. It was then he'd think about how everything might have been different if he'd only had someone constant in his life. Someone who knew him from the beginning. And cared.

It was May who haunted him, now more than ever. He thought of her whenever he smelled roses. A champagne glass was like the delicate curve of her breasts. The brush of a velvet curtain like the softness of her hair. All these years, whenever she came to mind, he told himself he had no choice but to let her go. *No choice.* He had made that same excuse for a lot of things he shouldn't have done—and for some that he should have but didn't.

But May was a million years ago. Now, with an hour to go until the first show, he laid his head on his hands and fell asleep.

"Hot off the skillet, my friend!"

Charlie stood in front of him holding a plate heaped with crisp fried chicken and mashed potatoes. The last show was over. The crowd, what little there was of one, had gravitated downstairs to the bar for a final drink before closing. Tonight, Mike didn't feel like mixing. Neither was he anxious to head home. The curtain had dropped fifteen minutes ago, but he remained seated at the piano as if waiting for an encore.

"Just give it to me here, Charlie."

"Come on, I'll set you up at a table."

"It's okay, don't bother." Mike raised a hand to his forehead, rubbing hard at the creases.

"You sure you all right?"

"Tired, that's all."

"Too many late nights with them young chickies, eh?"

"Ha. I'm a bit past all that now."

"Aw, no you ain't." Charlie handed Mike some silverware wrapped in a linen napkin and set the plate on the bench. "When you playing up a storm, tapping your feet, and them hands is flying—why, them ladies still is swooning. I seen 'em!" Charlie threw back his head and laughed. "Why, you is the one and only Mike Bernard, the man with the magic hands. On a good night you can still pack 'em in."

Mike glanced down at his hands. Charlie was right. They hadn't failed him yet. And the rings looked flashy as ever, the five-carat diamond and the gold lion's head with the ruby eyes.

Charlie wiped his hands on his apron. "Was telling my wife the other night, Mike Bernard the only one can play ragtime music the way it supposed to be played. Just like the old days."

Mike nodded, reaching for a chicken leg.

"Why, in all them playing contests, everybody was afraid to come up against you."

Mike licked the grease off his lips.

"You was the Ragtime King of the World!"

"I still am."

"That for sure! 'Course, I suppose one of these days you going to retire."

Mike's head jerked up. He put down the chicken leg. "I have no intention of retiring."

Charlie hastily backpedaled. "Oh, okay—sure am glad to hear that. After all, you's the granddaddy of it all. Why, you invented ragtime!"

"I didn't invent it, Charlie." Mike glanced down at the lion's head.

"Why, sure you did. That's what everybody around here say."

"Because they don't know any better. I never said I invented ragtime. Never did." He touched the beast's snarling mouth.

All of a sudden, he raised himself from the bench. Walking faster than he had thought he could, he headed for the stage steps.

"Hey," Charlie called after him, "where you going? Something wrong with the chicken?"

Something Lost, Something Found

Mike buttoned his light jacket against the brisk wind and headed south on Park Avenue, keeping an eye out for a cab. Damned if there was ever one when you needed it! He had no idea about the train schedule, just hoped he hadn't missed the last one tonight. But then, so what if he had to sit in the station for a few hours? One way or another, he was going to Philadelphia.

He hadn't been in touch with Jessie since she and Ben left New York. Hadn't responded to the one card he received from her, thanking him again for his generosity. But he'd taken note of the return address on the envelope, curious about where they had ended up. He remembered the name of the street, or almost. It sounded like *grass* . . . Gratz—that was it! North Gratz. Jessie had said their place was right across the street from some honky-tonk called Dido's. He supposed he could figure out the rest when he got there.

He turned onto a side street and headed toward Fifth Avenue, where he hoped to have better luck finding a cab to take him to Penn Station. The street was deserted; for some reason, several temporary barricades had been installed to close the road to traffic. Mike peered ahead of him, noticing now that the streetlamps were unlit as far as the eye could see. Must be some kind of a blackout. Though the sky was overcast, and there was only a half moon, he supposed he could see well enough. It was just a couple of blocks to Fifth.

He walked past a row of tightly packed buildings. All along the curb, bags of refuse were piled high, broken bottles left over from the weekend littering the ground. Out of the corner of his eye, he glimpsed a shadowy army of rats combing through the filth. Nothing unusual, but for a second it unnerved him.

His thoughts took a turn, back to what Charlie had said, how he'd tried to give him credit for originating ragtime. Just like the mayor had done. He chuckled to himself. He was no choirboy, nor was modesty his forte, but he wasn't about to claim that disputed territory. He knew where to draw the line. As for Ben, he was no more the originator of ragtime than Bach was the inventor of the fugue! But then, wasn't that Harney's genius? He saw an opportunity, and he took it.

He recalled the night he first heard Harney play at Tony Pastor's—the start of it all. Or maybe it began at that dump, the Eloise, when he put poor old Smokey on notice there was a new kid in town. The way he set that place on fire! He smiled, remembering himself down on his hands and knees, scrounging for pennies and nickels and dimes, never dreaming of what lay ahead. Ragtime King of the World! The Paderewski of vaudeville! There had been so many tributes over the years, so much success.

But he never said he was the originator of ragtime. Never! And Harney—well, maybe he didn't originate it, but, after all, he deserved some credit for having the guts to run with it the way he did. Ben must not have liked it too much when Mike came along, like the second man in a relay, eager to grab the baton. The thing was, he and Ben were never on the same team.

Funny how it hit him so hard tonight, sitting there behind the curtain at Bill's, listening to Charlie go on and on about his illustrious career. He looked down at the lion's head and felt ashamed. Whatever he'd accomplished, he hadn't done it completely alone. Nobody can, especially when it comes to music. Who knows where it all begins? Or where it's going to end. And that's when the thought came into his head. Just like Ben believed he owed his success to that black fellow Tom Strong, maybe Ben was owed something, too.

Hearing voices, he looked up. Three young men were walking down the middle of the street, maybe half a block away, their increasingly loud conversation punctuated with shouts and raucous laughter. As they came closer, he could see that each of them wore a similar outfit—plus fours with long socks and low boots, loose jackets, wool caps pulled partway over their eyes.

A ripple of fear went through him. What was he doing walking down a dark, empty street late at night, by himself? Was he out of his mind? His eyes scanned the buildings on both sides of the road, hoping to see a light, though he didn't expect there was any light to be seen.

They were right across from him now. He hated how nervous he was, like he used to feel as a kid in the old neighborhood. Back then, if you were alone and ran into some young punks like these, you hadn't much of a chance.

But this wasn't the old neighborhood, he told himself. Besides, maybe they weren't out to make trouble. Just drunk, having a good time.

Turning his head, he looked straight at them and smiled in the dark. "Good evening to you, fellas."

Next thing he knew, they had him surrounded, circling like a pack of wolves.

"Hey, what's going on here?"

One of them laughed. "What you think, man?" he said in thickly accented English.

"If it's money you want, I haven't got any."

"How we know that?"

His heart pounding, Mike tried to make himself sound gruff. "You're wasting your time. Now get out of here."

A second hoodlum grabbed him by the arm. "Take it easy, pops, and you won't get hurt." The third came at him, twisting Mike's other arm behind his back.

"Let's see what we got here." The one who had spoken first reached into the left pocket of Mike's coat and pulled out some bills, from the right side a few dollars more.

"Not much. But we take it," he said, nodding to the others. They let him go, giving him a shove that nearly sent him sprawling. He was relieved they were finished with him—but dammit! He needed that money if he was going to Philadelphia tonight.

"Wait a minute. What's that?" The punk who had taken the money was looking at Mike's hands. He quickly shoved them into his pockets.

"Leave me alone, will you? I haven't got anything more."

"Show me your hands! Now—or I swear I cut 'em off at the wrist."

Frantic, Mike tried to think of something he could do. Maybe grab one of the empty bottles on the ground, break it, use it as a weapon? But that would be crazy. They'd end up turning it on him, likely slit his throat in the process.

Slowly, he pulled his hands from his pockets.

"Well, well. Looks like some pretty fancy rings you got there, pops."

"They're fake. Got them at a carnival down in New Orleans." He pointed to the five-carat diamond. "Pretty good imitation, huh? Glass! Totally worthless!"

"Take 'em off. Both of 'em."

"Come on, let a fellow have his trinkets, will you?"

"Take 'em off!"

"Look, my wife gave them to me. She's dead now. It's all I've got left of her. You understand, right? It's got sentimental value. That's all." He was pleading now, but he didn't care. "You fellows got mothers, right? Grandmothers?"

"Take off them rings and do it now." The young robber's voice was threatening.

Mike's legs were shaking so violently he could barely stand. He shoved his hands down into his pockets. He would not give up those rings! Not like this.

"Get out of here, all of you!"

Before he could figure out his next move, they had seized him again. One held him steady while the other two grasped his wrists, dragging his hands from his pockets, twisting his fingers as they wrenched the tight rings over his knuckles. The five-carat diamond. The lion's head.

It happened so fast, like a sped-up movie reel, and then he was on the sidewalk, face down, unable to remember exactly how he got there. Had he lost consciousness? Was he still alive? He heard their laughter echoing from down the street. Thank God, it was getting fainter. He remained completely still, waiting until there was no trace, then struggled to his feet. The palms of his hands were bloody. Squinting in the dark, he tried to pick the tiny pieces of broken glass from his skin. But it was no use, and he began to walk, stumbling along, alert to every sound. A sharp pain in his knee stabbed him with each step.

Somehow, he made it to Fifth Avenue where, miraculously, a cab was at the corner. He told the driver to take him home, apologized for not having any money; he'd have to get it once they arrived, he said. The driver told him not to worry. He recognized him from the old days at Tony Pastor's, he said.

"Listen, you look pretty bad. Want me to take you to the hospital?"

"Thanks, but don't bother. I'm all right."

"You sure?"

"Positive."

The cabbie put his foot to the gas. "I'm telling you, I used to love that Tony Pastor's theater. Best time I ever had."

The rest of the way, the driver talked nonstop, recounting every time he'd been to Pastor's, every act he'd seen, every song he'd heard. When he finally let Mike off in front of the apartment house in Queens, all he asked for was an autograph. Mike was grateful. It wasn't only that his head hurt and so did his knee, and he wasn't even sure he could make it inside, let alone back out again. It was more than that. Maybe he was getting sentimental, or he was just relieved to be alive, but it felt good to be part of this fellow's fond recollection of the best time he ever had.

The lights were burning in the lobby and the elevator was working. He rode it to the second floor. At the door to 2C, he could barely hold his hand steady to insert the key. Once inside, he went straight to the mirror above the liquor cabinet.

It was worse than he'd thought. Blood dribbled from his nose and from a gaping wound over his right eye. His cheek was bruised and swollen. Strange, he didn't remember being hit. He didn't remember much of anything. Only what they had taken from him.

He tried to console himself. They were things. Just *things*. But no, he couldn't pretend. Those rings—they meant the world to him. He guessed he and Harney were alike that way.

He opened the liquor cabinet, poured from an almost-empty bottle of gin, then dipped the hem of his shirt into the glass and dabbed alcohol on his wounds.

"Well, Ben. Guess you're not getting your lion's head back after all," he said, addressing the mirror.

He looked down at his hands, flipped them over. The palms were scraped and bloodied. Seeing the sparkle of embedded glass, he succumbed to another rush of anger. Damn them for taking those rings! Just when he'd decided to give up one, now they were both gone. He had earned that diamond, worked hard for it. Every carat!

Suddenly, he swung around, his heart in his throat, his eyes on the door. He'd heard a knock, or thought so anyway. What if it was those thugs, coming to finish him off? But that was absurd! They hadn't followed him here. How could they? Was he losing his mind?

He crept to the door and, after fastening the chain bolt, opened it just a crack.

"It's me—Charlie."

Mike undid the bolt and let the door swing wide.

Charlie's jaw dropped. "Good Lord! What on earth happen to you?"

"Just a fall. I'm all right." Mike knew he should invite Charlie in but made no move to do so. He was too exhausted.

"Somebody drop this off for you at the club," Charlie said, handing him a small package wrapped in brown paper.

"Who?"

"Don't know. Left it with Jack at the bar. He forgot to give it to you, but I thought it might be important." Charlie regarded him with a skeptical eye. "You sure you gonna be all right?"

"I'm fine." Without thinking, Mike started to shut the door in Charlie's face, then stopped. "Charlie—thank you. Thank you, my friend."

"Sure thing. You take care of yourself now, you hear?"

Mike nodded, then gently closed the door. With a sigh, carrying the package between his raw palms, he limped over to the sofa and sat down. He hadn't been expecting anything. It wasn't his birthday. Even if it were, he couldn't think of anyone who would bother to send him a gift.

He studied the parcel's brown wrapping. His name was handwritten on one side. There was nothing to identify the sender. The package weighed less than a pound. Rectangular. Firm.

The wrapping came off easily. It was a book—a journal. He recognized it the moment he saw it. And in that moment, he felt a terrible sadness, followed by a sense of wonder that whatever was happening now was happening at all.

He ran his hand over the tooled-leather cover, noticing how the red had faded over the years. A long ribbon marker had been placed near the end. He opened to that spot and found a note between the pages.

May 27, 1929
Dear Mike:

I'm leaving tonight for Paris, after receiving word that my mother is ill and needs my help. I haven't spoken to her in years, not since she deserted the family. I didn't plan to forgive her, but perhaps it's time to let old wounds heal. I don't know exactly how long I'll be away. But when I come home, I was hoping we might sit down and talk. There's something I'd like to tell you, but it has to be in person. It won't be like the other times, I promise. I've come to realize that I owe you an apology. And the truth. But, for now, perhaps my old journal and the poetry within will remind you, as it does me, that once we were young—and entitled to be foolish. I trust you to keep it safe until my return.

May Convery

Curtain Call

AUGUST 1943

I t was a clear day in late summer 1943, one of those glorious sun-filled mornings that can tempt otherwise hardworking folks to call in sick, opting for a blanket under a shady tree in the park. Such dereliction of duty would never occur to Bert Bernard. He was late for work, and that upset him. Bert was well known around the office for being punctual, precise about everything. That was part of what had made him a rising star among the bevy of bright young attorneys at the US Department of Immigration.

He grabbed his briefcase from the kitchen counter. His young wife, Esther, was bathing the baby in the tiny bathroom down the hall. He called out his goodbye.

"Love you," she answered back.

Traveling at high speed, he flung open the front door of their Brooklyn apartment.

"Excuse me, I'm sorry." A man stood on the other side, his hand poised to knock. "I'm looking for Bertram Bernard. Are you, by any chance, him?"

Bert gave the fellow a quick once-over. He seemed harmless enough—about fifty, well dressed, clean shaven. Not a thief. Not a military man. These days, that was always in the back of Bert's mind. Quite a few of his colleagues at the Department had been drafted for the war effort. He'd go, of course, and be proud to serve his country. But so far, his name hadn't come up.

"What can I do for you?"

The man pulled something from his vest pocket, a newspaper clipping, and offered it for Bert's inspection. "That's why I'm here."

The short article was from the obituary page of the *Times*. The publication date was June 28, 1936, more than six years ago. Bert had seen it before.

"Ragtime King Dead at 60"

"Look, I know nothing of Mike Bernard's affairs, if that's what you're here about. I don't even know where he's buried," Bert added, just to underscore his point. The last thing he needed was some kind of trouble, somebody with a score to settle, an old debt never paid. He was not responsible for his father.

"Don't worry, I'm not a creditor. And I know—he's been gone quite a while. But it's only recently that I finally managed to piece it all together. Our connection, that is."

Bert had been looking closely at the man—his deep-set eyes, thin lips, narrow chin. He couldn't shake the feeling that they had met before. "Do I know you?"

"No, but hopefully you will. Maybe it's a little late, but I've always wanted a brother." The man smiled. "My name is Melvin Livingstone."

Author's Note

Temptation Rag draws on historical accounts in books, articles, and family records concerning the lives and personalities of real people of the ragtime era. While much of the story is fiction, and certain dates have been altered for the sake of continuity, many important elements remain strongly rooted in historical fact.

Among the people who actually lived, and were major musical figures, are Mike Bernard, Ben Harney, Will Marion Cook, Abbie Mitchell, J. Rosamond Johnson, Tony Pastor, and Willie Smith. Jessie Boyce (also known as Jessie Haynes) was Ben Harney's wife and performed with him. Strap Hill occasionally was his sideman. Dolly Zuckerman, Eli Zuckerman (his real first name was Benjamin), and Bert Bernard were some of the people in Mike Bernard's life. A few other minor characters are either completely fictionalized (for example, Teddy Livingstone and George, Isabelle, and Emily Convery) or loosely based on historical figures (Otis Saunders was a musician and friend of Scott Joplin, and Roy Baxter was inspired by the professional life of writer and muckraker Ray Stannard Baker).

A young May Convery was, according to public records, briefly married to Mike Bernard; the marriage was annulled by her parents. They may have married again a few years later and apparently had a son, Melvin, but it appears that the second marriage was also short-lived. Other than her name and the fact of her initial marriage to Mike Bernard, May Convery's life as depicted in this book is completely fictitious, and elements of the story line involving her career as a poet, her involvement in the women's suffrage movement, and her interactions with other characters (such as her deep friendship with J. Rosamond Johnson) are entirely invented.

Brief biographies of Mike Bernard have been compiled, but there are many gaps and contradictions in his personal information, even concerning his age. Mike Bernard's parentage is still in question, with official records inconsistent with one another. Mike's death certificate indicates his father immigrated from England and his mother from Germany; there are other documents that indicate both were Prussian. According to legend, at a young age Mike traveled by ship from New York to Berlin, Germany, to study piano at a conservatory, though precisely which one is not known. Records from the Berlin Conservatory do not show him in attendance; those from the Stern Conservatory are missing for the dates in which he would have been likely to study there. Though his ambition was the concert stage, at the age of nineteen (most likely) he was offered a position as musical director at Tony Pastor's vaudeville theater. There is evidence that Mike married at least three women and that he had three sons—Melvin, Bert, and Jules. Bertram "Bert" Bernard was Mike's son with Ziegfeld girl Dolly Zuckerman; while Mike and Dolly may have been married briefly, this cannot be documented. Mike's name does appear, however, on Bert's birth certificate as the baby's father. Dolly Zuckerman continued her career while Bert was raised by his grandparents. She died in her thirties, most likely of cancer. There was an effort by unscrupulous theater people to embezzle her savings, though the details are not exactly as depicted in my story.

Mike Bernard and Ben Harney most certainly were acquainted with one another. Mike apparently was first exposed to ragtime in 1896 or 1897 at Tony Pastor's theater when Harney played there as a headliner. As Mike became a major figure in the world of ragtime music in New York and nationally, presumably the two of them would have been rivals for bookings and renown; but the details of their relationship—whether they were friendly with one another or not—are unknown. Accounts suggest that Mike was not particularly well liked among his musical peers. While I don't have definitive information as to whether he was a good father to Melvin (that he did not know of Melvin's birth for three decades was an invention of my story) or to his third son, Jules, I do know from family accounts that he was almost entirely absent from Bert's life. As far as anyone in the family knows, Bert never had occasion to meet Melvin or Jules. It is possible he didn't know about his half-brothers, as no one can recollect him ever mentioning them.

I am not a scholar of ragtime music, but it was my aim to give readers at least a sense of its phenomenal popularity as well as the controversy surrounding this uniquely American musical genre. In the course of my research, a number of resources were extremely helpful. "Perfessor" Bill Edwards (www.perfessorbill.com) was most generous with his knowledge of the ragtime era and the musicians who populated it, including Mike Bernard. His research on Mike has been exhaustive and most certainly is the best I have found anywhere. I am very grateful to ragtime scholar Edward A. Berlin, especially for his monograph "Reflections and Research on Ragtime" which provides a wonderful factual account of the contest in 1900 for the title Ragtime King of the World. (The incident in my story involving a black contestant and the judges' selection of the song "All Coons Look Alike to Me" was based to some extent on a newspaper article covering the event.) Another noteworthy reference is *They All Played Ragtime*, by Rudi Blesh and Harriet Janis. Although not particularly complimentary of Mike Bernard's style, Blesh and Janis's work remains a staple of the literature about ragtime music. I am indebted to Joe Laurie Jr.'s *Vaudeville: From the Honky Tonks to the Palace* for its descriptions of Mike Bernard's years at Tony Pastor's; *Swing Along: The Musical Life of Will Marion Cook* by Marva Carter for further insight into the character and accomplishments of the great African American composer and his wife and musical colleague, Abbie Mitchell; and David Gilbert's remarkable book, *The Product of Our Souls: Ragtime, Race, and the Birth of the Manhattan Musical Marketplace*. None of the scholars or sources mentioned is responsible in any way for musical or historical inaccuracies, intentional or unintentional, within this book.

I was honored to include some of the works of the great African American poet Paul Laurence Dunbar in the pages of my novel. It is impossible for me to read his poem "Sympathy" without being moved to tears; it is this exquisite poem that so beautifully sets the tone for the fictional relationship of J. Rosamond Johnson and May Convery. I hope readers will be inspired to further explore Dunbar's remarkable poetry.

If you've noticed my name, you may have surmised that I have a personal connection with Mike Bernard. He is, in fact, my husband's grandfather. The two of them never met.

Bert Bernard (Mike and Dolly's son, and my husband's father) became a prominent immigration lawyer, as suggested in the final chapter of this book. He married Esther Levine and they had two sons. Bert died in 1988. His tombstone reads, "He loved his family with all his heart."

Unlike his own father, he truly did.

Acknowledgments

I am deeply indebted to my fabulous editors at Girl Friday Productions—Christina Henry de Tessan, Sara Addicott, Emilie Sandoz-Voyer, Laura Whittemore, and Nick Allison. Their insight and guidance were so important to me, and they made the entire process of bringing this book to fruition truly enjoyable. Many thanks as well to my incredible cover designer, Ghislain Viau, and to Paul Barrett for the lovely interior design.

This book is dedicated to my mother, who has always been my biggest and best cheerleader. She is also the one who taught me about music, introducing me at a young age to such wonderful and mystical compositions as "Afternoon of a Faun" (Claude Debussy) and "Pavane for a Dead Princess" (Maurice Ravel), pieces that stirred my imagination and undoubtedly started me thinking about all the stories there are to tell.

Thanks to the many friends who have encouraged me with their great enthusiasm for my literary endeavors—especially Mari Kent, Elisabeth Tyler, Tammy Moerer, the Book Belles, and the Black Mountain Ladies—and to my family and extended family for their support and kudos.

My incredible husband, Bob, believed in this project even when I questioned whether I could make it work. In more ways than one, he is my inspiration, and his love truly is the music in my heart.

Reading Group Guide

1. Each of *Temptation Rag*'s four acts begins with a chapter told from the point of view of Ben Harney's sideman, Strap Hill. What is the purpose of Strap Hill's character in the thematic context of the novel, and why is his point of view important?

2. As a young woman, May Convery is determined to have a life very different from her mother's, but are there any traits she shares with Isabelle Convery?

3. Is May's plan to elope with Mike Bernard justified by the prospect of an arranged marriage?

4. Why do you think the author chose to make Jessie Boyce a point-of-view character? Why not her husband, Ben Harney, who plays a more significant role in the story?

5. At several points in the novel, there is the hint that Mike Bernard and Ben Harney might actually face off in a ragtime piano contest, but ultimately the playoff never

materializes, perhaps leaving the reader to wonder who would have come out the winner. Besides an adherence to historical accuracy (there is no record of a contest ever occurring between Bernard and Harney), what other purpose might the author have in leaving unresolved the question of who is the better player?

6. The close relationship that develops between May Convery and Rosamond Johnson would be highly unusual for a white woman and a black man living in the early 1900s. What in May's character and background might explain her openness to a deep spiritual and emotional connection with Rosamond?

7. Jessie tells Lucinda Jones, "There's not a woman alive more independent than I am, dear." Is Jessie really as independent as she claims to be? Why, or why not?

8. Mike continually fails to establish emotionally satisfying relationships. At one point in the story, he wonders whether "there was something missing, some basic component of a human being that he was born without. Or maybe it was simply that there could be no room in his life for any love but music, an explanation he found far easier to accept." Do you accept Mike's overwhelming passion for his music as sufficient explanation for his emotional isolation? What other reasons might there be?

9. What is the significance of the book's title, *Temptation Rag*?

10. What did you learn from this novel about the history of ragtime music in America? How do you feel about Ben Harney's claim to be the originator of ragtime? Does the

turn-of-the-century controversy over ragtime's origins resonate in some way with modern-day concerns regarding the ethics of "cultural appropriation"?

11. In what ways are Mike and Ben alike? How are they different?

12. What is the symbolism of the gold lion's-head ring? To Ben? To Mike? To the story?

13. Mike is clearly a deeply flawed character, but does he have any redeeming qualities? By the end of the story, has he learned anything from his mistakes? If so, what? If not, does this inspire the reader to feel more sympathetic toward him, or less?

14. How does May feel about motherhood? Is she a "good" mother? Are the decisions she makes concerning her children, especially Melvin, the right ones? Do you think May eventually tells Melvin that Mike Bernard is his father, does Mike tell him, or does Melvin discover it for himself?

15. At the end of the novel, May seems to have found love, self-acceptance, and an ability to overcome the bitterness that has plagued her throughout her adult life. Which of the other major characters, if any, similarly come to peace with themselves? What reasons might the author have for leaving certain conflicts or situations without a clear resolution? Under what circumstances can ambiguity be an effective literary device?

ABOUT THE AUTHOR

A writer and musician, Elizabeth Hutchison Bernard lives in Arizona with her husband, Bob, and their black Lab, Pearly Mae. Her historical fiction has been recognized by the Eric Hoffer Book Award (2018, Fiction Finalist), the Arizona Literary Awards (2017, Honorable Mention, Published Fiction), and the Book Readers Appreciation Group (Medallion Honoree).

Visit Elizabeth's website and blog at www.EHBernard.com
Facebook at https://www.facebook.com/EHBernardAuthor
Twitter at https://www.twitter.com/EHBernardAuthor

7/19

CPSIA information can be obtained
at www.ICGtesting.com
Printed in the USA
LVHW091319031218
598372LV00041B/189/P

9 780998 440644